ENDORSEMENTS

The story of a father's deep love for his son and determination to rescue him. How far would you go ?

Drug cartels and hostage-taking are among the provocative plot elements in a tumultuous odyssey that takes you from snowy Russia to the highland jungle of old Mexico and finally to Jamaica's beautiful but troubled shores. Rodney Powell brings authority and vivid authenticity on par with the best of classic Tom Clancy thrillers !

Powell's Gospel-infused writing and character development make this a timeless literary work for all generations. **THE RANSOM** puts on full display the power of God to redeem the most vile of men, then leaves us marveling at the transformative efficacy of His love.

Cal THOMAS
Syndicated Columnist

Faith, emotion, anxiety, thrill, and a double dose of adventure ... **THE RANSOM** brings it all. Powell painted such a vivid picture that I could feel, smell, see, hear, and even taste the situations and settings.

As usual, Powell didn't disappoint my heart for Jesus — testifying of man's tribulations, our fleshly struggle with forgiveness, and most of all, the reliability of God's grace. This well-crafted tale revived my willingness to be more forgiving in my own life. **THE RANSOM** — not only entertaining but encouraging and personally inspiring.

Col Clinton "Sandy" McNABB
USAF, Ret

Rodney Powell has done it again! If you read **THE PARDON**, you'll be eager to continue the story. You're in for a double treat with **THE RANSOM**. These novels are exciting, fun, scary, and intriguing. More importantly, both give enlightening answers to how believers can live in a confusing and evil world. Most essential — how a very big, sovereign, loving, and good God deals so faithfully with His people.

Steve BROWN
Key Life — broadcaster, seminary professor, author

THE RANSOM

A PROFOUNDLY SATISFYING SEQUEL TO

THE PARDON

RODNEY POWELL

Published by RealMedia.US | 20831 Rosehill Church Rd, Tomball, TX 77377

Library of Congress Cataloging-in-Publication Data

POWELL, Rodney S.

The Ransom | Rodney POWELL

Summary: "A trip to paradise gone awry. The cartel took his son, but contending with a former Soviet special forces officer could be more than they bargained for." — Provided by publisher.

Subjects: Christianity — Mexico — cartels — Fiction | Christian Fiction | Historical Fiction

Library of Congress Control Number: 2023917070

ISBNs: 979-8-9876233-4-3 (hardcover); 979-8-9876233-5-0 (paperback); 979-8-9876233-6-7 (ebook); 979-8-9876233-7-4 (audiobook)

Publisher's Note: This novel is a work of fiction. Names, characters, places, and incidents are either products of the author's imagination or used fictitiously.

Printed in the United States of America

Dedicated to

Pastor Richard Caldwell, Jr.

faithful shepherd of our souls

USA
Sidera Islands
Atlantic
Ocean
Florida
Gulf of Mexico
Florida strait
Bahamas
Yucatan strait
Cuba
Campeche Bay
Yucatan
Jamaica
Mexico
Belliza
Caribbean Sea
Guatemala
Honduras
Nicaragua
El Salvador
Costa Rica
Panama
Pacific Ocean

PROLOGUE

March 12th, 1998

Many friends have asked me what became of Vladi and Marco. Some have inquired about Irina, Olga, and even me — although my story isn't half as interesting as theirs. Indeed, theirs is a fascinating account of the Lord's work and the sweetness of salvation. Little could we have known how their faith would be tested in the years that followed.

Even as I write this, I am reminded of Romans 8:28, the verse often cited when enduring hardship. God's Word tells us, "And we know that for those who love God all things work together for good, for those who are called according to His purpose."

That's a promise for the Lord's people, not a pithy salve for the world's troubles. It is given specifically to "the called," to "those who love God" — assurance that our Heavenly Father, who cares for His children, is sovereign in all things.

I couldn't imagine what it would be like to endure such enormous trials alone, without the Lord with me. The One whom "even the wind and the sea obey" — this is the Shepherd who walks with His people. That's not to suggest it is somehow easy — oh no! But it is a reminder to us that God is present and working, even in the darkest corners of the world.

Allow me to paint the picture of what happened next, as I believe it's important to provide a comprehensive understanding of the circumstances that led to their ordeal. Though some may find my explanation excessively detailed, I assure you that it's all relevant to the events that unfolded.

It was a time when the world was changing. As the Cold War slowly thawed, a new type of war was brewing — a crime war that soaked Latin America in blood. *Cártel del Golfo*, or the Gulf Cartel, was spreading its tentacles across much of Mexico's northeast coast and into Texas — insidious and deadly.

To fuel their expansion, the Gulf Cartel began recruiting special operations commandos with urban warfare training from the U.S. and Israeli militaries. For the same work, the cartels offered significantly higher compensation than the army. But they also made these trained commandos an offer they couldn't refuse. The decision was *plata o plomo*, silver or lead — coin or bullet. It was a simple ultimatum. The commandos could cooperate with the cartels and profit from it, or they could oppose them and die. You were either with them, or you died at their hands. It wasn't a difficult choice.

These criminal militias were nothing short of terrifying. They had the appearance of paramilitaries, donning army-style uniforms and wielding military-grade weaponry, including automatic rifles, belt-driven machine guns, and rocket-propelled grenades. They even built their own armored vehicles, narco-tanks that were aptly called *monstruos*, the Spanish word for "monsters." They were well-equipped, well-funded, and well-organized. And they were brutal.

The cartels rooted themselves in communities by bribing police and officials, but they also relied on intimidation, committing sensational acts of violence to establish their dominance. The harsh reality of the underworld was that the most terrifying cartels got the lion's share of the loot, giving rise to these apex predators. Wherever they had a presence, these criminal gangs left a trail of decapitated bodies and limbs severed with machetes and chainsaws.

The activities of these cartels would claim tens of thousands of lives year after year. Many disappearances and murders were not reported, so the true scale of the carnage may never be known. There were mass burial sites where victims were sometimes made to dig their own graves. The bodies of countless other victims were dissolved in barrels of acid, disappearing practically without a trace, and with no chance of justice.

The fact that such terrible violence occurred amid everyday life is a peculiar aspect of these crime wars. There was a war going on in broad daylight in the streets of Latin America, ruefully endured by those who simply wished to live their lives in peace. This war had its own rules — its own foot soldiers and leaders. Despite some of these locales having the highest homicide rates outside of declared war zones, markets continued to operate, and life went on.

In the land of cartel kingpins, power was not just a commodity — it was an obsession. They were the masters of their domains, the godfathers of a criminal empire that spanned the continent. They drew their strength from the villages and barrios. Crafting a façade that they were engaged in more than just wanton murder, these gangster militias portrayed themselves as freedom fighters trying to overthrow a repressive regime. But it was all a ruse. They had to maintain the pretense that they were more than just drug dealers in order to lure new recruits into their twisted fold.

These recruits were their pawns, mere collateral in their quest for ultimate control. They trained poor, lost teens to be heartless killers, *sicarios*. The barrios were fertile ground where cartels grew, a source of young blood eager to prove themselves. In these tiny pockets of the world where life was harsh and uncompromising, many young men idolized the wealth and power that drug lords bought with blood-stained money. But in their immaturity, these kids failed to grasp that the only way out of this lifestyle was death.

Like traditional warlords, drug kingpins ruled territories through both fear and organic support from some residents. Their grip on power was both insidious and absolute. The cartels even meted out their own form of "justice," conducting trials at remote locations in the mountains. In marginalized communities, where traditional institutions had broken down, this alternative justice system won a surprising amount of support. Mexico's poor rural areas have always been on the edge of the law. This was jungle law, but some people found it more effective and direct than the justice offered by the police and courts.

The cartel strategy was to control their territories by exploiting the weaknesses of a broken system. If the government resisted, the cartels launched insurgent-style attacks while claiming to fight for the poor. On the other hand, they also cut deals with government officials, controlling key figures by offering them a share of the spoils. So, it was common for politicians to be in league with the cartels, as cartel tendrils crept ever deeper into the halls of power.

But the devil always gets his due, and the scales were tipping. The cartels had long paid bribes to complicit officials. As the cartels strengthened their hands, they demanded more than just silence. They flipped the deal. They became powerful enough that they could strong-arm politicians into paying them instead.

Their stranglehold on the economy was equally unforgiving. No one was safe from their rapacious claws. Their extortion schemes bled people dry, siphoning money from taxi drivers, individual proprietors, and multinational corporations alike. The economic assets of entire industries, such as mining and agriculture, were practically taken over by cartels in some regions of Mexico and other parts of Latin America, leaving nothing but the husks of once-vibrant commercial enterprises. The entire commercial, political, and judicial apparatus — every aspect — was entwined in the web of money and services connected to organized crime.

Once merely a loosely organized network of drug traffickers, the cartels had become something greater, blurring the lines between crime and war. They're a cancerous growth, a parasitic force that has held Latin American cities and states in their thrall. Even the halls of *Los Pinos*, the presidential mansion in Mexico City, have been tainted by their web of dirty money and services. The cartels have held sway over all.

Warships and bombers are useless against irregular forces with scattered cells of ragtag combatants. The cartels became a shadow power, but their rule didn't constitute an alternate state. They didn't want that responsibility. Instead, they wanted a weak and corrupt government, which enabled them to thrive as a parasite feeding on a host.

Unlike traditional armies driven by ideologies like nationalism, the insatiable god of mammon motivates these criminal militias. The cartels diversified from drug trafficking to a portfolio of crimes, including extortion and kidnapping. And, without getting ahead of myself, this is where they ran afoul of Vladi Gavrilov.

In the third chapter of Ecclesiastes, under the inspiration of God the Holy Spirit, the wisest man who ever lived tells us, "There is an appointed time for everything. And there is a time for every matter under heaven—" But it's the words that follow, thundering like a war drum, that stir the blood. Here it is, two verses later ...

"A time to kill and a time to heal;

A time to tear down and a time to build up."

It's that first part, "A time to kill," that I struggle with. As a physician, I have dedicated most of my working years to healing and preserving life, so the idea of taking it is anathema to me.

For some, the choice is simple — a matter of duty or survival. Perhaps it was not such a moral dilemma for Vladi, a former military officer. As for Marco, the former prosecutor and my brother, I witnessed how his heart and mind were transformed after coming to know the Lord. The consequences of his past actions weighed heavily on his conscience. Maybe they had seen the worst of humanity — they were no strangers to violence — but I don't think anything could have prepared them for what was to come.

God commanded, "You shall not murder." Through the apostle Paul, in his epistle to the Romans, we are also commanded to be subject to the governing authorities — an avenger of evil, a minister of God for good.

But what happens when those institutions meant to safeguard us falter and we're left to fend for ourselves? It can all quickly become muddied and indistinct when we're faced with the breakdown of society's protective walls, leaving us exposed and vulnerable to the worst of humanity.

What happens when survival is at stake? When those we love are threatened by unspeakable horrors? When the only choices we have left are the ones that will challenge our core beliefs and perhaps define us forever?

As Vladi and Marco navigated the treacherous waters of a world gone mad, they were faced with impossible choices. What they endured is an evocative reminder that sometimes, there are no easy answers. They grappled with questions that have plagued humanity since time immemorial — what is right? What is just? What is necessary?

These are difficult questions to answer — ones that I myself struggle with. But they're questions that sometimes grab us by the collar, demanding an answer — refusing to be satiated by conjecture. For reasons we cannot fathom, sometimes sovereign God directs our lives into gray areas, not so clearly black and white. Amid the haze of conflict, the right choices are not always apparent.

This is no less true for new believers like Vladi and Marco, who got swept up in something much bigger than themselves. Grappling with unthinkable evils, they were thrust into a maelstrom of uncertainty, where the division between right and wrong became blurred like a fever dream. In the end, God will judge their decisions and their conduct.

As a physician, I'm acutely aware of the moral complexities that touch our lives. In areas where God's Word is silent, I am painfully conscious of my inadequacy to navigate them relying on my own theories and opinions. In the crucible of conflict, the strength of our convictions is tested.

So, I ask you, would you be willing to risk everything to protect those you love? Would you find the courage to contend with impossible dilemmas, the kind that wrench the soul? When I examine my heart, I wonder what I would do if one of my own children were threatened by unthinkable evil. I might have made the same choices.

Vladi and Marco's tale is not one for the faint of heart, but it's a story that needs to be told — for in their struggles, we see the very essence of what it means to be human. Theirs is a story that will absorb you. It has left me breathless at times. Their journey will take you to the edge of darkness and back again. It's a story that will stay with you long after you've turned the final page.

More than anything, these events have made me grateful for peace in my own life, and it has reminded me that when the world seems to be falling apart, God has not abandoned His children. Indeed, all things do work together for those who love Him, who are called according to His purposes — for God's glory and for our good.

Julio Rivera, MD.

Lakeland, Florida, USA

PART I

· REUNION ·

1

THE RAID

"T*odos, manos arriba!*"

Two dozen heads snapped toward the doorway. Spontaneous gasps were followed by an immediate hush. Most had expected this day to come. They just hadn't expected it to be today. Everyone in the small gathering froze except to comply by nervously putting their hands in the air.

"What have we here?" Marco inquired. "*Iglesia? Una reunión bíblica?*"

No one responded, but they didn't need to. The answer was obvious. Whispers of prayer hung in the air.

"Everyone, put your head down! I want to see your hands on the back of your head," Marco commanded again.

He proceeded to walk almost casually through the rusty, corrugated metal shed, searching the faces of those present. Would he recognize any of those in attendance? He strolled to the rear of the small structure, hands clasped at his back, and stood behind the man who had been leading the meeting.

"We have heard there are church meetings around Havana that are not approved by the government. Now ... you appear to be law-abiding people — I would not presume this to be such a gathering," Marco drawled with a detectable tone of sarcasm. A few people lifted their heads slightly, questioning looks in their eyes.

"Keep your head down!" Marco barked. "I want you to answer one question — and I want you to think carefully before you do. It is a simple question, but I insist on a truthful answer. We do not have any liars here, do we?"

No one responded.

"Here is the one question for you — 'Are you a Christian?' Keep your head down — I only want to see your hand in reply."

Only the man at the head of the room raised a shaky hand.

"Hmmm. This is a serious concern, *mis amigos*. Let me rephrase the question, so you understand the gravity. This '*Jesucristo*,' to whom many offer prayers — this man faced a tragic fate centuries ago. Are you willing to lose your freedom, your family, and even your life for this —" He hesitated, examining the room. "— fable?"

A woman at the back of the room quietly raised her hand — then another — then more. Before long, all but two men had their hands raised resolutely in the air.

"Well, well —" Marco spoke up. "It looks like we have at least a couple who are loyal to the party and the spirit of *la revolución*. You gentlemen may look at me," he said to the men whose hands were not raised.

A gentleman in his late fifties hesitantly raised his head. Another, a young man in his mid-twenties, did as well.

"I didn't think you were with these others." Marco nodded in approval. "Look me in the eyes. Do you respect the laws regarding assemblies and affirm your allegiance to El Comandante and those who are responsible for the welfare of our people?"

The men nodded their heads in affirmation.

"Then you are dismissed. Go quietly. Say nothing about what you have seen here today. If you are a *bembelequero*, talking about these operations that ensure our beloved Cuba is not overrun with unlawful assemblies, I will personally find you. Your cooperation is imperative."

The men nodded their heads again in assent.

"Then go — far away — where no one can mistake you for one of these so-called Christians." The men got up and hastily left the gathering. When he was sure they were out of earshot, Marco instructed everyone to sit up. His whole demeanor and tone of voice had changed.

"Take a breath, *hermanos*," Marco said with a smile. "One cannot be too careful."

The surprised group looked up, turning to one another with puzzled expressions and murmured questions. Should they be relieved, or was this some other trap? Was this not a raid? What was happening here?

"That said, I'm here because the Ministry of the Interior is actively suppressing Bible meetings like yours. You are on the list."

The meeting attendees straightened up, keen to hear what Marco had to say. Some remained suspicious, still wondering what he was up to.

"You need to meet somewhere else. Change your meeting times and frequently move your locations. Don't keep meeting in the same place regularly."

They understood. Many let out the anxious breaths they had been holding. Tension eased and parents hugged their children. Couples of all ages embraced. Their sense of relief remained palpable.

"For now, I need a couple of men to give me a hand with some packages. My brother, Julio, is a doctor in America. He has been sending medical supplies in parcels routed through Mexico. Julio also provided the funds for toothpaste, toothbrushes, and other basic sanitary items. He has asked me to distribute these to the Christian brothers here."

"Oh, *gracias*. *Gracias*," Marco heard repeated throughout the small room.

"I think there are a few sodas and mineral water in there too. Don't drink them all at once."

"*Sí, sí.*" Heads nodded in understanding.

"This will be all I have for a while. I will be traveling. So, try to make it last. God be with you."

So much had changed. Marco had lost his position as a magistrate after he pardoned Vladi. He argued some legal technicalities, but he was still demoted. He was back to being an *Inquisitor*.

Castro had gotten his show trial with Vladi. That was all that mattered. Almost no one knew what had happened to Vladi after he was sentenced, nor did they care much. So, Marco had gotten away with a slap on the wrist. If he wasn't such a good prosecutor, it could have been worse — but the Ministry of the Interior wanted to keep him around if they could. Meanwhile, they preferred that the case of the Soviet officer fade from the national consciousness like it had never happened.

In the end, it wasn't so bad. Marco was getting commendations for his work on trade relations with Prime Minister Norman Manley's new Jamaican government. *Pretty good for a fabricated proposal prepared in a rush*, Marco thought with some pride. Someone liked his work, so they sent him back to Jamaica as a liaison to the Minister of Foreign Affairs and Foreign Trade.

While in Jamaica, Marco arranged a meeting with a former "acquaintance" — Frank Díaz. The men sat together on Díaz's tiled veranda, both quite at ease.

"I have to say, I didn't expect to ever see you again," Díaz told Marco as he opened a bottle of sparkling mineral water and poured it into a glass of ice for his guest.

"Same. I never expected to return here, either. But since I've come back on business, I have a confession that will be of interest to you."

Díaz raised an eyebrow. "Oh?"

Marco divulged the whole story. Díaz was a no-nonsense man, but his stern expression soon broke into laughter.

"It's most surprising that someone would work so hard for a flight going to Cuba. My specialty is *de-fection*. Yours sounds like —" He paused with a smile and a slight roll of his eyes. "— *in-fection*. I can truly say I'm impressed with your ingenuity," Díaz complimented. "I'm rarely duped. Although, in my world, I might expect it to happen occasionally. On this, I tip my hat to you."

Díaz took a puff of a Cuban cigar and nodded appreciatively in Marco's direction. He tapped the cigar in an ashtray next to his coffee.

"I haven't come to relieve a guilty conscience with an empty confession," Marco assured him. "I understand there was effort, expense, and risk involved in aiding me — and I owe you for that. I propose that I could make it right by working with you as a legal advisor — for the cause."

Díaz looked down at his cup. His expression was hard to decipher, but Marco could almost detect a smirk on his lips. Of course, Díaz was skeptical. He was a man who had seen his share of double-crossing and betrayal.

"How do I know this isn't a setup?" Díaz finally asked. "You are, after all, still working for Castro's government." He wouldn't expect an honest answer from a mole, but he asked it more to make Marco aware that if he were, Díaz was no fool. More importantly, he wanted to gauge Marco's response.

"It makes the perfect cover, does it not?" Marco countered with a smile. His gaze and his pulse remained steady.

"That can go either way," Díaz smiled in return, though there was a hint of menace in it. Both men were adept at this game.

"If I am sincere and this is a legitimate offer, you stand to gain something invaluable, as do our people. My expertise and inside knowledge of the complex Cuban legal system will be a rare asset to you, one you will not likely find again," Marco told him.

"And if you are not sincere and this is not a legitimate offer?" Díaz asked as he sipped his coffee.

"Then you know where to find me. And I am sure you will have the ... resources ... to deal with me accordingly."

Díaz laughed, "It is true, though it will be a little more challenging to do from a rat-infested Cuban prison cell. But rest assured, if you are playing me, you will be on the run for the rest of your life — as short as it will be."

Marco nodded. "I understand your hesitation. You have no reason to trust me — in fact, so far, I've given you nothing but reasons to distrust me."

Díaz gave a single nod of acknowledgment but settled himself into his chair and steepled his fingers together pensively.

"Here is what I propose, then. I will let you test me out — to the extent that you feel comfortable," Marco offered. "The only way I can gain your trust is to show you my sincerity in action. If, after a time, you feel reassured that I'm truthful in my offer, we can work out a full arrangement."

Díaz studied Marco's face for several moments, both men unflinching. *He is so difficult to read*, Marco thought as he searched Díaz's face.

Without a word, Díaz put down his cup and reached a hand across to Marco. Their secret agreement was sealed with a firm handshake.

"I'll be in touch," Marco promised, "but for now, you'll have to please excuse me. I have a date tonight with the nicest travel agent in Jamaica."

2

BACK IN THE U.S.S.R.

Aeroflot Flight 379 made its final approach to Leningrad. Vladi looked out the window at the thick blanket of moonlit snow. *Ah, Piter,* Vladi mused, thinking of the name most Russians still called the city that had once been named Saint Petersburg. This was how he remembered it. He had grown up with snowdrifts piled on the roadsides and roofs, but his eyes had not seen snow like this for thirty years. *This is very different from the Florida "St. Pete" I have lived near for these last decades,* he considered.

As the wheels touched down and they taxied toward the airport terminal, Vladi's mind rehearsed what he would say. Various ideas ran through his brain. *There are so many ways this can go — it is impossible to know how this will unfold. I do not like all these unknowns.*

Vladi almost always had a plan, and executing a thoughtful strategy was his strength. But in this situation, he would have to improvise. That made him uncomfortable. Perhaps worse, he was concerned that perceptive Soviet customs and immigration officers might read the uncertainty in his face.

Shortly after landing, the passengers exited the aircraft. Vladi stepped off and took a moment to reflect. *I am under the sky of the USSR again, breathing in the air of Russia, standing on Soviet soil — the motherland.* "Rodina," he breathed out in an almost reverent whisper. He had to fight the overwhelming urge to fall to his knees and kiss the floor.

His eyes scanned the large room to which the passengers had been directed. He wondered how much the USSR had changed since he had been gone. *Not too much.* Vladi stood there alone, absorbing the moment while the other disembarking passengers busily collected their baggage.

Taking in a deep breath, he mustered the courage to queue up in the line for customs and immigration. *There is only one way out of here now.* Vladi shrugged his shoulders.

The officer was courteous but professional. Vladi was one of the hundreds of passengers he would process at his station during his shift — one of the thousands during a week of work. The routine was not much to get excited about.

"Passport and visa," he requested in a monotone.

Vladi reached into the pocket of his suit jacket and placed his documents on the counter. The officer opened the Cuban passport and examined it. Vladi watched him closely, a thin layer of sweat creeping up his neck. The officer thumbed through the pages, then turned it over and studied the outer cover of the passport. *What is he studying so closely?*

The officer looked up at Vladi without saying a word, but his gaze gave Vladi the uncomfortable feeling that the officer could read his thoughts.

"Welcome to the USSR, Mr. Rivera," he said with no inflection of suspicion or disapproval.

Vladi smiled back, somewhat relieved that everything was going well so far, but feigning a casual frame of mind.

"Are you here on business or pleasure?"

"On business," Vladi promptly replied. "Does anyone ever come to the USSR in the wintertime for pleasure?" He tried to make light of the subject, but the officer didn't seem to find humor in his remark.

Perhaps this is not the first time he has heard this, Vladi thought.

"What is the nature of your business here, Mr.— oh, *prostit*" the officer apologized, "— it is Sud'ya Rivera?"

Vladi straightened his spine more — he needed to remember that he was supposed to be a judge.

"I am meeting with Soviet advisors about the management of the Cuban prison system. They are involved with the training of personnel. I must say, we have learned from the best."

Vladi made use of a subject he knew something about — in fact, he could say he had empirical first-hand knowledge on the subject. *It is easier to lie when there is a touch of truth.*

"Your Russian is very good."

"Thank you," Vladi replied. *Oops, I am supposed to be Cuban.* "I have been working on speaking Russian for many years. It is nice to practice it now — thank you for noticing."

"Whom will you be meeting with about this ... prison consultation, you say?"

"Uhm ... his name is ... Colonel Boris Petrov." Vladi quickly retrieved a name from his memories, belonging to one of the men stationed in Havana with him back in the early days. He could only guess that Petrov might have reached the rank of colonel later in his career.

The officer picked up a pen and began writing notes. Then he opened Vladi's ticket jacket and thumbed through the contents.

"How long will you be staying?"

"Three weeks," Vladi answered as casually as he could muster, but he could already sense this interaction was taking a turn for the worse.

"Where is your return ticket, sir?"

"Is it not in there?" Vladi tried to stall for time to think of a better answer.

The officer shook his head in a negative response, looking intently at Vladi's face as though he were trying to read his eyes. Vladi patted his pockets, then opened his jacket as though he were looking for something.

"I do not know. Perhaps it is in my baggage." *You are a terrible liar, and you know it.* Vladi could feel the situation melting down in slow motion.

"Where is your baggage, sir?"

"Uh, well ... I do not ... have any." The words came out slowly. It was too late to try to come up with another answer, though. *These are things I should have expected and planned answers for*, Vladi reminded himself.

"You will be staying for three weeks, but you do not have any baggage? ... and you do not have a return ticket," the officer mused without a trace of humor. "You are aware that it is cold outside. Where is your overcoat?"

Vladi shrugged his shoulders. *Ughhh, no one in Cuba thought I might need a coat in the USSR? Of course, they would not even have a coat to provide. It is never cold there. And who thought about baggage?* Marco had been trying to get him on a flight out of Cuba. What he might need when he landed was not on anyone's mind. Vladi felt panic creeping over him. He didn't have answers.

"Have a seat right over there," the officer instructed. He flipped a sign over his kiosk, and immediately two armed guards appeared and stood on either side of Vladi where he was seated. The officer left his station and returned a few minutes later with a man in a suit.

"You come with us," the men told Vladi. Before he could think, the bulky armed guards had taken hold of him on each side.

KGB. There was no doubt. The thought was almost paralyzing for Vladi.

The cadre escorted Vladi down the dingy beige corridor, a labyrinth of offices and interrogation rooms connected by hallways with moldy tile. The whole place had a faint musty odor reminiscent of a teenage boy's locker. There were holding cells furnished with nothing but metal squat toilets and wooden benches, with handcuffs attached and waiting. Vladi glanced into one room and noticed dog cages, but no dogs. The canines were all out front, sniffing arriving passengers in the queue.

After patting Vladi down, the guards led him into a side room for what they called a secondary inspection. The officer accompanied them, but the man in the suit took over the interview. He questioned Vladi for several minutes while officers moved in and out of the room. They didn't say what they were doing, but Vladi could guess they were making calls to verify his statements.

At one point, he was left in the room for a half hour without explanation. It was just Vladi and the guards, neither of whom spoke to him.

This is my worst fear coming to life.

Come now, Marco, you could have sent one bag with me, no? Vladi gritted his teeth. *If I am coming in with a lie to Soviet officials, my story must have at least a shred of plausibility.*

Vladi kept his thoughts in check as they threatened to spiral into visible frustration.

There is no time for blaming. I must have my story straight before speaking again.

The man in the suit returned without an explanation of where he had been. This time, he came alone.

"You say you are here for a meeting with a colonel ..." The man in the suit looked at the officer's notes and raised his eyebrows while pronouncing the syllables. "... Boris Petrov."

"Yes," Vladi affirmed.

"You know this Colonel Petrov well?" the KGB man asked, tilting his head to the side as he awaited Vladi's answer.

"Yes, he is the foremost expert on the processing and management of the prison system. I must say, his counsel has been invaluable."

"Hmm, this is most interesting. We were unaware that Colonel Petrov had been involved with our interests in Cuba for some time."

"Oh, the operation has been classified, according to your military. Most of our consultations are secret. I am sure you understand," Vladi explained confidently, acting as though the KGB man would relate.

The KGB officer changed his facial expression into an appearance of sadness. He looked long into Vladi's eyes. He drew a deep breath and seemed almost physically weary.

"This Colonel Boris Petrov who served in Cuba was transferred some years ago — to Afghanistan. I regret to inform you that he perished in combat there. Indeed, we honor such a true hero of the *rodina*."

They are better liars than me. He could no longer tell if the KGB man was serious or making this up. He hoped it was the latter.

"We made a phone call to Havana. Sud'ya Rivera, it is highly unusual that we have such a distinguished visitor as yourself." The KGB man paused and inhaled dramatically. "It is even more unusual for a man to be in two places at once."

Vladi was caught. Of all people, he should not have been surprised to see the KGB follow up on everything he told them. *There is no other choice but to tell the whole truth and let everything play out as it will.*

He sighed and straightened up, looking the KGB agent in the eye. "I will tell you the truth."

The officer settled back in his chair, dangling his pen languidly from his hand with a somewhat bored expression. He always got the truth in the end, and today wouldn't be any different.

After telling his story and enduring two more hours of questioning, Vladi was arrested.

Well, at least I do not have to worry about where to find an overcoat or how to get a train ticket to Kavkaz with no rubles.

Over the next few days, Vladi received several visits from KGB personnel, who repeatedly asked him the same questions. In the adjacent cell was a man who claimed to be a dissident. A couple of times a day, the KGB personnel would come and remove him from his cell for a half-hour, then return him. Vladi was sure he was an informant put there to coax information out of Vladi and listen for candid confessions.

Then, on the third day, a man showed up. The guards unlocked Vladi's cell for him.

"Vladi — Colonel Gavrilov — is it you?"

Vladi stood up. "Yes," he answered, bewildered about how this meeting was beginning. It was taking on a completely different tone from anything that had happened up until now.

"You probably do not remember me. I am Misha Ivanov."

Vladi's eyes widened in surprise.

"Of course, Ivan!" A big smile accompanied his enthusiastic reply. "How have you been?"

Misha's last name was shortened to a nickname, so he was simply "Ivan" to old comrades.

The men embraced. It had been three decades since they had seen each other, serving together in Cuba.

"We thought you were killed in the Tu-114 crash out of Havana years ago. I cannot believe my eyes." Ivan was almost giddy.

Ivan had been a junior officer back in those days. Vladi remembered him as being bright — good to work with. It was not surprising to learn that he was now working in the Lubyanka as a liaison to the Kremlin.

"When I heard the name and the story, I told them I knew you. I have been assigned to accompany you back to Moscow."

"That is good news. So, what can be done?" Vladi asked, now trying not to appear as exhausted as he was.

"I am sorry to say they will keep you there until some decisions are made about how to handle this unusual situation," Ivan answered. "Try not to worry. I have connections all the way to the top."

The KGB officers provided an overcoat for Vladi — nothing stylish, but it was warm. Vladi, Ivan, and two military escorts left the jail and got on the rail for the eight-hour journey to Moscow. Vladi was allowed to wear his own clothes instead of prison garb, but he remained shackled. He spent the few hours of winter daylight gazing out the windows, absorbing the sights of the *rodina* as they whooshed by.

Between cat naps, Ivan worked on writing his report about the case. As soon as they arrived, Ivan saw to it that Vladi's file was forwarded to the Kremlin.

Word of recovering Lieutenant Colonel Gavrilov traveled fast throughout the Kremlin. In fact, President Mikhail Gorbachev was among the first to hear this amazing story. He remembered Vladi from their university days. As a young man, Comrade Vladi was someone he held in high regard. Gorbachev decided that an official pardon would be quietly issued. This would be a good test case for his *Perestroika* and *Glasnost* reforms and a way to help a former comrade.

Ivan personally delivered the good news to Vladi. "We are going to get you out of here. After a small mountain of paperwork is completed, of course," Ivan smiled.

There were always forms and delays in a bureaucracy, but a few days later, Vladi was approved to leave and move on with his life.

Vladi sank into his chair in relief, bowing his head to conceal the tear he felt threatening to run from one of his eyes. *I am finally going home. I was not sure this day would come. But wait —*

"Ivan, now I have a new problem."

"Tell me," Ivan responded.

"I will need train fare to Kavkaz and some rubles for something to eat along the way."

"Let me see what I can do," Ivan told him. "I am confident that we can take care of everything."

"Oh, and one more thing."

"What is that?" Ivan asked.

Vladi smiled back at him. "Can I keep the fantastic KGB overcoat?"

3
KAVKAZ

"We have a soldier coming in on today's run," the Russian Railways conductor at Kavkaz told his young station assistant as he returned from a lunch break.

"Do you want me to notify the mortician?" the assistant asked dispassionately. The corpses of Russian soldiers were regularly transported via rail.

"No. He does not need a mortician," the station conductor replied with a dry chuckle. "This is interesting, though. The whole nation thought he perished back when a plane out of Cuba crashed into the ocean during the Caribbean Crisis. Turns out, he is alive after all these years."

"What is his connection to Kavkaz?" the assistant probed.

"Family. He is from here."

"Really? Kavkaz is not a big place. Who would that be?"

"The wire says Gavrilov."

"*Oro*, that must be Erik Gavrilov's brother! I saw Comrade Gavrilov at the market on my lunch break. Should we try to let him know?"

"That is a good idea. Run over and see if you can find him. Here, take the teletype copy."

The eager station assistant stuffed the teletype message into his pocket and took off running as fast as he could. This was indeed big news. Nothing of this magnitude had ever happened in their tiny rural village, and the assistant was excited to be the bearer of such good news.

"Comrade Gavrilov, excuse me, sir!" He ran up to Erik, out of breath. "Your brother."

"My brother what?"

The young station assistant rapidly pulled the teletype message out of his pocket and shoved it into Erik's hands.

"This! This is your brother, is it not? He is coming to Kavkaz on today's run."

Erik looked at the teletype, reading it again. He was dumbstruck — his eyes like one who'd seen a dead man alive.

"*Ne mozhet bit* — impossible. It cannot be," he whispered under his breath. Without another word, he dropped the produce in his hands and took off running, leaving cabbages and turnips strewn onto the snow.

The door to Olga's home flew open with a bang. Erik ran in unannounced and panting — not so much from the exertion of running as from the shock of what he had just read. His startled sister looked up from where she'd been boiling eggs and diced potatoes on the stove to go with the cucumbers and radishes in her famous *okroshka* soup recipe.

"What? Are you having a heart attack? What is wrong, Erik?" She tried to get an explanation.

"You will not believe it, sister!"

Oh no, here he goes again. "Believe what?"

"Vladi ..." Erik got choked up. "... he is ..." He couldn't get it out. "He is ... coming home."

Olga's concerned look changed to a sort of angry skepticism.

"This is not funny. Do not do this to me, Erik! If you are lying, I will personally skin you like one of your wild hogs."

With a trembling hand, Erik handed her the teletype copy.

"Really," he said, his voice trembling as he held out the message.

"Oh, Lord — oh, Lord. How can this be?" Olga scanned the message carefully as if unable to believe her eyes. "Yet it says right here! Is this a mistake?" It wasn't her reluctance to believe — she just wanted to be sure. Her mind was having to adjust to the suddenness of receiving and accepting this news that seemed impossible.

"No — no, it is no mistake," Erik insisted. "The rail station assistant gave this to me. He ran to tell me himself. It must be true."

Olga fell to her knees, her eyes bright with tears and shock. She hugged the paper to her chest and rocked slightly. "Oh, thank You, dear Lord!"

In sudden realization, she screamed, "Irina!"

Irina ran into the room, alarmed, especially when she saw Olga kneeling on the floor.

"Are you hurt?"

Olga scrambled to her feet and hugged her sister-in-law like she would squeeze her to death. Irina was bewildered and gasped, trying to catch her breath after the overpowering embrace.

"What is the matter, Olga?" Then noticing Erik, "Erik, you are here ... ?"

Erik nodded, wordless, standing by the smoldering stove.

"Vladi is alive!" Olga sobbed, holding out the teletype copy. Irina looked at the paper without touching it as if it might burst into flames or turn out to be some kind of apparition.

"Vladi? My Vladi? Are you sure ... ?"

Erik and Olga both nodded solemnly in unison.

Irina began shaking and her eyes clouded over with sudden, overwhelming tears. She tried to speak, but no words came out, just a quivering of her lips. Her eyes rolled back, and she collapsed in a trembling heap. Olga and Erik caught her and laid her down on the sofa.

"Get a damp cloth," Olga instructed Erik.

Within a few minutes, they had her sitting up again. "Take it easy," Olga told her as she supported Irina's back.

"How?" Irina inquired, echoing Olga's disbelief. "How can this be after so long?"

Erik repeated the assurance he had given Olga, "I would not believe it myself if the rail station assistant had not told me."

"Oh, the Lord is so good," she kept repeating. It was all she could think. She couldn't process the situation further. Olga took charge.

"Erik, try to reach the girls. It will take them time to get here. As soon as she's back on her feet, we will go notify Aleksey."

Erik took off, running back to his apartment. Aleksey had his own apartment only a few blocks from where Olga and Irina lived. Whenever Irina recovered, she and Olga walked to his home to visit. Now, they moved along at a normal pace, stride for stride, allowing themselves time to talk and regain their composure. At the sound of their persistent knocking, Aleksey hastened to the door. He had been reading a Soviet-approved history of Cuba while sitting on an old armchair by the heater.

"Mama. Tetya." The young man of thirty greeted them with a smile. "This is a surprise. I was not expecting visitors today, but it is always nice to see you."

Neither woman moved to enter the apartment — they just stood at the doorway. Olga looked at Irina, waiting for her to deliver the news. Within a fraction of a second, Aleksey detected that something was awry.

"Did something happen to Dyadya?" he asked, using the name by which he called his uncle, Erik.

Irina took a deep breath. "No ... no. Aleksey, your Papa is alive ... and he is coming home." Irina could hardly get the words out, but once they left her mouth, she started bawling.

Aleksey looked up at Olga, who was nodding in confirmation.

"Oh, my —" Aleksey was stunned. The father who had left before his birth but never returned from his military post. This giant of a man, who had only ever existed in his imagination, was about to appear in the flesh.

"How ... ? I do not under—" He wasn't even sure what to think, much less what to say.

"We do not know," Irina told him. "All we know is that he is coming. The railway station was notified, and the assistant carried a message to Dyadya himself."

The two women looked at him as if expecting to see him jump for joy, but Aleksey felt like he'd taken a kick in his chest. He took a step backward and sighed.

"I am not ready for this," was Aleksey's reply. His whole life, he had wanted to know his father more than anything in the world. He just wasn't mentally prepared to have him show up in a moment. He needed time to think — for this to register in his senses. Olga and Irina could tell that the startling news was uncomfortable for Aleksey.

"The train arrives at fifteen o'clock," Olga told him — of course, everyone knew what time the fifteen o'clock train arrived in Kavkaz. "We will be at the station."

Aleksey stood and watched as they retreated into the snow, hugging each other and talking excitedly. Then he closed his door quietly and paced by the fire, his book lying neglected on the side table.

Irina, Olga, and Erik stood on the station platform as fifteen o'clock approached. Erik fidgeted restlessly. Irina closed her eyes and took deep breaths. Olga stood serenely, silently praying for her brother to arrive. Aleksey, however, did not appear.

Kavkaz was near the end of the line, so the Russian Railways train had fewer than six railcars on any given day. As the train came into sight, the three watched it intently. The train moved towards them as if in slow motion. It felt like it took an eternity for it to come to a stop.

The trio rearranged themselves on the platform so they were aligned with the doors where the two passenger carriages joined. Through the windows, they could see the silhouette of a tall man in an overcoat walking along the aisle toward the doors.

"I think that is him," Erik whispered and pointed. Olga didn't acknowledge him, though. That had to be him. Irina kept her eyes fixed on the moving figure. The tall man finally emerged from the door, keeping his eyes on the icy steps down to the platform.

Erik stepped forward, ready to rush his brother. Olga put her arm up to restrain him. She gave him a look of warning, and he stepped back. They remained where they stood and let Irina take a few timorous steps forward.

As Vladi stepped onto the platform, his eyes fell on a woman with graying hair, an older version of the same Irina who inhabited his memories every day and night. *She is here.* Vladi could hardly believe she was in front of him.

They paused for the briefest moment, meeting each other's eyes. Wordlessly, they both leaped forward, closing the remaining distance between them and embraced like they had waited thirty years to hold each other, which they had. Both sobbed heartily as they kissed and kissed again — and again.

Irina took his hand and turned toward Olga and Erik. They ran forward and held each other in one fantastic group hug. Not a word had yet been spoken.

"Where have you been?" Erik blurted out, breaking the silence. Olga gave him a disapproving look. "I mean, where is your baggage? Let me help you," he corrected himself sheepishly. Olga couldn't help the little smile that turned the corner of her mouth.

Vladi spread his hands with a wry laugh. "It is just me."

That beautiful, deep baritone voice fell on Irina's ears like music. Tears of happiness continued to stream down her frozen cheeks.

"Where — where have you been?" Irina held the rights to that question, and she couldn't hold it in longer, nor would Olga stop her. "Where?" she sobbed. Vladi hugged her close, wordless.

"Come," Olga said. "Let us go to my home, and we can talk where it is warmer."

Their daughters began arriving throughout the afternoon, which turned into an emotional and beautiful reunion. Vladi could hardly believe what splendid young women they had become — smart, tall like him, and each one was delightful in her own way. They brought their husbands and Vladi's grandchildren, ten in all.

Vladi was making a mental inventory of everyone present — there were the three daughters. A fourth offspring had not appeared, and Vladi felt a pang of anxiety. He was eager to know. What of the unborn child he had left behind? Yet, there was so much going on that Vladi felt it was prudent to wait until a more private moment to ask.

That evening, Erik was preparing a delicacy of smoked pork with Cubanelle peppers that he had been saving for a special occasion. This was about as special as any would ever be.

"Aleksey is quite the hog hunter — I taught him everything I know," Erik declared. "He is just like his father."

The crowded room suddenly got quiet at Erik's words. All eyes were on Vladi.

"Aleksey?" Vladi asked.

"Yes, Vladi. Your son," Erik reiterated but with a more prudent tone this time.

Vladi's eyes welled up as he scanned the room.

Irina slid over to his side. "Yes, Vladi, you have a son."

"And his name is ... Aleksey?" Vladi asked haltingly.

"Yes, his name is Aleksey," she said. "Formally Aleksander. You do approve of the name, I hope — no?"

Vladi looked around the room again, bewildered. The question about approving of the name didn't even register in his mind. "Well — where is he?"

No one spoke. Olga and Erik looked at Irina, waiting for her to tell him.

"He is not here," Irina explained. "He wants to meet you, I know, but he is not ready yet."

Vladi was confounded but did his best to be understanding. *He does not want to meet his father? Well, I am nothing more than a stranger to him after all ...*

"My son. Tell me about him," Vladi asked Irina in a gentle tone.

"So much like his father —" She looked deeply into his eyes with a tiny smile. "He was a military man too — a captain." Vladi's eyes widened slightly. "Two tours in Afghanistan —"

Vladi's countenance fell, suddenly anxious about what happened to his son.

"— an explosion ended his military career. But he survived."

Olga spoke up. "He has recovered from the injuries — it just changed things for him. He lives nearby."

"Will you ask him again to come? I wish to see him," Vladi persisted, anxious to meet his youngest child, the son he had only ever imagined.

"Soon enough," Irina tenderly touched him on the arm.

At that moment, there was a knock at the door. Erik got up to answer. "Well, look who's here," he stated with mild surprise. A cocked eyebrow was the only reply. Without saying anything further, Erik swung the door wider, and the room fell silent as all eyes went toward the door.

There stood a young man who looked identical to Vladi on the day he left home for Cuba. His eyes connected with Vladi's — for a moment, no words were said.

"Papa." Aleksey made a slight coughing sound like something was caught in his throat.

"My son," Vladi could hardly speak the words above a whisper. He stood and took a step toward him with open arms.

Aleksey ran to him as would a little child who had been waiting for his father to come home. He wrapped his arms around this man — this great man. His father was living, and he was here — he was *here*.

In his typical manner, Erik broke the silence of this precious moment. "Anyone ready to eat?"

"*Ara!*" went up the reply around the room.

Erik called the room to attention and then, as was their custom, turned the floor over to Olga.

Olga spoke, "Let us give thanks to the Lord, not only for our meal but for His goodness to us this day."

Vladi stood up. Olga's mind was yanked back to the contentious discussions of their youth.

But nobody expected what came next.

"I will pray today," Vladi declared.

Olga and Irina exchanged glances. They could hardly believe their eyes that Vladi stood before them. Now, they could hardly believe what they were hearing.

"We have much to be grateful for," Vladi told everyone, "and I will thank our God."

Olga wept and quietly gave thanks. *Oh, gracious Lord, this is Your mighty hand.*

4

THE LAND OF THE FREE

"Ladies and gentlemen," the captain's voice crackled over the intercom, breaking through the hum of the plane's engines. His tone radiated excitement. "If you look out the right side of the aircraft, you will be greeted by a breathtaking view of the Manhattan skyline. And there, in New York Harbor, stands our beloved lady, the Statue of Liberty!"

Passengers shuffled to the right side of the aircraft and craned their necks, eager to catch a glimpse.

"She is much smaller than I imagined," Aleksey remarked to Vladi. He had his face pressed against the window, taking in the iconic symbol of freedom and hope. Despite its diminutive size against a backdrop of skyscrapers that nearly reached into the clouds, its symbolic magnitude and significance were not lost on Aleksey. He shared the moment with his father. Vladi had his lucky aisle seat in the aft exit row. Irina happily occupied the middle seat between them.

They were on the second leg of their journey to America.

Over the few months spent in Kavkaz, Vladi had many opportunities to catch up on what he missed and share his story with the family. Aleksey was especially amazed by his father's experiences.

Vladi had told them about his life in Florida, and without pressure, he had also proposed the option of emigrating to America.

The girls had established families — understandably, they would stay in Russia.

Irina wanted to be wherever Vladi was — be it Kavkaz, Florida, or anywhere else in the world.

At this point in his life, Aleksey had no reason to remain in Russia. Like Irina, he was most eager to make up some of the lost time with his father and discover a new life. From how his father described Florida, it sounded far more interesting than Kavkaz.

Getting both the Soviet Union and the United States to agree to allow them to emigrate had been a complicated process. Vladi again went to Ivan for help. Vladi had favor with President Gorbachev, and the Soviet leader was eager to advance discussions with U.S. President-elect George H.W. Bush as a token olive branch demonstrating cooperation between the former Cold War adversaries. Quietly accommodating Vladi would circumvent any possibility of his situation drawing media attention and mushrooming into an international incident. At the same time, it would be a small step toward warming diplomatic relations with Washington.

Meanwhile, Vladi worked through other hurdles. For one thing, his bank in Florida had accounts in the name of his alias, Moses Moskowitz. To further complicate matters, he now had to legally prove that wasn't his given name, that he had done business for years under an alias to protect his personal safety and to avoid the risk of revealing his real identity. Simply making a withdrawal for travel expenses had also been an ordeal, as the bank manager was reluctant to release funds for an overseas wire to Russia.

At least they are protecting my money, Vladi reasoned.

Altogether, the process took about three months to work through. *It was all worth the effort*, Vladi thought later that day as he landed at the Orlando International Airport with Irina and Aleksey beside him.

Their hearts were filled with anticipation for what lay ahead. As they took those first steps off the aircraft, the moment almost felt surreal. With official documents, including letters from the State Department, they breezed through customs and immigration.

"Welcome to America," the immigration agent said with a friendly smile. Vladi translated for his wife and son. Irina and Aleksey's faces were filled with delight at hearing those words.

"You never thought you would have those words directed to you," Vladi remarked to Irina.

"No, I never could have imagined," she beamed in return.

Irina and Aleksey walked slowly through the Orlando airport, awestruck by all they saw around them. They were completely dazzled. Neither had ever been treated to such a spectacle of color, light, and modern ... everything.

"Papa, I did not know you lived at Disney World," were the first words Aleksey spoke in his new country.

Vladi laughed heartily, his eyes crinkling at the corners. "Wait until you see the real Disney World, my son."

Vladi had been critical of Ronald Reagan in times past. Looking back, he had to concede that there was much he appreciated about the former U.S. President. Reagan always upheld America as a place of opportunity — a place where decent, hardworking, God-fearing people would be welcome. Something Reagan famously said resonated with Vladi. As he recalled, it went like this:

"America represents something universal in the human spirit. I received a letter not long ago from a man who said, 'You can go to Japan to live, but you cannot become Japanese. You can go to France to live and not become a Frenchman. You can go to live in Germany or Turkey, and you won't become a German or a Turk.' But then Reagan added, 'Anybody from any corner of the world can come to America to live and become an American.'"

This proved to be true — it was the reality that Vladi, Irina, and Aleksey were about to inhabit. Previously, Vladi had heard Reagan's idealistic words more as empty rhetoric, but now he felt their significance.

As they left the airport and stepped out into the golden light of the warm Florida sunshine, the trio were about to begin a new chapter in their lives, and the possibilities were endless. But beyond the novelty and the excitement of their new surroundings, there was a deeper sense of possibility that filled the air.

For the Gavrilov family, America was not just a new place to live — it was a place where they could start over and where they could be together. The road to this moment had been long and winding, with hurdles that had tested Vladi's resolve. The future was uncertain, but they knew that whatever challenges lay ahead, they would face them together, as a family. For Vladi, Irina, and Aleksey, the adventure had only just begun.

Irina and Aleksey were no less amazed when they crossed the threshold into the grand foyer of Vladi's palatial abode — their new home. Their eyes widened with wonder.

"Papa, you live in a palace?" Aleksey remarked, in awe.

Their senses were overcome by the sheer opulence and grandeur of the space. The ornate architecture was nothing short of magnificent, with intricate details adorning every surface. The lavish décor was equally impressive, with plush furnishings and tasteful art pieces arranged in a way that made the space feel both regal and welcoming, a place where luxury and comfort blended seamlessly. Never had they seen anything quite like this in a private residence.

Vladi quipped, "My home is modest compared to some others. But I hope it will be comfortable for both of you."

"I can see it needs the touch of a woman," Irina teased, with a twinkle in her eyes.

For Vladi, this wasn't about a show of wealth and extravagance. It was the realization of a dream that had been elusive for so long. Having Irina and his son here, standing in his formerly lonely home, was more emotional to Vladi than it was even to them. This place that had always felt empty to him took on the presence of a home the moment Irina and Aleksey walked in with him. It was like an incomplete puzzle had finally been made whole.

Home. I am finally home.

Vladi's heart swelled as his eyes rested on the scene before him. He couldn't help staring at his wife and son. Their presence transformed the atmosphere into a sanctuary. It was as if the sun had burst through the clouds, flooding his home with light. The deep loneliness he'd felt in his formerly solitary life was now like the faint pangs of a half-forgotten bad dream. This was his life now, and he couldn't be more grateful.

As Irina and Aleksey explored the house, a woman bustled into the room. She screeched with excitement, "Señor Moisés!" Irina and Aleksey looked at Vladi, wondering who she was and whom she was talking about.

Vladi laughed. "She is our housekeeper — and a very good one at that," he added as he gave Marina a friendly hug that underscored his appreciation for her.

Marina chattered away in rapid Spanish. "Señor Moisés, where have you been?"

"That is the question I am asked everywhere I go," he replied with a laugh. "The story is too long for now, but thank you for taking care of everything in my absence. If there are any expenses that I need to take care of, please let me know."

The word spread rapidly among the refugees that Vladi was back. It was clear to Irina and Aleksey that Vladi was a man loved and respected by those around him. Before long, one of his best foremen, Antonio, appeared on his doorstep.

"*Jefe*, where have you been? You went fishing then come back eight months later! I've missed you, *jefe*," Antonio said, smiling and putting a friendly hand on Vladi's shoulder.

"I missed you too, my friend," Vladi replied, happy to see his loyal foreman.

"Except for a few, the labor hands took work with other growers. I, too, have worked other jobs to make money," Antonio admitted sheepishly, as if in some way he'd been unfaithful. "In your absence, I have kept the groves watered and ensured attention was given to basic maintenance. I kept telling everyone, 'Señor Moisés, he will be back.'"

Vladi was overwhelmed by the faithfulness of this foreman. He promoted Antonio to manager over all his field operations and tripled his pay on the spot. He also used the opportunity to introduce his son, Aleksey.

"I didn't know you had a son, *jefe*."

"I did not either," Vladi replied, smiling all the while. He was like a new man — a man who was more human, more relatable.

"Starting tomorrow, Antonio, I want you to take Aleksey with you to the orchards," Vladi instructed. "I want you to show him every detail of the field operations. Meanwhile, get the word out that we are back in operation. I want you to make wise choices and only hire labor hands who have good attitudes and will be reliable workers."

Just as Vladi had instructed, Aleksey followed Antonio to the citrus groves the next day. Although he knew neither English nor Spanish, he used a lot of pointing and creative gestures to communicate. The labor hands were highly amused by this. Despite the lack of words, Aleksey's warmth shined through. They all took an instant liking to him, and he to them.

Like his father, he was a quick and disciplined learner. Before long, he began picking up the basics of both languages, and communication became easier.

Aleksey took a keen interest in citrus cultivation. The warmth of the sun, the smell of the citrus trees, and the sound of his own father's voice as he patiently taught his son the business — it all added up to pure joy and contentment for Aleksey. When he wasn't in the groves learning how to put things together and keep it all running, he went everywhere with Vladi.

This kid is impressive, Vladi observed. *I am proud of him, truly proud — in a good kind of way. He could be even better than his father*, Vladi mused humorously.

Day by day, Vladi mentored him in how the free market worked. Aleksey didn't have the same initial resistance to a capitalist economy that Vladi had struggled over. Aleksey soaked up everything and then went to work implementing his new knowledge.

For Vladi, though, this was more than just a successful business venture now. It was an opportunity to build something together, something that he could pass down to his son and to future generations. He felt a sense of purpose in leaving something meaningful for his family. And now, with Aleksey at his side, Vladi knew that he was on course to accomplish just that.

Within days of their arrival, the Gavrilov family made the short drive to the home of Dr. Julio Rivera. The setting sun cast its rays in vibrant hues over central Florida, bathing their faces in a warm glow as they arrived at the doorstep of Vladi's trusted friend. Hearts were pounding with anticipation, and for good reason — Vladi and Julio hadn't seen each other since Vladi's disappearance nearly a year earlier.

Julio didn't even wait for them to reach his door. Impatient, he stepped outside to meet Vladi on his way up the driveway. Indeed, a melody of joy filled the air as Vladi and Julio embraced with the fervor of those who shared a deep bond. As they made their way inside, Vladi proudly introduced his family to Julio and his own family.

It was no surprise that the Rivera family's sweet nature and genuine love for one another were infectious, and this made the Gavrilovs feel at home despite the language barrier. The families felt an instant connection, as though they'd known each other for decades.

As they settled in for a cozy evening of catching up, Julio's curiosity got the better of him. He gently probed Vladi about his disappearance. Many months earlier, Vladi's unusually prolonged absence had prompted Julio to casually inquire as to the whereabouts of his old friend.

"I asked some of the orchard workers, but no one knew where you were,"

Julio told him. "They said you disappeared one day and never came back. You've made your way home, I see. You are doing well?"

Their comfortable setting filled with Vladi's warm, resonating voice. "Yes, I am well — better than ever. But there have been a few — I will call them miracles — along the way." He had been waiting for this moment to tell Julio everything that had happened.

"Oh?" Julio asked, intrigued.

"I have quite the story to tell." Vladi then recounted how he had been imprisoned in Cuba, how the Lord had rescued his soul, and about Marco's miraculous change of heart.

Julio's voice rang out with hearty laughter, almost disbelieving. "I'm not sure whose change of heart has surprised me more," he said, his smile reaching his eyes.

They talked over the details, and everyone wanted to know more. Vladi promised to explain it all in even greater detail soon.

"Now, I have news that may surprise you." Julio elaborated that he had received word from Marco, now living in Jamaica.

"Marco is doing well," Julio was pleased to report. "He intends to remain in Jamaica, where he can assist dissidents fleeing Cuba. He also plans on marrying a delightful travel agent there soon."

Vladi raised an eyebrow in surprise.

"Most of all," Julio continued, "Marco was asking many spiritual questions, and by all indications, he is walking with the Lord."

"This makes me very happy," Vladi said. While he was speaking the truth, there was a hint of hesitation in the statement, as if it were met with some skepticism.

"I am glad to have you both as my brothers now. Now, I only have to meet your wonderful sister, Olga, whom I have heard you talk so much about," Julio teased.

Vladi laughed, "In time, in time. I know she will come to visit us soon.

Then you can bask in each other's saintly glory." He never knew when his lame Russian humor might fall flat, but Vladi couldn't resist kidding with Julio.

Irina had also come to know the Lord during her time living with Olga. With Julio's help, Vladi found a healthy local church that he and Irina could attend regularly and where they could grow together spiritually. Aleksey went a few times, but he had little interest in church. He had long since grown weary of Tetya's incessant talk of the Bible.

The Rivera family were gracious hosts, who spared no effort in helping their guests feel at ease in their home. They had genuine curiosity and asked many questions, eager to hear about Irina and Aleksey's lives back in Kavkaz. They had to rely on Vladi to translate both sides of the conversation, which was a little awkward, but manageable. Much of their conversation centered around things of the Lord and His Word, which Aleksey found boring, although he remained polite and respectful.

Aleksey's apathy toward God weighed on Vladi's heart day and night. But Vladi thought about his own past — of all the years of resistance to anything of God — and how that had all changed when he had least expected. If God could rescue his soul, Vladi knew that no one was out of reach. He persevered in prayer for his son, realizing that God often answers in ways we would never anticipate. He felt a calm settle over him — *I will trust God to do what He knows best.*

As the evening came to a close, Vladi felt a deep sense of gratitude for his old friend and for the journey that had led him back home. He was grateful for the love and support of his new family in Christ. As he hugged Julio goodbye and the Gavrilovs walked out into the warm Florida night, Vladi was reassured that their friendship would endure through whatever trials lay ahead. This was only the beginning of a new chapter in their lives.

The next few months were filled with new beginnings for the Gavrilov family. They became part of the community, making friends with the workers and their families, growing to love America even more — both the land and the people who called it home. As Vladi looked out over his thriving citrus groves, reflecting on how life was going, he knew that Aleksey and Irina were home in every sense of the word.

5

A FATHER ... AND A SON

By 1994, the trees planted after the great freeze were bearing fruit, and Red Star Citrus was more than just profitable again — they were flush with cash.

In the roughly three years since they'd seen each other, Irina and Olga had written back and forth frequently. Irina would tell her about life in America, and Olga would share how various children were coming along in the orphanage. The ladies missed each other terribly — possibly the only drawback to Irina's new life in the United States. That, and the fact that she missed her girls and their children, of course. The women had been so close through the trials and the long years Vladi was gone.

Vladi was no longer bringing over refugees from Cuba. Instead, he provided private funding for much-needed capital improvements at the orphanage where Olga served. Vladi had confidence in Olga's ongoing ministry to the children there and wanted to invest his resources in the Lord's kingdom work. He made a practice of giving away more than he kept for himself, conscious that this demonstration of stewardship provided an example for Aleksey to follow.

Vladi's training of Aleksey was more than just giving his son a job — he wanted him to take over the Red Star Citrus operation in the future. Eventually, he would leave Aleksey in charge of the daily operations. As Aleksey's knowledge and management skills grew, it allowed Vladi more time for personal trips to the port. While Aleksey was growing more confident and taking on more responsibilities, he was also becoming more independent. Vladi had lived long enough to recognize that there were benefits to his zeal and confidence, but also pitfalls should Aleksey stray from his wisdom and guidance.

Vladi and Irina talked it over. He wanted to spend father-and-son time with Aleksey outside of work, and Irina loved the idea. Vladi didn't have to twist his son's arm too much. They were still in the long process of getting to know each other, and getting to spend more time together outside work was valuable to both of them. Aleksey took some time off, and they headed to the coast in Vladi's pickup truck.

"I have something for you," Vladi teased, dangling a lure in Aleksey's face.

Aleksey's eyes lit up. They were going fishing!

"I am sure you have been taught by the best," Vladi chuckled, referring to Erik. "However, the ocean is a different world than our little backcountry Sulla-Chubutla River in Kavkaz."

Aleksey chuckled in turn and said, "Well, then I will have been taught by masters of both river and sea. I am up for the challenge!"

Their first stop was Roy's Bait & Tackle Shop for "groceries." As they approached the weathered blue-gray building, Aleksey saw the blue marlin and exclaimed, "Look at that GIANT fish! Is that what we will catch today?"

Vladi laughed, "I would love that. Then we could show Erik who is truly the master of fishing!"

They walked across the boardwalk. Moments later, the tinkling bells on the shop door announced their entry. Vladi asked if Roy was there, hopeful that he could introduce his son.

"I'm sorry," the clerk told him with a disappointed tone. "Roy recently retired."

"Retired from what?" Vladi responded with mock contempt. "Retired from fishing?"

About that time, a cat emerged from between the aisles and rubbed against Vladi's ankles.

"Well, look who is here — Molly Brown. You don't have to trip me to get my attention." Vladi bent down and rubbed her head affectionately.

Aleksey was scanning the store with amazement.

"American fishing stores are fantastic! *Dyadya* will move to America if he ever sees this."

"He would not know what to do with all of this. If he is still anything like his younger self, he would prefer catching fish like a bear — with bare hands and his teeth," Vladi joked. "That would not work so well with the sharks."

"I think he would welcome that dare from you," Aleksey played along.

Aleksey walked up and down each aisle, studying the merchandise along the way and stopping to examine some particularly brilliant lures and other gadgets.

"I could spend days here. I have never seen such things. Do you know what all this gear is used for?" Aleksey asked, inspecting what appeared to him as strange and exotic fishing lures.

"I am flattered that you think your papa may know everything about fishing, but no, I do not know what fish every lure is used for. However, I used to fish with a man who did. And he taught me a great deal about fishing in the ocean."

Aleksey and Vladi wound their way through the aisle for a long while. Without thought, Vladi began singing to himself... "Back in the U.S.S.R."

Aleksey looked over at him. "Papa, you know that song?"

Vladi simply laughed.

Aleksey tossed some trivia at Vladi. "Did you know the Beatles never actually..."

"... visited the Soviet Union." Vladi finished his sentence. Again, Aleksey was astonished that his father knew this kind of thing.

"It always bothered me," Vladi remarked. "But they will never know what they missed." He winked at Aleksey.

Aleksey finally made his way to the back of the store, to the display of filet knives beneath the sign that read, "One cut and you're through."

Fascinated with the quality of American fishing knives, Aleksey made the tongue-in-cheek observation, "All these nice knives — but none of them are any good for hog hunting."

Vladi's mind was somewhere else. Memories unfolded at a rapid-fire pace — Dan saving him from a watery grave, then meeting him again all those years later, right here. His imagination carried him through the scene — where he'd been standing, where Dan had been standing. How they looked at each other. How they —

"Papa? Papa, are you okay?"

Vladi exhaled hard and swallowed, then answered. "Yeah. Yeah, I am fine. About ready to go? I have something else for you."

They arrived at the docks and began unloading gear.

"Where are we going with this?" Aleksey asked.

"Right here." Vladi stepped up on a new Viking Sport Fisherman boat. He felt the emotions well up in him as he scanned the craft. On the white bow was its name painted in bright blue: *Skipper Dan*.

"Whose boat is this?" asked Aleksey.

Vladi looked at him with a casual reply, "It is your boat, son. You just have to let me use it now and then." He smiled.

"Whoa, Papa. I ... I do not even know what to say."

"You do not need to say anything. It is yours."

"How can I even accept this? It is ... too much, I think."

"Think of it as a gift, after all the time we missed over the past thirty years. And as something we can finally share together," Vladi told him.

"Well ..." Aleksey began to respond.

Vladi interrupted, "Do not feel reluctant about accepting this. I insist and will not hear another word of protest. Captain's orders."

"Aye aye, sir!" Aleksey snapped straight and saluted with mock formality.

"I see you have picked up some of your Dyadya's irreverent humor," Vladi remarked with a chuckle. It was evident that Aleksey and Erik had spent much time together.

"I have another question, and this may be even more irreverent, but — do you know how to drive this?" Aleksey asked, motioning his arms like he was steering.

"Of course," Vladi replied, donning his skipper cap. "What do you think I have been doing at the port all this time while you were working? I have been under training — learning how to operate the boat, how to navigate, maritime laws, and most importantly, how to get back to port when the weather is bad."

Aleksey examined every nook and cranny of the boat, running his hands over the fiberglass and examining the bridge instruments. "I only know how to use oars. I am not sure I will be of much help to you."

"You will be my first mate, and I will teach you everything," Vladi assured him. "For now, we will go fishing."

They didn't go far. Vladi was careful not to get overconfident, so he stayed within sight of land. Still, they found a patch of aquamarine water over a reef teeming with fish.

"Papa, this is the most beautiful and peaceful place I have ever been."

"It is special, indeed." Vladi agreed.

"I always thought the Caucasus Mountains were beautiful — and they are, in their own way," Aleksey said. But then he added, "Perhaps, this is better because you are here too."

Those were maybe the sweetest words Vladi had ever heard spoken.

"I have something else for you," he disclosed to Aleksey.

"More? What about the boat? Do you have an airplane too?" Aleksey chuckled.

"No," Vladi answered as he sat beside him. "Something that means more than a fleet of boats and airplanes."

He reached into his pocket and pulled out the old watch.

"This watch belonged to your grandfather and his father before him. Even before I knew I would have a son, I dreamed of the day I would do what my own father did, what his father before him did."

Aleksey studied the watch closely, his eyes widening.

"I longed to place this watch into the hand of my own son and tell him where this part of our history has been. When I imagined this moment, I did not know it would have traveled with me from the beloved *rodina* and back again ... by way of Havana ... by way of the Atlantic Ocean ... by way of America. This day was long-awaited for me — the time to place our legacy into your hands. It is yours to keep. And perhaps one day you will pass this on to your own son."

Vladi put the watch in Aleksey's hand. Aleksey turned it over and studied it in the light of the sun. He rubbed his fingers across the etched surface, then looked up at Vladi and embraced him.

For as long as he could remember, Vladi had planned to give his precious heirloom to his son when he approached adulthood. It didn't matter that he was thirty years late and already over sixty years old himself. At long last, he and Aleksey were together.

Vladi had waited almost his entire life for this moment — a moment that had slipped into impossibility time and time again, finally restored to him now.

What does man control? Vladi mused. *Nothing. God laughs at our plans. The same God who controls all of history — He controls my life — and Aleksey's.* Vladi loved this young man more than he ever imagined possible. He would give him the world if it were his to give. But the world wasn't his to give, and neither was life or time — it was God's to give. *I will pray that God loves him more and leads him to understand who makes the time that the watch measures.*

They fished for a while — a while they never wanted to end. As the sun began to set, Aleksey got around to asking how their boat came to be named the *Skipper Dan*.

Vladi could have said something about how much Dan loved fishing and left it at that. But there was so much more to why he named the boat — or why he even had the boat — and he wanted Aleksey to know. He thought a moment about how he would answer this question before replying to Aleksey.

"We live in a world that is insane with sin. Men count God's patience as indifference. They try to imagine He does not exist. I wasted most of my life as just such a man."

Aleksey appeared befuddled.

"God? What does that have to do with this man, Skipper Dan?"

Vladi reached over and picked up the watch he had given to Aleksey.

"Once I almost lost this precious timepiece — it was taken away. But I received more valuable gifts. One was time itself. The greater one was the gift of faith. Other things were taken away that I can never have back," he lamented.

"What were those other things?" Aleksey asked, genuinely wanting to know where he was going with this thought.

"Like a friendship — a special person. Dan was a true friend in life — a friend who would die for my sake."

"What made Dan special?" Aleksey asked.

Vladi snorted a half-laugh — there was almost too much to tell. "Well, where shall I begin?" He paused. "Let me try."

Aleksey sensed the weight of this moment. Much like Vladi, he had yearned to know his father's heart his whole life.

"Dan had a son. A son he loved very much. His name was ..." Vladi's voice trailed off, choked with emotion.

"Aleksey. There is another gift I want you to have more than anything the world ever has to offer you." He had Aleksey's rapt attention.

He started over. "There was a Father. He had a Son whom He loved very much — and His name was Jesus."

6

SEAWORTHY

Over the next few years after coming to live in Florida, Aleksey continued to learn about his father's business and came to handle the management of Red Star Citrus almost entirely on his own. Vladi watched with pride as Aleksey designed new systems and processes, resulting in better quality and increased profitability. Coming in from the outside, he brought a fresh sense of direction and vision to the business. Aleksey readily adapted his mind to the tenets of capitalism and proved his ability to not only cope with market transformations and competition, but also profit from them.

Aleksey wasn't all work and no play, though. He was, after all, his father's son — and his uncle's protégé. He loved the outdoors as much as the other Gavrilov men. Continuing to spend time on the water, Aleksey had a chance to greatly improve his maritime skills. With Vladi's guidance, he evolved from a helpful first mate into a capable skipper. Vladi wouldn't always be there to help him, he knew.

Unlike some other nations, the United States didn't burden small-craft skippers with onerous regulations. Formal training and licensing were optional, but not requirements. Whatever its downside, linking freedom and personal responsibility fostered an ethos of self-reliance. The level of knowledge that Aleksey gained helped him develop the confidence to trust his own abilities. This paid off whenever conditions deteriorated unexpectedly out on the water. Fast thinking and well-honed skills were imperative for a two-man crew alone at sea.

Hearing cautionary tales from Vladi, he was ever mindful of safety. Vladi had recounted to him the story of how Dan lost his young son and the horrors of his own experience adrift at sea. These accounts left an impression on Aleksey, who was sure of himself but not cocky. He recognized the need to respect his limits at sea.

"It is a terror I would not wish on the worst of my enemies, let alone my son," Vladi told Aleksey. "At best, the ocean itself is aggressively indifferent to your survival. At worst, the life swimming within it can easily take your life. That is why you must learn how to protect the boat and ultimately keep yourself from such a fate."

Aleksey took the advice to heart. Being a voracious learner, he also read everything he could on the subject. One pearl of wisdom that lodged in his mind was a saying by Ernest Shackleton: "A good sailor isn't fearful of high winds and big seas — he's petrified of the deep!"

I wonder if Papa ever heard this quote, Aleksey mused. *It is the same thing he tells me all the time. "Have a healthy fear of the ocean, but do not have a paralyzing fear."*

A powerful survival instinct was imbued in Aleksey. Thinking back on the potentially dangerous situations in which he'd occasionally found himself did induce a twinge of anxiety. He often thought about the thin hull beneath their feet.

It is the only thing between our seagoing habitat and the great abyss below. For a long time, the thought would send a little shiver across his skin. *I cannot dwell on that,* he would remind himself. *Instead, I must focus on what is required to keep us safe from being swallowed by that liquid abyss.*

He understood that no matter how skilled he was, there might always be situations beyond his control. Like his father, he had a plan for everything — well, almost everything. When he didn't, Aleksey was adaptable enough to cope with the unexpected.

One of those details was making certain that they had a sturdy lifeboat on board that was regularly inspected and kept in a ready condition.

Aleksey spent many pleasurable hours tinkering with the boat and all the gear. He was technically familiar with every line, valve, and electrical cable on their vessel. He knew the deck layout so well that he could have worked on it blindfolded.

Like Vladi, he accepted the profound responsibility that came with complete control of their vessel. He was a prudent skipper who learned to match his decisions to the boat's strength, the conditions at hand, and his own abilities. He found his skills continuously tested. The ever-capricious wind and sea were unpredictable and could quickly become any skipper's ferocious adversaries.

Aleksey developed an understanding of how to interpret the signs provided by the wind, sea, cloud cover, barometric changes, and vessel dynamics. Such "tells" helped corroborate weather forecasts and hinted at the changes that may lie ahead. No two outings were ever the same.

"It is always interesting, Papa — never too boring. No matter how many times we run the same passage, the elements always bring new challenges."

Vladi returned a smile. "Good! Those challenges will keep you sharp. We do not want your brain to rot from looking at your office computer too much."

"Hmph, you old men just do not appreciate the usefulness of computers," Aleksey teased. "I do not just rot my brain with work on the computer. I play fishing games on it too!" Aleksey added, with an emphasis on the word "fishing."

Of all the seafaring attributes Vladi observed in his son, perhaps he admired his mental acuity most. Aleksey could diagnose problems and devise workable solutions, even when the resources seemingly weren't available. He possessed an innate reflexive wisdom that was tested, augmented, and proven in every new situation he encountered. Beyond versatility, Aleksey's acuity showed in his hair-trigger action toward correct solutions. He had his "mind in the game," as the Americans would say.

Aleksey had honed his maritime skills close to home, but long-range cruising was among his ambitions. He wanted more! After coming to America and discovering the wonders beyond Kavkaz and Afghanistan, the only places he'd ever been, Aleksey developed a wanderlust for exploring new places. Relaxing in the living room after a long day out in the groves, Aleksey broached the subject to his father.

"Papa, how about we take the boat out somewhere? You and me — kind of an adventure. I want to go further."

"You mean having the ocean on three sides of Florida is not enough for you?" Vladi half-joked.

"You know I love it, but we are good enough to venture beyond our own coast," Aleksey appealed. "The fish around here see our boat coming and think, 'Oh, these guys again.' They go find something else to bite because they are onto our tricks. We need some new places — new fish."

"That is ridiculous. You have spent too much time with Dyadya," Vladi quipped. Despite his somewhat dramatic assessment of the local fishes' thinking, Vladi understood what Aleksey meant — the need to challenge himself and push his limits a bit. He, too, sometimes craved fresh scenery and new horizons.

"Did you have someplace in mind?" Vladi asked.

"How about the Bay of Campeche, down in Mexico?" Aleksey proposed. "I heard big game fish are running along the Yucatán. And you have always wanted to try your hand at saltwater fly fishing for baby tarpon. The waters off Campeche are supposed to be among the best in the world."

"Mexico, hmm?" Vladi pondered the idea.

"We have done weekend getaways. It would take us just a few days more to go that far," Aleksey insisted. "Why do we have long-range tanks on the

Skipper Dan if we never use them? We can make it to Mexico, no problem, then refuel there for the return leg."

Vladi didn't share his son's enthusiasm for the plan. As much as he enjoyed a bit of adventure, he knew that a trans-Caribbean expedition was fraught with peril. And once they got underway, they were on their own.

"I can see on your face that you do not like this idea," Aleksey discerned. "You think it is too dangerous, and I am too inexperienced, yes?"

Vladi let out a soft laugh at his son's keen observation. "You are right," he admitted. "But it is not about me doubting you, son."

"Then what?" Aleksey asked.

"Maybe I have become more cautious at my age, but with good reason. It is not that I lack confidence in your abilities, Aleksey. I just have more awareness of the real dangers that lurk out there. Especially after what happened with Dan and Alex. I am not sure that I can ever get past —"

Aleksey cut him off. "Papa, you said Dan was inexperienced at the time, and I am not little Alex. I am a grown man who can help pilot the boat alongside you. Have I not been proving that to you? Do you feel I am still lacking in some way? If so, let me know — I will work on it."

Vladi gave a little shake of his head.

Aleksey attempted to lighten up the discussion again. "I know this old man still has a bit of adventure left in him," he said playfully as he shook Vladi's shoulder.

Vladi recognized the importance of allowing his son to prove himself. After all, Vladi had done many things in his youth that he would now consider risky or unwise. His son had been through a war — why would he hold him back from a fishing excursion?

Still, he knew such things were inevitable for any man who fully lived, and he couldn't shield his son from every potential trouble. With that in mind, for

Aleksey's sake, Vladi reluctantly agreed to talk over a workable plan for such a voyage.

"I would rather go with you now than have you go by yourself another time. But no more 'old man' talk. I am still tough — very rugged — and handsome. Your mother told me so," he jested. "But I still need to talk with her about it before committing."

When Vladi did talk with Irina about the idea, she was thrilled, a bit to Vladi's chagrin. He was holding on to the hope that she would feel hesitant about them going, giving him an excuse to postpone — indefinitely. Aleksey had confidence in their plans — Vladi, not so much. He continued to have an intuitive sense of concern but agreed to everything despite his reservations.

"I will miss you, but I think it is wonderful that you two can do this. After all the years without you, he wants to be with his father. That brings great joy to me!" Irina clasped her hands together, pleased that her favorite men had another opportunity to spend time together and enjoy that special bond.

"It is risky to cross the Caribbean, even for me. So many things can happen," Vladi pressed.

"Oh no," Irina said, dismissing his concerns with a wave. "What could happen that you cannot handle? You both are as good as anyone on the water. Has age turned my strong, confident Vladi into a mouse?"

Vladi chuckled and took her hands, "*Dorogáya*, you know I am impressed with everything about Aleksey, including his seafaring abilities. He has far exceeded what I have taught him myself. Yet I cannot dismiss a nagging concern about making such a trip. There are real risks. You are not worried about that?"

"Well, I do not know the risks of the sea as you do, but I know that you have handled many dangerous situations in your life with smart thinking, courage, and mental strength."

Vladi soaked up her praises. He liked hearing this. For her to express such thoughts was reassuring to him.

Irina continued, "People cross the waters all the time without problems — and they are not even you. Go, have an adventure with your son, and think only of the good things that will happen, not the bad things that are so unlikely to occur. You should spend time with him!"

Vladi gave a cautious nod of acknowledgment.

"I will pray every day that the Lord's perfect will be done on the trip. That should take care of any anxiety you have about going. I will pray for Him to go before you and behind you, as it says in my favorite chapter of the Bible — Psalm 139. There is no safer place for my beloved husband and my son than in the will and hand of God."

Vladi sighed. He remembered his days of anxiety living alone in Florida, wondering if he'd ever find out if he had a son or daughter or ever see Irina again. Now here they were. What was he so worried about now? He should go.

With Irina's blessing, Vladi's decision was sealed. Her playful mockery of him had, admittedly, spurred him to show that he wasn't afraid. He began to prepare for the trip, and a few days later, they were packed and ready to go.

They left Antonio in charge of operations in their absence. It would not be the first time Vladi's dependable foreman took care of business while they were away. He had already shown that he was a man with plenty of initiative and the willingness to embrace responsibility when it was presented to him. Antonio didn't even need to be asked to do anything. He would ensure it was done — and done well.

This gave Vladi peace of mind as the men started the *Skipper Dan* and pushed away from the dock, heading for the open water.

PART II

THE BAY OF CAMPECHE

7

OH, MEXICO

As Vladi and Aleksey navigated through the waters of the Caribbean, the island of Cuba came into view on the southern horizon. They passed at a distance that kept them well within international waters.

"I have so many memories of that place swirling through my mind," Vladi wistfully remarked to his son, who stood near him on the deck. "Some of the best and worst experiences of my life happened there."

Vladi's eyes remained fixed on the island, though he couldn't make out any details — but he didn't need to. Scenes from the past flashed through his mind — debates with Marco, swimming in the aquamarine waters with his comrades, the incredible food.

And then there were the memories that haunted his sleep — the gates of the Combinado del Este prison and La Cabaña as he walked through them, the stubby hand that confiscated his pocket watch, El Paredón — and the indelible images of Dan the day the Cuban coast guard raided his boat and brutally took the life of his dear friend.

Vladi couldn't shake the lingering, malevolent darkness of the island that had left its mark. Vladi shook his head without realizing it, wincing as if in physical pain.

"Are you okay?" Aleksey asked, noticing the strange and distant expression on his father's face.

"No, I cannot go back there," Vladi muttered, his eyes fixed blankly on the endless expanse of the Caribbean. "I cannot. I will not."

"We have no plans to go there, Papa," Aleksey reassured him sympathetically, assuming he was talking of Cuba. He was oblivious as to the true meaning of Vladi's resolve. Inwardly, his father was struggling to free himself from the memories of Dan and that fateful day — memories that cut into his soul so painfully.

"I do not like thinking about it," Vladi said, shaking his head again. "There were good times, to be sure. But the bad ... it was like the place was cursed or something." Vladi sighed, the weight of the memories pressing down on him. "It is hard to explain. Just ... things that should not have happened. Terrible things. And the way people acted as if under some dark spell ... I do not know — I just want to put it all behind me."

It was indeed a long stretch across the Caribbean, about a thousand miles altogether. Starting from central Florida's east coast, they had rounded the peninsula the day before. They passed Cuba on their second day at sea. The *Skipper Dan* was equipped with long-range fuel tanks, and Aleksey had carefully planned enough food and water to sustain them for the five days or so it would take to reach their destination. Once they'd sailed beyond the Florida Keys, there was nowhere to stop along the way.

With so much time and sun, Aleksey took the opportunity to relax. Feet up and hands behind his head, he closed his eyes and turned his face up to the warm, blue sky. He was thinking about a sweet young lady he'd met in Florida. He had always believed that Russia had the finest women in the world, but now he was beginning to change his mind. In fact —

He was yanked away by his father's stern voice.

"You are missing it all," Vladi growled, apparently irritated for no reason other than his "old man" prerogative to be grumpy sometimes. Maybe it was the salty sweat stinging his eyes, or maybe it was simply that he wasn't much of a believer in just lounging about doing nothing.

"What am I missing?" Aleksey asked drowsily, half-opening his eyes.

"Everything. The pod of dolphins that tried following us a way back, for one thing. And oh there — another flying fish!"

"Exocoetidae," Aleksey said without looking over.

"Exo—what?" Vladi asked.

"Flying fish," Aleksey smartly replied. "Latin — the scientific classification for flying fish."

"How do you know these things?" Vladi chuckled incredulously. He was such an adventurous and curious son. Vladi couldn't help but be proud of the young man Aleksey had become.

"Reading, Papa — I just read a lot," was Aleksey's smug reply. "I am sure it is all very exciting. But I am happy to have my eyes closed and not see or think about anything for a little while."

"In my day, we did not have this time to just ... lounge," Vladi said, rolling the vowels around in his mouth.

Aleksey gave his remark no consideration and shot back a snappy reply. "The good thing is that our business has picked up. The trade-off is that managing the orchards has been exhausting — for me."

Vladi sighed. *He wanted to go on this trip, and now he wants to sleep through it.* Raising a son — even an adult son — was harder than he'd imagined!

However, Aleksey's brain was too restless to allow him to keep his eyes closed for long.

"Listen to this, Papa." Aleksey looked up from the creased newspaper he'd picked up before they left port. "I am reading this disturbing article about the growing power of the Mexican cartels. It says they have become so large that they are even eclipsing the Colombian cartels."

Vladi looked over with interest.

"But here is the interesting part — it says their drug trafficking operations have spread beyond the U.S. into Eastern Europe. Can you believe it?"

Vladi sighed deeply. "It is a shame to see the Soviet republics being infected by such a terrible plague as this," he lamented.

"Growing up, drugs were rare, at least in Kavkaz. Now it seems like they are everywhere. Then again ..."

"Then again, what?" Vladi asked.

"My friends, my ... comrades. Back in Afghanistan, a few of them started smoking the local hashish. Some got into opiates and began using heroin."

"I know some of our warriors have struggled with drugs — fools as they were," Vladi acknowledged.

"Even after we came home, one comrade, Konstantin, was still hooked. They found him in his bathtub, dead at only twenty-six. I ... perhaps I should have known it would spread."

Vladi gave a groan.

"My time in the military is not something I think about so much anymore, but it is still something I carry in my heart. I have seen the problems men can get themselves into when they have poor judgment. There were issues with some of the troops in Cuba, but nothing like that. Too much vodka, maybe ..."

"There is no doubt — it is getting worse back in the old country, Papa," Aleksey said, his expression somber. "This article mentions that the cartels have found new markets in Belarus and Ukraine. When we were children, it was shocking to hear of anyone using or selling drugs. Now I worry for my nieces and nephews, who are growing up in a world with increasing access to drugs."

Vladi listened intently. He shared Aleksey's concerns, but it was hard to think about when they were so far away from his grandchildren and unable to be an active part of their lives.

"Your sisters are smart," he reassured Aleksey. "I am sure they teach their children about the perils of these things."

Vladi paused and looked over the vast blue of the Caribbean. "It is a shame," he said softly. "Like Cuba, México is such a naturally beautiful country that is also plagued by corruption." He knew of some of the hardworking men who had come from Mexico to work on his orchards. "I do not think it is quite as bad as Cuba, but they do face considerable hardships."

"Sometimes I think every place has its unique challenges," Aleksey astutely contemplated. "Even America."

Vladi agreed. "Life can be hard everywhere, I suppose." Vladi maintained a steady gaze on the horizon, satisfied now that his son was talking with him. That's why he came on this trip — it's what he'd cared about all along. He knew that sometimes the most important conversations were the ones that happened between a father and son.

He hoped that before the end of their journey, he would have opportunities to talk more with Aleksey about his faith. He knew his son well enough now to approach this sensitive matter with the gentle guidance he needed. Aleksey had heard the gospel — he had the benefit of clear teaching, but the truth was met with skepticism and indifference. Vladi understood Aleksey's reasoning, but he wasn't willing to leave him that way.

As their fifth day at sea came to a close, Vladi and Aleksey were getting antsy. They'd been on the water for days and were anxious to see land. Then, the men spotted flocks of seabirds returning to their roosts for the evening. Their dark forms flying against the reddening sky were a telltale sign that land was near. Vladi and Aleksey looked at each other with relief and excitement.

"Land ho! I can see it!" Aleksey pointed out toward the horizon, stretching forward with excitement. Vladi strained his eyes to see, but the setting sun made it difficult to discern the land. "There, portside," Aleksey directed him again. "That sliver of green."

"I believe you," Vladi finally said. He couldn't quite see it yet, but he trusted Aleksey. It was rewarding to know that Aleksey's charts had navigated them to their intended destination.

Aleksey was a master of both modern electronic navigation and traditional plotting techniques. He could fix their position and project course options based on weather data and the vessel's drift. Although celestial navigation was no longer necessary with all the new technology, Aleksey enjoyed practicing it for the challenge it presented to his mind. He was like an astronomer, meteorologist, and oracle rolled into one, applying his navigational skills to predict their future progress. Knowing their position at all times was essential for staying out of trouble.

Darkness settled upon them, and Aleksey was in his element. He consulted his star charts against the night sky and began identifying constellations. He spotted the hazy nebula wall running through the constellation Cygnus, and the bent limbs of Hercules. He found the Big Dipper inside Ursa Major and saw the star Vega beaming brightly in the corner of the constellation Lyra.

Aleksey marveled, "It is truly amazing to see the nebula dust stretching across the sky." Then he went on mumbling something about the wonders of the celestial spheres.

Always the big words with this one, Vladi thought.

"I often wonder how the ancients came up with these constellations," Aleksey mused to Vladi. "Would you ever look at that group of stars and think, yes, that is a bear?"

Vladi laughed, "Even where the charts tell me what it is, I cannot see any bears up there." Just then, a shooting star with a long tail streaked across the sky, and Vladi almost jumped out of his skin. "Ooh, did you see that? It is a ... a comet!"

Aleksey had his nose in his charts when it passed overhead. "Ah! I missed it! But we will probably see more. We are reaching the peak of an annual meteor shower."

"Americans say that if you make a wish when you see a shooting star, it will come true," Vladi said, kidding with his son.

Aleksey raised an eyebrow. "Did you make a wish?" he asked, a touch of amusement in his voice.

Vladi laughed. "Of course not, that is just silly nonsense. Wishes only come true when you take action to make them happen. Right?"

Aleksey nodded, although there was a hint of sadness in his response. Inside this young man, there was still a boy who would like his father to tell him that his wishes could come true.

"What about prayers, then? Do you believe in them?" Aleksey asked.

"Yes, I do. I believe the One to whom I pray," Vladi answered with confidence.

"But they are a type of wish, too. Right?" Aleksey was genuinely curious to hear his father's answer.

Vladi paused, thinking back to his own journey of faith. He remembered having these thoughts for many years before coming to know the Lord.

"Prayers are different, son — they are addressed to our Creator, the living God. It is not the same as a wish."

"How is that?" Aleksey persisted.

"Our Creator ... He is listening. What is more, He is wise — the answers to our prayers often do not come in the ways we expect. Sometimes God answers prayers, not by altering our circumstances, but by transforming us amid those situations He has ordained."

Aleksey rolled his eyes a bit. "Still sounds like wishes to me, Papa."

Vladi smiled but didn't reply.

Aleksey still has a lot to learn, but at least he is beginning to ask the right questions. The Lord must open his eyes.

As they navigated the Bay of Campeche along a stretch north of the peninsula, midway between Veracruz and Campeche, the soul-stirring beauty of the night sky filled Vladi and Aleksey with a sense of wonder and awe.

They set anchor for the night in the shallows, within sight of the Frontera coast in the Mexican state of Tabasco. It was a moment that would stay with them forever. It reminded Vladi of the vastness of God's creation, His goodness, and His sovereignty over all things. He prayed that Aleksey would one day come to understand that too — that the Lord would illuminate His truth for his son.

8

FRONTERA

The morning sun had just peeked over the horizon and cast a golden glow over the water when Vladi and Aleksey headed ashore to replenish their provisions before a day of fishing.

The calm waters of the Rio Grijalva inlet were eerily quiet as they navigated the short distance to the docks at Frontera. Vladi scanned the river banks as if some unseen presence were lurking in the fog. Nothing unusual caught his eye except for a crocodile atop a large rock waiting for the morning sun to warm its body.

As they came closer to the docks, Vladi locked eyes on a couple of heavily tattooed men standing near the pier, their gazes fixed intently on the approaching boat. The stares from the locals were intense and unyielding the entire time, even as Vladi and Aleksey pulled up and tied off.

"What is with these guys?" Vladi whispered under his breath. *All the Mexican people I have ever encountered were pleasant and welcoming — most friendly.*

He gave Aleksey a subtle nod to make sure he saw the lurkers. Vladi suspected the men might try to hassle them about buying something or hustle them for a taxi ride, and he steeled himself for their approach. But the men remained where they were.

Vladi and Aleksey tidied up and tended to a few things on the boat before disembarking. The men never took their eyes off them, nor did they try to hide that they were staring. One nudged the other with his elbow, some unspoken communication passing between them.

Aleksey, however, was undaunted. "These guys look like locals." Confident, he bounded ahead, trying to be friendly. "I will ask if they know where we can get supplies."

"No, I —," Vladi tried to stop him, but it was too late.

"*Perdón, amigos!*"

The two men glanced up languidly, and one chuckled and then spat on the ground. Aleksey remained unfazed.

"Where can we buy food?" Aleksey asked in Spanish, but with a thick Russian accent. The men looked Aleksey up and down more closely, sizing up Vladi as well. Remaining silent, one man scowled and pointed in the general direction of town in response to Aleksey's inquiry.

"Gracias," Aleksey said, turning back toward Vladi without showing any sign of the discomfort he felt.

As they made their way toward town, Vladi tried to brush off the uneasy feeling that they were still being watched. Determined to keep their business there brief, he and Aleksey made their purchases, gathered their supplies, and hastened back to to the boat. When they arrived, the men who had been on the docks were nowhere to be seen.

"Wonder where those guys went," Vladi muttered, scanning the boat to make sure nothing was missing. They were relieved to find everything as they had left it. *Maybe they just do not like tourists*, Vladi reasoned.

"Maybe 'El Cucuy' got them," Aleksey joked, trying to lighten the mood.

"Coo-Coo who?" Vladi asked, furrowing his brow in confusion.

"Cucuy. The Mexicans say it like 'coo-coo-ee.' He's the ultimate Mexican bogeyman, a mythological figure that snatches children who misbehave," Aleksey explained as they untied the boat.

"Ah, that is like Babay," Vladi chuckled, recalling the Russian bogeyman of his own childhood. "Same thing. Well, we are far from him," Vladi added with a wink.

"Finally, it is time to go on a fish chase!" Vladi announced enthusiastically as he pulled away from the dock. "Are you ready to hunt for the biggest fish in the ocean?"

Aleksey's enthusiasm was overflowing. "I cannot wait to catch the 'big one' and to prove that I am the ultimate fisherman!"

Vladi laughed at Aleksey's passion. "Well, I knew him, son — the ultimate fisherman. Let me tell you — you have a long way to go before you can claim that title."

Aleksey wasn't about to let his father's words dampen his spirits. "Come now, Papa! Where is your spirit of challenge?"

"Oh, I have plenty of challenge for you, youngster," Vladi replied, trying to keep a straight face. "Okay, we will see who can catch the biggest fish," Vladi declared, a glint in his eye.

Aleksey didn't stand a chance — Vladi knew all the tricks. "I will have you know, I am a seasoned expert at this," Vladi bragged, joking.

"Sure you are," Aleksey chuckled. "I bet the fish are shaking in their fins right now, knowing you are coming for them. It is your lucky day, though, Papa."

"How is that?" Vladi sensed from the tone of Aleksey's voice that he was being set up — he couldn't wait to hear.

"Yes!" Aleksey said enthusiastically, with a glimmer in his eye. "You must be willing to take risks and push yourself to the limit. And, I will do it." His eyes gleamed with determination. "I will catch the biggest fish in the sea and become the ultimate fisherman."

"That is the spirit, son. How are you going to do that?" Vlady asked with a wry expression following Aleksey's theatrical exposition.

Aleksey was waiting for him to ask — he wasn't done. "I brought my secret weapon to attract all the fish — my sheer force of will."

"What about bait?" Vladi asked skeptically.

"Bait is for amateurs," Aleksey scoffed. "I do not need any cheap tricks to catch these fish. They will come to me willingly, knowing that I am the greatest fisherman who ever lived."

"Well, no need to worry, son. I brought my own secret weapon to attract all the fish," Vladi said as he pulled out a plastic container filled with a neon-green substance and unscrewed the lid.

Aleksey wrinkled his nose, disgust etched on his face. "What is that?"

"That, my boy, is my special fish bait — made of equal parts rotten tuna, anchovy paste, and leftover garlic bread from last night's dinner. Trust me, the fish will be jumping into our boat," Vladi assured him with a wink.

Aleksey smiled and shook his head at the absurdity of his father's concoction. "This is going to be the best fishing trip ever!" he exclaimed with a laugh, already feeling the rush of excitement.

Vladi felt excited too as he navigated the *Skipper Dan* toward a secluded spot just off the shore. Vladi and Aleksey had decided on this location together — an area away from the shipping lanes and most tourist activity — remote and peaceful.

"The depth finder reads between twenty and thirty feet, but I can see right to the bottom!" Aleksey marveled while leaning over the side of the boat. Through the clear aquamarine ripples, colorful reefs appeared to be just within reach.

The blistering heat of the sun was inescapable on the deck of the *Skipper Dan*. Both men were dripping with sweat by now. Aleksey couldn't resist the allure of the relatively cooler water. "Maybe it is time to make like a fish and go swimming," he suggested with a mischievous grin.

"Why not?" Vladi replied as he cut the engines. He was already starting to peel off his shirt. "I was hoping you would ask. It is almost noon, and I bet the Mexican fish are taking a siesta anyway. This water is just calling to me."

They dropped anchor, and both men dove into the warm water without hesitation.

"Well, I am sure we just scared all of our fish away," Aleksey joked as they surfaced. "One look at your belly, and they will swim back to Florida without us."

"Are you calling me fat, boy?"

"*Nikogda!* Never!" Aleksey laughed, holding up his hands in mock protest.

"Hey now, watch it," Vladi guffawed. "I may not be as slim as you, but I can still out-fish you any day."

"We will see about that," Aleksey replied with a smirk.

"Want to know something very few people ever experience?" Vladi asked.

Aleksey nodded, "Sure, why not?"

"If you put your head underwater, you can hear the distinctive sound of parrotfish crunching on coral," Vladi told him, dunking his head under the water to demonstrate. Aleksey looked as if he wasn't sure whether to believe him, but he followed suit and dunked under to give it a listen. He resurfaced after a few moments.

"All I can hear is you splashing around like a wild boar," Aleksey reported with a big grin on his face. Vladi sent a wave of water his way and gave his son a playful push.

After about fifteen minutes, they finished their swim, but the water remained beautiful and alluring. This was so different from anything Aleksey had ever imagined back in Kavkaz. "I can easily spend hours just looking down at the reef and all the fish darting here and there," he remarked wistfully.

"Me too," Vladi agreed. "But we have some serious fishing to do."

The two men clambered back onto the boat, feeling invigorated from the swim. It was time to get down to business — fishing! Aleksey focused on the task at hand. He donned dry shorts and a shirt, then joined his father on deck, grinning ear to ear.

"We will get out into deeper water and see what we can catch!" Vladi said as he restarted the engines. "And I cannot wait to see the look on your face," he boasted, "when I haul in that giant mutant fish, thanks to my secret bait."

Aleksey felt grateful for this opportunity to bond with his father and experience the beauty of the sea with him. Despite not having caught any fish yet, they had already shared an unforgettable day together.

"Do not worry, son," Vladi added as he reached over and ruffled Aleksey's hair. "I will teach you everything I know. And who knows, maybe one day you will be almost as good — perhaps, even better."

9

THE PIRATES OF CAMPECHE

Vladi and Aleksey had prime fishing waters all to themselves. But there was a trade-off for their remote location. Aleksey was the first to spot the long, narrow, speed yacht approaching from about four hundred yards away.

"Looks like we have company," Aleksey remarked.

"Why do you say that?" Vladi asked.

"See the boat out there — that is fast! We might not have our 'secret' fishing spot to ourselves any longer," Aleksey groaned with just a hint of apprehension.

Vladi grabbed a pair of binoculars for a better look at the vessel. It was moving at a high rate of speed, bounding over the waters with its bow raised.

"Not a fishing boat," he informed his son, his voice carrying a note of concern. Aleksey immediately picked up on it.

"Mexican coast guard, maybe?" Aleksey called out, making an effort to be optimistic.

"I do not know. We may soon find out, though," Vladi remarked, seeing that it was coming closer.

"Any coast guard vessel would be plainly marked so it could be identified." Aleksey quickly assessed. "And that is not the Mexican Navy, Papa," he said, his voice rising along with his uncertainty.

Within fifteen seconds, the vessel had closed the distance. Vladi could see the boat more clearly — there were at least four occupants, two of whom were waving Kalashnikov assault rifles. He could also see the business end of an RPG launcher held by a man on the deck. The sight of their weapons sent a cold shiver down his spine. Vladi let out a muffled sigh. A second later, it became obvious that Aleksey was observing the same things he was.

"Go! Go!" Vladi shouted hoarsely.

Aleksey threw down his fishing gear and dove for the controls. He cranked the engines on the *Skipper Dan* and slammed the throttle full open. The boat lurched forward, the engines roaring.

Vladi watched their pursuers advancing — looming closer. "You cannot outrun them like this, Aleksey," Vladi called out over the noise.

"What do you want me to do?" Aleksey shouted.

Vladi's composure belied the turmoil within. The situation washed over him like a tidal wave. He clutched the railing, his knuckles white with tension. Flashbacks to the incident with Dan bombarded his brain.

At sixty-eight, I am getting too old for this, he lamented.

"It does not take a speedboat to outrun a sitting duck," Aleksey retorted. Gritting his teeth, he was gunning the *Skipper Dan's* engines so hard he thought he might break off the boat's throttle controls. The wind whipped through their hair.

Aleksey's heart pounded in his chest, his own experiences in Afghanistan returning to his mind. At least back then, he was armed and able to defend himself and his comrades. The violence had generally been brief, though overwhelming, but at least he'd been prepared for it. Now, he felt a desperate sense of helplessness and desperation. "Papa, we cannot take on four armed men with a few fishing rods. What do we do?"

Two can play this game, Vladi reasoned. *If we cannot outrun them, we must outthink them.*

"Aleksey, turn the boat around and head straight for them," Vladi said, his voice steady and decisive.

"What? Are you crazy, Papa? They have guns and an RPG!" Aleksey exclaimed.

"Aim for their bow," Vladi instructed, without a hint of emotion in his order, but raising his voice to be heard above the grind of the engine and the chop of the surf. "Steer straight into it as fast as you can. You seize control of the confrontation."

Aleksey hesitated for a moment, but then he nodded and swung the *Skipper Dan* around, heading straight for the pirates' boat.

Let us play 'chicken' — shall we? Vladi had a hunch these stupid cretins had never read *The Hunt for Red October*. Regardless, he was borrowing a daring tactical maneuver from Captain Marko Ramius. Audacious, but Vladi hoped it was just bold enough to shake them off.

The *Skipper Dan* was running wide open now, and the speed yacht was moving even faster. They were like two trains running on the same track head-on, closing in at nearly eighty knots combined. The men on the other boat fired several rounds toward their boat. Aleksey kept going with the fierce determination characteristic of the Gavrilov men.

This is it! Aleksey thought, bracing himself for the impact. Aleksey caught a fleeting glimpse of surprise on the faces of the men in the other boat when they realized he wasn't going to turn. At the last second, just as the two boats were about to collide, the pirates' confidence faltered, and they veered off. The close wake from the hard turn rocked the *Skipper Dan* violently. Vladi and Aleksey steadied themselves.

Cowards — I knew it, Vladi thought.

"Whoop!" Aleksey gave a triumphant shout. He looked at his father, who winked back. But the victory was momentary. The speed yacht made a wide loop and once again came back toward them.

"What now?" Aleksey shouted.

"Turn port and head straight for the shore," Vladi instructed.

"Ready? Brace!" Aleksey shouted, as he yanked the wheel to the left, and the *Skipper Dan* pitched wildly to the side. Reorienting, they made a beeline toward the shore as fast as her engines would allow. Aleksey could see the shoreline getting closer, but it wasn't close enough. The pirates' boat was gaining on them.

Seeing he couldn't win a match race against the speed yacht, he tried swinging the boat wildly from side to side, churning up even more wake in an attempt to evade their pursuers. His instincts had him fleeing. Deep down, though, Aleksey knew attempting to evade the speed yacht was futile. What would they do even if they did get to shore first?

Yet he was determined to try. Either way, Aleksey wouldn't make it easy for them. Gavrilov men were not the type to give up easily.

These modern pirates were part of the ruthless Gulf Cartel, operating a cell in the Mexican state of Tabasco, and they considered themselves the undisputed lords of these waters and all the lands around them. The military-clad predators fired their rifles into the air. A burst of gunfire echoed across the water toward the *Skipper Dan* — a warning. They wanted to get the Russians' attention, though Vladi and Aleksey were more than aware of their presence.

"*Alto! Alto!*" shouted one pirate, gesturing aggressively with his weapon.

"What do we do?" Aleksey yelled over the noise.

Vladi's face was grim as he motioned toward the radio. "Call for help, Aleksey," he ordered in a tight voice.

It was hard to focus and think because of the cacophony of racing engines and bursting gunfire that filled the air. The sounds of weaponry triggered memories that Aleksey tried to keep buried. He ducked down, attempting to catch his breath. His shaking hands fumbled for the radio, dialing in VHF channel 16, the maritime distress frequency.

"Mayday, Mayday, Mayday! This is the *Skipper Dan*. We are at position nineteen degrees five minutes north, ninety-three degrees seventeen minutes west. We are under attack by unknown assailants in a speed boat! They are shooting at our vessel! Repeat. We are under fire! Requesting immediate assistance. Over!" he yelled into the transmitter, hoping against hope that someone out there could hear their distress call.

As he spoke, Aleksey caught sight of a spray of water as several bullets hit the surface around the hull of the *Skipper Dan*.

"They are shooting at us!" Aleksey shouted to Vladi, his heart racing.

Too close. He felt like he was in a terrifying movie. How could this be happening? But this was all too real!

Like Vladi, this was not the first time Aleksey had found himself in a difficult and dangerous situation. It wasn't the type of thing he could ever have envisioned facing, though. He had left the battlefield and bullets behind him — or so he thought.

He looked back to gauge the gap between the vessels as more rounds threw up water in their wake. Aleksey was just in time to see one pirate level the RPG launcher and aim it toward the *Skipper Dan*. His heart skipped a beat.

We cannot outrun that. Aleksey realized that the only option they had was to stop or be blown out of the water. Reluctantly, he throttled back but left the engines idling. The *Skipper Dan* slowed to a stop, bobbing on the waves as the pirates' boat came alongside it.

He could see the pirates clearly now, their faces twisted in cruel grins as they closed in on their prey. Aleksey's mind raced as he tried to think of a way out of this situation, but he knew they were outgunned and outmanned. There was no way they could fight off these vicious outlaws.

Sweat dripped down Aleksey's forehead, and his body vibrated with adrenaline. His mind was running through an array of scenarios, each more chilling than the last. Robbery seemed the most likely possibility.

They can take what they want, but not this. Aleksey silently vowed that the pirates would not get their hands on the heirloom that meant so much to him and his family. He slipped the watch from his pocket and gently dropped it onto the deck, sliding it into a corner with his shoe, where he hoped to conceal it from the pirates' notice. At least it wouldn't be in his pockets if the pirates were looking for cash. They could take money or whatever else they wanted, but not the watch!

As the boats converged on each other, Vladi watched their rifles trained on him and Aleksey, and he could feel the blood draining from his face. His thoughts turned to his son — young, brave, and resourceful. He could only hope that Aleksey would be able to escape before it was too late. Vladi closed his eyes and said a silent prayer, bracing himself for the worst.

The other boat turned in a skid that killed its speed and left it almost parallel with theirs, the starboard bumping the *Skipper Dan's* port side. One pirate piloted from the flybridge as three armed pirates readied to board.

Vladi stood stoically, his gaze locked with that of the enemy. Gesturing aggressively with their weapons, they signaled for Aleksey and Vladi to raise their hands. Both men complied.

Without moving his head, Aleksey's eyes flicked to his right. Judging the distance, he estimated his raised hands were about eighteen inches from the 26.5 mm German Geco flare pistol mounted at eye level.

Definitely within reach if I am quick enough. It couldn't be depended upon for accuracy, but it was guaranteed to produce a diversion if he could fire it. Aleksey weighed the odds in his mind, hesitating for a moment as he calculated the risk.

Three pirates launched themselves across the gap between the two boats, boarding the *Skipper Dan*. Before he could talk himself out of it, Aleksey's survival instinct took control.

"Not so fast," he said, his voice cold and hard. Taking advantage of the few seconds it took the pirates to land on the deck and regain their balance, Aleksey made his move. Pulling in a deep breath, he snatched the flare pistol. His hand closed around the cool metal. For a split second, he met the eyes of the pilot.

You! Aleksey had a flash of recognition. The pilot was one of the men he had spoken to at the docks. *That creep!*

"*Mire aquí, capitán!*" Aleksey shouted. He swung the flare pistol up and then fired directly into the flybridge of the pirates' boat. The bright red flare shot across the gap between the two boats, streaking through the air with a loud whoosh and striking the pilot in the face just above his neck on the left side. The man let out a howl of pain and stumbled back, his rifle clattering to the deck.

Call it a lucky shot. The sudden flash of light caught the pirates off guard and momentarily disoriented them. They recoiled as the flare exploded, putting their arms up to shield their faces as a shower of sparks sprayed in their direction. Chaos broke out. Frantic, angry cursing and shouting ensued. The image of their compadre's face looking like a charred pizza was a disturbing sight. The pirates turned their attention away from Vladi and Aleksey.

One of the pirates leaped back onto the other boat. But he was not quick enough to save the pilot or their vessel. Within seven seconds, the phosphorus load burned through and into the cabin, where it ignited the pirate's entire boat. He dove into the water with his rifle and gear. Struggling to keep himself afloat, he clung to their smoldering boat, which was now dead in the water. This left his two remaining *compadres* to complete their dastardly business onboard the *Skipper Dan*.

Aleksey knew he had only seconds before the pirates regained their senses and retaliated with vengeful rage. Acting on pure adrenaline, he took full advantage of the moment. In a move that would have made the legendary Skipper Dan proud, Aleksey slammed the throttle open. He held onto the wheel as the bow reared up and bucked him backward. His feet stayed planted.

Aleksey cranked the control wheel to the port side, narrowly avoiding the burning boat and throwing their unwelcome guests off balance. Vladi's feet stuttered for only a second before he jumped into action to assist the tottering men over the side.

In one swift motion, he kicked the feet out from under the nearer man, sending him sprawling onto the deck. Vladi leaped toward his accomplice, arms extended, and tried to shove him into the water. But the pirate caught his arms and locked Vladi into a wrestling match. With his back bent over the edge, the younger man could see the absolute fury in Vladi's eyes and feel the hot breath huffing from his nose like that of an enraged bull.

With fierce determination, Vladi grabbed the man by the neck and pushed his head closer to the rushing water, hoping gravity would take over. The tension was broken by a loud crack. Vladi was so focused on getting the man off his boat that he didn't see the butt of the Kalashnikov rifle swinging toward his head — impacting his skull.

With a sudden heave, Vladi fell back. His vision flashed red, then black. Bloodied from the blow to his face, Vladi lay motionless on the deck. The pirate, now freed from Vladi's grip thanks to his *compadre's* intervention, scuttled to his feet. Both men turned to Aleksey.

Apprehension filled Aleksey's heart. Desperate to distract the pirates, Aleksey's mind scrambled for a solution. He had to do something, anything. He remembered his father's neon-green fish bait, the "secret weapon," guaranteed to turn even the most determined pirate's stomach.

In one whirl of motion, Aleksey snatched it up and spun around toward his attacker. Aleksey pulled the lid off the plastic container. The pirate lunged at him. Aleksey hurled the open jug of putrid concoction at the oncoming assailant. The stench of rotting tuna and anchovy mash filled the air as the mixture splashed across his face.

Revulsed, the pirate froze in his tracks, gasping and sputtering. Aleksey was sure the wretch would leap overboard in a frantic effort to wash it off. But when he instead acted as though he was immune to the disgusting smell, Aleksey knew he was in trouble.

Weapons leveled on them, the game was over. Vladi and Aleksey were outgunned, and their resistance, brave as it had been, failed.

The pirates thrust Aleksey to the deck, his face hitting the wood with a jarring thud. Strong hands pulled him upright and grasped his limbs to bind him with ropes.

Aleksey clenched his teeth, angered to be on the losing end of this battle. He glared at them with the same furious eyes they had seen on Vladi. Contemptuous spit flew from his mouth and landed on the man who bound him. He growled as they forcibly turned him over to lie face-down on the deck. Aleksey strained to meet Vladi's eyes, only catching a glimpse of his father's battered face before all went dark.

Upon regaining consciousness, Vladi was left to watch as the men pulled a black hood over Aleksey's head. Barely able to see what was going on, Vladi dragged himself up to a sitting position on the deck.

"Try to spit on us through this hood, idiot," they hissed at Aleksey. Vladi's heart filled with dread as he suddenly understood what was happening — they were taking his son hostage.

After the initial altercation ended, the spokesman for the pirate duo addressed them.

"*Buenas tardes, gringos,*" he said calmly, eyeing them with a sly smile, belying the danger they were in. "Do you speak Spanish?"

"*Poquito,*" Vladi replied, barely audible, before spitting blood onto the deck.

"What do you want?" came out in a gravelly rasp as Vladi spoke louder in the pirates' native tongue. "We do not have much money with us, but take what we have and go. You can have the fishing gear as well. Please, just leave my son."

The men laughed. "Do we look like fishermen to you, big man?"

The leader crouched down to meet Vladi's eyes as he sat on the deck. "I can tell by your fancy little boat that you have more than a few pesos, *señor*."

"Check my pockets. Check the whole boat. You will see that we are not hiding anything," Vladi insisted.

"Do you think I am *estúpido*?" the man shouted, pointing to his head. "You may not have money here, but you have it somewhere! Perhaps in your piggy bank? Perhaps under your mattress? Perhaps buried in your yard?"

"I do not have anything more to give you," Vladi said weakly.

"*Diablo, inferno!* Shut up!" the pirate captain yelled. Lowering his voice again, he muttered, "Let me tell it to you simple, *amigo*. Your son for your money. That is all."

"How much?" Vladi asked, eager to quickly resolve the matter.

"Hmmm, I think one million is a fair price for your son's life. That would be American dollars, not pesos. What do you say, gringo?"

"I'm sure this fat cat has enough to go around," his accomplice chimed in, a sinister grin revealing his yellow, rotted teeth.

"How am I supposed to get you a million dollars?" Vladi growled.

"That is your problem, *amigo*. If you value your son's life, you will find a way. But you had better hurry. The longer you take, the more pieces he will be missing. You wouldn't want us to send him home ... one piece at a time, would you?"

The other pirate was amused with his collegue's performance. Both cackled with glee, enjoying the power they held over their victims.

Vladi's heart pounded in his chest as he realized the gravity of the danger his son was in. These men were not rational. At once, he offered himself in place of Aleksey — anything to ensure this was not a repeat of what happened to Dan! He'd sacrifice his own life for Aleksey without a moment's hesitation.

"Please, just take me instead. I am more valuable to you. If you take me, I can get the money and give it right to you. It would be so much faster," Vladi implored. *I cannot lose another.*

"Don't give us any more trouble. Off you go," they told Vladi as they unceremoniously plopped him into the inflatable dinghy lifeboat and cut it loose. Setting him adrift, they waved. "We will be in touch! Paddle fast!"

Vladi spoke to Aleksey in Russian, so the pirates could not understand. "Do not fear, son. I will come for you, be sure of it." He kept his eyes on Aleksey for as long as possible. *Will I ever see him again?* Vladi's last glimpse of his son was of him lying face-down on the deck with that black hood on his head.

With that, the kidnappers abandoned Vladi in the water to find his way home. *At least this time, I have a lifeboat*, he thought. But his Russian humor was bitter.

A pirate grabbed the controls of the *Skipper Dan*. They turned back to pick up their stranded *compadre*, still struggling at the burning boat, before powering away at full throttle.

They had better run. Vladi ground his teeth. *Because when I find them, they will be the ones who pay dearly.*

10 NIGHTMARE IN MEXICO

Aleksey's head and ribs were slammed against the deck with every wave they encountered as the *Skipper Dan* coursed through the water. His left arm was pushed up between his shoulder blades. The cartel pirates bent his right arm over his shoulder and tied it to the left. His muscles throbbed and screamed in protest against the restraints that forced him into this contorted position. It felt like his tendons were stretched to their breaking point, causing him to cry out in pain. But the kidnappers denied him any relief.

Do not panic, Aleksey repeated to himself. He knew the drill. He had been trained for situations like this. Two tours in Afghanistan had prepared him for the possibility of being taken captive by the enemy. He closed his eyes and tried to focus on the procedures embedded in his brain about what to do to survive the ordeal. No matter if they were *mujahideen* or narco-terrorists, there were some things about human nature that transcended culture and geography.

There were steps he could follow to increase the likelihood that he would make it out alive. He knew that remaining level-headed was essential. The first and most important matter was to maintain his composure. But it was hard to keep his head straight when he was in such excruciating pain. Despite training for situations like this, the reality of being abducted was more frenetic and savage than he had anticipated.

Eventually, Aleksey heard the *Skipper Dan's* twin diesel engines decelerate back to a gentle purr. The boat slowed, and the rough ride became a smooth glide. They traveled for several minutes at this rate, so Aleksey inferred they were making their way into the Rio Grijalva inlet. He felt the boat bump against the pier as it docked.

In hooded darkness, he could hear men talking onshore, several speaking at once, but he couldn't discern how many there were. Then he felt a swirl of movement around him. Four hands, two under each arm, hoisted him off the boat and onto the pier.

The kidnappers dragged Aleksey across jagged bits of coral and shells. Bound tightly and under the darkness of the hood, Aleksey stumbled to his knees on the rough surface. His feet left the ground as they shoved him into the back of a beat-up Toyota pickup truck, his still-hooded face pressing against the rough metal surface of the truck bed. He was completely at the mercy of his captors — and Aleksey knew that mercy would be in short supply. True, raw fear began to set in.

The vehicle lurched into motion. One man drove while the other two guarded their prize. Aleksey listened to their conversation, trying to gather any information about where they were going. With the hood over his head, understanding the kidnappers' Spanish over the truck noise without any contextual clues was futile.

Aleksey turned his concentration to their route, hoping to estimate the distance they had traveled, memorize turns, or gather any clues that might help him escape later. Even that eventually became too difficult. The constant jostling made it impossible to keep track of direction — interminable hours of bumping along the road had left him disoriented. As the truck drove into the unknown, any hope of escape seemed to be slipping further away.

They sped away from Frontera, driving south and west across the coastal plain and into the foothills, toward a range of mountains. The deeper they went into the thicket, the more altitude they gained and the rougher the road became. The little pickup bounced and swayed along the jungle track, its suspension strained as the vehicle pitched and rolled, struggling to keep up with the uneven terrain. The constant bobbing of the pickup only added to Aleksey's feeling of unease. They had been traveling for much of the day, seldom exceeding thirty miles per hour as the track snaked deeper into Mexico's tropical interior.

Aleksey had lots of time to reflect on what had happened, second-guessing his judgment, and wondering about his father.

I cannot believe I have gotten him into this mess. He felt like everything was his fault. *I should have never talked with those men at the dock when we went in for supplies. But no, I had to go and open my big mouth — that was such a giveaway. I should have known better. What a grave mistake. Maybe if I had put on a tough face and stared them down ... Maybe we would have appeared more formidable ... Maybe they would not have dared to mess with us.*

Of course, shooting their boat pilot with the flare gun might have worsened the situation. That had been a rash decision. Should we have just quietly complied? Hah, I do not think so — it is not the way of Gavrilov men! But I could have gotten my father killed. Aleksey shuddered at the thought. All because of his mistakes.

Aleksey's mood grew gloomier and more foreboding. The thought of his father, injured and alone on the ocean — again — weighed heaviest on Aleksey's mind. He imagined his father struggling to make it to the shore and then wondered if he was even alive at all. He couldn't shake the feeling that it may have been the last time he'd ever see the man he loved so deeply.

I hope he is all right. How long could it take for him to make it to shore? Papa has endured tougher situations before — he will be fine. But then again, he was much younger back then. When he gets to land, will the locals help him or will they turn on him too?

And what of Mama? She will be so distraught. I do not know how much more strain she will be able to endure after losing Papa once already. So many thoughts were passing through Aleksey's mind, and he lost track of time.

Aleksey remained engrossed in thought as they crossed streams, inching the little truck through the currents, the wheels nearly disappearing under water and mud. The highland forest was filled with diverse flora. In hooded darkness, Aleksey couldn't see that Mexican rosewood, palms, and Castilla rubber trees thrived in the rich volcanic soil. They towered over increasingly dense shrubs and ferns, forming a canopy of foliage so thick that it almost blocked out the sun, creating an otherworldly atmosphere. It was an endless stretch of emerald green punctuated by the occasional village, although they were few and far between.

As they gained altitude, the jungle gave way to arid, rugged terrain. Craggy hilltops and sawtooth ridges replaced the rainforest landscape. Scrub pines stippled the slopes. If he'd been able to see them, they would have seemed to leer at Aleksey as they passed, as if they were mocking his despair. The kidnappers reached a point at the top of a gravel road where the truck could not drive any further and rolled to a stop.

Aleksey was torn from his thoughts when he heard the truck doors open. The kidnappers yanked him out of the truck by his legs and set him on the ground. They removed the hood from his head. He blinked heavily, his eyes adjusting to the sudden light. They untied his legs and then his hands. Aleksey's wrists and shoulders felt instant relief as he stretched out his arms. But his respite was short-lived.

"*Ándale!*" one kidnapper ordered, pushing Aleksey from behind and motioning him to march along a canyon trail. Aleksey noticed another man was staring at him from the side with a stony expression, his hand hovering over his pistol.

Whatever he is thinking, I do not think it is friendly.

Sweat dripped down Aleksey's face as he struggled to keep up with the pace set by his captors. The path was rocky, and Aleksey stumbled, to the irritation of his surly escort. He drew the pistol from his waistband and pressed the barrel against Aleksey's head, growling in Spanish, "Move faster and watch where you are going, *gringo* fool!"

After what felt like an eternity, they came to a clearing in a remote area. Aleksey's instincts urged him to make a run for it. But as he looked around at the foreboding landscape, he felt that he was already trapped in a hellish nightmare from which there was no escape.

Aleksey's attention was drawn to what the man directly in front of him was doing. When the kidnapper reached into the bag slung over his shoulder, Aleksey took a step back — his eyes scanned again for an escape route. To Aleksey's surprise, the kidnapper rummaged through his bag and pulled out a few chocolate bars and some bottles of drinking water. "Here," he said, "*agua* — drink."

Aleksey's first thought was disbelief, but the man motioned for him to take the items. Aleksey reached out and slowly took what was offered. The uncertainty on his face was plain to see, but the man gestured gently, and the soft expression in his eyes convinced Aleksey to accept.

This is ... surprising. I have no idea what they plan to do with me, but they would not give me food and water unless they wanted to keep me alive — at least for now.

"*Gracias.*" Aleksey thanked him and sat on the ground, but kept curious eyes on the small man, who had a bowl haircut and a mouth full of misaligned teeth.

This guy seems to have a bit of humanity in him. If I converse with him, I wonder if he will give me a little information.

"Where is your home?" Aleksey asked the man in Spanish with a low voice.

"My farm was in *valle*, vall-ee, you say English." He pointed off to the west.

"You are a farmer?" Aleksey asked.

"Was *granjero*, 'farmer,' *sí*," the man said with a heavy sigh.

Aleksey could sense there was more to the story, so he probed further. "You are not a farmer now? Why?"

The man sat next to Aleksey and lowered his voice even further, "My family still has a farm, but —" He stopped speaking when one of the other men in the band of kidnappers walked nearby. When the man had passed, he continued. "But I was do my own work when the *Golfos*, they show up in my village, saying we all go work for them. They are not good people, *amigo. No bueno.*"

"And you are different?" Aleksey asked.

The man ignored his question. He glanced around to ensure no one else was within earshot before speaking under his breath rapidly. "They will kill you — kill anyone who will not cooperate. I wanted to say no, but how they asked — stripping off my clothes, binding my hands and feet, killing my friends who say no — it make me think different."

Aleksey sat listening, stunned into silence, as the man told his story of how he was force-recruited by the cartel.

"They get my wife and son out of house, guns in their faces. They said, 'You can come with us now, or we kill your family together here.' I will never forget the terror in my wife's eyes." He nodded his head sadly. "No choice."

"I am sorry," Aleksey said quietly, feeling a deep sense of empathy for him. He couldn't imagine the terror and desperation the man must have felt as they threatened his family.

These are animals, he thought. He knew all too well the horrors of being forced into a life of violence and conflict. He had seen it firsthand when the *mujahideen* came into villages in Afghanistan, coercing poor goat herders into fighting in a war they had no interest in, promising them glory then burying them by the thousands instead. He felt at a loss for words to say to this man.

"Why do you stay with them?" he asked.

The man let out a long, deep sigh. "No choice. If I try to leave, they kill my family and me. I am *atrapado* — trapped."

"I am sorry for these kids — lured into this life in a different way," the man continued, nodding toward a group of young men talking into radios and patrolling the path with rifles. "Some dream of nothing more than being sicarios and narcos."

Hit men and drug traffickers — what a future! Aleksey felt disgust at the allure foisted upon impressionable minds.

"Were most of them forced, too?" Aleksey asked, his voice heavy with sadness.

The man sighed. "Most were not forced, but they do not have much of a chance to do anything else. They choose this life for the power or riches they think it will bring. It is the life they think they want, but few make it out alive."

Aleksey shuddered, rubbing his face in exhaustion.

He looked toward a teenager in a green ball cap who was standing with the other cartel members. "That boy, he has only fourteen years," the man said. "Was a good kid — wanted to be *veterinario*. He has no feeling now — killing people like animals while the others celebrate him."

Some of the *Golfos* were only in their teens, but they were already drug dealers and calloused murderers, at ease with a weapon in hand and a target to take out. They made no effort to hide themselves, sitting in the sun or shade with their guns and walkie-talkies. They were mostly on the lookout for gunmen from a rival cartel they were at war with.

It was hard to believe that so many young lives had been torn apart and ruined by the cartel. Aleksey contemplated how many others were trapped in this dangerous world, caught in a vicious cycle of violence and duress. These young men holding the guns had lived through this "pseudo-war" their entire lives. They had no concept of what peace looked like — this was all they had ever known.

As Aleksey sat with the man, he realized that he had just had a small glimpse into the complex and tragic world of the cartels — a world filled with desperation and coercion. Listening to his story and learning about his life, Aleksey couldn't help but feel a sense of admiration for this man's resilience in the face of unimaginable circumstances. It also gave him a glimmer of hope — that this man, who had been through so much, could still find moments of kindness and humanity.

They started walking again. Several hours after leaving the coast, they arrived at a small settlement bound by steep, rocky hills on three sides. Aleksey had no idea where they were, but there were women, children, dogs, and burros. The men looked to be a mix of peasant farmers and seasoned cartel operatives like his captors.

The air was heavy with the smell of goats and chickens picking at garbage and the faint, acrid scent of burning trash. Poverty colored everything. The rough, unpaved paths, children kicking up dirt as they ran barefoot, and the weary faces of the old all spoke of hard lives.

A collection of ramshackle huts stretched across a hillside cleared of trees. These dwellings were a hodgepodge of cinder blocks, wood, cement, and corrugated tin, all cobbled together on a haphazard sprawl with no sewage system. Most were just one room, with tangled electric cables overhead. Lights could be seen through gaps in the doorways, and thick, dusty blankets were usually hung across the entrances. Aleksey assumed they had to be stealing power from the grid.

Amid the squalor, he could see glimmers of technology — a small TV flickering through an opening in a wall, a telephone hanging on a hook by a door — reminders that they were not completely cut off from the world. Perhaps that could work to his advantage.

Locals looked up as the kidnappers brought Aleksey through the village, but none appeared surprised or concerned. He could see they were accustomed to the presence of armed men escorting strangers through their streets. With a sudden chill, Aleksey realized that he was in the heart of cartel territory. This was a community that had been fully assimilated by a crime syndicate that used a veneer of class struggle and quasi-socialist politics as twisted justifications to mask their drug trafficking.

Aleksey was led into a small shack and seated at a faded wooden table. He was confined to the cramped, stifling hovel, guarded at all times under the watchful eyes of three or more armed cartel operatives. It was like having been kidnapped by an army unit of some sort. To his surprise, they were extraordinarily disciplined, leading him to believe they had some real military training.

The blur of monotony in Aleksey's captivity was broken only by random bouts of hazing and regular meals. He was served freshly cooked *cabrito* — goat flesh — with beans, rice, and masa tortillas. Admittedly, the food was quite good — but it was the same for breakfast, lunch, and dinner. Aleksey could hear the faint sounds of children playing and dogs barking, but they seemed distant and dreamlike.

This was not the trip to paradise Aleksey had imagined when they left Florida — not even close. Instead, he was caught up in a nightmare from which he might never wake.

11

EL CUCUY

In the sweltering afternoon of Aleksey's second day in captivity, the flap over the doorway flew open, letting in a gust of hot air. A large, imposing figure stepped inside. His thick chest and broad shoulders seemed to fill the room — the man was a brute. His piercing gaze, scarred skin, and bulldog-like face expressed confidence and determination. He exuded an air of authority. As he looked at this man's jutting chin and hard, cold eyes, Aleksey couldn't help but think of Stalin. This man had an ominous aura. It was clear that he was not someone to be trifled with.

Most of the Mexican men were shorter than the Russian, Aleksey. The only one tall enough to look him in the eye was this one. Standing a head taller than his *compadres*, the giant's bulky frame radiated an air of undisguised menace.

For lack of a name, Aleksey dubbed him "Cucuy" in his mind — the ultimate Mexican bogeyman whom he'd joked about with his father only days before.

This beast was the one who drank all the milk when he and his siblings were growing up, Aleksey thought.

This hulking man was from the harsh and unforgiving land of Tierra Caliente, a seething hot valley in the Mexican state of Michoacán. His forefathers had been banished to this inhospitable land to eke out a living in the searing heat among the cacti and lime trees. It was also a major drug-producing area. His ancestors and *compadres* had grown opium poppies since Chinese workers had brought them to Tierra Caliente in the early 1900s. Marijuana plantations grew an abundance of marketable weed as well.

But Cucuy's personal history was even more fearsome than the place he called home. Born into a violent and impoverished family, he had witnessed firsthand the brutality and injustice of the world from an early age. He was one of twelve siblings abandoned by their alcoholic father. Cucuy's abusive mother smacked them so often that he and his siblings hid from her sight. The kids wore tattered clothes that were often ill-fitting. Subsisting on a diet of tortillas and dirty river water, they thought of the rich as anyone with bread and Coca-Cola.

Four of Cucuy's brothers were slain in a series of murders before he was even an adolescent — acts of treachery that pushed him over the edge. As a teenager, Cucuy himself was severely beaten and left for dead. In fact, Cucuy's forehead had been fractured as a result of repeated blows to the head. Surgeons had to insert a metal plate to hold his cracked skull together. These events affected him deeply during his youth and into adulthood, leaving him seething with ever-present, barely-repressed rage.

When Cucuy became agitated, the metal plate caused his brow to swell and his face to bulge, a testament to the anger that simmered just beneath the surface. He was a frightening man.

Working as a child laborer in the corn and lime fields, Cucuy was illiterate until he was ten. After that, he worked on another farm as a marijuana grower and began trafficking at sixteen. He eventually got a work permit that allowed him to legally travel back and forth between Mexico and the United States. He cultivated marijuana in Mexico to smuggle it north. On the return trip, Cucuy also ferried American cars and firearms to sell in the interior of Mexico. At the border, most vehicles weren't searched upon entering Mexico, making it easy to drive south with valuable firearms.

As a natural leader, albeit a terrifying one, people followed him either willingly or out of fear. Cucuy was intelligent and possessed an exceptional memory — he never forgot a face or a wrong that had been inflicted upon him. Because of his physical stature, it didn't take much effort to intimidate others.

This was a man who dwelled on the hardships of his past, using them to justify his own ideas about life. Cucuy saw himself as a poor rebel with the courage to fight the system of the rich and powerful on behalf of the downtrodden and marginalized — mainly himself. He was a victim who had fought back, and he believed that anyone who couldn't understand that was either privileged or stupid.

As Cucuy approached, Aleksey naturally shrunk back. Though the motion was tiny and almost imperceptible, Cucuy noticed. The reaction brought a twisted smile to the giant's lips. He liked the fear he caused in others. It was a tool he used to exert his power and control.

"Tie his hands behind his back," Cucuy told the two men guarding Aleksey, his voice like ice. A cold hand closed around Aleksey's heart.

The men obeyed, pinching his skin as they secured the rope and cinched it as tightly as possible.

Why must they tie my hands? Aleksey wondered. *They have no reason to be afraid of me.*

The men led Aleksey outside and around the back of the row of shacks to a clearing in the jungle foliage. There in the ground was a scene out of a nightmare. In the center of the clearing was a freshly dug grave. Aleksey had a sick feeling in the pit of his stomach. This all added up to one thing.

Is that for me? Is this where they will bury me?

Aleksey glanced around, taking stock of his surroundings. Behind him was Cucuy, the large Mexican's gaze locked on his pathetic captive. Alongside Cucuy were five other men, their faces also cold and unfeeling.

One man was wearing a Federales uniform. Aleksey had assumed that the Federales were above being bought off by the cartels. Apparently, some of them were not. Aleksey held out hope that, if what he heard was true, and the Federales weren't as corrupt as Mexico's local *policía*, there might still be a chance for him.

All were armed with assault rifles, handguns, or broad-blade machetes. *It is a lot of weaponry. I stand no chance*, Aleksey concluded. *Running would be suicide, as would be fighting. Maybe as a last-ditch option when the time is right.* Aleksey stood rooted to the spot as he juggled his options.

Cucuy pushed Aleksey down to his knees. *Now may be that time — already.* It was almost as if Cucuy could read his thoughts. Before Aleksey had a chance to react, his head felt a slam from the butt of a rifle — enough to knock him over but not hard enough to render him unconscious.

"What is your name?" Cucuy shouted.

Aleksey saw no point in lying. "Aleksander Gavrilov," he responded barely above a whisper.

"A Russian working for the U.S. government? Liar!" Cucuy shouted back in an angrier voice, smacking Aleksey a second time.

The U.S. government? Aleksey was taken aback by the accusation. *Why would they think a Russian would be working for the U.S. feds? I thought they wanted ransom.*

"Let's start at the beginning, *gringo*. Who do you work for?" Cucuy demanded, his patience clearly thinning.

"Red Star Citrus in Florida — growing oranges," Aleksey replied, trying to keep his tone calm, but the sweat gathering at the back of his neck gave him away.

"Red Star? Is that a code name for the DEA, smart guy?" Cucuy asked, his pistol now trained on Aleksey's head.

"The DEA?" Aleksey couldn't believe what they were asking. "No, Red Star Citrus! I grow fruit!" Aleksey's voice began to rise with the tension.

Cucuy struck him on the back of the head again even more forcefully, his anger mounting.

"Liar! What is a fruit farmer doing on our coast with a luxury fishing boat? Is that the best you can do? — because I find your story hard to believe, *amigo*."

"I — I can explain," Aleksey sputtered.

"You'd better!" Cucuy barked. "You were watching the port at Frontera from your boat — who comes and goes!" he shouted, growing hoarse. "Who do you work for? The FBI? CIA? You tell us the truth now because we have ways to find it out."

"The CIA? What are you talking about? This is insane — *loco*. No way. I am not even an American citizen," Aleksey insisted.

"Careful how you talk with me," Cucuy snapped.

"I am Russian. How can I be working for their government? I manage Red Star Citrus with my father in Florida. We do nothing but grow fruit." The barrel of a gun pressing against the back of his skull told Aleksey that they did not believe what he was telling them.

"Enough. The truth. Now!" Cucuy's eyes never left Aleksey's, his anger boiling over.

How am I going to convince these guys that I am just an ordinary person? These are dangerous men, and they are incredibly paranoid — I am not sure there is anything I can say to convince them.

Aleksey considered his next words carefully, making eye contact with the Federales officer. He wondered if there was any way to appeal to him. The officer did not return any sort of sympathetic response nor even acknowledgment of Aleksey's glance.

"Listen, I came to Mex—"

"I know things about you already. But I want to hear it from you," Cucuy menaced, waving a pistol in Aleksey's face. "Spill it!"

Trying to play it tough, Aleksey defied the assertion with, "Yeah, what do you know?"

Cucuy leaned in close to Aleksey, his hot breath on the young man's face. "Things about you. About your family," he hissed. "Things you'd rather I didn't know."

Aleksey met Cucuy's gaze without flinching. "You know nothing," he spat, trying to sound braver than he felt, "because there is nothing to know."

There was a brief silence as Cucuy appeared to be considering Aleksey's words. Aleksey dared to hope that he might be believed. But before he said anything more, the man in the Federales uniform stepped forward with his gun raised, a chilly glint in his eye.

"I am growing weary of this babble," the man stated with exasperation, appealing to Cucuy. "We have the boat. He's just another good-for-nothing gringo. We should just get rid of him and move on. That's the safest option. There are many fish in the sea."

Another of his captors spoke up, "Ah, don't be too quick. He might be useful. I have ideas. We make him an offer he can't refuse, and if he betrays us, well ..."

Another interrogator took over for Cucuy. It was turning into a sort of "good cop, bad cop" routine. His voice was smooth, almost too smooth, like a serpent's whispers.

"We know you work for the DEA, man. Just tell us you work for the DEA. Let's start with that, at least."

"I do not. I do not know how else to tell you." Aleksey retorted in a calm, measured voice that didn't betray his rising panic. "If I did, I would admit it right now. I am a Russian living in America who works in agriculture. That is the truth."

The man holding the gun was the one who had already suggested shooting him. He spoke up again as he pressed the barrel deeper into the back of Aleksey's skull.

"You think you're tough? You're nothing." The man's voice was cold and sharp as a razor.

Cucuy stepped back, rubbing his receding hairline and clearing one nostril of snot in a disgusting snort on the ground near Aleksey.

"He's of no use," the Federale said. "If he's an operative, he isn't going to talk, let alone work for us. Put him down now so we can go eat." The Federale wheeled and spat on Aleksey. The saliva ran down the Russian's face in a slow trickle.

"He is not useless," yet another man spoke up. "He said the other man on the boat was his father."

"What'd you make of him … the father?" Cucuy demanded.

"Rich. He'll pay to get his son back. We can still get a ransom from his family, regardless of whom he works for," the man responded.

This was met with a shrug from the Federale. "And just invite the U.S. government onto our turf if he does work for them? Don't be *estúpido* — his father will notify the agency he works for when we contact him for a ransom and come down on us — very risky."

"And what if he is telling the truth?" the second man asked, his voice gruff. "Are we just going to waste this opportunity for a big payday? Perhaps this goose will lay some golden eggs."

The debate continued, with each man trying to assert his point of view, deciding Aleksey's fate as if it were nothing more than a business transaction. Aleksey's sweat-soaked shirt clung to his back as he listened to their cruel deliberation, the man holding the gun on him growing more impatient.

"Enough!" Cucuy bellowed. His voice, like a thunderclap, silenced the men. "Enough of this bickering. None of you make decisions around here!" It was true — he called the shots, and no one defied him. "I will say what we do with him — and not right now. Hasty decisions are for weak men."

No one dared to say another word, and with that, Cucuy nodded his head toward the row of sheds, a gesture everyone understood except Aleksey.

Then, as abruptly as it had all started, the captors cut his bindings loose.

One man, a pudgy fellow wearing a Chicago Bulls jersey, offered his hand to Aleksey and helped him back to his feet. They walked back to the shack house without another word.

When the kidnappers parted the doorway blanket, the first thing that hit Aleksey was the mouthwatering aroma. A platter of roasted chicken had been set in the middle of the worn-out wooden table. It was dinnertime — for them, at least.

Lucky for me, they have their priorities straight, Aleksey mused with relief.

His kidnappers were already digging in and raucously complimenting the cooking of the Bulls jersey man's wife. They left Aleksey standing there in the room, watching them eat. It didn't take long for his appetite to reappear. He put a hand over his rumbling stomach. Watching these psychotic narcos eat was revolting, the way they wolfed it down, but he couldn't deny his hunger, nor the amazing smell of their dinner.

Since there didn't seem to be any food forthcoming, Aleksey was left alone with his thoughts, trying to comprehend the strange, violent world he had been thrust into. He used the opportunity of being ignored to get a better sense of his surroundings. Escape was never far from his mind.

There is nowhere to go if I run, he concluded. *Mister Federale was ready to kill me before dinner. I could take off running now, but they would shoot me before I got three steps out the door.* If they missed him by some improbable chance, the men patrolling the perimeter of the village would catch him without fail.

Aleksey looked on while the men took turns pulling pieces of chicken with their dirty fingers like vultures picking a carcass clean, indifferent to the flies buzzing around the food. Without even realizing he was doing it, Aleksey scrunched his face in mild disgust.

"Jersey Man" exercised more decorum than his cohorts, cutting his chicken pieces off the bone. He laid his knife on the table, and Aleksey dared to contemplate the eight-inch blade from a distance. He weighed his odds.

I could take the Bulls guy if I got my hands on his knife. It would be no more difficult than the many Russian boars he'd hunted growing up in Kavkaz. *But* — his imagination followed through on the idea — *the others would likely string me up and flay me alive with the same knife.* He couldn't win this scenario.

Papa could take them all, he thought with both pride and a pang of sadness.

Finally, as if they had just remembered he was there, one man tossed the remains of a half-eaten chicken leg at Aleksey without even looking in his direction.

"Have some cheeeken, *gringo*."

Gross — but Aleksey tried to look at the bright side. *It is better than starving — and at least it is not cabrito and beans again.*

"Mexicans are not bad people," one of his abductors said, still chewing his food between bites, "... just bad times." They'd just been beating Aleksey about the head and calling him a liar and a spy, and now this thug acted like nothing had happened. Aleksey was more than a little perplexed by the disconnect between the man's words and their actions.

"What were the good times like?" Aleksey loathed to ask.

The kidnapper thought for a second, then answered flatly and without a trace of humor, "Don't ask me. I can't remember any."

12

ISLA DEL CARMEN

With the tide in his favor, Vladi made it to land in a few hours. The raft had drifted east, coming ashore at Isla del Carmen. The sun beat down on him mercilessly, his wounds stinging with saltwater and sand.

Dehydrated and hungry, Vladi's weakened legs struggled to carry him across the beach, one heavy foot after the other. He trudged through the sand, his body trembling with exhaustion. Barely able to see through the haze of salty sweat in his eyes, he kept moving nonetheless.

Helplessness shrouded Vladi's mind, which was reeling with speculation about his son's fate. Getting help for Aleksey was the only thing he could think about, superseding any thoughts of food or water. His adrenaline sustained him. He needed to save his son at all costs. Nothing else mattered now.

"I cannot lose him. I will not lose him," Vladi repeated to himself as he stumbled forward until he came upon a winding road where he began to see more small shops and other buildings. He crossed the boulevard to the first place he saw, the Playa Norte Hotel. His steps stuttered as he came into the open-air lobby of the small boutique hotel. At first glance, the young woman at the check-in desk was alarmed by Vladi's appearance.

"Can ... I help you, *señor?*" she asked cautiously.

"*Sí, policía!* I need to call the police!" Vladi's voice broke, his chest heavy with grief. His red eyes were filled with desperation, darting around the lobby as though he were looking for something or someone who wasn't there. Vladi leaned on the counter, almost gasping and trying not to pass out. He felt dizzy and his head pounded with the worst headache he'd ever felt.

By that time, a male concierge had entered the lobby to assist. "*Señor*, are you injured?" he asked politely, although the answer was obvious. Vladi's clothes were torn and stained with blood, his face bruised and swollen. "I think we need to help you to the infirmary."

Vladi brushed the suggestion aside. "I am fine," he said through his busted lip. "It is my son — he has been kidnapped."

"Who? ... What happened, *señor?*" the concierge asked.

Vladi struggled to get the words out. "They have our boat an— and they took him! I need the police — *policia* — please."

Vladi could see the hotel staff exchanging glances, their expressions conveying concern. The young woman at the desk passed the phone to the concierge. He spoke in Spanish so rapidly that Vladi could hardly understand what he was saying. The concierge hung up then turned a sympathetic look on Vladi just as he collapsed in a heap on the floor. The hotel staff scrambled to help him, gently bringing him to his feet.

"*Policia* are on their way. Please take a seat here," the concierge ushered Vladi to a comfortable lobby chair. The young woman brought him a much-needed glass of water. Vladi tried to drink, but his hand shook so uncontrollably that he spilled water onto himself. He closed his eyes, trying to regain his composure, but images of his son and the attack out on the water kept replaying in his mind.

The reality of the situation hit Vladi hard — his son was gone, possibly forever. The weight of failure was crushing down on him now. He should have done more, he could have done more, to protect his son. His mind was battered by should-haves and could-haves.

I knew we should never have come to Mexico. Vladi berated himself over that same regret for at least the hundredth time. *I thought it would be too risky for other reasons, but I never imagined this. How stupid could I have been? I should have turned the boat around the moment I saw those men near the docks. Naïve! Overconfident! How can I face Irina? How can I tell her that I lost our son?*

After some time, two officers from the local police station sauntered into the lobby, their eyes scanning the room as they made their way to the check-in counter. *They do not look like they were in much of a hurry to get here,* Vladi observed sourly. He wasn't wrong.

The police briefly spoke with the concierge, leaning casually on the raised desk and keeping their eyes on Vladi while the concierge explained what he knew. The second officer, a young man with brown hair in a buzz cut and a clean-shaven face, went outside briefly to smoke a cigarette, gazing at the sky as if looking for rain.

About five minutes later, they both strolled over to Vladi, who was seated in the lobby chair. "It looks like you have had a hard day. How can we help you, *señor?*"

Vladi told the officer the entire story, including descriptions of the men who had kidnapped Aleksey. His voice shook, but he did his best to speak clearly and include any details he remembered. The other officer jotted down notes on a small pad.

"Did these men say what they wanted? Why were they taking your son?" the older officer asked, passing a hand over the balding dome of his head.

"They said they wanted a million dollars in ransom money, and they would be in contact with me," Vladi responded.

The officers looked at each other as if listening to something boring they'd already heard, but Vladi continued, "I do not know how they plan to contact me — they do not even know my name or where I live."

The older officer nodded, almost as if barely listening.

"What will they do to my son? Where are they taking him?"

The buzz cut officer put his hand up to signal that they would get to that. He continued with his line of questioning, his voice devoid of sympathy. "Tell us, besides the workers at the store, did you see anyone else?"

"There were two men on the docks at Frontera when we arrived. They had many tattoos on their arms and necks. They kept staring at us — I assumed because they could tell we were foreigners."

"What did you say to them?" the older officer asked, his bushy black mustache turning downward in disapproval.

"We had no interaction with them other than asking for directions. They never even spoke to us — they just pointed toward town."

With that information, "Señor Mustache" flipped his notebook closed and put it back in his pocket. He turned and spoke quietly to the other officer, "*De Golfo*."

"Sure?"

"Sí — Frontera — waiting for a shipment at the docks."

Turning back to Vladi, the officer spoke in a normal voice again, "I'm sorry, *señor*. There are many tattooed men around. It will be hard to figure out who exactly took your son."

Vladi bristled. "Who is *De Golfo*?"

The officer shook his head sadly as if refusing to give bad news to a child.

"What does that mean? I expect a real search," Vladi insisted. "I want help, not words."

"*Señor*, I suggest you lower your tone. You may disturb other hotel guests.

So, please, calm down." The officer went on to explain, "These things are not unheard of. Really, it could be just about anyone."

Vladi was surprised at the almost flippant way the officer spoke.

"So ... what do we do now?"

The younger officer fidgeted with his pack of cigarettes, and Señor Mustache made a sound, clearing his throat.

Like many police in Mexico, they were reluctant to get involved, either out of fear or because of their own collusion in organized crime. Many who were in the state government and police were either part of the cartels or were paid-off to do nothing. Police were sometimes complicit in kidnappings, either by turning a blind eye or actively assisting criminal groups in exchange for a cut or some private time with the cartel's women.

If anyone had dared to file charges, they might as well have signed their own death warrant. Either way, these officers made it evident that they were washing their hands of the matter.

"So, you cannot help me? Or you will not help me?" Vladi demanded.

"*Señor*, you need medical attention. Let's come back to this —"

"You will not help me find my son? That is it? Seriously?" Vladi growled.

"It is very dangerous business, *señor*." The younger officer spoke almost nonchalantly. "It seems like you and your son may have inadvertently gotten mixed up with some very bad men."

"You are the police. Your job is to catch very bad men," Vladi said as if talking to a kindergartener.

"Our police force does not have the resources to search all of Mexico for every kidnapped person," the older officer said gruffly. "Even worse, we'd be putting our lives in danger for very little ... incentive." The officer's emphasis on his last word did not escape Vladi's notice. He immediately caught on to the meaning.

"So, what you are saying is that you require money for an investigation? What is serious to you? This is my son — they took my son!"

The policemen both gave short laughs. "Of course it is serious, but it is also not uncommon. We are only saying that doing what you can financially to help us would also be of help to you. Those are simply the facts, *señor*."

Despite these words, Vladi didn't have any money on him, and he was confident that anything he gave to them would not get him one bit closer to finding his son.

"I cannot help you in that way. But —"

The officer cut him off. "I'm sorry, *señor*," he said, though obviously not sorry at all. "It may be best to call your embassy for help at this point. As I said, first you need to get some medical atten—"

"Wait ..." Vladi stared in disbelief as the officers got up to leave.

They turned their backs on him and kept walking, despite his entreaty. The sound of their footsteps echoed through the hotel lobby, a reminder of the futility of his situation. His heart felt like it was being ripped out of his chest. Vladi's sense of hopelessness deepened as the officers' words, still ringing in his ears, began to sink in. He didn't know whether the police lacked the skill, the inclination, or merely the ... incentive ... to do something.

Vladi knew that there was no point in arguing with them. The police were done and would have nothing more to do with it. On their way out, one officer signaled to the front desk staff to allow Vladi to use the phone to call whomever he needed. He felt defeated and alone as he watched the officers walk away, leaving him to deal with the abduction of his son on his own.

Vladi was disgusted at the officers' brazen admission of corruption — disgust that clung to him like a foul stench in his nostrils. He couldn't believe they were so indifferent to his son's fate. The way they spoke of the danger and their own lives being on the line made him sick to his stomach. The very people who were supposed to help were more concerned with lining their pockets.

He could feel the rage and frustration building within him as he grappled with the realization that, in this place, justice was nothing more than a commodity to be bought and sold.

As for their advice, Vladi decided it was best to contact U.S. authorities once he was home. Right now, his priority was to get back to the States and come up with a plan. He hoped that the kidnappers would be able to contact him there and that he could obtain some useful information about where they were keeping Aleksey.

He picked up the phone the concierge offered to make the most dreaded call — to Irina.

13

RACE AGAINST TIME

When Irina answered the phone and heard Vladi's voice, she intuitively sensed something was amiss.

"Vladi, what is it?" she asked, her heart already starting to race.

"I need to talk to you, I -"

"Why are you calling when you should be on the boat?" Irina asked, the pitch of her voice rising with the alarm she was already sensing.

"*Dorogáya*," Vladi's voice was strained, and Irina could hear the desperation in his tone. It was like a knife in her heart.

"There is no easy way to say this. It is bad, Irina, really bad.

"What? ... what is bad?" she pleaded.

"Please listen — I need you to help — and fast."

Irina felt numb as she listened to Vladi tell her what had happened. She couldn't believe what she was hearing. She could hardly breathe, and tears streamed down her face the entire time Vladi talked with her on the phone. Vladi knew it was important for him to help her think clearly, but he was having a hard time getting through it himself.

"Where are you now? What do you need me to do?" she asked between sobs.

"I am at a hotel in Mexico, the Playa Norte Hotel on Isla del Carmen. I notified the police, but they are not being any help. I need to get home as soon as possible to deal with this."

"Okay, yes ..." she said, barely able to speak.

"I need you to go to the bank and send me money for a flight home. And, I need to buy clothes and money for food, taxis, and the hotel. I do not have any cash."

"I will take care of it," Irina promised, her voice shaking. "But what if the bank does not give me the money? What if they do not believe me?" She was not experienced in dealing with American banks.

"There is no need to worry," Vladi reassured her. "I have done business with them for years. Just tell them it is an emergency. Tell them our son has been kidnapped, and I need to get home. They will help us."

"Okay, I will ..." Irina said weakly.

"If you encounter any problems, contact Julio or Antonio for help. I am not leaving the hotel now, so if necessary, you can contact me at the front desk."

Vladi's note of determination brought her some comfort, but there was a gnawing pain in her heart now that wouldn't go away. After getting Vladi's contact details, Irina hung up the phone, her hands shaking as she quickly dressed, grabbed her purse, and headed to the bank.

Rob Swindle, the bank manager, was a middle-aged man with a touch of gray. He was acquainted with Mrs. Gavrilov and waved a hand as she entered.

Vladi had proudly introduced Irina and Aleksey to the bank staff when they first arrived in America.

"Ah, Mrs. Gavrilov, it is nice to see you. What can I do for you today?" Rob folded his hands together and spoke most pleasantly, his silver tie clip glinting in the light coming through the streetside windows.

His smile faded and turned to concern when Irina explained the situation.

Rob was stunned. This was never the story he was expecting. "I'm ... so sorry, Mrs. Gavrilov. This is terrible," he sympathized.

"Please, Mr. Swindle, I need to send money to my husband in Mexico," Irina replied, her voice trembling.

"Mexico? How much are we talking about here, ma'am?" Although it was only a couple thousand dollars, Rob loosened his tie and conferred briefly with an associate, then returned. The bank had been reluctant to release the money to them out of the country before, and it was no different now.

"I want to help you, Mrs. Gavrilov, but it is against our bank's policies because of the risks with out-of-country wire transfers."

"Please, please," Irina pleaded. "He needs it."

"The thing is that I can't safely ensure that all or any of the money will reach your husband in Mexico," the bank manager said as courteously as possible.

"I understand the risks, but you do not understand the situation. This is an emergency, and he needs money to get home immediately. Our son —" Her voice was raw with emotion. She was unable to speak without tears returning to her eyes. "Our son has been kidnapped by the worst kind of men, and Vladi needs to return as soon as possible to speak with the authorities. You must help me. Please, I beg you."

"Maybe we should contact the police first," he rationalized. "Are you sure that your husband is not being held as well? I may end up wiring money straight to the kidnappers and cause even more trouble for you."

"I assure you that my husband is free. He called me from a hotel after speaking with the police there."

"I understand," Rob said sympathetically.

"Please, the kidnappers have taken their boat too. Vladi only needs the money to fly back home, and he will contact the authorities once he arrives. I beg you to help us," Irina said, dabbing her eyes with the tissue offered by the manager.

The bank manager was torn. He could see the anguished look in Irina's eyes and knew that every moment counted in a kidnapping. He didn't know if he should risk it, but something in his heart told him that he had to help this desperate mother.

Acquiescing, Rob decided to do what he could to make this happen.

"Okay, let me just make a phone call, and we will set up the transfer."

Rob quickly got to work, calling in associates to help ensure the money would reach Vladi as soon as possible. He knew it would not bring back her son or ease the pain of this tragedy, but arranging the transfer was the least he could do to help. He was prepared to stick his own neck out to make this happen, and if anything went wrong, he would personally make good on it.

Irina sat, trying to keep her hands from trembling as he made the calls. She craned forward as soon as he laid down the receiver.

"Mrs. Gavrilov, we'll do everything we can to help you and your husband during this difficult time," Rob said, his voice steady and reassuring.

"Thank you, Mr. Swindle. Thank you. Thank you," Irina told him, tears streaming down her face. "You are a godsend."

Back in Mexico, the staff at the Playa Norte Hotel had been gracious enough to allow Vladi to stay the night, providing him dinner that evening and a comfortable bed. Vladi now sat alone in his hotel room, staring out at the darkening sky. Feelings of hopelessness and dread further engulfed him. Thoughts of what his son might be enduring at the hands of ruthless cartel operatives were a constant presence in his mind, and he knew time was running out.

As the sun rose over Isla del Carmen, a wire transfer was waiting for him at a Western Union office just a few blocks from the hotel. With money in hand, Vladi made good on his expenses, and the hotel staff arranged a taxi to take him to the Ciudad del Carmen Airport. Aeroméxico had a flight with one connection in Mexico City that would get him to Orlando International Airport late in the afternoon.

As the Aeroméxico flight took off, Vladi closed his eyes and said a silent prayer. He knew that things were going against him, but he didn't fight alone. He prayed for wisdom and asked God to protect Aleksey.

The flight was uneventful, but the Aeroméxico agent at the small airport never asked for identification. Consequently, Vladi was able to board a flight out of Mexico with only his ticket. Upon arrival in Orlando, he was delayed getting through U.S. Customs and Immigration, which only added to his misery. After hearing his account of what happened, the agents either believed his story or were impressed that he could make up something so sensational. They filled out a report, verified his U.S. residence, let him sign an affidavit, and sent him on his way.

Antonio was waiting for him in the Arrivals section of the airport. Vladi apologized for the delay. Antonio could see the pain etched on Vladi's battered face and put a sympathetic hand on his shoulder. "I am sorry about Aleksey, *jefe*. But it looks like you did not go down without a fight."

Vladi could not help a tiny half-smile, even with his stinging fat lip. "You already know that I would not."

Irina, on the other hand, had a much stronger reaction to the sight of Vladi's black eye and fat lip. Clearly startled at first sight, tears quickly welled up in her eyes. Vladi reassured her, "I can eat soup for a few days. It is only a small thing."

Vladi took her in his arms and held her close, whispering soothing words and promising her he would do everything he could to bring Aleksey home safely. Irina's body shook with sobs as she clung to him, and Vladi knew that he would have to move mountains to ease her pain. She had been through so much already — and now this. Deep down, Vladi knew this was only the beginning of a long and difficult journey for everyone.

As he had planned, Vladi wasted no time contacting U.S. authorities once he was back on American soil. After several phone calls, he was told the FBI would be taking the case. Only a few hours after asking for help, two agents from the local field office came to the house to interview Vladi.

At least they seem to care enough to show up promptly. However, he didn't get quite the reaction he was hoping for from them.

They listened to him recount the events, saying they would pass on the information to their deputy director, who was in charge of international hostage situations.

"We will do what we can on our end, Mr. Gavrilov. But we strongly suggest you call the State Department and get them involved. They have more pull there than the FBI."

Despite being told there was no quick way to resolve the situation, Vladi thought how much more impressive these two were than the Mexican police. Whatever anyone may have thought about the FBI and the U.S. federal government, it was a lot more professional than the so-called authorities in Mexico.

The agent gave Vladi his card and told him, "Here's a number for you to call."

"We will be in touch. Good luck," the agent offered with a sympathetic grimace. Unlike the Mexican police, these guys at least appeared to care.

As soon as the agents left, Vladi called the number they gave him. Unfortunately, the State Department was not as helpful as the FBI had led him to believe they might be. After an odyssey of phone transfers and being placed on hold, Vladi finally got through to the right diplomatic relations office, only to have his request categorically dismissed.

"I'm sorry, sir, but the U.S. has a standing policy to not negotiate with hostage-takers," the State Department representative told him.

"Please, this case is urgent. It is critical. There must be exceptions for situations like this," Vladi pleaded.

"There have been rare exceptions for certain cases," the man on the other end of the line acknowledged. "But unfortunately, neither of you has U.S. citizenship," he stated matter-of-factly. Then, softening his manner a bit, he said, "I sympathize with your situation, Mr. Gavrilov, I truly do. But please understand that the U.S. government does not conduct rescue operations for hostages in Mexico."

Vladi could tell that this attempt to get help from the U.S. government was a waste of time. When he got off the phone, he felt the loneliness of this overwhelming burden drop onto his shoulders.

The FBI gave me no real assurances that they will be able to do much, and the State Department will not get involved. The Mexican police will not help. Our local police cannot do anything. Who does that leave? The answer became apparent — it left only him.

It is up to me to get my son back.

The abductors were not new to this game, and by now, they likely saw the advantage in whom they had taken. The fact that Aleksey and Vladi were Russian, ironically, made this situation more attractive to them since they would be without U.S. federal intervention.

The cartels' principal source of revenue was drug trafficking. Harassing Americanos drew unwelcome attention from the DEA, FBI, and other U.S. agencies. But victims of other nationalities were relatively low-hanging fruit that could be harassed, often without repercussions. The cartels knew this well.

These thugs had jumped on an opportunity that fell into their laps. They reasoned that the owner of a nice boat like the *Skipper Dan* would likely have the financial resources to make their effort worthwhile. The realization that they had no backup from the U.S. government to cause them trouble had undoubtedly come as an unexpected and welcome bonus, Vladi reasoned.

There was one thing they hadn't counted on — it was Vladi himself.

Meanwhile, Irina sent a telegram to Kavkaz via Western Union and a patch through Russian Railways to notify Olga:

ALEKSEY KIDNAPPED IN MEXICO. PRAY.

The Russian Railways station assistant delivered the message with a heavy heart. "I am so sorry," he told Olga, handing her the telegram.

Olga felt her heart drop as she read the words. She said nothing, stunned into silence. She stood tall, determined not to let the news break her, but her mind was awhirl with questions.

Erik was there drinking tea at the table and came to the door. He read the note over his sister's shoulder. "*Nyet! Not my nephew!*" he exclaimed, his voice filled with fierce protectiveness.

Olga insisted that they pray quickly, and then she and Erik followed the railway assistant back to the station to use the telephone for a collect call to Florida. The railway telephone was supposed to be for official use only, but the stationmaster made an exception for them because of the circumstances.

They got through to Vladi on the fourth ring.

"You think I will let you do this on your own, brother? You think I do not feel gutted about what these animals are doing to Aleksey?" Erik asked when Vladi refused his help.

"It is too dangerous. Do not come. There is no reason, I know ..."

"Come now — you need help — there is no one else. He is my blood too," Erik insisted, his voice growing louder and more passionate.

"He is your blood, yes. But I will not have your blood shed for my mistake," Vladi said sadly.

Erik would not be swayed. "I have been there since the day that boy was born, and I will not stand idly by to see the day he dies."

It was hard to refuse Erik's impassioned plea. And although Erik didn't say it, Vladi knew that his brother had helped raise Aleksey and viewed him as more than just a nephew. Touched by his brother's passion and resolve, Vladi gave in.

"I can see I will not stop you from coming. So, I might as well help, no?" Vladi conceded. "I will make the necessary arrangements for you to get here."

"*Och een' khorosho*," Erik said.

"I will be in touch very soon. I have to go," Vladi responded.

After getting off the phone with his siblings, Vladi made a call to Moscow. "Ivan, it is Vladi. Please, there is an emergency, and I need to impose on you once again for help." When Ivan heard the story, he felt sick for his old comrade.

"I will push Erik's passport and visa through as soon as possible," Ivan promised. "It is the least I can do to help. I wish you the best of luck, comrade."

With Olga flitting about contacting the girls and making care packages for everyone, Erik made his own preparations. He packed Vladi's old boar hunting knife and his own, rolling them up in his clothing to carry in his checked baggage.

Erik's heart was ablaze, and he was vibrating with ferocious resolve. His determination to rescue Aleksey was unwavering. He would stop at nothing to save his nephew — his blood.

PART III

TREACHEROUS NEGOTIATIONS

14

DEVILS AND MONSTERS

Things took a marked turn for the worse on the fourth day of the kidnapping. Aleksey drifted back into consciousness with his hands cinched to a hook in a rafter beam above his head. Resting against his upraised arm, his head lolled to the side, swollen and heavy as cement, and almost impossible to hold up.

How long was I out? How long have I even been here?

The thoughts muddled their way through his groggy head, and he wished he would just pass out again so the time would move more quickly. Having the dark hood on again made it difficult to tell whether it was day or night. The days had passed in a weird kind of swirling vortex — the hours crept by with eternal slowness.

Memories resurfaced from Afghanistan. He felt the texture of sand in his mouth and heard the crack of a rifle. He was back there, trapped in that ravine with his comrades. He heard the screams again. "*Davai! Davai!*" Rock splintering. The smell of blood in his nostrils. There was distant shouting … "No!" Aleksey began kicking his feet, jerking his head from side to side.

A swift kick to the ribs abruptly broke him out of the flashback, the painful start of a fresh round of beatings bringing him sharply into the present.

His cartel captors persisted in heaping all sorts of cruelties on him. They beat him with a rifle butt and thrashed him with a whip. Stretching him out, they repeatedly shocked him in the most sensitive areas of his body with a cattle prod. Aleksey's screams were dampened by the filthy rag they had shoved into his mouth, and the choice words he had to say about them stopped at the fabric as muffled grunts.

These disgusting beasts are worse than anything I encountered in a war zone. Have they no conscience whatsoever? Devils and monsters! How could they do this to someone who has never done a thing to them? They are nothing but savages. Are they even human?

Cucuy's devils weren't content with just physical abuse, either. They tried to break his spirit as well. They would take turns tormenting Aleksey with lurid descriptions of the terrible fate that awaited him and what would happen if his family didn't cooperate.

His captors weren't just ruthless criminals — they were outright barbarians. They took pleasure in inflicting pain, and they enjoyed seeing the suffering of others. They joked about whether his mother was attractive and leered at him in the filthiest way.

The beatings became more and more frequent, each one more brutal than the last. Aleksey's body became a mottled mass of bruises, cuts, and burns. He could hardly move without crying out in agony. He was barely conscious most of the time, driven in and out of a haze of pain.

Aleksey's muffled screams were futile as the cartel monsters worked to transform him into a broken, tortured shell of a man. Devoid of any humanity or compassion, his captors laughed and jeered as they took turns abusing him, reveling in the power they held over him.

Aleksey had become familiar with his various tormentors, so even though he could only see vague shapes through the hood, he recognized the voice of the man with the Bulls jersey. He seemed to be interested in proving himself to the other men and grabbed Aleksey's big toe with a pair of pliers, sharply turning it with no hesitation. The others cheered as Aleksey screamed with pain. The men seemed excited, ecstatic even, like this was some kind of sport to these freaks.

"I think this car needs some more work from the *mecánico*," the man joked. "Maybe we need to adjust his transmission, *sí*?"

The other men slapped their knees, howling with laughter.

Finally, they let him down, and Aleksey collapsed onto the dirt floor with a thud. Covered with red welts and dark blue bruises, his body throbbed from head to toe. Hitting the ground hardly registered in his mind — there was so much pain everywhere that it was barely noticeable. In fact, it was a relief.

It feels so good to lie on this cool ground, was Aleksey's desperate thought as his cheek pressed into the dirt. They did not allow him that relief for long, however.

Grabbing him roughly under his aching arms, two men hoisted him up and plopped him down hard into a chair. This time, he felt the landing as a sharp bolt of pain ripping through his lower body.

"Ahhhh!" Aleksey ground his teeth and cried internally, trying not to let his captors have satisfaction in their cruelty. But it was hard to keep tears of pain from misting his eyes. Onc of the imps tormenting him chuckled.

Taking the rope down, they now wrapped the rough, frayed bindings around Aleksey's feet, waist, and neck, leaving one arm free. They then dragged the chair near an open window, jerking it so hard that it rocked to the side, balancing on only two legs, before coming back down with a crack.

"Ugh!" Aleksey let out a groan this time.

Without warning, one of his captors ripped the black hood from Aleksey's head. The light streaming in through the window struck his pupils. He was momentarily blinded and felt pain in the sockets above his eyes. Aleksey snapped them shut, gradually opening them back up as they adjusted. Without having seen them, Aleksey could identify the sound of chickens scratching around and clucking softly outside beneath the window.

When he opened his eyes all the way, Cucuy was crouched down, very close. He pulled the rag out of Aleksey's mouth. Aleksey struggled to swallow — his mouth was dry, and his tongue ached. "What is wrong with you people? You treat me worse than an animal — and for no reason at all!" Aleksey managed to rasp out between heaving breaths.

Cucuy moved closer, spitting words into his face. "You are a *pollo*." The Spanish word for "chicken" was familiar to Aleksey, but he mistook the meaning.

"I am no coward," he whispered back. However, Cucuy had meant it in the slang way, "an expendable asset." It was a reminder of how the only value they placed on his life was as a hostage for ransom. They didn't see him as human, either — just a *piñata* full of money and a sentient object they could torment for their own amusement.

"I am no good ... to y— ... you unless you keep me alive," Aleksey said hoarsely.

"Oh, we plan on keeping you alive," Cucuy assured him. "You will just wish you weren't." The men around him laughed heartily at his joke, and Cucuy smirked with satisfaction. Then an instantaneous and dramatic change overtook his face.

"But ... enough with jokes, Junior. It's time to talk cash. If your *padre* doesn't come through with the money soon, we will cut you up piece by piece, like the *pollo*." He slowly brandished the tip of his knife in Aleksey's face, making slashing motions with it but never touching his skin. "When all your pieces are cut off, then we will gut you alive. You'll beg to die, watching your own entrails come out."

Aleksey muffled a groan, somewhere between nausea and rage.

"You think I'm joking?" Cucuy shook his head as if he were a teacher talking to an obstinate student. "This is no joke, *amigo*."

Aleksey searched the faces of all the men in the room, trying to find some shred of sympathy, an ounce of conscience, but all he found was cold, steely-eyed indifference.

Do these men even have souls? I do not think I could secretly convince any of them to help me. If only that farmer were here.

"My father will not leave me here," Aleksey stated with confidence, also reassuring himself.

"I guess we will see what your father loves more — you or his money!"

Aleksey was caught off guard as, out of nowhere, Cucuy's meaty paw grabbed his hand and slammed his pinky onto the windowsill, holding it there with his vise grip. He placed his knife just above the lower knuckle.

"Maybe you don't believe us. Maybe your father doesn't. But I assure you, this is no game. Maybe your pinky needs to be Exhibit A of my resolve."

The sharp blade was slowly pressed down onto his finger, beginning to sting as it cut in by a millimeter. Aleksey sucked in a breath and held it. He could feel the pressure of the blade and see a thin red line appear where it broke the skin. Aleksey said nothing. He wouldn't give them the satisfaction of pleading for his finger just so they could use him for their cruel, sadistic games.

Cucuy wants to see me beg, but nothing I say will change his mind. This bully does whatever he wants, and I cannot give him the satisfaction of seeing me reduced to that.

Cucuy released Aleksey's hand as quickly as he had grabbed it. He pulled the knife back and turned it around before plunging it into the rotting wood of the windowsill.

"Your precious finger is safe ... for now, *amigo*."

Aleksey groaned.

"I have given you my word that if you get us our money, we won't kill you. We won't cut you, either, unless you fail on your side of this deal. I am not a man that goes back on his word," Cucuy boasted.

Congratulations! You are a real moral hero, Aleksey thought, his inner sarcasm surfacing.

Cucuy threw a phone into Aleksey's lap. Pulling the gun from his waistband and cocking it, he pointed the barrel at Aleksey's head.

"Call home," he instructed. "Let your papa know it is time for him to pay up."

He does not need to point a gun in my face to get me to call. I will gladly do it. Mild relief at finally being able to contact his father lifted some of the crushing heaviness that had come over him in the past several days. The phone rang several times, and Aleksey began to worry that no one would pick up. Just hearing his father's voice would be a tonic to his weary soul.

I hope that Mama does not pick up. I do not want to put her through the agony of talking to me under these circumstances. Immediately following that thought, there was a click on the other end of the line and then a serious man's voice.

"Hello?"

"Papa," Aleksey spoke weakly, exhausted from the intense pain his body still felt.

"Aleksey! Aleksey, is it you? Are you all right?" Vladi shouted into the receiver.

"It is me ... I —"

"Where are you? Did you get away?" Vladi fervently hoped.

"No, I am still with the men who took me. They told me to call you."

Cucuy chambered a round in his handgun next to Aleksey's head so they could hear it on the phone. He then pointed the barrel out the window, and from behind Aleksey, he pulled the trigger next to his left temple three times in quick succession. Aleksey winced as the discharge deafened his ears, and a high-pitched ringing immediately drowned out all sound.

On the other end of the line, Irina put her hand over her mouth, and her knees buckled under her. Able to identify the sound, Vladi was horrified. At the same time, Irina's head tilted back, and her eyes rolled upward. He lunged forward to catch her. Torn between crises, he returned his attention to the phone, "Aleksey! Are you there?"

Then the line went dead.

Cucuy lowered the smoking gun and let out a guttural laugh. "Looks like your papa knows we're serious now."

15

THE DEVIL'S DEMANDS

Vladi dialed back for hours, receiving no response. Aleksey could hear the phone ringing, albeit faintly over the high-pitched ringing that persisted in his ears. The deafening gunfire had been close enough to cause a powder burn across the left side of his head between his temple and his ear. The pain seared through his skull, making it difficult for him to focus on anything else. Tension caused Aleksey to clench his jaw. He could feel sweat trickling down his face, mixing with the dirt on his skin, but he didn't have the energy to wipe it away.

Aleksey wondered what must be going through his parents' minds, the emotional ordeal they must be enduring, and what he would say to them if he had the chance. He wondered if he would ever get that chance.

It will devastate my parents if they know what I am going through, but I am still alive. I must focus on that. I would tell them I am being given food and shelter, so they need not worry. Believing I am okay will not diminish Papa's determination to get me out of here. Having peace of mind will help them to focus better on what must be done.

The phone continued to ring. Finally, someone picked up. It wasn't Aleksey.

"*Buenos días, Ruso*," answered Cucuy with feigned friendliness in his deep voice. "I have been waiting for your call. Do you know why? Because I want you to feel the same helplessness and despair your son feels right now."

"Who is this?" Vladi asked sternly.

"I have no intention of telling you! Are you an idiot? Oh, I see ... no, you think I am an idiot."

Cucuy's voice shifted to a low and menacing tone. "You want to know who I am? I'm the one who's got your son, and if you don't pay up, I'll make sure he's in pieces before you ever get the chance to see him again."

Irina put her hand over her mouth as if she could hold in the strangled sobs that burst out. Vladi motioned for her to sit down out of concern that she could faint again.

"You can let 'Mrs. Ruso' know I am the demon in her night, the bringer of death, the one who will make you suffer," Cucuy told him, having fun with it now.

"Get to the point," Vladi shot back through clenched teeth.

"Simple. I want one million dollars, Ruso. That ... is what is important — the price of your son's life."

Vladi placed a hand on Irina's shoulder, trying to offer some comfort. He looked at her and shook his head to indicate that this joker was just talking, trying to get under her skin. He was, in fact, succeeding.

"Have you hurt my son?" Vladi swallowed hard and asked, although he feared the answer.

"I'm not going to waste my time answering that."

The kidnapper on the phone was pushing all his buttons. Vladi felt his anger rising like molten lava, a hot volcano threatening to erupt at any moment. He sensed his rage creeping into his voice, and it took a conscious effort to resist the temptation to threaten the man at the other end of the phone line. Nothing good could possibly come from letting his temper get away from him. Vladi knew any misstep could cost his son's life, and he couldn't take the risk. He took a deep breath and spoke in a measured, controlled tone, trying to sound as reasonable as possible.

"It is clear you have the upper hand here." Vladi expressed deference to the caller while still insisting he didn't have the money. "But you have to understand something. I am a citrus grower. My business here is not just liquid capital. I cannot draw out anything near this amount of money you are demanding."

"Are you taking me seriously or not, Ruso?" Cucuy sneered at Vladi's words, toeing an empty beer can on the ground.

"I am explaining to you the realities of the matter," Vladi shot back at him emphatically, barely containing his anger.

Cucuy shook his head, audibly groaning. "Hey, Ruso, I don't want your life story, man. You will find the money, or you will never find your son!" he growled. "One million dollars, that's all you need to care about. I will allow you three more days. Make no mistake, Ruso, if you don't come through for me, I will make sure your son's death is slow and painful. I will make him suffer in ways you can't even imagine. You don't want this to get any uglier than necessary. Trust me, I'm ready to draw this out one body part at a time."

Cucuy placed a sinister emphasis on the last part of the threat, smirking darkly as he winked at his colleague and spat on the floor.

Vladi could feel the bile rising in his throat as the kidnapper's words hit home. His blood ran cold, imagining the horrors this cartel monster was capable of. He stared at the phone, fists clenched, trying to hold back the rage that was building inside him.

As Irina sat next to him, he sensed how scared and desperate she was. He put his hand over the phone and looked over at her. Tears streamed down her face, and it broke his heart.

"He is demanding money but has not even told me how to get it to them," he said to her, his voice low and tight.

He would never say it to Irina, lest she spiral into despair, but Vladi feared that the lack of instructions about delivering the money meant that these kidnappers were not serious about the ransom and were playing a sick and twisted game with Aleksey's life. Or perhaps they were just trying to see how far they could push things before killing him or demanding even more than the money.

Still, it is best to keep them thinking the money is coming and that I am doing everything I can to come up with it. Every moment counts. Working out the details may buy us precious time, even if it means negotiating with this monster.

Vladi uncovered the receiver, keeping his voice strong and steady.

"This is a lot of money you are asking for. I need more time," he told Cucuy. "It will probably take more than three days to get that much, especially with my situation — I am trying to explain to you."

"Stop explaining, start sending money. When you have the money, I will send instructions. And, Ruso, you need to follow every single detail," Cucuy crowed.

"I promise you I am working as fast as possible to resolve this," Vladi assured him.

Cucuy was a "no excuses" operator — he had no sympathy or patience for his victims. Instead, he pressed Vladi to hurry, his threats growing darker and more sinister.

"Put it to you like this, Ruso ... Junior has ten fingers ... at the moment. The longer you wait, the fewer he will have. A *ruso* with no fingers?" he followed with a bitter laugh. "That's a joke I haven't heard before, old man, but it's going to happen if you don't get me that money."

Click.

The line disconnected.

Vladi slammed the phone back into its cradle, fury boiling in his gut as he thought of the man on the other end of the line. He knew that even if they paid the ransom, there was no guarantee that Aleksey would be released unharmed. Irina's sobs filled the room as she clung to her husband. Vladi held her tightly. They were trapped in a nightmare with no way out. He knew they would have to make impossible choices to save their son.

16

A CALL FOR HELP

Julio Rivera's heart sank upon hearing news of the kidnapping. He learned what had happened from Vladi's orchard foreman, Antonio, with whom he kept in contact. Julio sat at the kitchen table, staring blankly at the wall, listening to Antonio's somber account of how the cartel pirates had taken Vladi's son. His dear friend, Vladi, was in grave trouble.

Julio paced back and forth in his small living room, replaying the conversation in his head. He knew just the man to call — Marco. Julio was confident that his brother, now married and residing in Jamaica, had good connections and might have some ideas that would help Vladi navigate the crisis.

When Julio called, the person who picked up the phone wasn't his brother — rather, it was the cheery voice of his sister-in-law, Jhas. Julio felt a momentary rush of joy as he heard his little nephew laughing in the background. Jhas quickly passed the phone along to her husband and went to put their youngster down for a nap so Marco could talk without distraction.

Marco received the news with a heavy heart. He could sense the gravity in his brother's voice, listening intently as Julio relayed the details. Marco mulled it over, restraining himself from making any overly bold commitments.

Marco didn't make any promises, but he didn't have to. Julio knew that when his brother said, "Let me see what I can do," he meant it. He was clearly taking this very seriously. This brought a measure of relief to Julio, knowing there was another competent head seeking solutions in this nightmare situation. At least they had a chance at turning this crisis around. As Julio hung up the phone, he knew he had made the right call.

Marco sat at the kitchen table, his head in his hands. The room was silent as he lingered, absorbing the weight of the news and contemplating the situation. The only sound was the clock ticking, counting down the moments until their lives would be changed forever.

Marco's wife, Jhas, had overheard one side of the conversation. She noticed Marco running his fingers through his hair as he held his head — a sure sign that something was bothering him. He could feel her eyes on him, but he didn't look up. Concern was etched into her face as she sensed Marco's disquieted spirit.

"What's up, honey?" she asked.

Marco looked up. "Remember me telling you about Vladi?"

"Oh, yes, the 'larger-than-life' Russian gentleman you and Julio are always speaking about."

"Uh, yeah, that's him." Marco had never told Jhas everything about their history. It was behind them — he didn't think any good could come from shining a light on their wretched pasts, particularly his own. Marco knew what a vile person he'd been. He was forgiven by the Lord, and this he knew. But he was also ashamed, and the emotional pain of his past dealings with Vladi still burned raw. He shuddered. Those recollections caused Marco actual physical discomfort. He had spent countless sleepless nights squirming, tormented by memories of his former self.

All he wanted now was a fresh start, not to unearth his bygone sins and have them back in his face again. Of all his wrongs, Marco particularly regretted the harm that he had caused Vladi.

Marco sighed. There was a temptation to just turn away from this and let it be somebody else's problem. He had hoped that he had already done what was best with that last act of pardon, and he preferred not to see Vladi ever again — it was just too painful.

Marco also feared Vladi's return would put him on another dangerous precipice. He'd admitted to Jhas that his former life had been bad, but he was a new man. He didn't want to tell her just how bad it had been. He didn't want to go back there and dig into that. Marco wanted to keep it buried, to forget about the person he used to be and what he had done. He didn't want to taint the present with the past — he wanted it to stay completely in the past.

I never actually told her the details of all the heinous things I was involved in. Will this force the complete truth to come out to my wife in all its gory details? I do not want her to know how long and how deep I was in such a dark life — I would almost rather die. How could she ever look at me the same way again? She is so good. How could she ever love someone who has committed so much evil?

Thinking about what this would do to his marriage and how he might lose her love and respect made Marco sick to his stomach. *She always talks about what a wonderful husband and father I am, but if she knew the former man, I'm sure she'd change her mind.*

No matter how far removed from his past Marco had become, there was still a chance that the ghost of his old self would return to torment him again. Would he ever be able to outrun it?

Marco suffered in his private thoughts. It had taken a long time for him to begin putting it all behind. He was a new man now, but Vladi coming back into his world threatened to dredge up things he would rather keep buried.

Marco sighed again. *But it is all here again. And once more, a life hangs in the balance. Can I just turn away from Vladi and his son and do nothing? That is the selfish, old Marco rearing his ugly head. Of course, I can't do nothing ...*

Marco hadn't said it, but what he really needed deep down was Vladi's forgiveness. He used to think that having Vladi pardoned would satisfy that — that he would have earned the Russian's forgiveness. *But has he ever actually forgiven me? I have not heard a word from him since he left Cuba again, and Julio has never mentioned anything or passed on a message from him. Might he still harbor resentment? One would not blame him. Even a lifetime of good deeds could not make it up to Vladi.*

Marco was torn between his desire to shield his new life and the guilt and responsibility he felt toward Vladi. But he didn't view this as just an opportunity to make further amends for the pain he caused — he was stung with genuine compassion for Vladi. *No one should ever have to deal with these low-life cartel criminals to rescue a family member from their clutches.* It was not a fate he would wish on anyone.

"Honey?" Jhas questioned him again, her voice laced with concern. Marco had been lost in silent thought.

"Oh, uh, sorry. I, um ... I'm just thinking. There was some bad news from Julio." His voice was low and tight with emotion. "Vladi was on a fishing trip in Mexico, and his son was kidnapped."

Jhas gasped, her hand flying to her chest. "Kidnapped? What in the world ..." Her eyes widened in shock.

"They were ambushed by cartel members," Marco continued, his fists clenched with anger and frustration. He continued, "They're demanding a steep ransom. I'm just trying to think of a way I can help."

"But how? ... How do you solve something like that?" Jhas asked.

"That's what I'm trying to figure out. Julio thought maybe some of my contacts might be of some use," he replied cautiously. "It may not be enough." Marco shook his head. "These cartel kidnappers are ruthless. They don't care about human life. They will kill his son without a second thought."

"Oh, I hope you find someone who can help!" Her empathy was sincere, as always. Jhas looked away, her thoughts obviously turning to their own son, Nemesio, resting in the next room. "I can't even imagine," she whispered.

Marco and Jhas had started a happy young family of their own. Hearing of this tragedy happening to someone else was horrific to contemplate. Marco treasured their little boy, Nemesio, beyond anything he could have ever anticipated. "Nemo," as his mother called him, would be three years old in a few days, and he thought his daddy was the greatest. He was Marco's little shadow, following him wherever he went and copying his every move. Jhas often laughed at her son's attempts to mimic his father. She enjoyed watching how inseparable they were.

As a parent now, Marco could empathize with Vladi's quest to find Aleksey despite all odds. As he looked at Nemesio, he felt compelled to take action. He still wasn't sure what form that would take, but he didn't intend to sit this one out, not with Vladi's son in mortal danger.

What if the situation were reversed? Marco could imagine what that would feel like if it were his own son in the hands of such monsters. Grief filled his heart at the very thought of it. In his former life as a prosecutor, Marco was familiar with the methods of torture used in Castro's Cuba. He shuddered to imagine what might be happening to Vladi's son.

Those cartel guys are far more barbaric than we ever were. He needs to be pulled out of there fast, and waiting for help from the authorities is not a viable plan. They don't have time to wait.

Marco knew there was one man on the island who might be able to help navigate this crisis — Frank Díaz.

Marco stood up, his chair scraping against the floor. "I need to go out for a while," he told Jhas.

She looked up from her housework with a mix of concern and resignation. "Okay, but please don't be too long. I need to run errands before my family arrives for Nemo's birthday."

Marco nodded, grinning. His heart swelled with pride at the mention of his son. "My big boy is growing up ..."

"In just a few days — the little man is going to be the big three. You know he's counting to three now on his fingers — smart like his daddy," Jhas remarked with a proud smile.

"I wish you wouldn't call him 'Nemo,'" Marco protested. "It always makes me think of Capitán Nemo in the submarine story."

Jhas playfully rolled her eyes. "It's Captain Nemo, silly. Besides, what's wrong with that?" she lightly countered.

"Nemesio is a strong name, more meaningful and dignified — 'he who gives justice fairly,'" Marco insisted.

"Like his daddy," Jhas concurred, her eyes shining with love. "All about doing what's right." Marco winced at the remark, but his subtle reaction was imperceptible to Jhas. She'd meant it truly, but the reality about the man he was — the man he had been — pricked him on the inside.

Marco pulled Jhas into a hug and pressed a kiss to her forehead. "I'm going to see Díaz now."

"Frank Díaz?" Jhas asked.

"They refer to him as 'The Boss' for a reason. If anyone knows what to do for Vladi, he will."

"I suppose," Jhas replied in less-than-cheery agreement. "Sometimes I wonder if that man has ice in his veins."

Ice in the veins might be exactly what is called for in this case, Marco thought as he walked out the door, closing it lightly behind him.

17
STRONG ADVICE

Díaz leaned back in his chair, taking a long drag on his cigar. Smoke curled toward the ceiling in thick plumes as he exhaled and let it slowly escape his lips. He furrowed his brow, pondering the story Marco had just shared.

"This sounds like the work of the Sinaloa or Gulf Cartel," he surmised.

Given their location on the north coast of Mexico, he put his bets on the latter. The kidnapping had all the earmarks of an operation headed by Osiel Cárdenas.

"Cárdenas leads the cartel, but I can tell you with certainty that he was not the one speaking to your friend on the phone," Díaz said. "It's highly unlikely that Cárdenas would be getting his hands dirty directly in a kidnapping. He's too insulated and surreptitious to be out front doing that kind of work."

Díaz's eyes were dark and serious. He was well aware of how the cartel boss ticked.

"The man telephoning Vladi was probably no more than a lieutenant, maybe a spokesman — head swollen with power, no doubt. But make no mistake, he's just as dangerous and unpredictable as Cárdenas himself," Díaz warned.

"From what I've heard, he's a nasty character," Marco agreed.

"They'll stop at nothing to achieve their goals," Díaz said. "They won't hesitate to kill you if they think you're a threat to their operation."

Marco felt the weight of Frank's words like a physical thing, pressing down on him. He was aware the stakes were high, and the dangers great. But for Vladi and his son, he understood there was no other choice.

"Is there a way to establish a back channel and go around this thug to make some progress?" Marco queried.

Díaz let out a harsh laugh and leaned in closer, his eyes scanning the room as though there might have been eavesdroppers.

"The one thing this cartel does well is smuggling, and we've used these guys to help us get dissidents out of Cuba — for a price, of course," Díaz whispered, affirming with a nonchalant wave of his cigar. "I have contacts, but those are some real bad *hombres*. Their 'friends' aren't much better. This cartel has arms-length ties with other local crime syndicates — Shower Posse here in Kingston in particular. 'The Shower' wants their guns, and the cartel wants Jamaican ganja, especially when marijuana is not in season in Mexico."

"The Shower Posse?" Marco was almost afraid to ask what that was about.

"Yeah, 'The Shower,' they call them," Díaz chuckled, "as in 'showering' their rivals with bullets." Díaz emphasized the point by using his cigar to mimic shooting. "These are some of the most ruthless and bloodthirsty thugs you'll ever come across. They're not to be underestimated."

These guys sound like some of the bands of rebels who did Castro's dirty work back in Cuba, Marco recalled.

"Are you sure you want to get involved with them?" Díaz asked, noting the serious expression on Marco's face.

"Are there any other options?" Marco asked, his voice barely audible, knowing the probable answer.

"Nope," Díaz bit down on his cigar, "at least not that I can help you with." Frank's words hung heavily in the air like the smoke from his cigar, as the gravity of the situation settled in.

"These cartel scum think they can just come in and snatch innocent lives like it's nothing." Díaz's eyes narrowed, his voice taking on a deadly tone. "We'll send a message they'll never forget — that they can't just take what they want without consequences."

He turned to Marco, his gaze intense. "Are you ready to do whatever it takes to save your friend's son?"

Marco's eyes met Díaz's, the fire of determination burning within them. "I'm ready," he declared firmly. "Tell me what we need to do."

With a final nod to Díaz, Marco couldn't help but think that, with Díaz by his side, the kidnappers had picked the wrong fight.

Díaz grinned, a dangerous glint in his eye. "That's what I like to hear. These cartel operatives may just find they messed with the wrong people."

As he did more planning with Díaz, what Marco learned was staggering. The situation with the Gulf Cartel was more complex than he'd ever realized. The cartels operating in Mexico had diversified their illicit businesses beyond drug trafficking. They found that kidnapping could also be a lucrative enterprise and incorporated it into their "business model."

Despite being the savages they were, these narco-terrorists were remarkably well organized. Many cartel operatives were former military, with training and access to military-grade weapons. The cartels operated with great efficiency because of their almost-perfect knowledge of their communities, the people, the roads, and the channels for goods and services through the territories they controlled. These were professional guerillas who knew the lay of the land and every nuance of the local environment.

Back in the old days, they were just smugglers, but Marco learned how they eventually brought the war home, preying on their own communities for profit and power.

Even Cancún, a fast-growing tourist area with large hotels and luxury resorts, was falling under the control of organized crime. Millions of visitors sunned themselves on the country's coral sand beaches, unaware that gangland wars and cartel schemes were taking place right around them. The influx of foreign money increased greed and led to a steady rise in extortion crimes. Restaurants and nightclubs along the *Zona Hotelera* were the primary targets of many cartel operatives and lackeys. They would offer "protection" in the form of an extortion tax, demanding a percentage of revenues. Those who refused to cooperate faced harassment and even death.

But the cartels were careful to maintain a façade of safety in these travel areas. If too many tourists got spooked, their extortion scheme would suffer. Homicide rates in these areas remained low, mainly because the cartels knew murdering tourists would be bad for business. If they killed anyone, it was usually in turf battles between rival cartels vying for control of the region.

Still, that didn't mean the tourist areas were all sunshine in paradise. Many low-level cartel operatives weren't always concerned with the bigger scheme. *Secuestro exprés*, or "express kidnapping," was a short-term hostage scheme that usually involved petty theft. Always looking for a quick score, these thugs prowled the streets like ravenous predators, seeking out their next unsuspecting victim. Tourists were easy targets, their wallets and valuables just waiting to be snatched in the blink of an eye.

The cartel's modus operandi was simple but effective when it came to express kidnapping. The members used borrowed or stolen taxis to do their dirty work, picking up tourists who thought they had flagged a legitimate cab driver. Their victims discovered too late that they were being driven by a criminal who only took them directly to an ATM, forcing them to withdraw as much cash as possible.

The driver would also take their valuables, with force if necessary. They might hold hostages for a few hours while calling family members to demand a ransom payment, but most of the time, they would release their victims after a trip to the cash machine. This was all about getting money quickly with as little fuss as possible. The criminals always got away with it, too, incentivizing this kind of quick grab.

The men who had Aleksey were not the petty "express kidnapping" bandits, however. They were next-level — a different type of criminal, more experienced and ruthless. They had a penchant for sophisticated schemes to extract ransom payments.

These armed bands of raiders were modern pirates. They had access to smugglers' go-fast boats with which they navigated the dangerous waters of the cartel's domain. It meant these kidnappers were the more experienced and trusted operatives in the cartel organization. They understood that to collect a large ransom, they needed to take high-value targets and hold them for extended periods of time.

As he and Díaz met over the next several days to discuss specifics, the genesis of a plan began developing.

"If you want something from them — in this case, your friend's son — you just need to give the cartel something they want," Díaz told Marco as he mashed his cigar out on the small side table ashtray. He leaned in, his voice low and serious. "The key is to let them feel that they got the best deal they could."

What do they want, other than money? Marco wondered.

"I've got some ideas about how to make that happen," Díaz said, answering Marco's unspoken question with a sly grin.

Díaz didn't elaborate on what he had in mind just yet. He did give a stern warning, though. "Listen closely. No matter what, under no circumstances do you meet on their turf. They have an unbeatable home field advantage, and not even the shrewd '*Inquisitor*' would be immune to trouble."

"How's that?" Marco asked.

"The problem starts before you even land," Díaz explained. "Private airfields throughout Mexico have cartel spotters. Their sole purpose is to identify ransom targets of opportunity or potential threats. So, if you charter a plane into Mexico without your own trustworthy security detail, you will become a new target for an even more sophisticated attack. They will take the ransom, the aircraft, and your boat for their own smuggling fleets. And they'll take more hostages — namely, you and your comrade. You will then be no help to his son — you won't even be able to help yourselves."

"Hmmm. But maybe someone with a Latin heritage like them has an advantage in this situation ... you think?" Marco asked, grasping at straws. "If they recognized I'm Cuban, perhaps they would be more inclined to deal well with me or at least ... see me as not a threat."

Díaz's laughter was bitter.

"Marco, Marco. I thought you were wiser in the ways of the world than that. Of course not. What is that to them?"

"Well, I just thought, maybe ..."

"Think about it," Díaz said. "Let me explain their 'business model' to you. The name of their game is to make as much money as possible, and non-Latino Americans are viewed as lucrative kidnap-and-ransom targets. It doesn't matter that your friend and his son are Russian and that you are a fellow Latino. It's just different ways to bleed money out of people."

"That makes sense," Marco conceded.

"Remember, the bottom line is that this is a business for them — nationality and culture mean nothing to them other than factors to calculate how and where to extort money."

"Money — money — money. It does always come back to that, doesn't it?" Marco mused.

Díaz nodded.

"But let me tell you something, Marco. The good news is they don't really want to kill this hostage — they don't even want to hold him. They want to leverage him to get paid. We can use this to our advantage."

"Right, so how does that work exactly?" Marco pressed for details — he had never dealt with anything like this before. "I'm supposed to gamble with someone else's life, bargaining on their behalf to get the ransom demands down?"

Díaz shook his head. "That's the thing," he replied. "It's not a gamble — it's a negotiation. And it's not so much about getting the amount down as it is about getting the hostage released. That's your goal."

Marco's stomach twisted at Díaz's words. This was a battle unlike any he'd ever fought before, and the thought of someone else's life now resting in his hands felt like an overwhelming responsibility. He couldn't help but think that he was in over his head. They would have to carefully follow Díaz's guidance if they hoped to locate Aleksey and get him out alive.

"You can keep negotiating with them and be firm," Díaz said, his tone devoid of any emotion. "They'll typically demand thirty thousand to one hundred thousand dollars for Americans."

Marco held up his hand, "They demanded one million dollars!"

"Perhaps Russians are worth more," Díaz quipped with a hint of twisted humor. "But here's the thing ... They're testing you first, counting on you to be irrational. They know that if the demand is excessive, you won't be able to come up with the money. You'll have to negotiate," Díaz noted.

"So what are the implications for us?" Marco pressed.

"They want you to pay, and they don't want to hold this hostage for more than a few weeks. They'll contact your friend again soon. You can count on it."

"Should I tell him he needs to negotiate? Do you think that's the best strategy?" Marco thought this might be the cleanest and most expedient route to take, but he was terrified of the consequences of getting it wrong.

"Yes, but you need to be careful and approach this with the utmost tact. It's not going to be easy, but if we play our cards right, we can get that young man back to his family. A few wrong, poorly chosen words could turn into a death sentence for his son. Just know," Díaz said, his tone heavy with warning. "Not every negotiation ends in a deal. If you're afraid, these guys can smell blood in the water. If you're too bold, they'll walk away. You've got to carefully balance your negotiations."

"We're treading the proverbial tightrope — a very thin wire here. That's a tricky line to walk when emotions are running high," Marco remarked bitterly.

"It is ... because here's the downside," Díaz continued. "Unlike the petty express kidnappings, many victims taken for ransom like this will never be returned to their loved ones."

"That's exactly what I'm afraid of," Marco said, shaking his head.

"After getting the ransom payment, the kidnappers cut all contact. If they get an early impression that the effort is a lost cause, they'll just kill him now. And they'll do it in a way that makes the most horrifying spectacle. Their intention is to instill fear in others, so next time, someone will pay them immediately."

Marco slowly let the air out of his lungs with a sick feeling. *Ughhh! Vladi could give these thugs his life savings and lose his son anyway.* It was clear that this was a delicate and dangerous game.

"It is probably worse than you're even thinking. They'll act with absolutely no scruples." Díaz spoke about it in an oddly casual manner. Over time, his interactions with the cartel had caused him to develop a callous acceptance toward how they operated. But he added, "I'm sorry your friend and his son find themselves in this situation. But you need to be fully aware of what kind of people you're dealing with and approach them accordingly."

He didn't expose Marco to further gruesome details, but Díaz knew that you could tell a lot about how these thugs operated by the barbarism used to kill their victims. If a victim were decapitated or put on public display, it was an execution ordered by the boss and carried out by loyal soldiers. If the genitals were mutilated, the kill was personal. If the mouth or tongue was mutilated, the victim had said something he should not have — this included the "Colombian Necktie," in which the victim's throat was cut open, and the tongue was pulled through the hole. If they left the victim lying where he fell, that might have meant the killer panicked, the kill was hasty, or it was just part of a larger rampage without any targeted hits.

Díaz was by no means a warm-hearted personality, but he earnestly hoped that none of these would be Aleksey's fate. Something about the story Marco told him struck a sympathetic chord. He did feel for all involved in this horrible situation. It disturbed Díaz to think of innocent lives caught in the crosshairs of these ruthless criminals.

18

UNFORESEEN FAVOR

The phone rang, and Vladi lunged across the room, his heart pounding in his chest. He hadn't left the house and was on edge, staring at the phone. He'd been waiting for this call for days, Cucuy's demands hanging over him like a dark cloud. When it finally came, the rush of adrenaline and nerves hit like a freight train. His shaking hand snatched the phone on the second ring.

"Hello?" Vladi growled into the phone, his voice rough with emotion. He couldn't even begin to imagine what the kidnappers were going to say or what they would want from him.

"Vladi?" The voice spoke with a Latino accent, but it wasn't the kidnappers.

"Julio?" Vladi asked hesitantly.

"No, actually, this is Marco."

Silence filled the line as Vladi's mind was scrambled by the surprise. Marco?...

Rivera? He was the last person on earth Vladi expected to hear from. He couldn't form a response as long, awkward seconds ticked by on the line.

Nervously, Marco broke the silence. "Julio gave me your phone number. He told me about what happened to you and the situation with your son."

There was a long moment of tense silence.

"What do you want, Marco?" Vladi shot back, his voice filled with contempt. "I am expecting a call from those miserable kidnappers. We are in the middle of trying to prevent this ... situation ... from getting worse."

"I'm very sorry. I know this is a difficult time for you. I just wanted to call and offer my help ... such as it is," Marco replied, his tone cautious and sympathetic.

"Offer your help? Like what?"

"That's what I'm calling about," Marco answered gingerly.

"You have some nerve, Marco." Vladi had justified concerns. He couldn't help but wonder if there was some ulterior motive behind this sudden offer of help. After all, the Marco he had known was cynical, cruel, cunning, and vindictive. They had a history — a dark and complicated past. Even if Marco sounded reasonable, Vladi had a deep-seated mistrust of the man who had betrayed him. It was hard to move beyond that.

Softening his tone a touch, Vladi continued. "I appreciate your offer, Marco, but . . . why are you really calling?"

Vladi's mind was in a fog as he tried to figure out how to process this conversation. Without waiting for a reply, he went on, "Marco, I am sorry. I just had not expected it to be you. I am surprised, I do not —"

"I know I may not be the person you want to hear from, Vladi ..."

"What I want is to get my son back," Vladi interrupted, his voice cracking with emotion. "I appreciate anyone who wants to help. Thank you for your kind offer. I am not sure what you can do, though."

"I've been thinking about this — I have contacts," Marco informed him.

"More than the FBI and the U.S. State Department?" Vladi asked with bitter incredulity. "Not even they are able to help. And the Mexican police have been indifferent at best. Worse than indifferent."

"Mexican police?" Marco scoffed. "No, no. That is not the way to go. They're a bunch of corrupt morons. Hear me out for a moment."

Vladi's stomach twisted with a mixture of hope and distrust. The thought of accepting Marco's help made him uneasy, but with his son's life on the line, he also couldn't afford to overlook any potential help, even if it meant working with the person he never wanted to see again.

"Would it be fair to say that I am skeptical? Maybe." It was a conversation Vladi really didn't feel like having right now. Marco couldn't see Vladi's face through the telephone line, but he could feel every word.

"I understand, Vladi." Marco softened his tone further, underscoring his serious intent. "We've had issues in the past. But I've changed. I know I don't deserve your trust. For now, let me help you get your son back."

Vladi sighed, his mind a whirlwind of conflicting emotions. "Go ahead," he finally conceded. "I will hear you out."

"What are the ransom demands and conditions?" Marco asked, his voice turning razor sharp as a man getting down to business.

"I have spoken to one of the kidnappers," Vladi replied, his own tone matching Marco's. "He said they want one million dollars in ransom."

"One million." Marco lingered over the words as if exploring them like a strange archaeological find.

"My son's life is worth more than all the money in the world, but I just cannot do it. I do not have access to that kind of money at a moment's notice. I own a home, land, equipment, but nothing I can sell overnight for cash, and the equity loan process is too long." Every turn was a futile dead-end alley. Vladi's voice reflected his frustration. "I have explored everything!"

"It is a lot," Marco concurred sympathetically. These were only a few words, but the way he spoke them carried an earnest compassion that was out of character for Marco. It lodged in Vladi's mind, although he didn't even acknowledge that he noticed.

"The representative I spoke to did not seem willing to negotiate. My brother, Erik, is en route from Russia. If we cannot negotiate, then once Erik gets here, we will take matters into our own hands and return to Mexico to find him ourselves."

Marco tensed up. He wanted to yell NO! — it was the very thing Díaz had said not to do.

Instead, Marco's voice came through the phone with a sense of calm determination. "Listen, Vladi, I can understand your wanting to go to Mexico and get things done," Marco empathized, his voice softer now. "If it were my son Nemesio, I would search every corner of the world for him and fight anyone who stood in my way. I would do things that ... well, you know ..."

"I do know," Vladi said, his voice darkening.

"But you must trust me when I say that storming into Mexico and trying to take matters into your own hands would be a mistake."

"What other option is there?" Vladi demanded.

"That's not the way to get your son back. I've learned a bit about the type of men who have your son, and now is not the time to be a cowboy. It would be suicide — a fool's errand," Marco warned. "And your son would end up just as dead as you and your brother."

"Then what else can I do?" Vladi growled, his voice rising in frustration. "Who else is going to save him? I have not heard from the kidnappers since I told them I did not have a million-dollar ransom. I am going crazy just sitting here. How can I stand by and just hope they do not maim or kill him?"

"This is why I'm calling," Marco said, his voice filled with a sense of purpose. "I know that you getting killed while looking for your son will not save him. It just means your wife will have two bodies to bury — if she ever finds them."

Marco paused for a moment.

"Vladi, I know you, of all people, are a man of action. This waiting must be anguishing for you. But this is a different kind of fight, and you're not a one-man army. Actually, I think I can help, but we have to be smart about this."

"Help how, exactly?" Vladi asked, still wary.

"Vladi, listen to me. You need to channel that desire for action into something smart, something calculated. It's important to remember that these kidnappers are criminals, and they're looking for easy money. We'll use that to our advantage."

Vladi listened intently, his hopes beginning to rise.

Marco continued, his voice taking on a steely edge. "We need intel. We have contacts who can give us information on his abductors, who they are, their whereabouts, where they're hiding ... their weaknesses. Carefully — together — we'll map out a plan to rescue your son and bring those kidnappers to their knees. But we can't afford to make any mistakes. We wait for the perfect moment — and when it comes, we move decisively, with precision, like a surgical strike. Most importantly, it will give us the best chance of getting your son back alive."

Vladi's eyes widened at the possibility. "How do we do that?"

"I went to see an acquaintance who has contacts within the cartels. He's quite familiar with how they operate, and he gave me some advice to pass along. He may be able to help us in other ways as well. More concrete ways."

Vladi's eyes narrowed again — triggered by the word "cartel." Just as he thought, this was the old Marco, back again with his tricks and schemes.

"Oh, great, so now we're seeking advice from a cartel insider. That sounds like a fantastic idea," Vladi retorted with sarcasm. "If he is involved with a bloodsucking cartel, he must be a shady character," Vladi noted, his voice rising in anger. "You expect me to trust someone who is associated with the very people who have taken my son? This is a mistake, Marco — a huge mistake."

"No, you misunderstand — it's not like that," Marco assured him.

"Why would you even consider trusting someone like that?" Vladi had a healthy amount of skepticism about anyone who was close to the cartel, and with good reason. "Who is this guy? What is his name?"

Marco hesitated for a moment as if weighing how much to reveal.

"Vladi, I can't tell you right now. But if anyone can help you, this is the man to make it happen. You can be sure, in his circles, they call him 'The Boss' for good reason."

Marco couldn't see Vladi rolling his eyes on the other end of the phone line, but he could sense that Vladi wasn't convinced.

"Hear me out, Vladi. This guy is a Cuban attorney — and he's a covert operator, but that is exactly who you need right now. He's navigated situations like this before, faced the worst of the worst, and come out on top."

"Well, if he is acquainted with the worst of the worst, then these will be just his type," Vladi agreed.

"He's just a man who knows how to survive in a dangerous world, and I believe he can help us do the same. He's discreet, he's smart, and he's our best shot at getting your son back alive. But that doesn't mean he's in league with the cartels, not like you may be thinking. He's not like the corrupt Mexican authorities and politicians. He has connections because he's used the cartel guys to help him with his, uh, business."

"Used them? Used them for what? Are you suggesting we get on their level and somehow use these criminals? My son's life is on the line here. Are you out of your mind?" Vladi exclaimed.

Marco wisely kept quiet, concerned that anything he said would be misconstrued. He allowed Vladi the moments necessary to process this conversation in his mind.

Vladi didn't think that after all that happened, Marco would call him out of the blue to lead him into even greater danger. Even so, he was dubious of Marco's proposal.

"So, let me get this straight," he finally spoke again. "You are asking me to trust an attorney who uses cartels for his 'business?' And you expect me to believe he is not corrupt? You have got to be kidding me."

This is strange, Vladi's mind was whirling with the implications of this new development, and he was cautious about believing anything right now.

"It's ... well, certainly it's not ... typical, and he's not your average guy. But you won't regret agreeing to his help, and you can trust me on this, despite ... well, despite our history," Marco ended rather awkwardly.

As Marco explained in more detail, Vladi couldn't help but feel a persistent sense of unease. But as he listened, he understood the logic behind it, and he also knew he didn't have any other options. He would have to put some trust in this unlikely ally — he had to trust Marco, and he might need to trust this mysterious attorney, too.

Vladi considered Marco's words carefully. He had to admit that he was moved to see Marco standing with him in this trial. He still felt the sting of the wounds from their past and the betrayal that had torn them apart. Could it be said of both men that they turned away from their former selves to a new life without looking back?

Vladi wondered if it was possible to forgive Marco without removing the boundaries that ensured he couldn't get betrayed again. Vladi was a new man with a new spirit, through and through — and he didn't want to be held hostage to unforgiveness. He would seek to forgive, even if he struggled to do so.

"Fine," Vladi gritted out. "What did this 'clandestine counselor' have to say?"

19
NEGOTIATIONS

The next day, the sky outside was dark and stormy, mirroring the turbulent emotions raging within Vladi. The wind howled, and the rain pounded against the windows as if trying to beat its way into the room and join the heated conversation within. The lightning illuminated the room in bright flashes, casting the faces of Vladi and Irina in an eerie light.

The telephone rang at the Gavrilov home again, just as Díaz had predicted it would. There was no introduction, but Vladi did not have to guess who was on the other end of the line. A gruff, soulless voice announced itself without ceremony.

"Where's the million, Ruso?"

"I want to speak to my son. How do we know he is alive?" Vladi countered.

There was a moment of silence on the other end of the line, followed by some scuffling sounds and a grunt. Faintly in the background, Vladi heard, "Tell him." More noisy scratching filled the line before a clear voice came on. "Papa, I am here. I —"

"That's enough!" barked a voice in the background. The line crackled as the phone was pulled from Aleksey's hand.

Vladi felt a wave of relief wash over him, knowing that at least his son was still alive. He didn't sound well, though. Vladi could perceive that much, even with only a few words.

The kidnapper's tone was like ice when he came back on the line. "Do not test my patience, Ruso. You have a situation right now — and it's about to get a lot worse if you don't cough up some *dinero*. Where is the money?"

Vladi felt the weight of the circumstances squarely on his shoulders, yet he tried to keep his voice calm.

"I am sorry. As I told you, we are not able to do that. I do not have access to the million dollars you are asking for," Vladi appealed. He kept his words steady, attempting to mask the dread that crept into his mind.

Cucuy's voice dripped with sarcasm. "If you want to negotiate, we can make it two million dollars. I can play that game too, but I prefer to be reasonable."

Vladi began to think he might be outmatched. He was just a desperate father trying to save his son, up against a manipulative psychopath who had no scruples and played by no rules. He tried to follow the advice Díaz had given Marco for him, but it was much harder now that his nerves were frayed. Such tactics threatened to make him beg or yield. He had never felt so helpless, utterly at the mercy of another person.

I used to believe that anyone who succumbed to this type of manipulation was weak, ignorant, a coward, or all three. But now that I am in this situation and the fate of my son is at stake, I realize how difficult it is. Vladi's military training had prepared him for how to respond when his own life might hang in the balance, but when his child was in mortal peril, it was a different matter.

"I am glad to hear that you are a reasonable man." Vladi's heart was in his throat. He wanted to choke on those words he knew he had to say, although, in his mind, they were spoken with sarcastic emphasis.

"I am willing to work with you, and I think together we can come up with a solution that will get you plenty of money to make it all worthwhile. The issue is timing," Vladi appealed. "Simply put, I cannot give you what I do not have access to right now. Not yet. With more time —"

"Okay, Ruso … I am hearing what you say, *sí*? I tell you what, you bring us three hundred thousand dollars, and we'll call it good," replied the cool voice on the other end of the phone. "See, I'm easy to get along with."

Vladi was seeing right through the approach. *Marco's man, Díaz, was right again.* His trust in Marco and his contact went up a notch. *By anchoring their demands at one or two million dollars, it makes three hundred thousand seem more reasonable.*

"Okay, we are getting closer to what is possible." Vladi was still telling him no, but he tried to maintain a positive tone.

"Closer?" Cucuy growled.

"Look, I've got bad news. After carefully going through what I have, the most cash I can get on short notice is fifty thousand dollars. I hope in your reasonableness you will see it is all I can do." Vladi's heart was pounding in his chest, and he could feel the blood rushing in his ears. He knew he had to keep it together.

Having to play nice with this animal is almost unbearable. I would tell him to forget it, if not to save my son.

"What part of three hundred thousand do you not understand?" Cucuy snapped. "Do not mistake my 'kind offer' for weakness. Do you think that because you are in America, the world plays by your rules? … that your wishes just come true? Well, this is my world, and you are now in it. I set the terms — all you can do is comply. Or, perhaps you don't love your son as much as you would have everyone to believe?"

"I hear you," Vladi responded with a cool tone that belied his inner agitation.

"Make no mistake, Ruso, this is not a negotiation. This is me giving you a choice. You either pay up, or your son dies. Piece by piece. Simple as that."

Cucuy's words were like daggers, twisting in Vladi's gut. "You should consider yourself blessed, *amigo*. The last man I dealt with, I never offered this kind of..."

"As I previously stated, I do appreciate you being reasonable on this," Vladi reminded him. "I only wanted to say ..."

Vladi could feel the storm within him reaching a crescendo, as he fought to keep his temper in check.

"Let's forget what you want to say ... and keep it simple," Cucuy menaced. "I will give you another day to come up with the money before we start sending him home, one piece at a time. Or ... we can start now if you want to keep telling me how this is going to go."

Vladi could hear what sounded like a chair being knocked over in the background. Several voices shouted at once. Vladi was unable to tell if Aleksey was among them, but he took Cucuy's threat seriously.

Just then, a bolt of lightning lit up the room. "No! No!" Vladi shouted into the phone. He could see Irina startled by the panicked rise in his voice. He reined it in and shifted back into a neutral tone. "I am not trying to tell you what to do. This is your game — I am working with you. We both want this resolved. I just need a little time."

"No. No, you see, Ruso. This is not a 'game.' This is real life," Cucuy communicated in a low growl. "And it's going to be the real end of a life if you don't get the money as soon as possible — whatever it takes."

"I am going to do this, I ..."

The wind and rain outside had reached a frenzied pitch, battering the windows as if nature was in league with Cucuy and his threats.

"By all means, take your time," Cucuy drawled sarcastically, "When Junior runs out of fingers, he has a couple of ears we can send home too. We will continue to send you parts of your son until none are left except his lying tongue."

"He ... what in the world ..." Vladi was struck with bewilderment. "He would never lie."

"He says you'll do what's necessary to save him," Cucuy said, chuckling. "Sounds like a lie to me!"

Vladi could feel the tension in the air as if the storm outside were brewing within the room. Irina stood close, her breathing shallow and labored. She listened intently, straining to make out every word on the other end of the phone. The sound of her rapid heartbeat thundered in her ears as the kidnapper's demands echoed through the receiver. Her sudden gasp confirmed she had heard this last statement.

Vladi's eyes shot to hers. What he saw was more than he could bear. Her body trembled — raw grief written on her face. The pain in her voice cut through Vladi, and tears welled up in his own eyes, spilling down his cheeks. And he felt responsible for this nightmare.

Vladi straightened his back to regain his composure, trying to calm the surge of emotion that threatened to overpower him. He still had work to do, and Díaz had said not to exhibit behaviors that could be perceived as weakness. Vladi mentally switched gears, doing everything to keep it under control.

"Then we need to talk specifics. I do not even know where or how to send the money," Vladi said, his voice tight and controlled. "You have not given me any instructions."

Vladi had a notepad in hand, ready to write. He hoped this would help them talk and ease the tension that had developed over the amount of money. He knew that if he continued to argue back and forth right now, he risked making it appear as if there was no resolution. And Díaz had warned them about the dangers of this scenario.

"When you have the money, Ruso, I will tell you what to do next," Cucuy barked, not showing any more of his hand than necessary.

CLICK ... *dial tone* — the phone disconnected. This was the kidnapper's game, much as he claimed it wasn't a game. Cucuy played it by his own rules, and he determined when the conversation started and ended.

Vladi put a hand to his tensed jaw, clenched so tightly that the veins in his head bulged and throbbed. He stared at the phone, squeezing the receiver harder as if to crush it in a bear-like grip. The ticking of the clock on the wall seemed to mock him, reminding him of the precious seconds slipping away.

When he finally put the phone down, Vladi noticed his hand was trembling — a combination of strained nerves, anger, and frustration. He looked down at the blank notepad. Tearing the top page out, he crushed the paper in his hand.

The storm outside had subsided, but Vladi knew the real storm was just beginning. He took a deep breath and steeled himself for the fight. Thinking about Aleksey — and thinking about the kidnappers — he whispered through gritted teeth.

"I am coming for you."

20
CABRITO

Nights in the "Cartel Hilton" were nothing short of a waking nightmare for Aleksey. The darkness brought little respite from the constant torment of his captors and only amplified the hopelessness that consumed his thoughts.

With his hands tied — and sometimes his feet — Aleksey remained under guard throughout the night as the men took shifts. The guards never fully extinguished the light so they could continue playing their endless card game and maintain a watchful eye on their prisoner. Furthermore, the hovel was never quiet and restful, as the guards talked loudly and laughed at their own crude jokes throughout the dark hours.

Aleksey's bed was nothing more than a pitiful pallet of dirty palmetto fronds, a dusty, thin goatshair blanket, and a burlap sack he rolled up for a makeshift pillow, all of which reeked. The foul odor emanating from his "bed" was suffocating, making it impossible for him to get a decent night's sleep.

The flies that plagued Aleksey by day were replaced by hordes of cockroaches that came at night to feast on the pus from his unwashed, bloody sores. Repulsed by the sensation of their tiny legs climbing across his body, Aleksey brushed them away — but that was difficult, if not impossible, when he was bound.

Whenever Aleksey did finally doze off from complete exhaustion, he snored. That was the cue for the guards to come over and kick him or deliver a surprise wallop with a rifle butt.

Between the guards, the smells, pests, and pain, Aleksey struggled to get any semblance of rest. He never slept completely through the night and would awaken fitfully every hour or two. He closed his eyes, trying to shut out the world, but all he could see was the twisted face of Cucuy, looming over him like a demon.

It was all part of the psychological and physical torture, and Aleksey began to lose track of where he was or whether he was awake or asleep. The lack of sleep had taken a heavy toll on his mind.

Cucuy arrived early on this morning, while Aleksey was still on the pallet. Cucuy looked like he'd been awake all night, mulling over a fiendish plan. He barely tried to hide the sinister grin on his face as he relished Aleksey's suffering.

The massive Mexican pulled up a chair and straddled it backward, spitting to the side and eying Aleksey with amusement. Aleksey struggled to sit up.

"Tell me, this citrus farm you said you manage for your father, what do you grow there?" Cucuy's voice was cool and shrewd as he interrogated Aleksey.

Aleksey rolled his eyes, partly from pure exhaustion and partly from disbelief at Cucuy's stupid question. It was a citrus farm. They grew citrus fruits. Obviously.

Cucuy gave a slight grunt, then went on. "Being the intelligent young man you are, I am sure you are an effective manager of your family business," he continued to prompt.

Aleksey said nothing, muffling a groan, and closed his eyes briefly. He pondered lying down again. Perhaps if he pretended to sleep, or blessedly fell asleep, the dumb questions would stop.

"It must be quite a responsibility for you," Cucuy almost seemed to sympathize. Or did he sound impressed? Aleksey wondered. *What is his deal?*

"Tell me, how large is this operation?" Cucuy pressed.

Aleksey realized Cucuy was fishing for insights about his father's financial assets. He turned his head aside and didn't answer, knowing that any information he gave would only be used against him and his family. Cucuy wasn't so easily discouraged, however. He persisted, his questioning becoming more aggressive and to the point.

"Does your father have valuable assets, such as property or investments? What would you say is his ... net worth?"

Aleksey remained resolute, still refusing to talk, his obstinate silence driving Cucuy to greater frustration.

From his hip pocket, Cucuy pulled out a device that resembled a prehistoric wrench, a stick of wood with a short rope tied on its end in a loop. He put it under Aleksey's chin and forced him to look his way.

"Know what this is?"

Aleksey shook his head faintly, playing along.

"We twist this on a burro's lip when it is stubborn and will not open its mouth. This instrument—the *vaqueros* call an *arcial*—to American horsemen, it's a twitch. We've also found it effective in getting prisoners to open their mouths. After it's been wrapped around your tongue, you'll be quite ready to talk."

Cucuy's voice was low and menacing. He was determined to extract information from Aleksey by any means necessary.

"Let me get to the point, Junior. Your father tells me he doesn't have the money to pay the ransom. We are just trying to be ... helpful?"

"Okay," Aleksey said listlessly.

"So, if he doesn't deliver soon, you will help motivate him. So be thinking about that." Cucuy spat out the last word, visibly frustrated as he gave a signaling nod to the guards and tapped the tool in the palm of his hand.

The guards nodded back. They were just as sadistic as their leader, ready to carry out Cucuy's twisted plan. He threw open the doorway flap and stormed out of the shack.

Aleksey refused to be broken by his captors. They gagged him again. Two guards worked together to hang him from a wooden beam in the low ceiling of the shack. The pain was excruciating as his flesh stretched, tearing and bleeding from the rough ropes digging in deeply and cutting off circulation to his hands.

Aleksey's body ached as he hung from the beam, his arms stretched taut above his head. His shoulders felt like they were being pulled out of their sockets. Each breath was a struggle as he tried to take the weight off his overstretched arms by standing on the tips of his toes. His bare feet hardly touched the ground, making it impossible to find relief from the searing pain in his shoulders.

He knew what was coming next. Another round of torture — even more devious forms of mistreatment. He'd lost count of how many times he'd been gagged and tied up like this, and how many burns and whip marks decorated his skin. He had been through everything from having cigarettes extinguished on his flesh to shocks with a cattle prod, but what would it be this time?

Had I answered his questions about Papa's business, it would be the same right now, only I would have compromised my family. Do they think I am the same kind of scum they are?

Even if he had been tempted, betrayal brought Aleksey no benefits or relief. His captors took pleasure in inflicting suffering, deriving satisfaction from his cries of distress and pain. Aleksey had long since realized their hazing had no purpose other than for their own sick amusement.

More often than not, Aleksey was sure that Cucuy did and said things just because he could. With Aleksey bound and gagged, Cucuy held all the cards. He might not express it in words, but Aleksey was convinced. For Cucuy, this was all about power.

Why is this ransom payment taking so long? Aleksey wondered for at least the hundredth time. In fact, there were so many questions. Not knowing what was going on was torture in itself. *Does Papa have the money they demand? Is anyone going to get me out of here? Maybe I am the only one who can rescue me,* he considered, also for the hundredth time. *How can I —*

Aleksey's wandering thoughts were interrupted by a man carrying about ten feet of hemp rope and a short wooden stool. The man casually hummed a tune as he stepped onto the stool and twisted the rope around itself, fashioning it into a noose. He then tied it to a beam a few feet in front of Aleksey. The man stepped off the stool and walked out of the shed, leaving Aleksey alone with the noose hanging in front of him. The message could not have been clearer, but as to why they were bothering? That was more of an open question ...

Aleksey recognized this as a form of psychological torment. *Hmph. These psychos are trying to terrify me. I must not react, no matter what. Do not give them what they want.* The military had certainly taught him at least that, even as a young recruit — *Do not show the enemy fear ... ever.*

For a moment, the only sound Aleksey noticed was his own labored breathing. He could feel the rope taunting him, daring him to react. He closed his eyes and tried to block out the impression of the noose, but it was etched into his mind as an afterimage. The rope seemed to be calling out to him, beckoning him to surrender to his fear.

Is that it? Are they just trying to scare me by leaving me with a noose?

A short time later, he got the answer. The flap across the doorway was pulled open, and a cute gray buckling goat was led in. The little goat looked about the shed curiously, bleating, oblivious to Aleksey's dire circumstances ... or its own.

In one swift motion, one guard reached beneath the goat and pulled its hind legs from under it. He slipped the noose around them and dangled the little goat head-down right in front of Aleksey.

The goat struggled, twisting and swinging from the rope. Its eyes filled with panic bulged — the buckling's distended tongue hung out of its mouth as it swung there ... helpless.

Charming bleats turned to pitiful cries that sounded eerily indistinguishable from a child screaming. Aleksey had to make a conscious effort not to wince with revulsion.

The man placed a metal bucket below the little goat. He reached for his blade, bent over, and slit its throat.

"*Misericordia para el cabrito*," the man said, winking. "Mercy for the little goat."

Blood splatter hit Aleksey all over his face and body, the coppery smell at once assaulting his nose. He turned his head away, concerned he would vomit and choke while gagged.

His entire life, Aleksey had field-dressed deer, wild hogs, and small game with Erik, but this was different. It was the warped satisfaction these barbarians derived from killing that was so disgusting.

When the adorable buckling ceased struggling and twitching, the man stood upon the short wooden stool and proceeded to skin, disembowel, and quarter the carcass. Severing its head, he held it up by Aleksey's gagged mouth.

"Don't like seeing where your dinner comes from, Ruso?"

Aleksey, of course, understood that for people to eat, something had to die. He had never taken that for granted — he just didn't think of killing as amusement. Where he came from, you didn't take the life of a living creature thoughtlessly. In contrast, these cartel operatives were desensitized, seeming to enjoy it.

That's because they did.

In fact, Osiel Cárdenas, the Gulf Cartel kingpin, had recently begun working with trained paramilitary soldiers under Guzmán Decena. These ferocious "narco-mercenaries" carried out the most brutal of the cartel's dirty business. For them, killing a human, a chicken, a goat, or any other living thing made absolutely zero difference.

As part of their initiation rites, they would assign each recruit a puppy to care for. After several weeks, the recruit was ordered to kill the puppy in some savage way. The blood needed to flow, or the oxygen needed to be cut off. That precious puppy needed to suffer and die horribly. This accomplished two things. First, it proved who would obey orders, no matter how outrageous. Also, it conditioned these cartel operatives to be callous — to kill anything they were told, however innocent ... however harmless.

Evidently, these brutes met Guzmán Decena's requirements for cruelty.

The guard's blood-soaked hands wrapped the butchered goat in burlap. He held the pail of blood and entrails in Aleksey's face, snickering, hoping to get a reaction. The odor of the goat's intestines met Aleksey's nose.

It is certainly foul, just like his mind, Aleksey thought as he tried to block out his sense of smell — impossible to do since his mouth remained gagged.

The only thing Aleksey would give this man was a stony face and a cold stare. He was a Gavrilov man — and these monsters didn't know a thing about just how tough he was.

21

SERPIENTE

A couple of hours went by, but when one is hanging from a rafter, every minute is interminable. Sweat poured down Aleksey's face in rivulets, stinging his eyes and blurring his vision. Every muscle in his body screamed from being strung up to the overhead beam, the ropes digging into his flesh. The gag in his mouth made it hard to breathe, and angst gnawed at his mind.

A few thin rays of sunlight filtered through cracks in the walls, casting twisted shadows on the ground. This was Aleksey's only means of gauging the passing of time. Suddenly, he noticed a quivering in the sunlight seeping in below the roof's eaves. Then he saw something move.

At first, he thought it was a bird or a rodent. He strained to see what was happening in the narrow gap at the top of the wall. Whatever it was, it moved slowly, cautiously, as though it were inspecting the environment of the room before proceeding.

What in the world is that? With growing dread, Aleksey watched as the creature's form became visible to him — *a snake!* Its head emerged only a foot or so through an opening at the top of the wall at the end of the rafter to which Aleksey was tied, probing the surroundings with its flicking tongue.

Its head wound and bobbed under the eaves. Once it grew comfortable, it moved more rapidly along the rafter, heading straight toward Aleksey. He kept his eyes glued to its movements, watching with fascinated horror as the snake's body emerged through the hole.

It keeps coming! Will the end of this snake ever appear?

The creature's body was thick and muscular, its scales a deep brown that glistened in the shafts of sunlight. Aleksey grew more uneasy as the snake approached. The serpent inched nearer to Aleksey, its forked tongue tasting the air, and its beady eyes fixed on him with what felt like a glint of malevolent intelligence.

The more motionless Aleksey tried to be, the more conscious he became of the blood rushing through his ears and his own heart, threatening to burst out of his chest.

Growing up in Russia, Aleksey didn't know much about the snake species in this part of the world, but he didn't need to know much. As the snake fully emerged onto the rafter, Aleksey saw something that sent a chill down his spine. Beads adorned the serpent's tail, marking it as a rattlesnake.

Every instinct in Aleksey screamed at him to move, to do something, but he was powerless. Trapped, gagged, and strung up — hanging from a beam with a venomous snake inches from his face — time seemed to slow as the serpent crept closer.

Aleksey kicked his feet down low and made noise through his gag, trying to get the guards' attention. A lot of good that did. They were as cold-blooded as the snake slithering its way toward him. Instead of intervening, the men sat at the rickety wooden table and pointed it out to each other, chuckling at Aleksey's predicament. It was obvious they intended to let nature take its course — even wagering on the outcome.

As the rattlesnake inched nearer to Aleksey, the men jeered at the spectacle, and one raised a bottle in a mock toast to Aleksey's fate. Another one made hissing sounds, imitating a snake. "*Ssss, ssss!*" One crooked the pointer and middle fingers of his hand, mimicking fangs, and shook them toward Aleksey. The men laughed, finding themselves supremely witty.

The snake, for its part, appeared faintly annoyed by the fuss Aleksey kicked up. The snake's unblinking eyes seemed to fixate on Aleksey, determining whether the slight commotion posed a real threat. It was not to be deterred. It stopped only momentarily before proceeding.

Aleksey tried to suppress his natural trepidation. *Do not panic*, he reminded himself. *The snake is probably curious because of the little goat they butchered in the shed.* He reasoned that the viper was hunting for a meal, its keen sense of smell drawing it to the lingering odor of the little goat.

The serpent drew closer, its undulating body gliding along the rafter with a fluid motion that was both mesmerizing and terrifying. Directly overhead, it stopped at the rope that bound Aleksey's hands. Aleksey tilted his head all the way back, eyes looking straight up. *Do not come down here*, he begged silently. *Do not do it. Go away!*

The snake neither read nor cared about his thoughts. With a graceful spiral, the snake began its descent down the rope onto Aleksey's arm. His arm reflexively tensed, and he mentally steeled himself for the ordeal.

Aleksey forced himself to remain immobile, knowing that any sudden movement could provoke the snake. *As long as I do not move, it will not know me from a piece of furniture.* He closed his eyes, summoning memories of past encounters with vipers in the deserts of Afghanistan. But this was different. It was much easier to stay calm when he wasn't hanging helplessly from a rafter.

The snake seemed momentarily intrigued by the hot breath pouring through Aleksey's nostrils. The sweat on his head turned icy as the viper stopped at Aleksey's face for an eye-to-eye inspection — flicking its black tongue at his nose and tasting his eyelashes — each movement sending another jolt of fear through Aleksey's body.

The snake's cold, black eyes studied him. Aleksey held his breath, hoping to mitigate a sneezing disaster and trying to keep himself as still as humanly possible.

The guards, meanwhile, were in hysterics, laughing at Aleksey's predicament. They were enjoying the show, but Aleksey could only focus on the slithering reptile inches from his face.

After a thorough inspection of Aleksey's face, the snake moved on. Aleksey could feel its belly softly brush against his neck, sending a wave of terror through him as the snake continued its descent down his body. He could feel the snake's muscles writhing beneath its skin as it moved over him.

This thing is heavy, Aleksey thought. He couldn't help but marvel at its heft. He slowly and cautiously dropped his eyes and chin, following the course of this unwanted guest. *Its midsection has a greater diameter than my arm!*

The snake paused at Aleksey's waist for a long while. Venomous fangs inches from his exposed abdomen, Aleksey could feel himself starting to shake, his breath coming in ragged gasps. Perhaps it was contemplating whether to proceed down his leg or take a concealed route through his trousers.

Come on! Just take the direct route and get out of here! Aleksey allowed himself a small breath of relief when the snake chose the former option and continued onward down his leg.

And then, with a suddenness that took Aleksey by surprise, the entire five feet of snake dropped to the floor at his bare feet. The rattles on its tail passed his nose on the way, leaving behind a musky odor that Aleksey knew would be forever seared into his memory.

The soft sound of shuffling cards filled the air as the guards returned to being semi-preoccupied with their card game. Several bets were settled discreetly. They weren't too worried about the snake in the room. Living in Mexico, encounters with rattlesnakes were a fact of life. Everyone had a story or two, and it wasn't very remarkable for any of them. They learned about these creatures from childhood and did not fear them any more than an American might dread a squirrel.

Satisfied that the show was over, one of the guards stood up and carefully pinned the rattler with the butt of his rifle. The snake had been docile while everyone had just been minding his own business. But now it was threatened, and the snake's agitation was palpable. Its rattling conveyed an intimidating warning. Despite this, the guard reached over and grabbed it behind the head, lifting the monstrous serpent off the floor.

Realizing he had not extracted the last ounce of entertainment value from the situation, the guard walked over close to Aleksey and held the snake's bared fangs inches from his face. This time Aleksey flinched just a little.

"Ssss, ssss," the guards laughed, repeating their unoriginal taunt. "Maybe it wants another chance to give you a kiss and taste your pretty face, Junior!" Both roared with laughter.

The snake made three firm wraps around the guard's arm as he continued goading Aleksey. The other half of the snake dangled down to the ground. It was then that the guard realized that he had no way to get the snake loose without help. His gleeful expression quickly dropped, turning to panic. This joke was getting out of hand. Literally.

"*Ayúdame!*" he called over to the other. His fellow despot was now watching with a new level of amusement and appeared disinclined to give the requested help.

Aleksey had enough. If they were trying to get a reaction out of him, they had succeeded. He pulled back on the ropes to gain some momentum and swung forward, kicking the snake-handling guard's feet out from under him. The guy collapsed to the floor and in the process, let go of the rattlesnake's head as he instinctively tried to break his fall.

That was all the time the angry rattler needed to strike. Like lightning, it lunged, sinking its fangs like driving hot nails into his flesh. The big rattler got two good punctures before the guard could react. He cried out in pain. The first one might have been a warning, but the second bite was for keeps. The snake had latched onto him and wasn't letting go.

"*Víbora! Víbora!*" The guard screamed as the venom coursed through his body. With the rattlesnake still latched on, he scrambled to his feet and exited the shed in a panic, dancing in a kind of looping trot that had the other guards caught between laughter and wide-eyed alarm.

Moments later, Aleksey heard a commotion outside. Naturally, he assumed it was about the rattlesnake incident. He instantly regretted that brash move.

Ugh, I only brought more trouble down on myself. This guy is definitely coming back for revenge. They will torture me for sure after this.

At this point, Aleksey wondered if all his resistance was only delaying the inevitable.

22

GLADIATORS

The sudden commotion followed an unexpected turn of events. As it turned out, the Gulf Cartel soldiers had captured several members of the rival Sinaloa Cartel who had ventured onto their turf. Bringing them into the village created more of a stir than when Aleksey had been escorted in more than a week earlier.

The low-level Sinaloa captives were of no value as hostages for ransom. Their own group already considered them dead and gone. Instead, the cruel hand of the Gulf Cartel had other plans for these men. They were prisoners of war, and their fate would be decided in the most barbaric of ways. First, the captives were dragged through the streets with their hands bound behind their backs and their heads hung low, eliciting jeers from the gathering crowd of villagers, who spat at them as they paraded by.

A guard entered the shed and spoke with the one who watched over Aleksey. Aleksey's heart raced as he listened closely, trying to make out any clues as to what they planned to do with him. But the only word he could make out this time was "*gladiadores.*"

So strange. Are they really saying what I think they are saying?

The guards walked over to Aleksey, and adrenaline caused instant tension throughout his body as he waited to see what they were going to do with him. To Aleksey's surprise, they ungagged him and untied him from the beam, then bound his hands behind him. They forced him out of the shed at gunpoint and into the bright sunlight.

I am not sure that I am going to like this. In fact, I am sure I am not going to like it! Aleksey prepared for the worst. He knew the dark depravity of men often emerged when they had absolute power over other humans. He was completely at their mercy.

Aleksey's bare feet were ill-suited for the rough terrain and unpaved ground. Small, pointed rocks pressed into his bare soles, issuing darts of pain, constant reminders of his vulnerability. There were also mud patches that he couldn't avoid, the squishy coolness of which brought relief, although Aleksey was concerned that his feet might get infected from animal dung mixed into the mud. His guards didn't care what he had to walk across or through as long as he kept moving.

Aleksey scanned the surroundings for any opportunity to escape, but the guards watched him closely and started to walk faster, prodding him with their rifles. He picked up chatter about something going on in the village, and he'd definitely heard the word "Sinaloa" being repeated, but he was unable to piece it all together. Aleksey looked around for any indication as to what might be happening.

As he walked, he could feel electric excitement in the air. The wind carried whispers among the villagers about the fate of the captured men — it was evident from the looks on their faces that they were relishing those thoughts. The anticipation of what was to come was palpable.

In the distance, Aleksey could see a makeshift arena, crude but adequate. He could tell from the trampled area that it had been used many times before.

He was led to the center of the village, where all the locals were assembled, forming a perimeter around a ring of sand. The sky was darkening with an afternoon storm, mirroring the darkness in the hearts of the villagers. The wind picked up, whipping the sand.

"The big man said to bring you," one guard crowed to Aleksey. "He doesn't want you to miss this." Aleksey gave him a sidelong glance before returning his attention to the crowds. *What now?*

Aleksey couldn't help but feel a sense of dread creeping up on him as he remembered the word he overheard earlier — "*gladiadores.*" He had heard rumors of the Gulf Cartel's tradition of forcing captured cartel members to fight to the death. Was this real?

Aleksey realized the captives were from the rival Sinaloa cartel and were heading for a brutal public execution known as *El Juego de Muerte* — The Game of Death. He had a sinking feeling that he was also about to be thrown into the arena to fight for his life.

Aleksey slowly walked over to the circle and nudged through the gathered crowd. He could hardly believe what he was seeing. Each of the three Sinaloa captives stood in the sand, armed with a blade, like a butcher knife, taped to his hand and wrist. The blades glinted in the light, reflecting fear in the eyes of the contenders.

Aleksey couldn't help but think of the dark irony of being in a remote Mexican village, yet seeing duct tape. It truly was universal.

What are the chances one of these Neanderthals has a can of WD-40 around too? He shook his head, trying to stifle a chuckle.

Aleksey's solitary levity was short-lived as he took in the various implements in the center of the ring that could be used as weapons — a hammer, a four-foot piece of steel rebar, and a three-foot length of heavy chain. The sight of these bludgeoning instruments sent a chill down Aleksey's spine as he contemplated the brutal nature of this tournament. He just hoped the guards weren't going to compel him to participate.

A couple of cartel henchmen stood at opposing points in the inner circle, stone sentinels with sneers carved in their faces as they watched the Sinaloa captives. The guards ensured their three prisoners stayed where they should and did what they were told. The henchmen had no mercy in their eyes, which gleamed with sadistic pleasure. They held guns at the ready, fingers hovering over the triggers, ready to kill anyone who dared try an escape.

The Sinaloa captives were pitted against one another in combat, like gladiators of old. Stripped to the waist, beads of sweat glistened like diamonds on their foreheads. They stood juddering in the inner ring, each man's eyes darting between his opponents, knowing that only one would come out of this alive. The one who prevailed would be spared but compelled to swear allegiance to the Gulf Cartel. It was a brutal ultimatum — fight or die.

The entire village had shown up to witness the gruesome spectacle. Even the young men who usually guarded the mountain path left their posts to watch the macabre event.

Aleksey's heart thumped hard in his chest as he tried to make sense of what was happening around him. He knew that the Gulf Cartel had a reputation for barbarism, but he never thought he would be a witness to this spectacle of savagery firsthand.

The sickly-sweet smell of sweat mixed with the acrid scent of tobacco smoke was in the air. That thick haze hung about the ring as men held out money to one of the henchmen and placed bets on who would be the last one standing. Aleksey found the attitudes of the spectators disturbing — they were wagering on the death game as though it were a cockfighting tournament.

The crowd parted as Cucuy strolled to the ring, where he then stood with his feet apart, his face almost aglow with deranged pleasure. His voice boomed like thunder as he laid out the rules. Punching the air to accentuate his points, Cucuy's maniacal drill-sergeant persona caused Aleksey to narrow his eyes in ever-increasing revulsion.

"Today, we will show the Sinaloa Cartel what happens to those who dare to cross our borders. Only one of you makes it out of this ring alive. As for the other two ... we will dispose of your corpses. Who that will be is entirely up to you."

A raucous cheer arose from the crowd, a susurrus of bloodlust. The Gulf Cartel was determined to make an example of the Sinaloa captives.

Cucuy continued, "These men will fight for their lives, but there will be mercy for the victor. The winner lives on one condition. Your life belongs to the *Cartel del Golfo*, and you will now work for me. If you refuse ... you will have been better off dead in the ring."

"Vamos! Vamos!" The crowd pulsed with a frenetic energy — the call for blood was growing louder as the guards pushed the Sinaloa captives into the center and stepped back, leaving the three men to their fate.

The involuntary gladiators faced off in front of each other, taking their fighting stances, weapons waving in their half-outstretched hands. Their bodies were slick with sweat and their muscles were taut with surging adrenaline. Labored breaths now came in short gasps.

Aleksey wondered how this would end. Would one take on the two others simultaneously? Would two team up together to take down the one that would otherwise dominate? Aleksey's stomach turned even to think about the horrific spectacle unfolding before him.

"Comienzan!" The signal was given by Cucuy — The Game of Death had begun. Shouts filled Aleksey's ears as the crowd erupted in wild cheering. The scene was a blur of blades, fists, blood, and screams as the three fought for survival. The fighting was brutal and intense, each fighter going all-out to emerge victorious. The sound of flesh hitting flesh, the grunts of exertion, and the cries of pain were a symphony of violence.

One of the gladiators was a relatively tall, muscular man. He was most fierce and quickly gained the upper hand. His opponents, younger men with less experience, were no match for the older man's skill and strength, but the younger fighters had the advantage of lightning-fast reflexes. The larger warrior landed a series of powerful blows, driving his smaller opponents back and leaving them vulnerable.

By all appearances, the largest of the gladiatorial contenders would prevail over the other two. The tension was electric. The villagers watched with rapt attention as the fighters exchanged blows, not one able to gain the upper hand. It seemed as though the battle would never end.

As the spectators' excitement reached a fever pitch, Aleksey knew he had to act fast. While they saw entertainment, he saw an opportunity — one he had patiently waited for.

I did not think it would be this, but there is no complaint.

While everyone was enthralled with the bloody event playing out before them, Aleksey quietly backed away from the crowd. Looking about quickly, he found just what he needed.

In their haste, the guards had not checked Aleksey's bindings again before leaving the shed. His hands were already more loosely tied than usual after being stretched overhead for so long. With all the stealth and innocence he could muster, Aleksey squatted near the ground beside a large rock with a squared-off corner. While the audience yelled and twisted their faces with bloodlust, he quietly rubbed his bindings on the square edge. Nobody among the villagers or his cartel captors was paying him the slightest bit of attention. They wanted blood — and, fortunately, he wasn't the subject of that right now.

Aleksey's wrist restraints snapped loose without a sound. He kept his hands in position behind him, giving no indication that he was now free. He kept his eyes on the crowds, the cartel henchmen in particular, looking to make sure they were fully engrossed in their violent amusement.

Aleksey watched as the largest gladiator, who had been dominating, suddenly and unexpectedly turned on the rowdy crowd and started attacking anyone within reach. As if by a secret signal, his opponents spontaneously joined the melee. The move was suicidal, but the short-lived attempted massacre created complete chaos. Aleksey's guards jumped into the fray.

From the ground, Aleksey couldn't see exactly what had happened next, but the ensuing chaos was all he cared about. As people ran, Aleksey saw his guards were distracted by the commotion. *This is it. I may never get another chance like this.*

A bold decision was made — *escape. Now.* It was a risky choice — getting caught would, without a doubt, be regrettable. But even that sure knowledge gave Aleksey only a moment's pause.

If I stay, I will likely die here. And I will not leave this world at the hands of these fools if I can help it. I would rather die trying to escape. It is not the end for me yet!

Even though his body was on the verge of breaking, the survivor within him was reinvigorated at the prospect of freedom. Aleksey believed he had been wise to patiently bide his time, waiting for the perfect opportunity to flee. This was it. He had one chance, and he was going to take it.

Vamos! he whispered to himself, as he made a break for freedom.

23

ESCAPE INTO THE JUNGLE

His heart pounding in his chest, Aleksey pushed himself to his feet and darted into the dense foliage behind the makeshift dwellings. He could hear the shrieking and shouting of the crowd receding as he bolted into the undergrowth, ducking under branches. He didn't care that vines and twigs whipped into his face as he fled. The undergrowth of the forest and the dead, fallen log debris that littered the ground beneath the canopy of trees snagged at his clothes, scratched his skin, and dug into his pounding feet.

But Aleksey barely noticed — the burning pain in his feet, the fatigue in his legs, the ache in his chest — because all of it was nothing compared to his dread of being caught. It was a small price to pay for freedom.

Just keep going — cut-up feet are the least of your problems! Aleksey pushed on, driven by the adrenaline that coursed through his veins. He knew that his captors would be hot on his heels. Ragged breaths huffed from his mouth as he strained to put as much distance between himself and them as possible.

The jungle, however, was not on his side. Thick foliage hindered his progress. The humid air, heavy with the scent of vegetation and decay, made it hard to breathe. Sweat from his forehead slid down in streaks, stinging his eyes. One hand tried to wipe the sweat as the other batted obstacles away from his face, yet his feet never stopped moving. Aleksey knew his life hung in the balance — every second counted.

Above the sound of his labored breathing, Aleksey heard rustling leaves and snapping twigs as his pursuers crashed through the trees like oxen. The sound of their voices calling out to each other grew louder, a war-like drumbeat in his ears, driving him to run faster. The thought of being caught, of being dragged back to his makeshift prison, propelled him forward, pushing himself to the brink of exhaustion.

How in the world are they catching up to me so fast? Aleksey couldn't fathom how the lazy oafs could be gaining on him. *Someone must have seen me run and told the guards right away. I was hoping for a little more lead time. Ratting weasels!*

His thoughts stopped short at the same time his feet did. Skidding to a halt, Aleksey found himself at the edge of a ravine. It was narrow but deep, with steep walls on either side. The ground was rocky and uneven, jagged boulders and twisted roots jutting from the earth. He hesitated for a moment, looking down at the daunting terrain below.

What other choice is there? Ugh, here goes. Aleksey took a deep breath and started to climb down, using roots and vines to steady himself as he descended. Muscles burning with strain and fatigue, he struggled to keep his grip on the steep incline.

One hand and one foot slipped away from the slick, muddy rocks as the other hand clung on, momentarily supporting his weight. He could feel the jagged edge of rock cutting into his palm as he heaved his free arm back up in search of a secure hold. A split second after he regained his footing, Aleksey returned to his treacherous descent.

He gashed his arms and hit his face on exposed shale as his descent bordered on recklessness. The rough bark of the trees and the jagged, rocky terrain scraped his skin raw, leaving him covered with cuts and bruises. A copper-tasting trickle of blood mingled with dirt and perspiration made its way to his mouth.

Finally, Aleksey reached the bottom of the ravine. His exhausted body — sweat, dirt, and blood-caked — collapsed onto the ground and rolled under some fronds, his breaths coming in ragged gasps. He lay there for a moment, listening to the sound of his own breathing and the faint rustle of leaves above him. The smell of moss and decaying leaves filled his nostrils.

Turning onto his back, he peered up through the foliage, trying to see if anyone was looking down from the top or was attempting to climb down after him.

No one ... not yet. They are coming, though.

For the first time in days, Aleksey felt a glimmer of hope. He had escaped the grasp of his ruthless pursuers, at least for the moment. But he knew that the respite was fleeting. That could all change in a heartbeat. Cucuy didn't seem like a man who let his meal ticket just run into the forest and disappear.

His goons will be just as afraid to go back without me as I am to go back with them.

The jungle itself was a treacherous place, and death could be lurking in many forms. He also knew that he couldn't lay hidden among the fronds forever. Furthermore, he was concerned that he might be near a trail. He imagined the spectacle of automatic rifle barrels snaking out of the underbrush toward him. The worst thing that could happen would be running right into their path.

Aleksey pushed himself to his feet and scanned the ravine, searching for a way out. His eyes fell on a narrow path winding through the rocky terrain. With renewed determination, he followed it deeper into the jungle.

The rocks were slippery, covered with moss, and the damp earth squished beneath his stinging, lacerated feet as he stumbled through dense undergrowth. He had to be careful not to lose his footing. The rocky path eventually became more dirt, but the adrenaline high was wearing off, and he felt the pain begin to set in. He had run until his legs gave out and his lungs felt like they were on fire.

Aleksey was lost in the jungle with nothing but the clothes on his back and his own wits to guide him. But he was determined to survive, even in an unfamiliar environment. Was it possible? He would be the one to find out. He had heard accounts of people surviving for weeks in the forest, but he knew it was a different story when it came to being hunted.

Psshh, I can do this. Even if it takes three weeks or more ... Aleksey cut off his thoughts there. He had no idea where he was or how he would get back to civilization, but for now, he was free.

As the sun began to set, he knew he had to find a place to hide for the night. *Shelter is a priority for now*, he remembered, thinking back to his military survival training. He pushed himself harder as he scanned the jungle for any sign of shelter.

I do not have the strength or tools to build anything, but if I can just find a secure little nook somewhere ...

Aleksey spent some time searching in vain for shelter. Eventually, he collapsed to the ground again from utter exhaustion, his body completely spent. He groaned and rolled onto his side. That was when he spotted a small hollow behind a thicket of vines. He crawled into the little space and collapsed again. He had no food or water, and he knew he wouldn't be able to go on much longer. Before he could even give it much thought, he was fast asleep, curled up in the fetal position.

Aleksey dreamed of a delicious *medovik*, a Russian honey cake that his mother used to bake when he was a child. The sweet smell of honey and the warm aroma of baked dough filled his senses as he dreamed of it dissolving in his mouth. But when he was snapped awake by the whistling, firecracker-like sound of curassows doing their morning rounds, there was no food to be found.

"Have you eaten my cake?" Aleksey joked to the frenzied birds, a moment of levity amid his dire situation. As he laughed, he realized that despite the perils and uncertainty, he was alive, which was something to be grateful for.

One must focus on the blessings — that is what Tetya would tell me at a time like this.

He could see hints of the morning above the canopy, but it was still mostly dark. A light mist hung in the air, filling the forest with a ghostly aura. He felt like going back to sleep but knew that wasn't a good idea.

A low-pitched guttural growl silenced the birds. It was soon joined by several other animal noises. Aleksey instinctively stiffened. There were large cats in the Mexican jungle — solitary hunters. Had they picked up his scent?

I will never outrun a jaguar or puma. My best option is to stay here and remain still, he concluded.

Heavy rustling in the canopy told him that the creatures were just above. Aleksey lay on his side holding his breath, hoping to remain as still as possible. The chorus of growls grew louder, but Aleksey's view from his alcove was limited, and he couldn't detect the source.

This sound is all around me, but I can see nothing.

He was quietly repositioning himself to get a better view of his surroundings when there was a splat from above followed by another. Warm, smelly, dark brown mounds landed next to his head and shoulder. Looking above, he saw four howler monkeys scowling down at him, the intruder. Aleksey breathed a little laugh and crawled out of his spot. He stood hands on hips and looked back up at the angry primates.

"You could have at least thrown me something I can eat!" he hollered to them.

As speckled sunlight filtered through some of the sparser growth, Aleksey felt a sense of hope and began to explore his surroundings, foraging for something edible. His stomach rumbled with hunger, and the parched dryness in his throat made it hard to swallow.

Foraging proved to be a difficult task. Aleksey searched for sustenance, but unfamiliar plants and insects were risky fare. He had no idea what was edible or poisonous around him, and the thought of eating something that could make him sick was a real concern. He plucked a berry from a bush and examined it closely.

How ironic it would be to escape my captors only to perish in the forest from eating berries. Maybe I am not at the point where I need to take that risk yet, he concluded. For now, his thirst was more pressing — water was essential, or he wouldn't make it out alive.

Within a half-hour of wandering about, he detected the sweet sound of trickling water nearby. Aleksey felt a surge of relief and excitement. He plodded through the foliage and came out of the dense underbrush to a stream, its cool waters moving swiftly over the rocks. He had a passing thought that amoebas or a stomach bug could render him helpless on the forest floor, but that was a chance he would have to take.

I doubt the water in the village was filtered. Well, by the brownish color I know it was not. If that has not made me sick yet, there is a fair chance I will get by fine with the running water in this stream. He also remembered military training about whether water was potable or not, and he vaguely recalled the maxim — *if it runs, it will not run you down.*

Aleksey approached the edge of the stream. He was stepping down into the inviting water when he felt something slimy and cool brush against his foot. He instinctively recoiled, and his heart felt a surge of panic. Perhaps just as afraid of Aleksey, a beleaguered snake speedily slithered away from him. Aleksey shook off the moment of surprise and cautiously stepped into the stream.

Finally, a bath! ... sort of. Aleksey splashed into the water and washed his bare feet, now bloody from the rough terrain. The water quickly soaked through his clothes, but he didn't let it slow him down. He was so thirsty that he drank greedily, barely pausing to take a breath. He felt invigorated by its coolness. It was also a welcome relief to his aching feet and sore muscles.

Aleksey waded on through the stream, using it as cover, his eyes scanning the banks for any sign of his pursuers. Finally, he emerged from the stream and took one final look behind him, but there was no sign of his captors.

Aleksey resumed trudging through the jungle. He followed the path of the stream, trying to find his way back to civilization. For a while, he took solace in the beauty around him — the sounds that enveloped him were vibrant. Small mammals chattered in the trees above, and exotic birds called out from the branches, a reminder of the freedom he was striving for.

Soon the comfortable morning gave way to extreme heat and humidity, the kind of weather that made it difficult to breathe and once again caused sweat to pour down Aleksey's face. He felt as though he were being pursued again, but this time by the heat — and there was no escaping it.

Without nourishment, he was also running out of energy. Oppressive fatigue sat heavy on him, and his feet began to feel more leaden with every step. Even so, Aleksey was determined to make it out alive. His will to survive burned bright within him.

I am not going to die here — not today.

Meanwhile, Aleksey's captors had not given up either. The manhunt continued, led by the determined and furious Cucuy, and fueled by a dangerous mix of anger and pride. He was bent on tracking down his valuable hostage at any cost.

Constantly cursing under his breath, Cucuy's rage seethed as they pushed through the thick underbrush of the steamy jungle, the heat and humidity feeding his furor. He had a reputation to uphold, and letting a hostage escape was a grave embarrassment and a personal affront.

A ragtag contingent of heavily armed cartel operatives trudged alongside Cucuy. The scowling wretches weren't happy about this little escapade either. They carried a panoply of weapons that might as well be out of a scattered collection of arms catalogs from the past four decades, including some top-tier weapons like the Israeli Galil ACE and M16s. Their rifles were at the ready, and their irritation made them all the more apt to use them.

One grizzled scout wearing a sweat-soaked bandana sneaked a drink of tequila from his small hip flask and suppressed a yawn, only to be thwacked in the back of the head by his *compadre*.

Cucuy's band of men stomped over to the nearest neighboring village, deep in the jungle. Approaching the outskirts of the settlement, the cartel operatives expected that their escaped hostage was close. They spread out, surrounding the area and preparing a pincer trap.

He could hear faint sounds in the distance, voices barking out commands. *They are close. They are about as subtle as a wild Russian boar in the forest.* The voices grew nearer. Aleksey scrambled for somewhere to hide.

He huddled behind a banyan tree, pressing himself against the coolness of its massive damp trunk. He held his breath as a group of four or five passed only a short distance from him. Rivulets of salty sweat dripped down his face, but he didn't dare make a move, not even turning his head to get a better look at his pursuers.

Aleksey felt sure the whole jungle could hear the uncontrollable pounding of his heart. He squeezed his eyes shut, desperately wishing he were invisible. He heard the loud snap of a branch, and his eyes flew open. The footsteps stopped. The cartel soldiers were close — so close he could hear the heavy breathing of his hunters.

Aleksey waited for several tense seconds that felt like an eternity. *I need to have an escape route.* His eyes darted around, searching for a way out, but all he saw were towering trees and dense underbrush. *I am trapped*, he realized. There was almost resignation in the thought. There was nowhere to run and no one to help him.

Finally, he heard their footsteps fading away into the distance. They hadn't seen him for the simplest reason of all — not a one, including Cucuy, could imagine a man brave and brazen enough to hide right in their path with only a tree concealing him.

The cadre of cartel operatives tracked beside the stream, which ran all the way to the village. Several men stopped to drink, their water flasks already mostly empty. The hours of tracking the escapee had taken a toll on Cucuy's men, and their frustration was starting to show. One murmured profanities under his breath, but the others hushed him. Their fear of Cucuy's growing wrath was also growing, and nerves were on edge.

It was slow going, and Cucuy was determined to be thorough. He refused to give up the search after they lost Aleksey's trail. He occasionally held up a hand to signal quiet as he listened for any sounds in the distance and examined potential tracks. The men then doubled back without complaint, covering again the path back to the village from which they came. They knew well that if they didn't locate the escapee fast, he'd be lost to them forever.

Once again, Cucuy held up his hand, signaling for his men to stop. He had heard something up ahead. Cautiously, they moved forward, rifles at the ready. Cucuy smirked triumphantly and motioned for his men to approach, a sadistic grin on his face as he savored the moment of capture.

"Going somewhere?" Cucuy sneered. "We've been looking for you."

24

THE BETTER MONSTER

Cucuy stepped into the shack, his presence commanding attention. Aleksey felt the hairs on the back of his neck stand up, as the man's aura radiated evil. Clapping his hands together, Cucuy called out, "*Buenos días*, Junior. I see you're hanging in there," he said, a smirk playing on his lips.

A single flick of his wrist ordered the guards to untie Aleksey. They loosened the ropes and scurried out of the way of their boss. Cucuy dismissed the guards with a sharp nod, his eyes never leaving Aleksey's.

As the guards shuffled out of the shack, Aleksey noticed an odd shift in Cucuy's demeanor from previous encounters— he detected the change right away. Aleksey's eyes darted around the room — intuitively, he sensed something was up. Cucuy no longer appeared to behave as a ruthless tyrant but instead as a relaxed and almost casual host. Aleksey rubbed his sore wrists, giving Cucuy a wary look. He'd anticipated suffering unthinkable torture after being caught, but Cucuy had something else in mind.

What is going on?

Moments later, a woman entered the shed carrying a platter of sizzling rattlesnake meat. Cucuy gestured for Aleksey to take a seat at the wooden table.

"Go ahead. Enjoy." He encouraged Aleksey to have a bite. "It's yours ... your snake friend, to be specific," Cucuy purred. "A little something for our guest of honor."

Cautious, Aleksey slowly moved toward the table. The gnawing pain in his empty stomach overruled his wariness. He sat down and reached for the meat, pensively at first. He took a bite and was pleasantly surprised. The rich and spicy flavor exploded on his tongue. He couldn't remember the last time he'd tasted anything so delicious. Greedily shoving it into his mouth, he let out a sigh of appreciation.

"You like it?" Cucuy asked, a look of amusement on his face. "I hear you Russians have a taste for exotic cuisine."

A delicacy, fit for a king ... or a pawn, depending on your viewpoint, Aleksey mused.

"I am impressed." Cucuy leaned forward, his eyes gleaming like the flickering of candles. "You Russians are a remarkable people," he remarked, pouring himself a shot of mezcal. "Always so courageous. Always so intelligent. Tough as nails. This is my first time doing business with your people. So far, you live up to all I've heard."

He offered Aleksey mezcal. Aleksey put up a hand to decline.

"No? What about a little *cheeba* ... weed? It'll loosen you up."

Aleksey shook his head, again declining the offer.

"Ah, come on, man! Live a little!" Cucuy watched Aleksey's face carefully to read a reaction, then shrugged. "Suit yourself." Cucuy then paused as though considering how he wanted to continue the conversation.

"I wondered, how far will you go to protect secrets?" Cucuy continued. "It's now clear to me — as far as necessary. This makes you trustworthy, *comrade*."

Cucuy only got an emotionless stare from his hostage. Aleksey perceived this to be a novel psychological ploy to make him feel good before breaking him down.

"You sniff coke?" Cucuy asked with a mischievous grin, producing a small bag of cocaine.

Aleksey didn't break eye contact, his voice firm, "Never. I prefer to keep a clear head and my wits about me."

Oh yeah, go on, Aleksey thought sarcastically. *That is what Cucuy would like — to give you a taste of the dark side. Once you experience it, you will never be able to turn back.* Aleksey intuitively recognized he was being lured into a trap.

"Oh, that'll clear you right up — keep your wits up also," Cucuy continued to press, his laughter ringing hollow in the small shed. "Wise choice. You understand the value of keeping control. It can get you into a bit of a habit. Always better to be a supplier than a customer."

Aleksey remembered his comrades in the Soviet Army in Afghanistan who suffered from heroin addiction long after they had returned. He knew of others who got into the habit of using hashish while away from home. Momentary lapses in judgment had resulted in a few losing their lives.

"It seems your 'Papa,' as you call him, doesn't think your life is worth much," Cucuy asserted. "Perhaps you have been too much trouble for him?"

These are mind games, Aleksey knew. *Come now, does this Mexican "paleto" not comprehend who he is trying to manipulate? I am Russian — not one of his impressionable lackeys. He is no match in this game.*

"He does not truly love you. You know that, *sí*? Why does he not want to buy your freedom?" Cucuy probed, taking an almost sympathetic tone.

"Maybe he does not have the money," Aleksey replied coolly.

"You *rusos* — always so poor," Cucuy sighed sarcastically. "You're a terrible liar."

Is that a compliment or a criticism? Aleksey wondered.

"You and your Vladimir Lenin, *sí*?" Cucuy continued mocking.

"Actually, when it comes to communism, we came to America because we ..."

"Hey, I don't care!" Cucuy barked. "Listen — pay attention! I'm trying to talk about something important."

Aleksey felt his blood boiling but kept his expression neutral — Cucuy had a devilish way of getting under his skin. "What do you want?"

"*Dinero*, of course," Cucuy replied, as if it were obvious. "Let's not pretend. We both know your father is a wealthy man. One would think that a man with the means to have such a nice boat would value his son even more."

"How do you know that is even his boat?" Aleksey challenged.

Cucuy paused and pursed his lips. He continued without arguing the point. Aleksey sensed he was going somewhere with this conversation.

"For the sake of this discussion, let's assume your poor Papa doesn't have the ability to pay. Maybe we can work out something ... agreeable."

"Like what?" Aleksey asked with an almost amused curiosity. *What could this Neanderthal possibly have in mind?*

"You're not like the others — more intelligent than many *Americanos* — the *turistas*. That's why I've taken a special interest in you," Cucuy said, his voice smooth as oil. "A business associate in Florida could do very well. We have the goods — you have the customers. Someone like you can become wealthier than you ever dreamed in no time."

Aleksey raised an eyebrow and pondered, *Really? How long is "no time" in Mexican-mobster time?* He couldn't help but think, *I am already wealthier than I ever dreamed of being when I was back in Russia, but that is no help in my present circumstances.*

Still, he wondered, *will they release me if they believe I will be a player in their game?* Either way, he wasn't too quick to take the bait. If he showed interest too soon, it would be obvious. He tried turning the table on Cucuy's proposition. *How badly does this criminal want to recruit me?*

"What makes you think I'm interested in that kind of arrangement?" Aleksey replied, keeping his poker face intact.

"You're a smart man. I know you recognize the opportunity in front of you. And let's be honest, we both know your options are limited at the moment," Cucuy said with a smirk.

"They are limited," Aleksey conceded.

"Listen. Your father may not value your life, but I do. I see potential in you. With the right push, you could go far in this business," Cucuy hinted.

Aleksey was appalled. "Why would I ever want to work with people killing each other? Who would voluntarily want to be a part of this madness?" Aleksey muttered, his voice tinged with disgust. "I end up dead either way."

"No, no," Cucuy contended. "Look at me. I'm practically an old man over here."

"Everyone is fighting everyone — like the entire country is in a gang war, no one caring who they hurt as long as they come out on top," Aleksey countered skeptically.

"I like to think of it more as a family feud — like a *telenovela*, a Mexican soap opera, but ... with more guns," Cucuy grinned wryly. "It amounts to a *revolución* of sorts, where we fight for what's rightfully ours."

"Really?" Aleksey rolled his eyes. "Do you really want a country run by drug lords? That is your idea of progress?"

Cucuy didn't look offended by Aleksey's accusation.

"You seem to forget that great nations are born from the ashes of rebellion — built on the backs of so-called rebels and outlaws. We've been called guerillas. Who is to say if that description applies? I'm not a moral philosopher."

A gorilla, alright, Aleksey mused to himself, but he said nothing, and Cucuy went on pontificating.

"You live in America. A bunch of rich men refused to pay their taxes and took up arms. They started your adopted country with their guns. So, I guess that makes them criminals too. But hey, what do I know?" Cucuy shrugged casually, though his eyes carried a hint of madness. "History repeats itself, doesn't it? Or don't you know history?"

Aleksey wasn't convinced. "I doubt your followers are taking a history lesson. None of your men are thinking like that," he fired back. "They don't care about history — they just use it as an excuse for their criminal activities."

"They don't need to, *amigo*. They follow me because I'm the one with the plan, the strategy. You don't understand. It's about reclaiming what's rightfully ours. We've lived for countless generations under a corrupt regime — far too long. We're simply fighting for our families and for the next generation."

Aleksey rolled his eyes. "So running a criminal empire is okay as long as you believe in the cause?"

Cucuy's expression darkened. "They don't need to believe. All they need to know is that the end justifies the means. And if we need to sell a little bit of white powder to gringos to finance that, so be it. Perhaps not ideal, but it's what's necessary. Besides, the gringos crave to buy it. We offer, they choose to partake," he countered with a smirk. "We're not holding a gun to their heads, forcing them to buy it and use it. It's economics — we merely supply what they demand."

He leaned back. "It's not just about the cause. It's about survival. You do what you have to do to survive in this world."

"And what about the innocent people caught in the crossfire?" Aleksey asked, clearly frustrated by Cucuy's warped logic.

Cucuy shrugged, "Sometimes sacrifices must be made — the cost of doing business. We can't control who gets hurt, but we're fighting for a better future."

"So that makes it okay for your death squads to behead people and leave the corpses swinging from overpasses or chopped up for dog food? You call that a revolution?" Aleksey retorted. "It is nothing but a cruel game of power, where innocent lives are mere pawns."

"Innocent lives? Pshh," Cucuy waved his hand dismissively. "In this world, there is no such thing. Everyone has a price, and I have the means to pay it. Fear is my currency, and violence is my tool."

Cucuy leaned forward, his eyes narrowed. "You either play the game, or you get played. Remember, only the strongest survive, and you're a fool for thinking otherwise."

"I think I understand your perspective," Aleksey said, feigning respect.

"It is a sad fact that in this business, the only way to build respect is through fear." Cucuy's expression turned steely. "You have to make your presence felt, and sometimes violence is the only language that's understood. If we must spill blood to assert our dominance, so be it. Sometimes you must order an execution or a beating to ensure cooperation. You must show that you won't hesitate to order a hit. It's all in the mind, *amigo*."

Cucuy bent forward, tapping his temple with a cold, calculating finger, and winked. "Control the mind, and you control everything."

Aleksey tilted his head as though he were taking it all in. This gave Cucuy all the encouragement he needed to keep talking.

"You see it as murder — to the cartel, it's righteousness. Execution — it's justice. Extreme perhaps, but effective."

Aleksey shook his head in disbelief. "You truly believe this is what it takes to succeed in this world?"

Cucuy's eyes glinted with a dangerous light. "I don't just believe it, I know it. And I will do whatever it takes to come out on top."

"How about an abuse of power that you have no right to use?" Aleksey dared to challenge.

Cucuy shot him a disdainful look. "Who is to say whose 'right' it is? Rights are a matter of perspective, *amigo*. Those in power often think they have the right to do whatever they please. Give me a break. Who's keeping track of who has the right to do what? Yankees attack countries and overthrow governments while claiming to be the 'good guys.' Please, who are you kidding?" Cucuy casually waved off the statement. "As for those so-called 'good guys' ... well, let's just say their hands are often far from clean."

Cucuy continued, "The powerful make their own rules, and the weak obey. Why bother with right or wrong? ... false premises for weak men who need some clever means to manipulate others. The strong will always prevail."

"Who are 'the strong?'" Aleksey enquired.

"Easy — whoever can stay on top. This is the problem," Cucuy replied. "Wealth and power breed a thirst for more, a desire to control and dominate all that lies within reach. The world is full of those who believe they have the right to rule, to control, and to abuse their power." With a smirk on his lips, Cucuy added knowingly, "But, in the end, it's a mirage that inevitably crumbles."

Aleksey leaned forward in fascinated horror. "Is that how you see yourself? What makes you different from those in power?"

"I understand the game," Cucuy said with a nonchalant shrug. "Money and power, they intoxicate you. And when the high wears off, you're left with the consequences of your actions."

"You've tasted the poison, then?" Aleksey probed, intrigued by the man's confession.

"I have, and I've looked over into the abyss," Cucuy replied, his voice growing colder. "You have no idea what real power is. You don't know what it's like to have the power the bosses have."

"Is that so?" Aleksey feigned casual interest.

"All of my life, I have known these guys — and I know them well. At the top, the drug world is like a fever dream. But it all comes at a cost."

"And what cost is that?" Aleksey asked.

"Insanity," Cucuy stated matter-of-factly. "The rich and powerful become delusional, thinking they can do anything they want. This drug business is a strange beast — its money gives it the power of a god. This god, it makes millionaires and billionaires stupid fast — a quick ticket to wealth. Wealth turns to power. It allows them to buy political favors and live a life of luxury — cars, boats, airplanes, bodyguards, mansions, exotic animals, and racehorses. The world becomes your playground, where you can indulge in any vice without apparent consequence ... at least for a while."

"Sounds like a dream," Aleksey remarked.

"Dream? A mirage maybe," Cucuy opined. "They believe they can do whatever they want — whatever they ever wanted — and get away with it. Because, why not? They lose touch with reality. That kind of power corrupts even the strongest of men. They become megalomaniacs — I think that is the word — drunk with power, consumed by their own delusion."

"Ah, yes. We have those kinds of people in Russia, too," Aleksey nodded. "And what happens to those who become corrupted by power?" he asked, delving further.

"Some of them, they go crazy for sex. They find it's limited, and their insatiable appetites always end up frustrated — they never find what they're after," Cucuy recognized. "Whatever they're chasing just gets farther away, no matter how hard they try. Drives them mad — or rather, deeper into their madness.

"Many turn to violence — some start there. They get a rush from killing. But unless you are a particular type of psychopath, the act of killing becomes boring. It is so — how do I say this? — anticlimactic. You get used to it."

"Boring? ... an interesting choice of words," Aleksey remarked.

"Sí," Cucuy whispered, as though he were digging deeper into his own thoughts. "Because they don't understand all this, many turn to their own drugs. That's where the real destruction begins ... and ends ... and that never ends well. It's like they want to kill themselves. But hey, more money for us, right?"

Cucuy perceived that Aleksey was genuinely intrigued, so he continued discoursing.

"We're talking about the kind of power that can bend the law to your will and make entire countries bow to your command. These men, they are no better than the liars and thieves who govern us. They're all puppets, dancing to their own destruction. When you have everything, there's nothing left to chase. That's when the game becomes most dangerous. You start to see enemies everywhere, and soon you're trapped in a cycle of violence and fear. You lose sight of what's real and what's not, and before you know it, you're the one being hunted."

"And you think you're different?" Aleksey mocked. *My move. Check*, he thought.

"Oh, I know I am," Cucuy purred with confidence. "I've seen the other side — I've already been there. I've tasted the forbidden fruit, and I want more. I want it all. I'll stop at nothing to get it. You see, I know that about myself," Cucuy readily admitted, his eyes taking on a far-off look.

"What happened?" Aleksey asked, surprised by how much Cucuy was telling him.

"I realized I had fallen into the dark and terrifying maze of fantasy worlds and futile pleasures. The constant pursuit of gratification, the never-ending search for the next hit, the next thrill. And then the crash. The emptiness that follows. I've learned from my mistakes, unlike these guys. And, unlike others, I was able to exorcise many of the ghosts in my head."

Aleksey considered the irony of Cucuy's demented musings. *An exorcism is probably exactly what this vicious beast could use.*

"I don't pretend to be anything other than what I am," Cucuy said with a chilly smile. "I'm a predator, a hunter. I do what I do because it's in my nature. And I don't apologize for it."

Aleksey swallowed hard. He had stumbled on a candid moment — a portal into the raw evil within this man's deranged psyche. He knew he was playing with fire, but he couldn't help but be fascinated by the man's words. Aleksey had walked into a dangerous world, a world where morality carried a loose definition and where power was the only language spoken.

"I hear everything you're saying," Aleksey said slowly, trying to mask his growing unease. "But I can't get past the consequence of your actions — the violence, the killing — it is wrong."

"Wrong?" Cucuy repeated, giving a humorless laugh. "I told you — in this world, there's only power and the lack of it. Only the strong survive. And I, *señor*, am the strongest of them all," Cucuy declared, his eyes alight with madness. "I am the very embodiment of power and control. My wrath is swift and merciless — my will unbreakable. I bask in the fear and suffering of my enemies, reveling in their despair."

"It sounds like it is you who thinks you are a god," Aleksey stated bluntly.

"Am I such a madman? No, I'm a visionary. I see what others cannot. I see a world where fear is my loyal servant and where chaos is my symphony."

Aleksey suppressed a shiver. In his own mind, Cucuy was completely rational, and his violence was justified. He saw the world as a struggle. He was an untamed noble fighting in a savage world. He was a warrior, and his aggression was a natural and healthy dimension of his masculine design. This perspective allowed him to feel no guilt about torturing or murdering anyone who crossed him. They considered themselves soldiers — killing on orders made them feel like it took away part of the responsibility.

Aleksey wondered what toxic combination of factors had come together to make Cucuy so vile and heinous. Did a lifetime of physical dominance allow his depraved nature to reign unchecked? And what wretched environment fed that inner depravity? He shuddered at the thought of what kinds of horrors Cucuy must have endured to make him this way. He played along, though, reasoning he was in less danger as long as he was part of Cucuy's plan.

"I have my reasons for telling you this, Ruso. As I said, there are some opportunities coming up. Opportunities you might be able to ... assist ... me with."

"So, what is in this for my trouble?" Aleksey asked as if tempted.

Cucuy rubbed his forefinger and thumb together and leered.

"*Dinero*, first of all, *amigo*. A lot of *dinero*. And you'll be free to go, under condition of your ... loyalty."

Aleksey forced a smile. "I see your point. And let's not forget the sweet smell of American dollars," he added, trying to sound more avaricious than he really was.

Cucuy chuckled and gave a satisfied nod with a wink. "That's the way, Ruso. I like a man with backbone and ambition."

"Well, then we should talk. What can I do?" Aleksey asked, endeavoring to show that he was buying into the proposition.

"Not too fast. There are some simple tasks I need done."

"Such as?" Aleksey pressed, knowing he was edging himself toward the cusp of the abyss.

25

REBEL CAPITALISTS

The next morning, Cucuy returned to the shed once again, carrying two cups of coffee. This time, he wore an odd smiling expression — out of place and unsettling. He greeted Aleksey by holding out a steaming cup of coffee to his nose.

"Drink."

The warm coffee was of poor quality, but it soothed Aleksey's aching body slightly. He wondered if Cucuy was going to pick up their discussion from the previous day and continue his recruiting efforts again. Yesterday, before Cucuy had ever got around to specifics about what he wanted from Aleksey, he left the shed to attend to other matters and didn't return for the rest of the night.

"You know, Ruso, I was awake last night, and I was thinking — you give my men a hard time, sí? A very hard time ..." Cucuy grasped his coffee cup and nodded as he circled Aleksey. "I met many people, sí. And where do you get skills like that? To evade my men like that? To hide your tracks?"

This ogre has changed his mind. Yesterday he wanted me to work for him, now he is complaining about how I gave them a hard time.

Aleksey grunted. "If you are going to kill me, just do it."

Cucuy cleared his throat gruffly and sat on a battered chair in the corner, crossing one of his legs over the other and tapping his hand on his knee.

"Kill you?" he chuckled. "That's not what I have in mind ... at this moment. What I'm thinking about is, who exactly are you? Who trained you? And ... how, perhaps, you may be useful to me in other ways."

You think your flattery will make me like you. Such a fool, the Russian mused to himself.

"I have a prize rooster — cockfighting." Cucuy arched an eyebrow indicating he took satisfaction in dominating the cruel tournaments. "His name is Gigante. And you know why he's so strong? Because I teach him to kill. I train him to survive. So, tell me, who taught you?"

Cucuy penetrated his Russian pride, if only for a split second. Aleksey lifted his chin and looked the man in the eye — *"Rabóčekrest jánskaja Krásnaja ármija."*

"Hey, hey. If you can't speak *español*, at least speak English," Cucuy growled.

"The Red Army," Aleksey shot back.

"That some kind of *ruso* thing?" Cucuy demanded.

"USSR — the Soviet Union, yes," Aleksey answered.

"And what did you do in that 'red army'?"

"Defender of the motherland," Aleksey responded in a brusque manner.

"Uh-huh. I knew you had ... skills ... some type of extra-crazy, icy *ruso* training. Those communists — where did they send you?"

"Afghanistan." Aleksey spat the word out bitterly.

Cucuy whistled softly. "Uh-huh. I see. You have been there, hmmm." The monstrous Mexican looked distinctly impressed. He eyed Aleksey with new respect, nodding slightly and squinting his eyes like he was seeing something new.

"That explains a lot. You know, a *soldado* ... *sí*, very useful to me. A *soldado Ruso*, no less ..." Cucuy seemed to be talking more to himself than Aleksey.

At this point, Cucuy brought up the work opportunity again — now even more laser-focused on transitioning Aleksey into this role. Aleksey again wondered what would happen if he played along.

"Listen well, *soldado*," Cucuy spoke sternly. "I will instruct the men to treat you exactly as they would treat me. I have something in mind."

"So ... how about telling me what is the 'something' you have in mind?" Aleksey probed, not attempting to hide his disdain.

"I need someone who can be my eyes and ears in Florida. Not the whole state. I have in mind *medio* ... *medio*. How you say it? ... central — Tampa, Orlando, *sí*? You are responsible to keep business running smoothly. I return you to Florida — you do as I say."

"Okay," Aleksey answered, listening intently now.

"There, in Florida, I will have a trusted associate waiting. You will be in his charge — he will arrange everything. But make no mistake, they serve only me."

"Yes, that is clear," Aleksey responded curtly, hiding his nerves behind a facade of professionalism.

"You don't get into trouble up there — understand, *sí*? The American donut gang isn't like Mexican police. They're hard to bribe ... and even harder to kill," Cucuy laughed.

"So, you need ... an accountant ... for your business in Florida?" Aleksey spoke slowly, indicating he was trying to grasp where Cucuy was going with this.

Cucuy was humored.

"Think of yourself as our ambassador to the Sunshine State — simply act accordingly. Remember, you're a marketing executive, not a criminal. You maintain some connections for me, keep some property under your name, and let some money move."

Aleksey nodded. "Right, I see."

"You're my front man. You make everything look legitimate and ensure no one gets suspicious, sí? The rules are simple. Don't mess up — stay out of trouble. Dress smart, pay cash for everything, drive the speed limit, and avoid conflicts — there will be no problems. Most importantly, no tattoos — we want to keep a clean image. *Comprende?*"

"Well, I am not planning any tattoos. But once I am there — well, what happens if I do get caught?" Aleksey asked cautiously.

"You won't," Cucuy assured him with complete conviction.

"I am glad you are confident in that. I just know that the Americans, they are strict, and ..."

"Listen ... if you slip up, we don't know each other. If you go down, all we have to say is that you were some small-time hustler, a drug lord wannabe, trying to make a name for yourself."

"Okay," Aleksey said, exhausted by Cucuy's aggressive barking voice and domineering control.

"If our phone number shows up, I'll swear you were hounding me, begging for someone to take you on — but we refused. If it ever comes down to it, don't expect any help from me," Cucuy added with gravity. "I'll deny any connection to you and leave you to face the consequences. In other words, you take the fall ... alone. Got it?"

Aleksey saluted like he was getting the picture. *When do I pick up my scapegoat costume? Apparently, he is looking to setup a stooge to take the fall when they get caught.*

"Besides, they have to worry about warrants and probable cause and all that. They're no problem. Our fixers will take care of any legal troubles, but one misstep and you'll answer directly to me."

"I understand," Aleksey said.

"As long as you continue to do exactly as we tell you, there will always be insufficient evidence to proceed with an investigation."

Of course. What was I thinking? As long as I do exactly as I am told ..., Aleksey chuckled to himself. *Such a comforting thought.*

"You'll serve as my eyes and ears in Florida, ensuring everything runs smoothly. You do what I ask, and I'll make sure you reap the benefits."

"I see no reason not to follow your orders and do things right," Aleksey said, injecting a note of confidence into his voice.

"But make no mistake ..." Cucuy leaned in, his cold eyes locked onto Aleksey's. "Cross me, and the authorities will be the least of your worries. Let's just say that I have ways of making people disappear, and those who betray me never resurface. Serve me well, and you'll be rewarded beyond your wildest dreams. The choice is yours."

"So, you have a bigger organization already in Florida?" Aleksey probed.

Cucuy shrugged. "We have a small organization in Florida — loyal men who'll do anything to protect our interests. Our operations stretch far into El Norte." He made no effort to hide the pride on his face. "And if you play your cards right, you could be part of it all."

"Why me?"

"Why not?" Cucuy countered. "You have discretion, you have skills, and you have a head for business. But most importantly, you already know what's going to happen if you ever cross us, and you know we're not joking."

Aleksey returned a serious look, pausing. "This 'front man' role — I want to know what that means. What exactly is my job?"

"You are a businessman — experienced and organized, I assume. We need that up there. Think of yourself as a rebel capitalist."

"And ... ?" Aleksey assumed there was more to this.

"And you are not Latino," Cucuy said with a shrug. "Mexicans, Cubans, Puerto Ricans — we tend to run in our own circles. You know, they say *los pollos* scratch around with other *pollos* with the same types of feathers. Mexicans generally just sell to other Mexicans and so forth. Nah, but see ... you wouldn't try selling on the street in Little Havana or Memphis, would you? There are lots of buyers, they're just not for you."

"So, what are you saying ... ?"

"So, we need to move into central Florida and north, into the areas where the money is. When people want drugs, they will find a way to get them — and people always want drugs. Users are there, and dealers are there, separated by a cultural divide. Our operatives in Florida tend to be Latino-American men in their mid-twenties. They're street tough, which makes people nervous. They attract too much attention — the wrong kind, if you know what I mean."

"So, you want me pushing this stuff on the street, selling it out of my house, or what?" Aleksey asked.

"No, no, no," said Cucuy in a tone that Aleksey thought was supposed to be reassuring. "We need a guy to be the face of the franchise — you know, window dressing. You've got the Russian thing going — the real tough-guy image. You don't handle any product. Your job is a gateway. You will own some homes for us, various small businesses, and a few vehicles for transportation purposes. You will also recruit for our fulfillment operation in central Florida and interact with regional operatives. You are the grease for the wheels ... tough grease ... *ruso soldado* grease."

"I do have the Russian thing going," Aleksey agreed with a forced smile.

Cucuy laughed, clapping him on the shoulder. "You got it, Ruso," his expression turned grim. "Besides, we have enough Latinos who are addicted already. I have no desire that more of my people should fall prey to drugs."

Yeah, right. Such a humanitarian — protecting his 'people' from getting hooked on the drugs that fuel his own wealth. I see how that works. Aleksey stifled a sarcastic smile.

"So, here's the thing ... We insulate organization members from each other

— they only know what they need to know to carry out their business — our business. Our preference is to have more ... let's say, diversity.

"We want dealers on the street to include people of all races and social classes, just with no knowledge about their actual suppliers — *sí?* No worries, you won't be anywhere near the street. The customers don't need to deal directly with you. They just know that you're there, and they see some different shades and hues when they're out picking up the product."

This guy is incredible, Aleksey thought. *Equal-opportunity drug dealing? 'Diversity?' This conversation would be like something out of an American sitcom if it were not so deadly serious.*

"Stick with me, and you're going to make more money than your poor papa ever dreamed of in his miserable communist life, *amigo.*"

Aleksey nodded as if lost in bitterness at his absent father, all the while thinking, *And you do not know my papa, 'amigo.'*

Aleksey put his face in his hands. He had the sense that it would be impossible to refuse Cucuy and get out of Mexico alive.

"Your offer is interesting. Let me give it some thought," he said.

Cucuy stood up, took a hand-rolled cigarette from the table nearby, and scowled. Aleksey absently wondered how his sausage fingers could even roll it.

"Oh, *amigo*, no, no. I don't think so, *amigo*. There's been more than enough time for you to think already," Cucuy said, shifting his weight between his feet as he stood up and paced, dragging on the cigarette.

"Listen, I think we need to plan it out more carefully. Maybe you can tell me mo..."

Cucuy cursed loudly and threw his barely half-smoked cigarette at Aleksey.

"Think? Think? Ruso. No. Don't think more. Trust me, that would not be good for your family. Wouldn't be good for you, either."

"My family?" Aleksey asked, confused.

Cucuy approached and pushed one of his giant chicken tender-sized fingers on Aleksey's sternum.

"Your family. Sííí."

"What about them?"

"Ohhh, Ruso ... poor Ruso. You still think you are dealing with a fool here, hmmm? A real village clown or — rodeo clown — what do you call it in El Norte?"

"No, I never said th ..."

"I can hear your thoughts!" Cucuy shouted, his eyes blazing demonically. "I know what you're thinking. You think you can lead me on and find some way out of this? Some easy exit? Never gonna happen, Ruso," Cucuy asserted. "My offer to you is in good faith — not a game."

"Who ever said it was?" Aleksey replied.

"Remember your papa's boat? Yeah ... ? Well, my guys found some interesting mail in one of the compartments. It had an address ... a Florida address with information about one *mujer*, a nice lady perhaps, a Mrs. Irina Gavrilov, hmmm? What do you think about th ..."

"Do not bring my mother into this!" Aleksey pounded the scarred top of the table and shouted, his face reddening. It was exactly the reaction Cucuy had wanted.

"Sííí. That is indeed what I would prefer — not to need to involve her. But you're starting to make me wonder about ... whether I should make a little call to my guy in Miami, and ..."

Aleksey was furious that this monster would threaten his mother. Cucuy's evil knew no bounds. Aleksey's only consolation was the thought of his father, an avenger, arriving to set matters right.

If he ever gets wind of this, Cucuy's entrails will be scattered to the four ends of the earth! His sausage fingers would be ...

Aleksey's fantasy of vengeance was broken by Cucuy's ugly voice.

"Well?"

Aleksey groaned, wisely controlling his tongue and resisting the urge to curse at this beast.

"Enough of the threats, *amigo*. Yes ... I will do it."

26 DEALING WITH THE DEVIL

Another day passed, and Cucuy was increasingly optimistic about Aleksey. He had already worked on recruiting him, and the younger Russian seemed like he might be game. Grooming a new member required a lot of time and effort, but it was a viable backup plan if the ransom didn't work out.

It looks like I will have some use for our hostage no matter what, Cucuy thought, pleased with himself. He never allowed himself to lose the upper hand, but always stacked the odds for a win. This young man could be a useful recruit, and there was no need to throw him away too easily. For now, his intentions were to double down on getting the immediate payoff.

"If his family doesn't pay, he could be a valuable accessory for us in *El Norte*," one of the smarter of Cucuy's men suggested. He was the fellow fond of wearing the Bulls jersey.

"Sí, we can play this many ways ... but don't tell me what to do. I would prefer a payoff right away," Cucuy warned his confederate.

Cucuy placed a telephone call to the Gavrilov home in Florida. As the phone rang, he hoped "*Papa Ruso*" was on the other end, waiting to cough up plenty of US dollars.

"Hello?" Vladi answered. This time, there was more confidence in his voice. After his last conversation with Marco, he felt more composed and certain of himself.

"Hey, Ruso, got the three hundred grand?" Cucuy demanded, wasting no time with formalities.

"How am I supposed to do that?" Vladi replied right back, then he didn't say another word. There was a long silence. *He probably was not expecting that response*, Vladi thought with a grain of satisfaction. Vladi replayed Díaz's advice in his head — *Show no weakness.*

"We do understand," came the surprisingly calm reply on the other end of the line as Cucuy batted away a fly. "We can accept two hundred thousand — our best offer — but we need it now. No more stalling."

"I am not stalling," Vladi replied with a calmness he didn't feel. He had faced down dangerous men before, but never with his son's life on the line.

"Don't lie to me. No games. Just accept this kindness, and you can still see your son in one piece," Cucuy insisted. "See, we are easy to work with, Ruso. You just need to have respect."

Does he think that by constantly telling me that they are easy to work with, I will believe it? He almost acts like he is doing me a favor, Vladi found himself frowning, his brows knit.

"The money you want, two hundred thousand, it is —"

"It's my best price, Ruso. I told you. My last offer."

"I am afraid I will not be able to do that," Vladi said firmly. He was so focused on this conversation that he had tunnel vision.

Despite his steadiness and focus, his emotions ran high, and he felt like he had a fever. Only a few feet from him, Irina was physically shaking. She chewed the nail on her index finger and nervously fidgeted with her other hand. She could hardly bear to listen, but she dared not step away.

At the other end, Cucuy raised his eyebrows, momentarily distracted. The pointy toe of his alligator cowboy boot made a crunch as he squashed a cockroach. He was surprised and aggravated by the change in Vladi's demeanor from the last time they spoke. At the same time, he held some admiration for the Russian's resolve. This guy had some grit. Did his son have some of the same fighting spirit? The hint of a smile twisted the corner of his lips, but he betrayed no trace of amusement to Vladi.

"My patience with this is not infinite," Cucuy stressed. His tone was icy and laced with threat. "When I say final offer, I mean fin ..."

"It seems we are coming closer to an agreement." Vladi cut him off this time, in an assertive but polite way, endeavoring to maintain the right balance and buy some time. "I found another twenty thousand since we spoke — I can offer seventy thousand."

"We will only agree when you do as I tell you, Ruso. I have now lowered the price twice. Do you think I am some fool who will feed and care for this son of yours for weeks while you dawdle around, only to end up with a measly seventy thousand for my trouble?"

Vladi was concerned about pushing too hard and setting him off. Yet he did have one advantage — when pressed, Vladi could be quite adept at understanding the enemy. Taking time to analyze his foe, he could discern how his opponent thought and operated. In this case, he understood that the abductor had an obsessive need for what at least appeared to be absolute control of the situation.

"You say you want the money now." Vladi steeled himself for the negotiation and made another run at it, appealing to the kidnapper's impatience. "I am telling you exactly what I can get you now — seventy thousand."

Vladi figured Cucuy was making certain assumptions about how he would act — like any other father who was desperate and would do anything he was told to get his son back. Granted, some of that was true — but Cucuy had no real idea of Vladi's background, intelligence, or what his resources might be if he was squeezed hard enough.

Indeed, Vladi was not like the other fathers Cucuy had dealt with. This man had a spine, a determination to protect his family, and a cunning mind. Cucuy had underestimated the man, and it was starting to show.

Cucuy took a deep breath, eyeing the cockroach's mangled remains. "Two hundred thousand is the deal, or your boy's blood is on your hands," he pressed.

"How am I supposed to do that? As I said, I cannot give you what I do not have," Vladi told him. Once more, he shut up and waited for whatever the scum on the telephone had to say.

"We will take your offer into consideration," came the reply from Cucuy. "You are to charter a flight into Chetumal. Let us know when you have made arrangements. We will meet you. The port is near the airstrip. You bring the money, Ruso. I want every *centavo*."

"How do I know you will bring him out alive?"

"Just show up, and you can pick up the boy and your boat."

Vladi rubbed the back of his neck, carefully choosing his next words. He needed to find a way to take control of the situation.

"I will tell you what," Vladi said, a cold, hard edge to his voice, "if I meet you in Chetumal, you had better have my son with you. No money changes hands until I see him with my own two eyes."

Vladi waited for the kidnapper's response, the seconds dragging on. He could almost hear the man's mind working, trying to contrive a way to outmaneuver him.

"Fine," Cucuy finally spat. "But I expect the money as soon as you land. No tricks."

"No tricks," Vladi agreed, his tone leaving no room for argument. "Just you, me, Aleksey, and the money."

Vladi could smell a setup, but he decided to play along for now and feign naïveté until he could devise a counterplan.

"I need another couple of days to make arrangements, to get the cash and charter a plane. How about telling me your name since we are getting to know each other now?" Vladi was working to buy as much time as possible and establish human connection and trust, two things he felt sure the goon was genuinely incapable of. *But at least if there is some pretense ...*

"Pablo Noriega," came the curt reply, then the telephone disconnected.

"Pablo Noriega," Vladi whispered to himself, memorizing the name. He looked down at the phone, a sneer curling the corner of his mouth, and he gave a sarcastic laugh. *So, I finally have your name, you arrogant cretin. See you soon.*

27
BREAKING POINT

Irina was curled up in the easy chair, her head buried in her arms. Her body convulsed with sobs. Vladi approached her to offer comfort and put his arm around her. She shook him off, too consumed with grief to accept his touch.

Being a military officer, Vladi was a man of responsibility. He was trained to take ownership of problems and not shift blame. He had not underestimated the dangers of making the trip — he had most certainly voiced his concerns, but he couldn't have foreseen this situation. *There is no one else to blame.* Even though Aleksey and Irina had pressured him to go, he had taken full responsibility the moment he conceded. He made no excuses — he was ultimately in charge, and he felt the weight of what had occurred on his watch.

"I am sorry. I have let you down," Vladi whispered, his voice filled with regret as he apologized for the dozenth time. "I should have prevented this — I know it. I should have protected Aleksey, but I failed."

"We ... could not ha— have known," Irina muttered between agonizing sobs.

"I was right there though!" Vladi declared adamantly. "Perhaps God may forgive my failure, but I can never forgive myself for this."

Irina did not respond further, only continued to shake with tears.

Vladi felt awkward. *What else should I say to her?* He racked his brain, groping to find the right words. Her tears also caused him much discomfort. *I do not know how to help her. What will make her stop crying?*

Irina's tears fell harder. Vladi wished he could be a better support for his wife, but he didn't know how. He wanted to be a good husband and father, but it didn't come naturally. At best, he was way out of practice. There were no military manuals with procedures for keeping a wife happy, and he had minimal life experience in this role.

Their marriage, only seven years strong when he left for Cuba, had been strained by the long periods of time they spent apart. In reality, they had spent a relatively small portion of their lives together. And of course, after Cuba, Vladi had essentially been "single" for three decades. Time had created an unusual gulf, and now it was being fully exposed.

The years apart had created a gap between Vladi and Irina that he didn't know how to bridge. Neither was the very same person they were before, and their former selves were only shadows in the other's memory. The time apart had changed both of them, leaving them feeling like strangers in each other's lives. It felt like they were starting the relationship all over again, and Vladi was struggling to find his footing.

But now, in this moment of crisis, all that mattered was their son. With a broken voice, Irina lifted her tear-streaked face, her eyes swollen and red, pleading with Vladi about the call they'd just received from the cartel.

"Why? Why must you argue with him? Why are you being so stubborn?" she demanded, her voice trembling with anger. "You have the money now. Give this monster whatever he wants and get Aleksey back. Please, Vladi, bring him home! It is enough! You are risking h— his life! Our son!" Her voice was a desperate wail, the sound of a mother at the end of her rope.

Irina's words sliced through the air. Vladi listened but remained silent. His heart ached at the pain in her voice. He longed to ease her fear and make everything okay, but he couldn't. Even if he paid all the money now, what incentive did the cartel have to keep up their side of the bargain? Nothing ensured Aleksey's survival. He felt a crushing sense of helplessness as he struggled to find the right response.

Irina is a good woman — she just does not really understand what is going on. It is not as simple as she imagines, Vladi thought. *She has a naïve perspective of the situation. She does not have much experience with real-life villains. Giving them the money they want right now would be the worst choice I could make. They have too much power in the situation as it is.*

Irina could not be faulted for panicking as any loving mother would. Consumed with frustration, her accusations intensified. Vladi attempted to explain the danger of blindly giving in to the kidnapper's demands, but she saw things from a different perspective, one born from desperation and fear for her son. They were both anxious and stressed about the situation, which was placing a strain on their already fragile relationship. The simmering tension between Vladi and Irina over how to deal with the kidnappers was beginning to erupt.

She is thinking with her emotions right now, Vladi understood. *I wish she could be more clear-headed and trust that I am making rational decisions given the circumstances.*

"Please, *Dorogáya*, it is more complicated than you think. I am working hard on the best solution for our son," Vladi said. He turned to pour himself a glass of orange juice from the fridge, hoping for a momentary respite from her accusations.

Vladi had been trying to help her grasp the complexity of the situation, but her words pierced him to the core. *Is Irina right?*

"It is a simple transaction," she insisted. "Give the kidnappers the money, and get Aleksey home safely. Stop treating me like an idiot, Vladi."

He shook his head.

"Love, this kidnapper is on a serious power trip — money is not all he is after. These are very bad people, and you cannot trust one word they say."

"Maybe they would like you to just give them the money and be over with it," Irina protested.

"Well, I would like that too," Vladi explained. "But giving him money does not obligate a bad guy to reciprocate honorably. He can take the money and do whatever he wants — he then has all the power over the situation ... even more power. He could ..." Vladi was reluctant to say the words out loud, but he knew Aleksey's life hung on the whim of a psychopathic killer.

She lashed out, "Power — power in the situation — that is all you ever say." Irina's face contorted with anger and pain. "You, Mister Commander, let your ego get in the way of paying the ransom and settling the matter! Who cares who has the power? I only care who has Aleksey!"

"Irina, please listen to me." Vladi spoke softly, trying to calm the tension between them. "This is not about my power or ego. It is about making sure our son comes home safely. It is not ..." Vladi attempted a better explanation, but Irina cut him off. Decades' worth of built-up pressure came gushing out in a torrent of grief.

"All those years you were gone, you put me in the unwilling position of making all the decisions. All I wanted was for you to be there to take care of things. You left me alone to figure out everything! I had to decide what was best for them."

"I know, I know, but —"

"Now you are here, trying to tell me what is best for my son — how to save and protect him? What do you even know of him?" Sobs strangled some of Irina's angry words, but Vladi understood the force of her emotions quite clearly.

Tears still streaming, Irina continued, "I had to adjust to making difficult decisions on my own, and we managed. I did grow accustomed to that being the case."

"I realize that, and I am truly grieved for it," Vladi whispered, but the damage had been done.

"For many years, you have been making decisions based on what is good for you and you alone. Now, it is hard to trust my husband — someone I have hardly known. I am sorry this is not what you want to hear, but I cannot trust you to do what is best."

"I understand," Vladi said, although it came out more coldly than he intended. He was having trouble expressing the emotions he felt within himself.

The pain of Vladi's absence was still raw, and Irina's anger and distrust poured out of her. "I want to trust you, Vladi. I really do. But every time I try, I am reminded of all the times you were not there for us."

Vladi bowed his head and sighed. That hit him hard. Hearing his wife say she didn't trust him to make the right decisions stung. It hurt like a thousand knives thrust into his heart. The room was deathly silent, save for Irina's quiet sobs.

Her criticisms hung between them like a heavy curtain. The weight of her indictments was like a physical blow to his chest. The accusations echoed in his head.

Vladi struggled to control his emotions. He understood she was speaking from a place of fear and desperation, but her words still crushed his soul. He knew she was right.

The tension between them thickened with each passing moment, while the thought of their son being in the hands of a madman was tearing them both apart inside. This ordeal was affecting Vladi's relationship with the one person he wanted to trust him most.

She is not altogether wrong. Maybe I was away from them too long — maybe I am no longer fit to be a good husband and father. What do I know? Vladi was tormented by the reality that Irina's words revealed. He already felt remorse about being away from his family for all those years, leaving Irina to shoulder the burden of raising their children alone. He struggled to make up for the time apart that could never be recovered. Now, this.

Vladi had always known that his time away would have consequences, but he never imagined it would be like this. Irina's words were rooted in a deeper pain.

This was just the tipping point for all the hurt and resentment she had been carrying. The situation hit Vladi from all sides, as he struggled to save Aleksey and repair his relationship with Irina. He felt like he was losing the only people who mattered to him.

Irina desired to honor the Lord in her role as a wife. She prayed daily for grace and strength to honor her husband and submit to his leadership, recognizing this as God's design for the family. At first, she had adjusted to Vladi's presence rather well. The joy and relief she felt at his homecoming had carried her through the initial challenges she faced.

But this — this was different. She was frightened to her very core, too frightened to trust the decision-making of a man she'd just grown reacquainted with. Her desperation was driving her to her knees. And it was driving her and Vladi dangerously far apart.

A biting realization hit Vladi. *I do not think she will ever forgive me.* After all, he found it hard to forgive himself. He wasn't the kidnapper, yet he was consumed with guilt. The situation had been avoidable. Even the port they'd docked in — why that one? Should he have recognized something was awry with the shady men on the pier sooner and moved to another location that might have been safer? He kept reliving the abduction, beating himself up over what should have been done.

But it is more than just this situation, is it not? He grappled with the reality that she hadn't really forgiven him for his prolonged absence. *This was just a catalyst for all the grief she has been carrying around. And now the truth spills out — the bitter truth about how she feels.*

The thought that Irina might never forgive him was a harsh reality that Vladi couldn't escape. He ached for forgiveness. If only he could turn back the hands of time. But he couldn't undo her suffering — that was impossible. He was vexed by the thought that the Lord would forgive him, but perhaps his wife would not.

"I am sorry, Irina," he whispered. "I am so sorry for everything. I never meant for this to happen. I never wanted to put you in this position. You have suffered enough already. I am here now. I just want Aleksey back. I will do anything to make it happen."

"Anything?" Irina challenged, her voice rising. "Can you guarantee that he will come back to me safely? Can you promise me that?"

Vladi's silence was answer enough. He had no guarantees.

"Irina, I cannot promise an outcome, but I can promise you this. I will fight for him until my last breath. I will do whatever I can to bring him back to you, no matter what." Vladi's voice was filled with determination, but even as he spoke the words, he wasn't sure they were enough.

Vladi was desperate to save Aleksey, but with Irina's mistrust weighing heavily on him, he wasn't sure how to proceed. Now he was torn between the need to save his son and the suffocating fear of making the wrong decision. He felt like he was drowning in a sea of emotions and uncertainty, with no way out.

Until now, Irina had often spoken of her trust in the Lord. She trusted the Lord when everything was good before Vladi and Aleksey left, but life had since taken a downward spiral. Now, she struggled to trust anyone, especially the man who had vowed to always be by her side to love and cherish her.

"I want my son," Irina said, leveling puffy, red eyes on Vladi. "I want him home now."

28

LAST RESORT

Vladi was at his wit's end. He agreed with his wife — he just wanted Aleksey home, safe and sound. He was weary of deliberating and trying to figure out what to do, but it seemed like no one with any authority was willing to help him. He was left feeling increasingly frustrated and helpless as the days wore on. Minute by minute and hour by hour, his impatience grew. This was enough! Even after his best efforts, there was still no definitive plan for getting Aleksey back.

Despite saying he agreed to Cucuy's plan of flying down with cash in hand, Vladi had no intention of carrying it out ... at least not that way. Meeting a madman on his own turf, giving him a large sum of money while hoping he'd get his son back and they'd both leave alive — insane. *I would be naïve to think that would go smoothly.*

As a commissioned officer, Vladi had studied in the *Akademiya*, a compulsory post-graduate military school in the former USSR. The young officers had surveyed an array of world leaders, ancient to contemporary, including the American military officer and statesman, Dwight Eisenhower. At the time of Vladi's tutelage, Eisenhower had been a general, before ascending to the presidency.

Being the supreme commander of Allied forces in Europe during the Great Patriotic War, Eisenhower was of great interest to the budding Soviet officers. He once said, "In preparing for battle I have always found that plans are useless, but planning is indispensable." As a seasoned military officer, Vladi concurred with that wisdom. Now he understood better what Eisenhower had meant.

Vladi needed a plan, but not Cucuy's plan. He devised various scenarios in his mind, but they always had holes that were too big to ignore — flaws that were unacceptable to him. He needed to do everything in his power to tilt the situation in their favor, ensuring they would come back with Aleksey alive. The persistent obstacle that hampered his plans was that he couldn't do this on his own.

Meanwhile, he was feeling pressure from Irina, who was on the verge of a nervous breakdown. She was barely sleeping or eating, and she was constantly begging Vladi to do something.

"Please, please, you have to get him back," she pressed, day after day, hour upon hour. Her urgency was human — Vladi naturally felt the urgency as well. He also knew how disastrous it could be to act on their emotions and intended to refrain from making consequential decisions in haste in the hopes of avoiding regrettable outcomes.

"*Dorogáya*, I am doing all I can," Vladi explained with all the patience he could muster. He struggled not to betray his own frustration. Both were dissatisfied with how slowly things were moving, but he was perhaps even more so because he felt the burden of needing a more viable solution.

"These are not reasonable men. We have no choice but to wait until they call me to discuss the matter." He tried to placate her while buying some time to think of a workable solution.

Irina shook her head, frustrated.

"We talked about this," she insisted.

"Yes, I know we did. And I will take action ... soon," Vladi assured her.

"I think you need help, Vladi. This is not the type of thing to do alone. Waiting is the last thing we should be doing. Can you not —"

"I know! I am try —"

"Is there not someone else to call? Maybe the state police?" Irina offered.

"My love, the state police will not be able to help," Vladi said, calming his voice. "As you know, I have asked the federal authorities and even the Mexican authorities, and no one seems to have the ability to do anything, not even the desire to help ..."

"That is unbelievable! He may not be a full citizen yet, but Aleksey lives in this country legally. How can they not help the people whom they are supposed to protect?"

"I know ... I know, of course. And I agree about —"

"They are being lazy!" Irina cut in. "We have seen these things in Russia. What about money? We can get someone to listen — pay someone to make things happen — to ... well ..." She was feverishly grasping for answers. "Maybe try again, and next time you will get someone willing to help."

Vladi recognized her desperation and could not fault her. But he also knew he couldn't just call up the FBI and demand that they work faster or bribe them.

"The FBI are the only ones who told us to wait for them. They said they would do what they could to help," Vladi explained patiently yet again. "They told us they are working on it."

"More lies. What are they doing? There is nothing. We have heard nothing," Irina reminded him.

Vladi muttered in agreement, only to repeat that he was doing all he could.

"They do not care what happens to Aleksey. There is no time to wait for their slow bureaucracy. Call them. You can make them understand. They must move faster."

Irina slammed a hand on the breakfast table and got up to pace by the window. She could see workers gathering in the distance to begin the day's work in the citrus groves, but her eyes were still blurry from tears.

"*Dorogáya*, please be reasonable ..."

"Do you even want to get our son back?" Irina screamed, wheeling on him. "Are you just planning to leave him there to die? If I spoke better English, I would be on the phone with them day and night until something got done. Make them do their jobs!"

Vladi held up a hand to try to get her to calm down, but her eyes bulged, and her body trembled as though she were losing control.

"Our son is going to be killed because you did not want to make more phone calls!" Irina was bordering on hysterics, and the pressure of her words squeezed the breath out of his lungs.

She is right, they are infuriatingly slow. I cannot just sit here and do nothing but wait for those kidnapping barbarians to call again and hope they will somehow turn reasonable.

The more Vladi reasoned, the more he saw no alternative except to increase the pressure more and more, until ... until ... what, exactly?

The authorities were dragging their feet, and the longer Aleksey was missing, the more discouraged and hopeless Vladi and Irina became.

Flustered, Vladi conceded, "I will make more calls." He sat down stolidly at the phone, getting right to it.

Irina shook her head and sighed, walking back to the bedroom and slamming the door behind her.

As before, the FBI staff were initially cordial and sympathetic. But when Vladi asked about their progress, they didn't appear to be doing anything that would lead to his son's safe return. The ordeal was infuriating for Vladi — this was taking them nowhere.

"I understand your frustration, Mr. Gavrilov, but please understand that we are needing to work through another country's agencies. Going through diplomatic channels and working with the Mexican FMP takes time," the FBI investigator calmly explained.

"But it is time we do not have," Vladi pressed. They needed to see that the situation was critical.

"Those monsters could kill my son at any time — on a whim. They could be torturing him to death right now. Every minute is precious. There is no more time to waste on bureaucracy."

"I understand your worry, sir. It is a troublesome situation. We just have to trust the procedures we have in place for these types of cases."

"Trust them? For what? Your procedures are impotent. There are no tangible results from th—" Vladi was growing belligerent.

"It may seem like nothing is happening, but internally there is plenty going on. Be assured that we are doing our best," the investigator said, trying to placate him.

"Your best is not good enough," Vladi bit back.

As the conversation continued, a sense of helpless frustration washed over him. What were their empty promises to him? He wanted results. Aleksey had been kidnapped for the better part of a week, and despite all the supposed efforts of the authorities, there was no verifiable progress in the case.

Vladi was fast losing hope in the authorities.

It is not the FBI agent's son being held hostage. It is my son in grave danger out there … somewhere. The feeling of helplessness turned into a bear-like rage that brewed inside him.

That evening, in the stillness of the night, Vladi and Irina had lain in bed, their minds swimming with uncertainty about Aleksey's fate. Through it all, they held on to their trust in an all-powerful and loving God, crying out to Him to protect and keep their only son safe. Prayer brought a few hours of rest.

But the next morning when Vladi found himself on the phone once again, imploring the FBI to take action, his faith was tested. He was left grappling with the question of whether God intended for him to be the one to rescue Aleksey.

Something had to be done. Something ...

Vladi hadn't eaten in several days, apart from a quick frozen dinner. In his increasing desperation, he had begun seriously considering what it would take to bring his son home, even if it meant going against the authorities' will. He was determined to do whatever was necessary. But what to do, exactly, he didn't know yet.

The phone call just kept dragging on. The investigator let out an audible sigh before Vladi informed him, "I will just have to take matters into my own hands then."

"Don't do that, sir. Trust me, that is exactly the opposite of what needs to happen right —"

"So, tell me what will happen instead, then. Just tell me real answers, not speculation — give me facts!"

"Please, Mr. Gavrilov. I know you understand the gravity of this situation and the danger posed by the perpetrators. We ask that civilians do not become involved with these people. Please let us handle it," the investigator pleaded. His exasperation was also becoming evident. They'd had civilians interfere in hostage situations before with catastrophic results.

"This is Lieutenant Colonel Gavrilov, formerly of the SPETSNAZ — I am no bumbling civilian," Vladi blustered. "In fact, I have connections in the Russian military all the way to the top. I am sure my old comrade, Premier Gorbachev, would not be happy to hear that you take the grave situation of our people so casually, especially after such an olive branch has been extended between our nations."

The agent cleared his throat.

"Well, I do thank you for bringing up your, uh ... Soviet ... connections, sir. Perhaps they could lend you a hand?"

Having been a hard-charging former Soviet officer, Vladi was used to giving orders. Maybe he had stepped over the line here? When he had orders, he followed them. Likewise, he was accustomed to having people do what he said. But the U.S. authorities, including the FBI, didn't seem to care about him or his demands, no matter how reasonable they were.

But when Vladi grew belligerent, he didn't help the situation. The conversation took a troubling turn. The investigator began to question Vladi's own actions and motivations, leaving him feeling even more helpless and desperate.

"Lieutenant Colonel Gavrilov — or should I perhaps call you Moses Moskowitz?" the investigator retorted. Vladi's heart skipped a beat. They already knew he was a former Soviet military officer and recognized he had used an alias for years. What else did they know about him? It was obviously intended as a warning for him to back off.

Vladi hadn't wanted to make this personal, but his frustration had boiled to the surface.

"What? So, you can look up a file — what do I care? So what — you think that proves something? It does not help my son. Perhaps you are so smart — graduated at the top of your class in spy school, right? Impressive ..."

"I'm not trying to impress you," the man answered coldly. "I'm trying to get you to calm down and stop being reckless. This is a sensitive international situation."

"Highly sens—!" Vladi shot back before he was abruptly cut off.

"Listen, I didn't want to go there, but I'll be straight with you," the investigator continued. "We have been looking into this matter, Lieutenant Colonel Gavrilov. And frankly, the more we look, the more questions it raises ... about you."

29

BYGONE DAYS

Kingston was coming alive with the sights and sounds of a new day. Marco ambled along the familiar route through the city, making his usual stops along the way. He knew each street and alley, each vendor and vagrant. They'd been part of his daily routine for years.

He exchanged a warm smile with his favorite street vendor, Renford. As was his custom, he bought two ripe bananas for $20 Jamaican. He always made a point to pay Renford double and insisted that he keep the change.

Marco then proceeded along a side street where most other pedestrians were reluctant to venture. There, he would usually give his extra banana to one of the vagrant men he regularly encountered. But this morning, the homeless men Marco had previously befriended were missing one of their own.

Maybe he had a rough night, was his passing thought, but Marco didn't give it much more consideration beyond that as he continued on his way to the market. It was common for vagrants to disappear and then reappear.

Marco peeled a banana, eating it as he walked. He tucked the extra fruit into his pocket. He walked onward to the market, where he bought his usual copy of the *Daily Gleaner*. He normally would have scanned the headlines on the front page, but he was trying to steady the half-eaten banana in one hand, so he simply paid, then tucked the folded newspaper under his arm and continued on his way.

Instead of retracing his steps, Marco took a different route back. This took him past the travel agency where his precious bride had once worked.

Marco's eyes fixed on the blue cinder block walls of the building that brought to mind so many memories. He let out a wistful sigh — those memories were still so poignant. That had been such a wild episode, some aspects of which he would prefer to forget.

He paused at the steps and looked up at the door, still locked at this hour. He was momentarily transported back in time. A montage of the events that led to their coming to meet each other flooded his mind.

What a crazy set of circumstances — and to find love in the middle of all of it! Marco envisioned that moment when he'd sprung up the steps and laid eyes on his sweetie, Jhas, for the first time. His heart swelled with warmth and gratitude for the life they had together. He laughed to himself. *Oh, I was in rare form that day.*

Then Marco's conscience was struck with an unexpected pang. He couldn't escape the reality of Michael Cervera's death, an ever-present shadow that loomed over his life and tormented him whenever it got the chance.

It was an accident, he repeated to himself. He had tried to rationalize it, a desperate attempt to ease the burden of guilt. In a way, yes, it was an accident. But deep down, he knew it was more than that.

He had kept the truth locked away — not even confiding in Jhas. He had told no one. *I was a different man back then*, he reminded himself for the thousandth time. Now, the thought of the legal consequences terrified him, knowing it could destroy everything he held dear. What that would do to Jhas, the first and only love in his life, was a constant fear that never quite subsided.

It wasn't only the fear of earthly punishment either. He feared God's dread judgment on his wrongdoing. He was no longer able to afford the atheist's expensive luxury of insisting God was not real. There was indeed a God. Marco knew Him and, more essentially, was known by Him — the One who saw all and judged all.

Marco was tormented by the thought that he would never be free from the grip his past had on him. The image of Michael's face haunted him — the memory was a noose around his neck, one that was now tightening. He tried to push the thought away, but it kept returning. Guilt gnawed at him with relentless ferocity — and nagging worry swirled inside him, a never-ending vortex of regret and anxiety. The terror of being discovered consumed him in the moment, as it did whenever it reared its ugly head.

Even as the wind blew past his head, he swore it whispered his secrets. He put his hand up to his ear to stop it. He felt like a monster, unable to shake the self-disgust that ate away at him.

Marco turned from the building to walk across the street. He tried to put one foot in front of the other, but his legs felt like lead, slow to respond. Most of the time, he went about life like anyone else, but occasionally the memories of that fateful night floated into his consciousness like an undercurrent that refused to let him go. His mind was still trapped in the past — his conscience imprisoned him in those fateful moments.

The screeching of tires jolted Marco back to his senses. He looked up just in time to see the little truck that was barreling toward him. Marco winced and reflexively put up his arms to protect himself as it braked to a stop. Cautiously looking up, he found the bumper only an arm's length away from him. Angry words were hurled from the cab of the truck as he sheepishly peeked through the windshield. Then he did a double-take.

Wait a minute — these guys look familiar. Can it be? Marco strained to look more closely through the glare on the dirty glass. Tendrils of smoke curled out the window.

"Hey, mon, is Cheeko! You almos' run over Cheeko, mon!"

Marco's suspicions were immediately confirmed by those words. They were the same Rastafarian ganja farmers who had given him a ride out of the mountains several years earlier. How was it possible that their old truck was still operating?

The passenger quickly stuck his head out the window, smiling from ear to ear and waving enthusiastically. The driver pulled over to the side of the street, carefully avoiding a homeless man sitting on the curb, and Marco approached the little truck. There were two familiar faces beaming back at him from the cab.

"Hey, hey! What are the chances? I can't believe it's you guys here! You almost ran me over — again!" Marco's grin was genuine.

The Rastas erupted in laughter. "Mon, you almos' get yuself run ovah! Why yu walkin' in di street actin' like nobody else around? Di road is fa car, mon!"

Marco joined in their laughter. "How's business?" he asked.

"It good. Kyaan't complain," replied the passenger. "Wi a grow di sinse right now. Lamb's Bread. Di bes'!"

These guys sure take pride in their work. He couldn't help but feel simultaneously impressed and amused.

The sinsemilla ganja they grew took some skill and extra care to cultivate. It required them to separate the female plants to keep them unfertilized, resulting in the finest seedless buds that fetched premium prices. Lamb's Bread was a spicy Sativa strain named for its buds that looked like balls of sheep's wool. This is what they called "high grade" — at least, that was what they told Marco.

"You know, I never got your names," Marco prompted.

"Mi name Delroy," replied the passenger. "Mi fren, him name Ras Iyah." The driver smiled and gave a half-wave.

"Good to see you gentlemen again." It was a humorous surprise to start out, but it quickly turned into something more for Marco as he stood beside the little truck chatting with the Rastas. An idea started to form in his head.

Remembering the story he hoped they'd forgotten, he brought up the prospect of a deal with Señor Moisés.

"We may be able to make a deal — a whole boatload," Marco enticed with a mischievous grin. Their eyes widened with excitement.

"By di boat? Now we talkin' mon," Delroy said.

"Maybe worth your trouble, eh?" Marco teased.

Delroy reached over and poked at Ras Iyah. "See it deh, I knew dat Cheeko wudda have all kine a connection fo wi," he remarked.

"Let me work out the details. Where can I find you?"

Delroy rummaged through the glove compartment and fished out a scrap of paper and a pencil. He scribbled an address in Tom's River.

"Use dis yard," he said, handing the address to Marco. "Dem will fin' us."

And with that, Delroy and Ras Iyah drove off, merrily singing reggae tunes, the little truck chugging and sputtering down the street.

Marco went on his way, handing his extra banana to the homeless man still sitting on the curb.

30

DREAD JUDGMENT

Marco hurried to meet up with Díaz, eager to share an idea that could change everything. But he needed Díaz on board. As he was being escorted through Díaz's expansive Hellshire Hills compound, Marco's pulse pounded in his temples. He entered the room and spotted Díaz, deep in thought, staring into a glass of Scotch as if it held all the answers.

"I've got it, Frank!" Marco declared, his voice filled with determination. With a flick of his wrist, he cast aside the newspaper that had been tucked under his arm.

Díaz looked up with a momentary frown, startled by Marco's boisterous entrance into the room. "I'm listening," he told Marco, intrigued but cautious.

Marco wasted no time laying out his idea, his words tumbling out in a rush as he explained a plan he had conceived. "We need to get these guys to Jamaica for the handoff, and it will be one for the books," he explained with zealous enthusiasm.

"You're dreaming," Díaz replied, his tone flat. "It'll take more than just an idea to get them out of their comfort zone. These people are highly distrustful and don't like venturing away from their own turf. They prefer the home field advantage, where they know the terrain and have the authorities in their pockets."

"I know it won't be easy," Marco ventured.

"Quite an understatement," Díaz warned.

"That is why we need to make it worth their effort. We sweeten the deal — make an offer they simply cannot pass up," Marco pressed, his voice growing more confident by the second.

Díaz raised an eyebrow. "And what kind of offer would that be?"

"Think about it — we dangle the carrot." Marco's mind was already working out the details. "If they're picking up a shipment of premium ganja, it might be enough temptation for them to step off their turf," he conjectured.

"And where exactly are you going to get that?" Díaz asked with a hint of dismissiveness.

"I happen to have connections to inland growers," Marco told him proudly. "These guys trust me, and I'm confident they can deliver."

"Well, I'm sure they aren't in the business of donating their premium crops to a worthy cause such as kidnapping victims," Díaz remained dubious.

"No," Marco agreed, "but I bet they would make a trade for a cache of handguns they could peddle for top dollar."

Díaz let out a derisive laugh, "Are you telling me you have connections to arms dealers now, too?"

"Well ..." Marco stared at him with a pointed look. "I know someone who does."

Díaz smirked. "Sounds like a tall order, my friend."

Marco was undeterred. He leaned forward, his eyes blazing with fierce resolve. "I'm sure it's nothing more than a finger snap for a resourceful guy like you. Weapons and dope — that's their business. So we offer the cartel some ransom money plus the premium weed."

Marco paused for a moment to confirm Díaz was paying attention.

"I'm listening," Díaz remarked, "... skeptically, I might add."

Marco was satisfied with that response, so he proceeded. "We tell the kidnappers that Vladi can secure the ganja in lieu of the rest of the money they demand. The street value of a shipment of authentic Jamaican Lamb's Bread is way more than what they can get out of Vladi. That's an offer they can't refuse. They'll be crawling over one another to get in on it."

"Lamb's Bread, eh?" Díaz shook his head gravely, his hand tightening around the glass of Scotch. "The cartels aren't to be trifled with. They've got eyes and ears everywhere, and they won't hesitate to take you out if they even suspect anything's amiss." His eyes narrowed as he spoke. "It's risky, Marco," he muttered, swirling the amber liquid in his glass in contemplation.

"Aren't you in the business of risk, boss?" Marco replied, holding his palms up. "We have the opportunity to get Vladi's son back to him. They think they're untouchable. We may be able to play on that and tempt them to be overconfident. With a sweet payoff, it might be the right combo to get them to agree to a place where they have no advantages."

"Like ... where do you have in mind?" Díaz inquired, his tone now neutral.

Marco knew just the place. "Oracabessa Bay," he suggested, grinning slyly.

Díaz nodded, "Oracabessa, huh?"

"It's the perfect location for the handoff," Marco asserted confidently. "It's remote enough that they'll feel secure, but still accessible enough that they won't feel like they're out of their depth."

Díaz's expression remained impassive, but Marco could see the wheels turning in his mind. He was silent for a moment, studying Marco with a newfound respect. Finally, he nodded, a hint of a smile creeping onto his lips.

"Bold ..." he paused. "This plan just might work, Marco. I still have my reservations. Elements of risk are always there. The devil, as the saying goes, is in the details. Let's see if we can firm up a solid approach." Díaz drained his glass and stood up, clapping Marco on the shoulder.

With that, Marco launched into the ins and outs of the daring rescue mission, laying out each step of the plan with the precision of a seasoned strategist and the passion of a man determined to make things right.

Time was of the essence — Marco moved with the speed and urgency of a man on a mission. Getting Díaz on board was the first big hurdle. Still, a sense of unease washed over him. He knew he would need to talk to Vladi again, and that induced more than a bit of anxiety. But he knew what he had to do, and he had to be man enough to do it.

Marco's next hurdle was that he didn't even know how to contact Vladi except through Julio, so he called his brother first to propose the bold strategy. Julio's response was cautious. "I'll reach out to Vladi, but we need to be careful. This is a delicate situation. We need to find out if Vladi is on board with this idea."

"Of course," Marco agreed.

"Don't do anything until I talk to him. After that, one of us will be in touch with you," Julio urged before hanging up.

As he listened to Julio offer a brief overview of Marco's idea, Vladi's first reaction was skepticism and, frankly, anger at Marco's involvement. From Vladi's perspective, Marco was a dangerous wildcard who couldn't be trusted. He might only exacerbate an already complicated situation. With Aleksey's life on the line, the stakes were too high for Marco to bedevil.

Why is Marco so eager to help? Vladi couldn't help but wonder if he had a hidden agenda.

Julio gave Vladi a phone number to call Marco directly. The thought of contacting his former comrade-turned-enemy-turned ... who knows what? — it all made Vladi uneasy. His hand hovering over the phone, Vladi dreaded making the call. But Aleksey's life was on the line — and Irina's sanity, for that matter. Was that more important than an uncomfortable phone call? Besides, what other options did he have?

Marco greeted him warmly. "I'm glad to hear from you again, old friend. I wish it were under better circumstances, but my associate and I may have a plan to help. However, there are significant risks, and it will be important to follow our instructions closely."

The advice Marco had passed along before seemed to be effective and on point — however, Vladi was reluctant to agree to anything concrete until he heard the particulars of this proposal.

"I am listening, but I want to hear the plan before I commit to anything."

When Marco was finally given the opportunity to begin unveiling his idea, the first words out of his mouth only added to Vladi's distrust.

"First, you will need to get on a flight to Kingston," Marco instructed.

"Kingston?" Vladi did not hide his surprise and mistrust. "You want me to come to Jamaica? Now? Are you out of your mind?"

"Vladi, please hear me out —"

"Aleksey is in Mexico. We need to get there, get Aleksey, and get back — as directly as possible."

What in the world is Marco thinking here? Vladi was almost too frustrated to contemplate any convoluted scheme that originated with Marco Rivera. The Russian weighed his options, wondering if he was crazy to even consider whatever Marco had to say. Part of him wanted to hang up.

How much can I really trust Marco? This guy tries to get me killed for no reason other than jealousy, and then one day, he waltzes back into my life and says he wants to help me? Julio says he has changed, but can a leopard really change its spots? Maybe he got in trouble for letting me go in Cuba and is trying to take me back to redeem his reputation with the Castro regime?

Vladi grappled with the idea of relying on Marco, blindly trusting someone who had caused him such trouble in the past. All sorts of ominous thoughts crept to the forefront of Vladi's mind at this turn in the plan. Marco wasn't surprised at his reaction but tried to reason with him.

"I know, but remember, you absolutely cannot meet them on their own ground. It would be a death sentence."

"Speaking of death sentences, Marco ..." Vladi shot back, every word laced with derision.

"Let me tell you the rest before you decide," Marco implored him patiently.

Vladi's mind was a tempest of conflicting emotions. Trust and caution, hope and fear, all clashed within him as he tried to make the right decisions. But with Aleksey's life hanging in the balance, Vladi didn't have the luxury of waiting around. If this audacious plan offered a glimmer of hope in an otherwise dire situation, he had to hear Marco out.

Marco flushed out the details, but they didn't allay Vladi's worries. "You want me to bring five thousand dollars in cash through customs? And what? You will be there to greet me with open arms? How do I know you will not take the money and run?"

"Come on, Vladi. What else can you do —"

"Or what else?" Vladi snapped. "I do not know what else. But I do not have time for these games, Marco!" Vladi couldn't contain his stress any longer. He didn't know what to believe. All he knew was that he didn't really trust Marco.

Vladi's distrust carried a bitter sting for Marco, but he also couldn't fault Vladi for feeling skeptical. "Listen, Vladi," Marco persevered, speaking with a steady, reassuring voice. "I understand your reluctance. But think about it — the alternative is to hand over seventy thousand dollars to the cartel, the same known murderers who have your son. Can you trust them to release him unharmed?"

"Of course not. But your idea is a complete shot in the dark, and that does not inspire confidence in me," Vladi pointed out.

"I'm proposing a safer, more controlled solution where you have a fighting chance of getting your son back. I'll be there every step of the way," Marco assured him.

Marco hoped to make a logical appeal to Vladi and soothe his concerns. "I know, I know — I have given you little reason to trust me, and I regret it deeply. But has Julio not told you that I am a different man now? He knows I would never intentionally lead you wrong, especially about something this serious," Marco desperately tried to reassure him.

He is not wrong, Vladi conceded. *If Julio trusts him and his plan, it is probably okay.*

"I need to think this over," Vladi told Marco, his voice betraying his inner turmoil.

"Take your time, but remember, time is not on our side," Marco replied.

He is also right that I cannot trust the cartel. Really, he is my best option. Actually, at this point, this may be my only viable option to get Aleksey out of this alive.

"Okay, then. Explain to me, what happens after I get to Jamaica with the money?"

"My associate will arrange the details of the rendezvous through his own contacts."

"I am listening to your loco plan — continue," Vladi insisted with a mix of caution and hope in his voice. His mind was still churning with uncertainty.

"We will give you details and further instructions once you are here. Just get on that flight, and I promise, everything will fall into place," Marco assured him.

Vladi knew that this was a crucial moment, that his decision could mean the difference between life and death for Aleksey.

Marco hung up the phone, feeling satisfied that this was all coming together.

It was a delicate balance, but Marco thought he had hit the right notes. *Vladi doesn't know what I know, but if his oversized ego will allow him to trust someone who really wants to help him, I think there is a good chance we can get his son back.* He breathed out a sigh of relief. *The greater feat may be mending my relationship with Vladi.*

Marco thought he was doing what he should do to make amends. Having caused so much trouble in Vladi's life, whatever he could do would never be enough to make it right.

Finally relaxing after several busy hours, Marco got around to looking at the newspaper he'd picked up that morning. The headline stared back at him in bold black letters: *Homeless man hacked to death. Suspect detained.*

Marco read on, his heart sinking with each word.

> Kingston police have detained a person of interest as part of their investigation into a deadly overnight attack on another homeless man this week.
>
> While Jamaica has one of the highest homicide rates in the world, this attack was particularly grisly. The victim suffered chop wounds to the head. The attack was among the bloodiest they had ever seen, police stated.
>
> Still more worrying to the local homeless population is the fact that this was not the first such occurrence and could be the work of a serial killer.
>
> The unnamed suspect is in custody and is under investigation in connection with a pattern of similar attacks in the area, dating back to the murder of Michael Cervera at an area travel agency nearly a decade ago.
>
> "We will spare no effort in investigating such heinous and barbaric murders of those among our society's most vulnerable," said Winston Cato, a Detective Inspector for the Jamaica Constabulary Force.
>
> Over a thousand people were murdered last year in Jamaica, with criminal gangs to blame for much of the violence. Several communities remain under emergency watch by security forces.

"Oh, no!" Marco whispered, horror-struck. "Oh, no." Marco felt his hands shaking — he was reading about his own personal nightmare come to life. His worst fears were rearing their ugly heads. His mind raced with a million different thoughts, each more horrifying than the last.

There were hundreds, if not thousands, of homeless people in Kingston. What were the chances? The homeless guy that he'd been giving breakfast to — was this him? He didn't seem like a killer — was he the victim? Whomever the suspect is, he may be a real killer — but they were trying to pin Michael's death on him too.

The fate of the homeless man, and Michael Cervera, and now possibly himself, were all intertwined in this dark and twisted web.

This could be the thread that unravels it all.

Marco shuddered. He felt a cold sweat break out on his forehead. His stomach clenched as a wave of nausea rolled over him. Marco felt the room spin as anxieties that had loomed over him in the aftermath of Michael Cervera's death came flooding back.

He stumbled into the bathroom. The sickening taste of bile filled his mouth, and he retched before he could even get to the toilet, vomit puddling against the wall. His knees buckled beneath him, and he slid to the floor. The cool tile against his skin offered little comfort as he lay there gasping for breath and shivering, sick with fear.

As the fetid smell of puke reached his nostrils, it became evident that no matter how he tried to hide from the past, it was always there, waiting to catch up to him. The truth and all its far-reaching consequences had a way of eventually finding their way to the surface.

The line between reality and horror was suddenly blurring. Marco didn't know what the future held, but he knew the past wouldn't allow him to ignore it any longer.

31

WINSTON CATO

The towering frame of Detective Inspector Winston Cato cut an imposing figure as he strode through the streets of West Kingston. Cato was a robust man with a flat nose, thin brows, a large jaw, and a narrow head topped by close-shaven, graying hair. He had grown up in the Tivoli Gardens garrison community, and his hard features were etched with the sharp lines of a legacy both brutal and revered. On this day, however, he looked every bit the part of a typical homeless man.

Cato was currently overseeing the investigation into a rash of recent homicides among Kingston's indigent population. Drifters and panhandlers tended to keep to themselves and avoid the police, so he wasn't getting any leads coming in formally — he needed to bust this open from the inside.

A suspect was currently in custody, a man who was among the homeless himself, but Cato wasn't satisfied with the arrest. Cato's professional sensibilities were piqued by the string of cases — he attempted to draw conclusions by putting them together, but it didn't all add up. It was likely that this was a serial killer — a term almost never needed in the Jamaican context — but for how long had he been at work? Cato would leave no stone unturned in his mission to find the answer. He wasn't one to sit behind a desk waiting or to settle for partial solutions.

That pursuit had led Cato to the dusty file on Miguelito Cervera, a homicide linked to a travel agency break-in within the same neighborhood as the more recent stabbing deaths. No one was ever convicted. In fact, a suspect was never even identified. This bothered Cato immensely. Cold cases like that were rarely as random as they seemed.

From what Cato could determine, the Jamaica Constabulary Force [JCF] had bungled the investigation. The victim's driver had run into someone fleeing the scene, but he hadn't been able to identify the murderer in the dark office. DNA testing had been done on the murder weapon, a knife used as a letter opener. There was also a handgun and a broken lockbox in the office. But the case hadn't gone anywhere.

First, Scotland Yard was backed up, and it took months to get results from the lab. The DNA identified on all the evidence belonged to the victim as well as a man of colonial Spanish ethnicity. By the time all this reached the hands of JCF investigators in Kingston, the case had grown cold, and they had neither the manpower nor resources that they were willing to spend on an old case.

Cato was stumped by the fact that everything pointed to the suspect they were holding except that he was a Jamaican of African ethnicity, not colonial Spanish. There was no match on the DNA — and DNA never lied. Cato always used every opportunity to link criminals to their crimes by using DNA evidence for the very reason of its infallibility, and he wasn't about to just let this one go. Furthermore, Cato ensured that the results of his work were always made public so that criminals could see that they could no longer hide.

Cato had an unyielding devotion to his duty, which was evident in every step he took and every move he made. His passion for justice burned like a fiery inferno within him, fueling his relentless pursuit of those who dared to break the law. He was a force to be reckoned with, a hunter of criminals, a warrior who would stop at nothing to bring them to justice.

That was what brought him here today, disguised as a homeless man. He was holding several plastic bags and roaming up and down Duke Street and Johns Lane, the area where these crimes had occurred. For one, he wanted to see if anyone would attack or threaten him. Was there still a killer on the streets, threatening the homeless community? Based on the DNA results, he wasn't convinced the police had the right man. That meant there was a possibility that a killer was on the loose out there. He also wanted to see if the locals interacted with him, perhaps uncovering latent details that might prove helpful. Cato intended to see firsthand if anything unusual turned up in this locale.

Cato made himself appear vulnerable and affected a slight limp, but beneath his tattered disguise was an intrepid soul. His unwavering self-assurance and unshakable resolve had consistently allowed him to remain calm and composed even in the face of the most dangerous situations, and this was no different.

He would walk alone into the lair of the Shower Posse without hesitation, his duty as an officer of the law driving him forward. The word on the street was that Cato was obsessed and fearless. Those who played fast and loose with the law just tried to stay out of his way.

Beyond his immediate motive of observing the neighborhood, Cato wanted to authentically experience what it was like for those who lived a dark existence in the shadows without drawing attention to himself as an officer of the law. This morning, it paid off.

As he sat on the curb in front of the very travel agency where Miguelito Cervera had perished, Cato was witness to another important event. A small, beat-up pickup truck pulled up to the curb nearby. A Latino man stepped out of the shadow of the next building and walked over to chat with the two Rastafarians in the truck. Cato's interest was piqued.

What do we have here? Cato strained to listen while giving the appearance of paying no attention. He couldn't make out every word, but he heard enough — a deal being arranged between a Latino male and two Rastafarians for a boatload of cannabis. This may be Jamaica, and Cato was well aware of the reputation that went along with that — but these guys were now playing on his turf, and he didn't make any exceptions.

Not on my watch, fellas.

He noted the appearance of these individuals as well as the license plate number and description of their compact truck. He would follow up on that when he returned to his office. This was worth checking up on, but he couldn't allow it to distract him from his main goal of the day.

For the moment, he was focused on solving this string of homicides and getting to the bottom of how the Cervera murder had occurred and why. The next step was to interview the travel agency's employees, everyone who had worked there when the murder occurred. Cato missed nothing, and he felt a surge of adrenaline as he contemplated what was next. There was no way any culprit would escape his investigation.

He stood up from his perch on the curb, peeled a banana, and headed directly to his office ... trying not to forget to limp.

A RANSOM FOR MANY

As the providence of our Lord would have it, on that Sunday morning in Florida, Pastor Gerardo took to the pulpit with a sermon entitled "The Ransom."

"Our Scripture reading today is from the Gospel of Mark," Pastor Gerardo told the congregation. "I'll be reading from chapter ten, verse forty-five."

Allowing a moment for everyone to turn to the passage, he read, "For even the Son of Man did not come to be served, but to serve, and to give His life a ransom for many." The pastor prayed and then began to preach.

"Dear brothers and sisters in Christ," Pastor Gerardo began, "the Bible uses the term 'ransom' to illustrate the high cost of our salvation.

"Why a ransom?

"We are all captive to sin, unable to redeem ourselves, held in the grip of our sin nature and the power and dominion of Satan. The only way a sinner can be rescued is by the payment of a ransom — someone must pay to secure your release.

"But there is hope. For we read from God's Word this morning that the Son of Man came ... 'to give His life a ransom for many.'"

Seated in the congregation, listening to the Scripture, Julio knew this was God's message to him as Pastor Gerardo continued.

"To whom was this ransom paid?

"At the crucifixion, the Son of Man paid this ransom to our gracious Heavenly Father — for His justice, holiness, and wrath must all be satisfied."

Julio nodded his head in agreement. Every word of the Bible was true.

"You see, our Creator is a moral being. He gave us His Law so that we could understand His moral character. He endowed us with a conscience to know right from wrong. And He has told us in His Word that there will come a day when we will all stand before Him to give an account."

The congregation was attentive, soaking in the truth of God's Word as the pastor continued.

"This same Word of God repeatedly describes how Christ Jesus gave Himself. He came into this world for the express purpose of dying on the cross as a ransom to redeem those who were hopelessly lost.

"Christ Jesus took the punishment we deserved for our sins, beloved," the pastor declared. "He gave His life as a ransom. He stood in the place of sinners, taking our punishment upon Himself to suffer and die our death on the cross. This substitutionary atonement is a truth often disregarded and even rejected in our time."

Julio could sense that God the Holy Spirit was impressing this message on him. This was precisely what he needed to hear at this moment.

Pastor Gerardo concluded by reminding the church, "Christ Jesus paid a real and specific price at the cross. In this ransom, He purchased with His own blood all those whom God the Father had set apart for Him. This was the highest price ever paid for anything in the history of the world, and it will not be wasted. No, not a drop. And we, dear brothers and sisters, are His purchased possession, redeemed by the blood of the Lamb. Amen?"

Toward the end of the church service, Pastor Gerardo's voice grew solemn.

"My brothers and sisters," he proceeded, "I come to you with a heavy heart. A fellow servant of Christ, Vladi Gavrilov, has had a trial placed upon him, a test of his faith and the faith of those around him. Many of you may be familiar with Vladi, affectionately known to some as *Señor Moisés*. If so, you know how the Lord has done an amazing work in his life. Once lost in the ways of the world, he was brought to the sweetness of salvation by the grace of our Lord and Savior, Christ Jesus, and now he walks in obedience to His will. He is not a member of our congregation but a brother in Christ. I ask that you keep him and his family in your prayers."

A cold chill swept over Julio as the matter was brought before the Lord's people.

"This morning, Brother Julio shared with us the devastating news that Vladi's son has been taken from him. He has been abducted in Mexico and is in grave danger."

A collective gasp was heard throughout the congregation. Every eye was fixed on Pastor Gerardo, each member feeling the weight of the situation on their hearts.

"We do not know all the details," Pastor Gerardo continued, "but we know this much — the situation is dire. We also know that Vladi and his family need our support. They need the love and comfort that can only come from the Lord and His people.

"Let us not despair. Let us instead turn to our great God, the One who hears our prayers and answers them in His perfect timing and wisdom. So, will you, the Lord's church, commit with me to pray for them? We can be praying fervently for his safe return and their strength in the face of adversity. Will you lift your voices with mine and petition the throne of grace on their behalf?"

The congregation responded with one voice, "Amen!" Tears rolled down the faces of many as they joined hands in prayer for Vladi and his family. It was a testament to their faith in the Lord and the unwavering love of His church in times of need.

At the close of the church service, the Lord's people began to collect their belongings. Jorge, the former boxer whom Julio and Marco had met on their treacherous journey to America, was among them. He emerged from the crowd as they made their way toward the exit, approaching Julio. His heart ached for Vladi.

"Dr. Rivera, I must speak with you," Jorge implored. "Please put me in contact with Vladi. I want to assist any way I can," he said with genuine concern.

"Jorge, brother, thank you for your desire to help out."

Jorge took Julio by the arm and guided him into a quiet alcove where they could speak privately, away from the other church members who were still milling around. "What can you tell me about the situation?"

Julio quickly explained that Vladi, along with Marco and his associates, were planning to go down and either try to negotiate Aleksey's release or extract him themselves.

"What do I need to do to help?"

"Well, you can be praying for him. That is the very best we can do," Julio replied. "It is in God's hands."

"I understand that," Jorge said with a nod, "but I want to offer myself to go on this rescue mission. We will get his son back."

Julio was overwhelmed to hear this offer from Jorge. "That is courageous of you, Jorge." Moved by his compassion, Julio put his hand on the man's thick, muscular shoulder. "I know your heart is in the right place, but this situation is complex and dangerous, and I don't know that Vladi would want you to put yourself at risk."

"I'll do whatever it takes," Jorge declared without hesitation. "I'll go and rescue him myself."

Jorge was resolute. "Dr. Rivera," he appealed, his eyes softening as he spoke, "do you remember when the Lord brought us together on our journey to this great country? It was through the kindness of a mysterious Señor Moisés."

Julio nodded. "I remember, of course."

"At the time, we didn't know who had come to our rescue. We later learned that this same Vladi was our generous patron. He gave me freedom and a new life," Jorge said with a grateful smile.

Again, Julio nodded slowly — touched.

"As for myself, I would surely have been killed on the streets of *La Habana* or imprisoned in Cuba. Instead, we stand here together in the Lord's church. I would do anything to repay his kindness.

"I cannot pay his ransom, nor could I pay mine," Jorge said, his voice filled with conviction and passion as he continued. "But I am physically strong. For many years, I used my strength for nothing of value. I fought for money, power, and notoriety — in and out of the ring. Now, I want to use whatever God has given me for a noble purpose."

"I appreciate that, I do. I —"

"I can be a valuable asset to Vladi and the mission. Please, don't turn away my help — I completely understand what I could be walking into."

"You're truly a man of honor, but these cartels are monsters, Jorge — the things they do, the things they threaten to do — you cannot imagine ..."

"Dr. Rivera, I know — and you know too," Jorge insisted. "Growing up where I did in Cuba, I saw the worst of such animals. But I am not so concerned for my own well-being. If my life is of any value to me, it will be to protect the life of my brother in Christ and, Lord willing, to bring home his son."

The words struck a chord in Julio's heart as he listened to Jorge's selfless offer. He could see the passion and conviction in Jorge's eyes. Julio considered this for a moment. He knew he couldn't deny such a determined and lion-hearted man.

He has come so far — what a completely different man than the one we met on the boat from Cuba. He still has fight in him, but at least now he wants to use it for the good of others. Who am I to keep him from doing what he thinks is right? I'll let Vladi decide whether he wants the man's help.

"Please, Dr. Rivera — I'm serious about this."

"All right, I'll put you in touch with Vladi," Julio finally agreed. "Ultimately, it's up to him to decide whether he wants you to accompany him."

Jorge wrapped his strong arms around Julio in a heartfelt embrace.

"You're a true friend, Jorge — and a priceless brother in Christ. There are not many like you."

"Thank you, Dr. Rivera ... thank you," Jorge replied. "Let's help Vladi get his son home."

33

A MASON JAR

The wind was intense as an afternoon thunderstorm blew through Kingston's suburbs. Trees and power lines swayed beneath the heavy rainfall, thunder shook the air, and threatening flashes of lightning lit up the sky.

A firm knock came at the door of the Rivera residence.

"Honey, can you answer that?" asked Jhas.

Marco opened the door to see a tall man with such a neat appearance that scarcely a single wrinkle was visible in his clothes.

"I'm Detective Inspector Cato," the man said, introducing himself and flashing a badge. "I'm looking for a J ... J-Has Campbell."

"Hello, I'm Jhas," came her melodious voice from behind Marco. "It's pronounced 'jazz,' like the music. And it's Jhas Rivera now," she added. "This is my husband, Marco."

"It is a pleasure to meet you ... Mr. Rivera." Cato's words slowed as his eyes fell on Marco. Cato instantly recognized the face of the man standing before him.

Something in the manner of the man's pleasantry made Marco's blood run cold ... a certain glint in the man's eyes. Marco mustered a nod and a forced smile.

"Marco, why don't you let the man in? He's getting soaked out there," Jhas said hospitably.

"Oh, yes. Uhm ... do come in," Marco invited him with some reluctance.

Cato wiped his feet on the welcome mat and stepped inside. Marco closed the door behind him.

"What's this about, Detective?" Jhas inquired in her usual cheery manner. "You know, I did run a stop sign one time. I was so ashamed, but I paid the ticket. Haven't missed a stop sign since."

"Yes, ma'am, there's a reason they're called stop signs and not 'suggestion signs,'" Cato responded dryly. "But that's not why I'm here."

Marco remained stone-faced, while Jhas gave Cato's remark a tiny giggle, just to be polite.

"You used to work as a travel agent, yes?" Cato inquired.

"Oh, yes, loved it," Jhas replied. "I went to school to be a nurse, but I always said the travel business was much more enjoyable than emptying bedpans and ... you know."

"You worked at Ultimate Destination Travel in downtown Kingston, yes?" At her nod, Cato continued. "And how long has it been since you worked there?"

"Oh, a long time. Years ago. Not since Marco and I married," she answered enthusiastically, without a hint of guile. "Would you like some coffee, Mr. Cato?"

"Detective Inspector Cato," he corrected her gently. "And no, thank you."

"Yes, sir, uh ... Detective Inspector Cato. So, what can we help you with?"

"I have several questions about an incident that occurred in the past at your former place of employment."

"Well, go ahead, of course," Jhas said, eager to be helpful.

"Were you working at the travel agency at the time of Miguelito Cervera's death?" Cato asked.

"Oh ... yes. I mean I wasn't there when it happened, but I had worked earlier in the day." Her tone instantly turned somber. "He was such a sweet man."

Marco turned pale, and his heart sank to his stomach. His initial unease with the man registered in his mind. He felt like he would be sick and considered making an excuse to dart into the bathroom.

No, that's too suspicious — besides, upsetting or not, I need to hear everything.

"I'd like to ask you some questions about that if you don't mind," Cato continued.

"Sure. I'll tell you what I know," Jhas said modestly. "Please, have a seat. I — I know you said you didn't want any coffee right now. Can I offer you some iced water or tea?"

"Is that sweet or unsweet tea?" Cato asked as he and Marco took a seat at the kitchen table.

"Any way you like it. Honey, would you like some tea too?"

"Sure," Marco croaked out. He was intensely stressed, and his throat was feeling dry. Something to drink would help.

Across the table, Cato noticed Mr. Rivera's discomfort, although his stony gaze betrayed nothing.

"Mr. Rivera, what kind of work do you do?"

Marco was caught off-guard by the turn of the inspector's attention. His immediate reaction was to question the investigator's motives. *Why does he want to know what I do? Is he just being polite? Or is he digging?*

Marco thought for a second about how to answer. It came across like he wasn't sure what he did for a living. "I'm an ... attorney?"

"Oh? Another man of the law like myself," Cato replied with obvious pride and approval. "What kind of law?"

"Immigration law," Marco answered curtly.

"Oh, really?" Cato pressed, "Here in Kingston?"

"That's right," Marco said, his voice evening out a bit.

"Which firm do you work with?" Cato shot back smoothly.

"I'm, uhm, independent." Marco wished he'd stop prying. Thankfully, Jhas brought three glasses of iced tea to the table in mason jars, providing an interruption that ended the questioning.

"Look at that. I haven't seen tea served in old-fashioned mason jars in forever," Cato remarked. "How delightful."

"Yes, sir. I went to nursing school in North Carolina. That's the way everyone does it there."

Cato nodded, punctuating an end to the commentary about glassware. He immediately snapped back into full official mode, pinning his eyes back on Jhas.

"Was there anyone you could think of who might have had the motive to kill Mr. Cervera?" Cato got right to the point.

"Oh no, Detective ..."

"Inspector Cato." He finished the sentence for her.

"No, no. Mr. Cervera ... we called him 'Michael' ... he was the nicest man. He was always entertaining important people. Business, you know."

"Yes. We are aware of Mr. Cervera and his ... business," Cato said, clearing his throat gruffly.

"Yes, so ... I understand that a lot of his business was hush-hush, kind of secret. He kept that office in the travel agency because he had friends in high places."

"Like the prime minister?" Cato asked.

"Exactly," Jhas answered with some delight that Cato knew that fact.

Cato went on. "So, what do you remember about the day 'Michael' was killed?"

"Oh, it's a day I'll never forget. In fact, that was the day I first laid eyes on my honey," Jhas turned loving eyes to Marco and put her hand on his. "He visited the travel agency to get some passport photos done."

Marco winced internally. *Did she have to tell him about the passport photos? Please stop, Jhas. Please.* He silently wished he could somehow derail this conversation.

"Is that a fact?" Cato asked, looking over at Marco — this time staring at him even more intently. Marco wanted to make himself invisible, though he kept a cool, collected outer appearance. *Oh Jhas, what are you doing to me?*

A tremendous clap of thunder suddenly shook the house, then rolled off in the distance. Jhas jumped. "Woo, that was a big one!" She looked at the men and gave a nervous giggle. Cato was steely, as though he had heard nothing — but, of course, he had heard everything.

"Mrs. Rivera, since I now know that you will remember some of the details about the victim and that unfortunate day, would you mind if I follow up with you again later? If I stay here much longer, that fording down the road is likely to flood."

"Oh no, not at all. I'd be happy to do anything I can to solve that murder. If I could get my hands on whoever did that ..." She didn't finish the statement but made an angry face.

As Cato stood up to leave, he swung his arm out just enough to knock Marco's jar of tea off the table. It landed on the floor with the crash of breaking glass.

"I am so sorry, ma'am! Let me help you clean this up. Please forgive me."

"It's not a big deal. Just a mason jar. I buy them by the dozen," Jhas remarked as she pulled out a trash can and a broom.

"Do you have any paper towels?" Cato asked, already kneeling over the spill. Jhas pulled the whole roll off the dispenser and passed it over the table.

Cato wiped up tea and melted ice cubes with one sopping paper towel, then reached for another. With it, he reached for a chunk of the glass jar, specifically taking a piece of the rim from which Marco had been drinking moments earlier. He wrapped it in the paper towel and then turned away from Marco and Jhas toward the trash can with both paper towels in hand. He dropped the dripping paper towel into the trash, simultaneously slipping the other with the broken glass into his pocket.

"Well, it looks like I've caused you enough trouble for one day," Cato apologized again. "I'll just be heading out now. It looks like the rain is clearing, but if it's still falling further up the hill, I may have to swim back to the office."

"No need to rush off," Jhas said.

Marco just wished the detective inspector would hurry up and get out of their house, and that Jhas would quit running her mouth. His nerves were about to short-circuit.

"I'll just let myself out," Cato offered, still feigning embarrassment. "I must get back to the office, but you've been most helpful."

Exercising good manners, Marco got up and let him out the door. Cato turned and looked at Marco again, taking his time, and studying Marco's face.

"Thank you, Mr. Rivera. We'll be talking."

Marco didn't know whether it was what Cato said or the way he said it, but he didn't like how that sounded. Not one bit.

34 THE COFFIN

Aleksey languished in a stupor inside the sweltering hovel. He was untied but guarded by Cucuy's men, who were leering smugly. The still, thick air was filled with the acrid smoke from their cigarettes. It hovered over them like a toxic cloud.

Crumpled in the corner, Aleksey struggled to hold onto consciousness, his mind flickering in and out of awareness in a haze of pain. Perspiration dripped down his dust-mottled face. Every inch of his skin was slick with sweat and grime, the oppressive heat seeping into his bones. His battered form was racked with marks from his injuries and the cumulative agony from wounds inflicted upon him since his capture. Each beat of his heart caused the wounds to throb, a constant reminder of his grim predicament.

A rustling noise caught his attention. Through his burning, dirt-caked eyes, Aleksey could see the flap over the doorway swing open. Cucuy stormed in with three of his most brutal henchmen. Aleksey summoned all his strength to sit upright, but his body felt weak and heavy. He was determined to project a façade of strength and confidence in front of his captor, but it was becoming more difficult with each passing moment.

He must not know the extent of my weakened state, Aleksey vowed. *I do not want Cucuy to sense it or think he is getting the better of me.* Aleksey had no idea what Cucuy had in store for him, but he was resolved not to show any signs of weakness.

Every time the man came in, Aleksey's heart would race. The mere presence of Cucuy put him on edge. The guy was volatile and an absolute psychopath. Aleksey never knew what to expect when Cucuy entered. He was a mercurial monster, capable of lashing out with psychotic threats of violence, then flipping in mere seconds to exude a disarming charm. The visit could go either way — it could be another round of torture, or it could be a seemingly polite and reasonable chat. By all appearances, Aleksey had a bad feeling that things were about to get worse.

The men carried a well-crafted, wooden coffin — a six-sided death box. Without a word, they set it on the ground at Aleksey's feet. This didn't look good. His heart sank as he felt the gravity of this foreboding addition to his already dismal situation.

The wooden box seemed to exude ominous energy, almost alive with some dark force. Aleksey's ears started ringing. Some kind of oncoming shock, maybe? This felt oddly surreal, a walking nightmare from which he couldn't escape. By the look in Cucuy's eyes, Aleksey firmly believed his torment was about to reach new heights, perhaps its finale.

"Tie his hands behind his back," Cucuy commanded, his voice cold and emotionless. "We're leaving."

The men moved to obey. They pulled Aleksey to his feet and wrenched his arms behind his back, binding them tightly. He fought to keep his wrists turned outward, hoping to leave more slack in the ropes, but it was useless. He was at the mercy of Cucuy and his men, who forced his wrists inward and bound him as tightly as possible. For now, though, Aleksey focused on trying to talk his way out of this situation.

"What happened to our business relationship? When do I start?" Aleksey asked with a croaking and raspy voice while trying to keep a brave face and sound nonchalant.

"You took too long," Cucuy snapped back dismissively. "Things have changed."

Some business partner, Aleksey thought wryly. *I think I would have a hard time working with him.*

Aleksey could only shake his head in disbelief. If he'd ever foolishly thought that he could trust Cucuy, to make a deal with the devil and come out unscathed, how wrong he would have been.

"You are a monster," Aleksey whispered, his voice dripping with disdain.

"Ah, but what a glorious monster I am," Cucuy replied with delight, a twisted smile playing on his lips.

Aleksey thought he noticed a trace of white powder under Cucuy's large, square nose. Not surprising that Cucuy had been lying about supposedly overcoming the vices that had gripped others in his profession. Cucuy might be a hypocrite, but his fearsomeness was all real.

Aleksey could feel the cold, clammy grip of horror squeezing his chest, slowly suffocating him as if the walls of the coffin were already closing in around him. His mind swarmed with dreadful imaginings of impending doom — how it would feel to be entombed within that coffin, the lid slamming shut, sealing him in darkness. He imagined being trapped, alone, and at the mercy of this sadistic monster. A mocking chorus of laughter from Cucuy's imps echoed in his mind as he sensed the last vestiges of life slipping away. He was a dead man walking, and there was nothing he could do to change his fate.

After tying Aleksey, Cucuy and the other men grabbed bulging burlap sacks. Aleksey speculated it was food, but he couldn't tell what else it was — perhaps other supplies. Then, Cucuy and his men left the shack with Aleksey and the coffin in tow. By all appearances, he was destined to be in that box before the day's end.

They trudged down the trail away from the village. The rocky path beneath

Aleksey's feet felt like it was moving, shifting, and trying to trip him with every step, a metaphor of his life these past two weeks.

Along the way, Aleksey caught a glimpse of the farmer who had been kind to him. The man looked up from his work and met Aleksey's eyes. The man's visage was laden with sadness.

Is it sadness for himself or for me? Maybe both.

Aleksey felt a pang of regret that he had not sought the man's help while he was being held in the village, but this was the first time he had seen him since they arrived. He knew it was a futile thought.

He is in just as tough a situation as I am — just as trapped. There was probably nothing he could have done, and it could have put his life in danger if I had asked for his help, Aleksey reasoned.

The farmer's sorrowful gaze lingered on him — it felt like a harbinger of things to come. With the man still staring at him, Aleksey turned his head forward again, his eyes fixed on the men struggling to carry the coffin. *Something seems off about this,* he assessed. *Their arms are pulled low, and their muscles are taut like the coffin is heavy. And when they set it down, it made a solid thud rather than the hollow sound of an empty coffin.* Aleksey was curious, but he didn't dare ask any questions.

The criminals and their cargo descended deeper into the dark jungle, the dense foliage reaching out like grasping hands to ensnare him. The jungle was a treacherous maze. Aleksey dodged low-hanging branches and thick vines that tangled underfoot. He stumbled often, his strength sapped by the heat. But the men pushed on.

As the distance dragged on, Aleksey struggled to keep up. When he tripped over a fallen log and collapsed on the ground, the man behind him kicked him with his steel-toed boot, sending a jolt of pain through Aleksey's otherwise half-numb body. Another spat at him, hitting Aleksey's shoulder, relishing the show of power.

Even though every muscle in his body ached with exhaustion, Aleksey struggled to his feet quickly to keep going. Resistance would only invite more punishment. He knew what these men were capable of, and he didn't want to tempt their brutality.

Eventually, they reached the battered gray Toyota pickup at the top of the gravel road. Aleksey's mouth was so parched from the heat and lack of water that he felt as if he were choking on sand. For days, he had hoped to get out of the stifling shack, but he was not so happy about the situation he found himself in now. Strangely, he longed to be back in the village, in the cramped, dilapidated hovel where he had been held. Compared to this it would be a godsend. He watched as the men loaded the coffin into the truck bed.

"Climb up and sit on the coffin," they ordered. Aleksey stared at them briefly before tilting his head to remind them that his hands were bound. Annoyed, three men grabbed Aleksey roughly and shoved him onto the truck, face down on his stomach. He gasped as the impact on his ribs knocked the wind out of him.

"I'll take it from here," he told the men as two of them climbed into the truck bed with him. Despite his remark, they hoisted him atop the coffin before covering his head with a black hood. Aleksey couldn't help but feel a sense of panic rising within. Sweat stung his eyes, and he struggled to catch his breath. The heat was suffocating, and when he tried to move his head around to get some fresh air, it just made him feel even shorter of breath.

Flashbacks from his time in Afghanistan flooded Aleksey's mind. Strangled cries and dry earth spitting into the air as bullets chewed up the ground, the strange quietness and slow-motion of it all as he woke up tied to a drainpipe, his face hooded in darkness, with the sound of water dripping nearby ...

No, now is not the time for that. He tried to shake off those thoughts.

Unfortunately, some psychological triggers were hard to suppress, and they didn't care whether it was a good time to show up. His mind began to swirl. He battled to keep his panic in check, focusing on regulating his breathing using a technique a Soviet army psychologist had taught him. Slowly, his racing heart began to calm. He knew he needed to keep a clear head if he wanted to have any chance of escaping, although the odds seemed slim. He just hoped that a chance would come before it was too late.

The two men who rode in the back with him had no idea what was happening to Aleksey and, even if they did, would not have cared. They'd never asked about his background, and he assumed they wouldn't even know where Afghanistan was, let alone about the Soviet campaign there. Despite Cucuy's previous acts of courtesy, the driver and Cucuy, riding in the cab, were equally indifferent at this point.

The truck rumbled to life, and Aleksey braced himself as he was transported toward an unknown fate. He would get out of this nightmare, or die trying.

Aleksey strained his ears, trying to piece together any bits of conversation between his captors, hoping to get some clue about what was happening. Despite his efforts, their words were muffled and indistinguishable, lost in the cacophony of the truck's engine and the crunching of tires against the gravel road.

What were these men planning to do with him? Where were they taking him? The thought of being executed was becoming increasingly plausible. But if that was the plan, why not just pull the trigger and be done with it? The idea of a bullet being the swift end to his life seemed almost preferable to the unknown fate that awaited him.

The ride out of the highland jungle was as treacherous as it was endless. The truck pitched and rolled over the rough roads, each bump sending a fresh wave of pain through Aleksey's already aching body.

Aleksey rode across the plains of the Yucatan's northern coast unprotected in the open truck bed. He felt his body wilting under the scorching direct sun, which only amplified the thirst that clawed at his throat. Sweat and fear commingled in a stifling mix. He wondered how much more he could bear.

At last, they arrived at the docks of Frontera, and Aleksey was unceremoniously unloaded from the truck, along with the mysterious coffin. As they walked, the hood still covering his face, Aleksey tuned his senses to gauge his surroundings.

He could hear the gentle lapping of the water, but these sounds were now terrifying. The eerie cries of seabirds overhead seemed to mock his hopelessness. The cold metal of a gun barrel remained pressed against the back of his neck, a persistent reminder that his life was in their hands.

He could feel the change in the surface beneath his feet as they walked across gravel and shell. Then wooden boards of the dock creaked underfoot.

Are we getting on a boat? he guessed. *Oh, no ...*

Aleksey knew he was being taken on a boat, but he was sure it was not for a leisure trip. The men transferred him to the *Skipper Dan*, which had been kept safely at the port in a protected harbor at the mouth of the Rio Grijalva.

Cucuy's men kicked Aleksey's feet from under him. He was thrown to his knees alongside the coffin, the omen of his own death looming before him. Then they shoved him backward onto his rear against the gunnel and tied him where the life raft had previously been stowed, leaving him to contemplate his fate as they prepared to get underway.

The minutes ticked by. The familiar sound of the Skipper Dan's twin diesel engines roaring to life, once a source of thrill and adventure for Aleksey, now rang like a death knell in his ears. The low chugging sound as they idled was like the steady beat of a funeral drum.

This is bad, he thought. Aleksey's imagination ran wild with the terror of being sealed in the coffin and tossed overboard to drown. His heart sank as he realized that he was completely at their mercy with no way out. He was a doomed soul hurtling toward his fate. He had never felt so alone — so utterly helpless.

The boat plowed through the waves, seemingly taking Aleksey further and further from any chance of salvation.

35

THE HEAVENS DECLARE HIS GLORY

The briny scent of the sea filled Aleksey's nostrils, a bitter reminder of the vast expanse of water that lay between him and safety. It made him feel small and insignificant. The sea, a monstrous, unforgiving, inky black void, taunted him with its infinite depth, reminding him that he was subject to powers beyond his control.

Regret gnawed at Aleksey's mind as he lamented every decision he had ever made that led him to this moment. He bemoaned missed opportunities to bargain more with Cucuy. Aleksey replayed their conversations in his mind, wondering if there was anything he could have done differently. Maybe he could have manipulated Cucuy, somehow convinced him, or possibly even found a friendly side to him ...? *Cucuy? Friendly? Ridiculous!* — Aleksey realized he wasn't even thinking rationally.

Time dragged on. Aleksey lost track of the hours while his anxiety only grew.

Meanwhile, he appreciated finally being able to inhale some of the cooler ocean air that found its way under his hood, clearing his head and allowing him to breathe better.

The men ignored him as though he were a lifeless object, talking casually amongst themselves as if he weren't even there. Maybe they already considered him dead and were acting as such, their nonchalance like a macabre dance around his inevitable demise.

It does not matter what you say in front of a dead man, Aleksey told himself wryly.

Yet Aleksey always kept his ears attentive and his senses sharp. *Anything could be an opportunity to get out of this. I cannot let it pass me by.*

Eventually, he sensed that night had fallen. *Maybe they are waiting until dark to do their dirty deed?*

Without warning, the black hood was yanked off his head — the man who did it stared at him for a moment. Aleksey's heart raced.

This is it, he thought.

Instead, the man led Aleksey to the head and untied him so he could relieve himself. It was a welcome chance to stretch his aching limbs. He splashed his face and lapped up some water from the lavatory to slake his thirst. Aleksey couldn't help but think of the irony in being given this small freedom before meeting his end at the hands of these men. Even the mujahideen in Afghanistan had been known to grant a small kindness before carrying out a death sentence.

I must escape, Aleksey told the reflection in the cloudy mirror. But there was nowhere to go. *These fools are at sea without even a lifeboat,* he scoffed.

A lot of good my military training does. I cannot overpower four men. In his best days, Papa could take them all. That would be a sight, Aleksey thought with dry amusement.

Vladi was a formidable man who could have overpowered their captors in his prime, and Aleksey found second-hand pride in that thought, getting lost for a moment in the reverie.

Even now, I cannot match my father's strength in his younger years, but still, I can outsmart these dull-headed goons. His mind was the only tool he had left. Taking one more glance in the mirror, he sighed and resigned himself to submission for now.

The smuggler pointed for him to take his place again on the deck. Aleksey slumped back against the gunnel. He tossed Aleksey a bottle of cool water and a couple of rolled-up masa tortillas filled with cold cabrito.

Ah, all the luxuries of home, Aleksey mused, too hungry to care about how it tasted. Although, the thought crossed his mind that this may be the last taste of anything he would ever experience in his lifetime.

As the night wore on, nothing happened. They didn't land anywhere, and the men on board eventually grew quiet, leaving only the occasional murmur of small talk. They didn't bother putting the hood back over his head. It was a small relief, but one Aleksey clung to nonetheless.

Aleksey knew this vessel from bow to stern. After all, it was his boat and one he'd spent countless hours on in happier times. He listened to the powerful thrumming of the engines and tried to gauge their speed. He judged they were cruising at nearly thirty knots, a fast pace for the *Skipper Dan*.

I hope they don't break my boat. It was a sour and relatively petty thought, but Aleksey couldn't help but feel even more violated that these Neanderthals haphazardly operated the vessel he had maintained with such meticulous care.

Aleksey racked his brain for a plan, none of which seemed plausible. He searched for anything he could use as a weapon or a tool, but he had nothing. He was outnumbered and outgunned. It seemed like there was no way out.

What are my options but to sit and wait for them to kill me? There must be a way to either take control of the vessel or maybe signal for help.

His thoughts turned to his father and the lessons he had taught him about resilience and determination, even in the short few years they had spent together. He owed it to himself and to his father to fight until the end.

The night stretched out before Aleksey. He looked up at the bright stars scattered across this clear sky, twinkling like distant beacons of hope. The same constellations he'd admired some nights ago stood watch over him again. He felt a sense of wonder and awe at the sheer scale of the cosmos.

Perhaps this was the last night of his life. Not knowing whether he would ever see them again, he mentally traced the lines of the Bears, the Dragon, and the Hero, and soaked in the faint glow of the galaxy dust. He knew them all by name, having studied their paths with a scholar's dedication. A sense of calm descended over him.

How beautiful, Aleksey admired. *If this is the work of a Creator, as Tetya and Papa always say, He is quite the exquisite artist.*

Being a student of celestial navigation, Aleksey tried to piece together any clues from the stars. He determined they were moving in an eastward direction. *But to where? And why?* He wondered what could be waiting for him there.

The *Skipper Dan* continued onward with no changes in direction or speed. Eventually, Aleksey's fixation on the enchanting beauty of the night sky was broken by the aching he felt in his neck.

He stretched out on the deck alongside the coffin, an ever-present reminder that death was but an arm's reach from where he was now. Even so, the stars provided a comforting blanket that lulled him into a deep sleep under their distant light.

36

THE LONG ARM OF THE LAW

Winston Cato was a lone wolf — he was used to working solo, isolated in his pursuit of justice. He thrived on that solitude. He knew that the law was under attack in the Cervera case, and now he felt he was the only one who cared about bringing the killer to justice.

Cato often imagined himself to be the solitary crusader with his convictions, but not without cause. He had seen it all — the corruption, the greed — too much to trust the system. His blood boiled at the thought of the incompetence and apathy that allowed criminals like Marco Rivera to roam free for so long, endangering the innocent. This case had gotten under his skin in a way that few others had. The rest of the world seemed to be moving on, oblivious to the magnitude of offenses that had gone unpunished.

He stared at the evidence before him, a sense of urgency and frustration building inside him. Fate seemed to have brought him to this case. Cato knew it had the potential to change everything, to right the wrongs of the past, and to make sure that justice was served. He wasn't about to let it slip through his fingers.

We cannot be delayed another year or two while results come back from the lab. How many more innocent lives might be lost while we wait for the slow-moving wheels of justice to turn? The thought gnawed at Cato's gut. *Not on my watch*, he vowed.

Cato seethed with impatience as he took the weight of sole responsibility heavily on his shoulders. Long delays on this DNA analysis were unacceptable, an affront to his sense of duty. This case had grown cold once before because of bureaucratic red tape. He couldn't bear the notion of a cold-blooded killer remaining on the loose. He moved with the precision of a well-oiled machine to ensure it didn't happen again.

Cato fancied himself a living, breathing juggernaut of justice — no obstacle could stand in his way. Determined to cut through the endless layers of incompetence and delay, Cato used every ounce of his influence to move things along. He pulled every favor he had and called every marker owed to him.

He even went directly to the superintendent of London's Homicide and Serious Crime Command, demanding immediate action.

"I'm sure you can appreciate the urgency of the case," Cato told him. "We potentially have a serial killer roaming our streets. We have a suspect already in custody. But there may be another who has been right under our noses — ten years — if you can imagine that! I would put my badge on the line for this one," Cato added, underscoring his vehemence. "This warrants immediate attention — not another one or two years. It will be a miscarriage of duty of the highest order if we neglect to act with expediency and get this DNA analyzed now."

The superintendent was a steely-eyed figure himself, a man with a reputation as hard as the city he served. The man promised to do what he could to help, but even with his connections, Cato knew it was a long shot.

For that reason, Cato took matters into his own hands. The DNA analysis was a matter too urgent to leave to chance. He wouldn't settle for anything less than excellence, and the only way to achieve excellence was to do it himself.

Ignoring protocol, Cato swabbed the evidence from Marco's glass with a surgeon's precision and expedited it to the lab, ensuring that there would be no mistakes or delays.

While he waited on the results report, Cato followed up on other loose ends with burning, relentless determination. He worked tirelessly to build a case, pushing himself to the brink of exhaustion. He barely slept, and he ate on the run, while his head swirled with ideas and possibilities.

Consumed with the thoughts of catching this fugitive, Cato's bloodshot eyes assiduously pored over every scrap of evidence including crime scene report minutiae that seemed insignificant. What he found compelled him to follow every lead and pursue every avenue with unyielding fervor. Every detail mattered, and he refused to let anything slip through the cracks in his quest for the truth.

With each piece of evidence he uncovered, Cato surged with a renewed sense of purpose. He saw the darkness that had lurked just beneath the surface, waiting to be exposed. And he knew he had a duty to bring it all to light and put Rivera behind bars. As he dug deeper, he found himself unraveling a web of lies and deceptions that only reinforced his suspicions.

First, there was JAMBAR, the Jamaican Bar Association, a reliable source of information on registered attorneys. He combed through their registry, yet there was no Marco Rivera listed as an active attorney. His gut told him that something was amiss. Cato's intuition was like a sixth sense that never failed him.

It was his half-second of hesitation in answering — I knew he was hiding something. Cato thought smugly. He reflected on their conversation in the Riveras' home. It was a small detail, but it raised a red flag and sparked a chain reaction of questions in the mind of the seasoned detective.

A man of the law, hmmm? Why did Rivera lie about his occupation, and being an attorney, at that? If he was connected to this murder and trying to play it cool, why slip up with such an amateur mistake? Nerves?

These questions vexed the detective, reminding him once again that the world was full of deceit and treachery. He was a man who had seen the worst of humanity, and he knew that when someone was hiding something, it was usually for a bad reason.

Marco had lied, and Cato was left to wonder what other lies he had told. *What else is Marco Rivera hiding?*

Next, he pulled the plates on the compact truck driven by the Rastafarians he'd seen Rivera conversing with on the street in front of the travel agency.

These Rastafarians are a thorn in the side of the law. Cato ground his teeth. To him, they were a reminder that Jamaica was never truly under control.

Whether Rastafarians should be allowed to cultivate and consume cannabis for "religious purposes" had always been a matter of public debate in Jamaica. Nevertheless, Cato knew the law down to the letter, and while some of his colleagues might turn a blind eye to the odd spliff now and then, there were absolutely no provisions for anyone to export marijuana commercially from Jamaican shores.

This chafed Cato in two respects. First, to him, the law was absolute. His convictions on this were unshakable. He believed that his duty as a servant of the law was to impose it upon all who dared to cross its boundaries, no matter how insignificant the transgression.

Second, illegal drugs were a scourge in Jamaica. It was a systemic blight that had infected every part of society, and he considered cannabis a gateway drug leading to nothing good. He aimed to eradicate this plague from the streets of Jamaica, no matter the cost.

Cato was a man of principle. He'd always had high regard for Ronald Reagan, whose ideas resonated with him. Cato lived by the former American President's words: "We must reject the idea that every time a law's broken, society is guilty rather than the lawbreaker. It is time to restore the American precept that each individual is accountable for his actions."

Cato embodied that statement in his work. For him, this was no less true for Jamaica. He was fueled by his strong resolve to rid Kingston of the drug dealers and other scum criminals he believed were lurking on nearly every corner. He wouldn't rest until they were brought to justice — until every last one was locked away for good. He saw himself as a soldier in the war against drugs, a warrior fighting to protect the people of Jamaica and bring down those who profited from the misery and vices of others.

Lives were utterly destroyed by illegal drugs. Family problems and unemployment were worsened by the heavy use of cannabis and other substances — an epidemic across Jamaica, especially Kingston — and Cato abhorred the abuses. It defined his life's story, and he would stop at nothing to put an end to it.

This Rivera case had Cato firing on all cylinders, which is why he was willing to make an exception and break protocol in getting the DNA analyzed. The wait was tormenting him, but he had done all he could.

Ten agonizing days later, the DNA report from Scotland Yard landed on his desk. *That was record time.* Cato scooted forward in his office swivel chair with a satisfied grunt. Had his shortcut paid off? Cato's heart raced as he tore open the envelope. Despite his effort to remain calm, his hands grew clammy. His breath grew short as his eyes moved over the pages as fast as he could read. And then, just like that, he had his answer ... and it was crystal clear.

37

BREAKING THE BLOOD CURSE

The man called Cato was a paradox — a man who lived between two worlds, torn between a despised legacy and the desire to be something more. He was a complex and troubled soul, driven by a fierce sense of justice and a deep-seated need to distance himself from the shadow of his father's deeds.

For Cato, the act of upholding the law was not just a duty, but a way to prove to the world and to himself that he was decent, upright, and worthy of respect — the polar opposite of his father.

As Cato walked through the bustling streets of Kingston, his mind wandered back to his childhood. He had always known that his family was different from others. For one thing, the blood of the Shower Posse ran thick in his veins and, growing up, no opportunity was ever wasted to remind him of that. He was born the illegitimate son of a notorious drug lord, known to all as Dadda, a man who commanded fear and respect in equal measure. Dadda was responsible for a long list of atrocities that had stained the streets of the city with blood.

Cato knew firsthand how West Kingston could chew people up and spit them out. Savage brutality left a stream of broken lives, broken hearts, and broken bodies. It was a harsh reality that he had come to accept. The garrison communities of West Kingston were places where hope was a luxury few could afford, where danger waited around every corner, and where the shadows held secrets no one dared to uncover.

He thought of the kind and watchful eye of his mother, Cedella. Thanks to her, he had been spared the full brunt of the violence that plagued his family, as she had done her best to shield him from the worst of life's harsh realities. Despite his father's connection to the criminal underworld, Winston had grown up with a sense of safety and security that few others in his family could claim. Cedella had raised him with a fierce love, determined to keep him away from the criminal activities that consumed his father's life. And for a time, it seemed to work.

All of that changed in an instant when the deaths of his preteen half-brother Devon and half-sister Jada shattered his sheltered world, both felled by bullets on the very streets he had been kept from during his earliest years. The violence that had always lurked on the periphery of his life had finally pierced its core. There was nowhere left to hide, no false normalcy left to cling to.

For Cato, their deaths were a wake-up call. The violent reality of his family's legacy came crashing down on him. Devon and Jada were just children, but in the garrisons, the bullets didn't have eyes, nor did they have age limits.

Cato's remaining half-brother Tarone turned to a bitter form of activism, encouraging crime in the name of justice. He was sort of a Robin Hood figure in his own mind, but in reality he was exploiting the anger and frustration of the downtrodden residents of Tivoli Gardens to fuel his own misguided crusade and personal gain.

Meanwhile, their father's suspicious death in prison had left a power vacuum in the Shower Posse. Tarone's street smarts and activism led in only one direction. Soon after Dadda's death, he took up the mantle of his father's criminal enterprises, ascending to the head of the Shower Posse.

For a moment, Winston himself had been at a crossroads. He was forced to confront the question that had always hung over him — would he follow in his father's footsteps or not? Tarone demanded that he join in and stop playing coy. He needed to "step up" — as Tarone put it — and get used to "di big man ting."

His father's untimely death dropped the weight of expectation heavy upon him. Would he join his brother and continue the criminal legacy of his family? He could have followed this course, using his family's criminal connections to carve out his own place in the world. It would have been a tempting proposition for many.

"Come, gwope!" Tarone demanded, implying that Winston was being stupid. "Find your way home."

But such pressure only strengthened Winston's resolve. For him, there was hardly a question. He knew he wanted to break the cycle of violence and crime that had consumed his family and community. There had already been enough heartache, misery, and destruction — he wouldn't be the one to add more to it.

It was a radical choice, one that would change the course of his life forever, taking him down a very different path from Tarone and the rest of his family. Winston wholeheartedly embraced the authority of law and order, turning his back on all but his mother. He'd seen the byproduct of ineffectual law enforcement — indeed, he had lived the results of it.

No more. He would be the one to change the system, even if he had to do it alone. For him, this was the path of redemption for the sins of his family ... past and present.

But even as he took on his new life, Winston Cato was a man plagued by the shame of his heritage. Memories of his criminal father loomed large in his mind. The specter of his father haunted him at every turn and sometimes mocked him in nightmares. The only way he could quiet the voice in his head was by doubling down on his devotion to the law.

The blood coursing through Cato's veins was not so different from that of those he pursued, and that's what scared him the most. As a man living on the edge, Cato was consumed by the conceivability that he might one day fall into the same darkness as his father — that he, too, would cross that thin line and become what he despised.

And so, he ran as hard as he could in the opposite direction — from one extreme to the other, believing there was nowhere in between. You either abided by the law, or you were a criminal. Full stop.

Cato's allegiances were tested and proven on that point. He would have arrested his own flesh and blood ... in fact, he had done exactly that.

It had been a cool night, the kind that awakens the senses and makes one feel alive. But Cato felt nothing — as always, his mind was focused on the job.

In close proximity to the port, the industrial warehouse complex off Marcus Garvey Drive backed up to the May-Pen Cemetery. The graves stood as stark reminders of so many he had known from the Tivoli Gardens garrison who were laid to rest there, including Devon and Jada. It felt as if the ghosts of those who had been lost to the unforgiving streets still lingered in the shadows.

As Cato stepped out of his car and started toward the warehouse, the sea wind whipped sand into his face, stinging his eyes. His vision blurred momentarily, but he rubbed his eyes and scanned the decaying landscape, taking in the rubbish and "grassphalt," where vegetation had sprouted through pavement cracks to reclaim patches of earth.

Storage facilities that once bustled with commerce had long been abandoned, broken into, plundered, and turned into hangouts for drug addicts living on the streets of West Kingston. The skeletal frames of derelict warehouses formed the cavernous walls of alleys, where darkness stretched out like a living thing.

The rusted siding of the warehouses flapped in the howling wind like a chorus of angry ghosts. The sounds of the rustling metal, the random mewling of a feral cat, and the echoes of his own footsteps disturbed the night. The crunch of broken glass and debris under his feet was magnified in the near blackness.

Cato's eyes narrowed as he surveyed his environment. Shadows danced around him as he walked through the forsaken streets. His heartbeat quickened as he got nearer to making his move. He'd been tracking the ruthless drug lord for weeks, gathering intel and preparing for the inevitable showdown.

He was about to do something he'd hoped never to do. It was a dirty and dangerous game, and Cato understood the rules and the risks. Still, the weight of his badge hung in his pocket heavier than ever. Cato had never expected being on the right side of the law to get this personal, though he probably should have. He couldn't back off, though — not now. Brother or not, he'd come too far to let this criminal slip away.

Cato took a deep breath and stepped out into the open — exposed. The city was alive in the distance, with only faint sounds of sirens and far away shouting that were dampened in the night air. But all Cato could hear was his own pulse rushing through his ears as he approached his target. He could feel the tension building in his muscles, the adrenaline surging through his veins.

And then, he saw his mark. His eyes fixated on the towering figure standing at the end of an alleyway. Even in the dark, he could sense the cold, hard glare and the mocking half-smile. Cato stood there for a moment, his chest heaving, as he stared down one of Kingston's most infamous felons.

The Shower Posse was responsible for violence that laid waste to everything in its path, and this criminal beast was at the top of the food chain. At one time in their lives, they had been close, playing together as kids. But tonight they stood on opposite sides of the law.

Now, when he looked at his half-brother Tarone, he saw only a menace, a danger to society, a man who had lost his way. The emotions Cato felt were a tangled mess — anger, sadness, and guilt were all churning inside of him. How had they ended up here? Why did it all have to come down to this?

Cato's heart pounded in his chest, but his face remained stoic and unmoving. His job was to take this man into custody, a sworn duty he couldn't ignore.

"Why yu come here, Winston? What yu think yu gonna do, huh?"

Tarone likely had spotters watching and trailing him to this location, so Cato said nothing to escalate the situation. Plus there were still at least ten yards between Winston and Tarone.

"Yu gon' lock me up and throw away di key? You don' have to do dis, Winston. I'm giving yu a courtesy as a family member."

"Courtesy? What kind of courtesy comes from pushers but the first taste of your poison?" Winston intoned in perfect, clipped sentences.

"Here's di ting, lil' breddah. I am di law here. I'd prefer not to kill you," Tarone warned, trying to appeal to their shared history. "I've watched yu from afar ... same guts and intuition about di street dat our fada had."

Cato felt a wave of resentment at the mention of their father, but he pushed it aside. He knew it was all a lie — a facade of promises that concealed a blood-soaked reality. He couldn't compromise his values or his commitment to the law. There was more than just his brother's freedom on the line — it was his own integrity.

"How about you stop talking and put your han—" Cato demanded.

"Hush. Hush, bredda police man. Yu can put dose traits to better use, workin' wit me," Tarone interrupted. "We can be partners — dis city could be yours, and it wouldn' deny yu anything."

"I told you, put your hands where I can see them," Cato said, his voice hard and unwavering.

Tarone sneered at him, his eyes filled with contempt. "Yu think yu better dan me? Yu just a pawn, Detective man Winston Cato ... puppet on a string. Yu tink yu in control, but yu a zero. Yah jus anadda cog in a broken system."

A surge of anger was rising within Cato, but he kept his emotions in check. He had heard these taunts from countless criminals trying to play with his mind.

"I'm not here to debate the merits of the justice system," he said, his voice steady. "Tonight, I'm the law — here to arrest you."

His half-brother laughed, but there was a hint of concern in Tarone's eyes. He knew that Winston was formidable and that he wouldn't hesitate to use force if necessary.

"Yu don' scare mi, Winston," his half-brother spat. "Yu think yu so tough, so righteous, but yu jus as dutty as di rest of us. Yu got blood on yu hands, jus like our ol' man."

Tarone was throwing every manipulative trick in his direction, but Winston couldn't afford to let his emotions best him now.

"I'm here to do a job, not to debate our family history," Cato replied, his voice hardening.

"Can't run from it either, can yu, little bredda?"

"I am nothing like your father," he said, his voice cold and hard, dismissing the familial connection. "I'm a servant of the law — the law you've broken — and now the bill comes due."

"Look at yuh, even usin' them fancy words now, hidin' away under that big white mon talk," his brother said with a chuckle. "A 'servant' dat's right, exactly, yu is a slave again to a broke, rotted out system —"

Cato continued to let his brother's words roll past him. "You can come quietly, or you can make this harder than it needs to be," he said.

"Yu is nuttn but a coward, little bredda — always have been — jus hidin' under yu mumma dress. Yu tink yu so tough, but yu is nuttn widdout dat badge."

"Enough," he said, his voice low and menacing. "You're under arrest."

Tarone hesitated momentarily, then slowly raised his hands in surrender. Cato moved quickly. There was a certain satisfaction as Cato felt his handcuffs snap shut around the wrists of a known criminal, knowing that he had done his job.

"Yu is nuttn — nuttn but a traitor, turnin' yu back on yu own blood," his half-brother snarled, eyes filled with contempt. "Papa mus' be turnin' in his grave down at May-Pen Cemetery on a night like tonight. Come to tink of it, it's a good ting him dead, because seein' yu like dis wudda certainly kill him."

Cato's heart shattered into a million pieces at those words. He had to admit — if only to himself — that the encounter was tinged with the shame that hung over him, leaving him with a gnawing emptiness inside. He wanted to scream, to lash out, to tell his brother that he was doing the right thing, that he had to uphold the law. But the words died in his throat.

As he led Tarone away, his brother's taunts stung and echoed in Cato's mind. He wondered just a bit if he had made the right choice, betraying his family for the sake of the law. His brother's verbal shots held a kernel of truth that he couldn't ignore. Maybe he was nothing but a pawn, a cog in a broken system. Maybe he was just like his father, tainted by the sins of the past.

Sitting in his favorite cafe over green banana porridge, Cato rubbed his eyes and snapped out of the memory of Tarone's arrest. It had been several years ago, but the pain was still fresh. He knew this battle was far from over. For now ... for now, regrets stayed with him — never letting him forget the price he'd paid for his convictions.

Personally, Cato could live his own life following a strict code of law — that was almost easy for him. The trade-off was that there was no room for leniency and mercy in his world. These were character flaws in his eyes, avenues by which lawbreaking and backsliding could easily worm their way in. The only security against it was the emotionless hand of justice. He couldn't afford to be soft.

Cato was determined to prove to the world that he wasn't just the son of a drug lord, even if it meant sacrificing his own humanity. But the truth was that he was already lost. Hatred and vitriol had poisoned his soul, turning him into a different sort of monster — one nearly as terrible as his family on the other side of the law. Being a prisoner of his own ideals had turned him into a heartless, unfeeling machine.

As the years went by, he watched as his colleagues married and had kids. They formed bonds with each other, something he'd never been able to do. His self-imposed isolation had turned him into a shell of a man, lacking emotion or feeling. He had long ago abandoned any hope of love or companionship, accepting his loneliness as a necessary sacrifice for the greater good. He found solace in his work. All the years had been spent chasing criminals and pushing people away. It was too late now. The damage had been done. In the end, he'd lost sight of what really mattered. He lived a solitary life, lacking meaningful connections, convinced that he could never be anything other than what he was — a man forever alone.

Cato was also a man without vices, or so he thought. He was steadfast and incorruptible, his integrity unshakable. His existence was characterized by privation, isolation, self-denial, and chastity, shunning all forms of amusement and pleasure. He believed in living his life without breaking a single rule, and his devotion to that purpose was evident in every step he took. He lived, breathed, ate, slept, and would die for justice in the form of the law and all it implied.

He had sacrificed every pleasure, every comfort, every relationship, and every joy to uphold the letter of the law and his fanatical devotion to it. His body was a temple of self-punishment, his mind a fortress of rationality, and his heart a frozen lake of detachment.

Whether intentional or not, his home was barren and devoid of any warmth, reflecting the austerity of his own desolate soul. He spent his days poring over legal documents and case files, his only company being the sound of his own breath and the scratch of his pen.

Cato's underlying wounds only seemed to deepen and fester as he grew older. Despite his inner turmoil, Cato was a force to be reckoned with. His steely commitment to justice made him a formidable opponent for anyone who dared to cross him.

While he was feared by the criminal underworld, Cato's peers viewed him in another light. His single-minded obsession alienated him, making him an outcast among fellow law enforcement professionals. He was seen as a zealot, a fanatic, and a lone warrior driven mad by his own quest for redemption. His peers kept their distance from him, repelled by what moved him — his own self-righteousness.

Finishing off his porridge, Cato sighed. It wasn't just about the law, no — deep inside, his conscience told him there was something more, but he had no sense of what to do about it. He paid the bill and got up, heading to his office. There were DNA results calling his name. Once again, he reflected with satisfaction on his work in obtaining them.

Beneath the surface of Cato's stoicism and righteousness lurked a dark desire for vengeance, for retribution, for dominance. Each arrest and conviction was not just a triumph of justice, but a personal victory, a chance to prove himself superior, to inflict pain on those who had dared to cross the line. These served as his validation — stamps of approval on his life — evidence that the proverbial apple did sometimes fall far from the tree.

He saw himself as a hunter, stalking his prey with ruthless efficiency. That hunt for justice had become a war, a self-imposed battle for his own sanity, his own redemption, and his own identity. This was the hidden side that he buried deep within his soul, but which fed his obsession.

He believed that by capturing and punishing every lawbreaker, he could redeem his family name and exorcize the shame that had plagued his soul from birth. It was validation of his self-worth — proof that he was not his father — not even close. This was his way of coping with the crushing self-reproach that consumed him, with the poisoned roots of his family tree that bedeviled him.

But in the end, it was a futile mission — hopeless. He was applying useless salve to hurts that would never heal — wounds that would define him until the end of his days. His heart was a stone, his mind a labyrinth of dark thoughts, and his soul a bottomless pit of despair. His passion had become a curse. This was his drug, and he needed another fix. Cato's obsession had sadly blinded him to everything else, making him a lonely figure doomed to wander the earth in quest of a purpose that would never be realized.

And now, as he went after the elusive Marco Rivera, Cato's obsession had turned into a single, all-consuming goal, to see him punished. He would not rest, he would not relent until he had pinned the charges on his quarry.

Cato's pursuit of justice and Marco's evasion of it had brought them together, entwined in a dance of fate. Cato's destiny was to bring justice to the world — and Marco's destiny was to be brought to that justice. Simple. The corner of Cato's mouth turned slightly upward, the closest he ever got to a smile, as he imagined finally putting an end to this man's criminal ways.

It's time for that shifty Rivera to go down, and go down hard. He has eluded the law for far too long! At his desk, Cato clenched his teeth with a resolute scowl, scanning the DNA results for the hundredth time. *This guy needs to be shackled up for the rest of his natural life like the worthless animal he is.*

A fire burned in Cato's eyes as he stared at the mounting evidence. There was a twisted elation in the thrill of this chase, even if it had begun in earnest ten years too late. After all, justice delayed was still better than no justice at all.

CONFESSION

Vladi booked the first Monday flight to Jamaica for himself, Erik, and Jorge. Julio took them to the airport in his trusty blue Buick. For most of the drive over, he contemplated what he and these men were about to do. Their mission was life or death for those involved. Despite the risks, he knew they had to do it. The weight of the situation hit him hard.

Vladi had something else weighing on his mind — facing Marco again. Julio knew the situation and the two men's history. Recognizing Julio's wisdom, Vladi seized the opportunity to talk about it on the ride to the airport.

"I want to forgive Marco, but ..." Vladi tried to think of a deeper way of expressing himself, but he couldn't come up with anything more than, "... it is not easy."

"Hmmm, I understand your struggle," Julio empathized. "I've had to forgive him also. Let me ask you this — would you rather live with bitterness?" Vladi responded by shaking his head no, as Julio had expected.

"That's the problem. If you don't forgive, it will weigh down your soul and only make you miserable." Julio paused. "Jesus commands us to forgive — He said we must forgive. When the apostle Peter asked our Lord how far he was required to go with forgiveness, the answer he was given was 'seventy times seven.' That is, we shouldn't be limited in our willingness to forgive."

Vladi indicated with a nod of the head that he heard what Julio had to say, but he left the conversation there. Moments later, Julio pulled up in front of the Departures area and got out of the car with the others.

The terminal was a hive of organized chaos. People of various nationalities rushed past each other, wheeling their suitcases, pulling their carry-on bags, and looking at the flight information screens. The air was filled with the sound of chatter, beeping carts, and the occasional announcement over the intercom. But for Julio, time stood still. The airport noise faded into the background as he processed his emotions.

Julio's eyes met Vladi's momentarily, and he could tell his friend was thinking the same thing. This was "do or die," and it was time to find out which. The Russian pulled him in for an uncharacteristic bear hug.

He must be worried if he is hugging me, Julio thought.

The men slapped each other on the back and parted. Julio shook hands with Erik and Jorge, wishing the men success on their mission. Jorge's request to participate had been unexpected, but Julio didn't question his decision at this point. The boxer's commitment was unmistakable.

"I will be praying for you," Julio reminded the men earnestly as he bid them farewell.

As Vladi walked through the airport doors, Julio felt a lump in his throat. This was no ordinary trip — he considered this might be the last time he would ever see his friend. But just as Vladi was about to disappear into the airport terminal, another familiar voice called out.

"*Jefe!*"

Vladi turned in surprise. It was Antonio, speed-walking toward him.

"Antonio, what are you doing here?" Vladi asked in a manner that conveyed his high regard for his foreman.

"*Jefe*, I'm here for the mission — to get Aleksey."

"What?" Vladi was flabbergasted.

"You think I would leave you in a time of need? I'm here to go with you," Antonio proffered, his voice resolute.

He lowered his head and smiled — no further words were needed between the two men. Antonio was a good man, and the trust between them was solid. But Vladi knew he had a family and didn't want this fine man to put himself in danger. Vladi held up a hand and calmly placed it on Antonio's shoulder, pulling him nearer.

"I cannot let you come," Vladi told him sincerely. "What I truly need from you is to stay here and care for your wife and kids and to keep my business operating."

"Someone else can do it, *Jefe*," Antonio insisted. "We have other good men. They have worked with me — I taught them — they know what needs to be done."

"Well, nobody else does it half as good as you, *amigo*," Vladi said.

Antonio's cheeks colored a bit as he heard the praise, and he pursed his lips. He put down the carry-on bag he was holding.

"Someone has to look after Irina. Can I rely on you to do that?" Vladi already knew the answer but phrased it as a question to keep Antonio from pressing the matter.

"You can count on me, *Jefe*." Antonio put his hand on Vladi's shoulder in turn.

"Good man. I will see you when I get back." Vladi wanted to end the matter with a hopeful remark.

"I will be praying," Antonio said, his words weighted with the gravity of the situation. "We all will."

As Vladi and his team finally walked through the airport doors, Julio tried to keep his emotions in check, but his eyes betrayed him as they welled up with tears. The gravity of the situation had fully caught up with him.

The sound of the airport slowly returned to Julio's consciousness as he turned around to leave. He knew whatever awaited them would test their mettle and resolve. As he returned to his trusty blue Buick and drove away, Julio prayed that the Lord would give them success and these brave men would return home safely.

Within an hour, the trio boarded an Air Jamaica flight and were en route to Kingston.

As soon as Julio returned from the airport, he called Marco to let him know the men were on the way. But Marco's mind was elsewhere. Far from his usually confident demeanor, his voice was hollow and laced with tension, distant and distracted — like that of a completely different person. Julio sensed that something was off with Marco, but he didn't push it. Marco wrote down the information regarding what time the men would arrive in Kingston but then turned their conversation to another topic.

His mind was consumed. Since seeing that newspaper story in the *Daily Gleaner*, Marco had been miserable, gnawed by guilt that threatened to destroy him from the inside out. He struggled with what was right or wrong. Now, he wanted to talk — he needed to talk. And Julio's understanding voice on the other end of the line was exactly what he longed to hear.

"There's something I need to tell you, Julio," he said. Marco's words were slow and deliberate. "... something I should have told you long before now — and I don't know how to say it."

Julio's breath caught in his throat. He could tell it was serious.

"What is it, brother?" he inquired gently.

Marco drew a deep breath as if gathering his thoughts. "Remember when I returned to Cuba?" he began.

"Yes — you said it was nerve-racking, but not much else," Julio recalled. "Why?"

"I was desperate, and I thought it was my only way out. But I was wrong. I was so wrong."

"Knowing you, I didn't ask anything beyond what you had to say at the time," Julio said, trying to keep his voice steady. "I expected you to have your reasons."

"I ... I did." Marco hesitated for a moment before continuing. "I unlocked a travel agency after hours to prepare some documents to get past officials, and I was looking for a passport. You know, *inventado*."

"You broke into a travel agency? That's a serious crime, Marco."

"It was ... well ... other things happened. Very bad things."

"I figured if it had anything to do with returning to Cuba, conceivably it had something to do with your safety," Julio said, his voice low. Marco had always been cagey about his return to Cuba, but Julio had assumed that it was simply because of the danger he had faced.

Marco's voice trembled. "What happened was horrible. I can't undo it." He exhaled hard. "I don't know how to say ... I ..."

"Take it easy, Marco. We'll get to it." Julio was reassuring.

"Yeah." Marco paused again. "Well, there was an important piece of that story that I left out, and it has been eating me up inside. I can hardly bear it anymore," he confessed, his voice strained with emotion.

"I was afraid, Julio. I didn't want to get you involved. And I was afraid of what would happen if anyone else knew," Marco said, his voice trembling. "But now, with everything happening, I can't keep it to myself anymore."

"Oh?" Julio asked. His interest was piqued, as was his mounting concern. He knew that whatever Marco was about to reveal was going to be heavy.

"I got cornered in a man's office when he returned that night. There was a brawl, a fight. I was just trying to get out ... and we were wrestling in the dark office. Then I pushed him, and he fell. When I looked, he was struggling but unable to move, and there was blood ... a lot of blood ... He fell onto his own knife."

"You killed someone? Marco, what have you done?" He tried to keep his voice steady as he spoke, but his words came out in a shaky whisper.

"He ... yes, he died, but I didn't kill him. I swear. We fought, and then he fell and ... and really, that's how it happened. But I know it was wrong to not say anything ..." Marco's voice cracked with distress as he recounted this part to his brother — he paused before continuing.

"I ran and was never caught — never even pursued, as far as I know — except ... by my own conscience."

Julio's heart sank at Marco's words. He sighed on the other end of the line, cradling his head in his hands and laying down the phone receiver for a moment. His mind was reeling, and he felt a wave of nausea wash over him.

"Who was the man, Marco?"

"Miguelito Cervera, but everyone called him Michael," Marco said. "He was an important man, and now it's catching up to me."

Julio had known his brother was capable of reckless behavior, but this was beyond anything he could have imagined. He'd always wondered if there was more to the story than Marco had let on before, but he never dreamed it would be so grave.

"Julio, I've never breathed a word of this to anyone before now. And that wouldn't have happened except that now another man is being investigated for the incident."

"Another man? Oh, no," Julio said in a hushed whisper.

"Yes, in this exact case ... He's a homeless man — lives on the streets."

"Back up, back up," Julio said, his mind spinning. "What are you talking about?"

"There have been a number of homicides, and police are looking for a serial killer who's murdering homeless people in Kingston," Marco explained. "They think this incident is connected. I have no idea who's doing these other killings, but if the police charge someone else in this particular death, I know they're wrong. I saw Michael Cervera die. The suspect they've arrested may be a serial killer, but he didn't do this. If I say nothing, he'll take the fall for at least one death he didn't cause."

There was silence on the phone line. Julio didn't know how to respond. His mind raced with a million questions, but he couldn't bring himself to voice them. Julio's heart sank even lower as he thought about the man who was killed. He had a name, a face, and a life beyond that dark office. Marco had taken that all away, even if it had been an accident. And now, years later, another man was being blamed for his brother's mistake.

Marco's actions had far-reaching ramifications. This was so much bigger than Marco's culpability — this was about justice, about truth, about exonerating another man. If he kept silent, a man would be prosecuted and perhaps convicted for a crime he didn't commit. If he spoke up, his brother's life would be shattered, and he would have to face the consequences of his actions. Either way, someone would suffer.

Julio felt as if the ground had fallen out from under him, his own emotions roiling within him as he tried to grapple with the enormity of the situation. He felt horror and dread and sorrow, all mixed in a potent cocktail. But above all, he felt a fierce love for Marco. There was no easy answer, no simple solution. All he could do was promise Marco that they would navigate this together. No matter what, they were brothers, and Julio would be there with him.

When Julio finally spoke, his voice was steady and reassuring. "We'll get through this, Marco." The words were simple, but they held more weight than anything Julio had ever said.

39

BIBLICAL COMPASSION

"Julio, let me state upfront — I am resolved to do what is right — whatever that is. Help me to know what's right."

"Brother, I can't make decisions for you," Julio sympathized with him, realizing this was his brother's battle. "You know, all I know to do is ask, 'What does the Bible say?' Even at that, where do we begin? The police are after a killer, and you know that even if he really is guilty, he's not guilty of this."

"Exactly," Marco said, his tone hushed.

"And you don't want to be the cause of a false accusation. Is that correct?"

"Yes," Marco said, almost whispering, hoping his brother could save him from this moral trap.

"The first thing that comes to my mind is Proverbs 28:13. 'He who conceals his transgressions will not prosper, but he who confesses and forsakes them will receive compassion.'

"This verse calls for confession, indicating that it will be met with compassion. It's a proverb, not a promise — that doesn't make it any less true. It's still God's Word."

"What exactly does it mean?" Marco asked, willing to learn from his brother, who was older in the faith than he was.

"The first part of that verse warns us about concealing transgressions. This happens when we hide them, justifying our sins with excuses and living our lives filled with lies rather than the truth given to us in God's Word. Sin thrives in darkness. Satan deceives men by making it appear you're getting away with sin — and maybe the people around you never know. But when it is time to answer to God, all our deception and lies will be exposed naked before Him."

"I know I have sinned," Marco admitted. "And I know I've rationalized what happened to myself by saying it wasn't my fault. But I also know I should never have broken into that office in the first place."

"I hear you, Marco," Julio empathized. "What really helps is to recognize that all of life is lived within sight of God — even our deepest thoughts, motives, and attitudes. Knowing that changes how we live."

Julio's speech was deliberate and measured.

"To walk with the Lord is to do so with the awareness that you're always before His face. It means a transparent, submissive life — ready to be corrected and willing to be directed. There's no alternative plan and no way to escape judgment. We'll all face this."

"I can't do this on my own," Marco cried.

"True," Julio agreed. "You don't have to, though. You have to remember that God is here for you. We need to listen to Him and trust Him through everything. This is also why we need to be in a healthy church, among people indwelt by God the Holy Spirit. Are you still going to the church you began attending when you got married? You need a pastor who will pray with you and give you sound Biblical guidance."

"No," Marco answered reluctantly. "Well, I visited the church Jhas had been attending before we married. But I have to say, it's not the same as your church. In retrospect, I regret that I scoffed at Pastor Gerardo. Now I can see that he was preaching straight from the Bible. That's rare — even more special and uncommon than I ever imagined."

"I understand," Julio commiserated. "But you do need to find your place in a local church. God doesn't leave His sheep wandering alone."

"I know. I know," Marco humbly acknowledged. "Perhaps I'm more like a stupid sheep than I assumed — I keep finding myself in trouble. But really, even if we had a church already, I'm not comfortable confiding in anyone besides you, brother. That's all I can do for now. No one else needs to know — at least not at this point."

"Well, God knows — we're not hiding anything from Him," Julio reminded him understandingly. "He's given us a verse in the fourth chapter of Hebrews that says, 'And there is no creature hidden from His sight, but all things are uncovered and laid bare to the eyes of Him to whom we have an account to give.' Ultimately, everything will be revealed, Marco. As surely as we're having this conversation today, we will all appear before Christ Jesus to give an account for the deeds of this life, whether good or bad."

"I know it's true," Marco admitted.

"So the good news, Marco, is that God already knows everything," Julio continued. "He won't be surprised like I was. He already knows us better than we know ourselves — you wouldn't be keeping anything from Him either way. He does call us to confession and repentance, though. You have to be honest with yourself and with God. Remember, we belong to a Heavenly Father who is both just and merciful. He knows our failures, and He still loves us. He won't turn you away."

"But what about justice?" Marco asked. "We have a system of justice." His voice trembled. "If I confess —" He left the statement unfinished.

"That's a difficult question," Julio affirmed. "I wish I could tell you that everything will be fine, but the truth is, you've gotten yourself into a grave predicament."

"That's what I'm scared of. My family ... they need me here."

"I understand," Julio sympathized. "We have to trust that God is ultimately in control and that justice will be done in His time. We can't predict the future, and we can't control the actions of others, but we can control our own actions — we take responsibility for our own choices. And right now, we do whatever is right and trust that God will take care of the rest."

"Julio, I'm afraid," Marco told him, speaking frankly.

"Understandably so, brother," Julio commiserated. "Fear of the Lord is the beginning of wisdom. Once we understand that God is real and is in control, we know that He has all power over us, including to condemn or deliver our souls. To keep things in perspective, let's think about what's most crucial. We know we are to fear God over man."

"Okay, so I have confidence that God is perfectly just, but men are not," Marco replied. "I don't know how Jhas will take this news, but there's no way it's good. She'll be crushed."

"I understand," Julio reminded him, listening intently.

"In my imagination, I can almost hear her now, 'I don't even know who you are!' She'll wonder what kind of monster she's married to. Let's not forget that this all happened in the office where she was working at the time. She knew Michael Cervera personally. We never discussed it, but she may have lost a friend that night. She'll never understand what happened. Once she knows, she will always see me as the man who caused Michael's death ... and on the night after we met, no less. I will have ruined everything — my life and her life too! She didn't deserve this."

Julio concurred. "Marriages depend on trust, so discovering your spouse has been harboring secrets can be devastating. Especially something this dark ..."

"What's more," Marco went on, "I'll be convicted for a murder I didn't commit. I've done so much wrong in my life, Julio, but killing Michael Cervera wasn't among those things. With God as my witness, it was an accident. Really, I ... I swear it was an accident, I would never —"

"I understand," Julio said patiently, letting him talk. "I believe you."

Marco was almost frantic now, stumbling over his own words. "But ... but I was in the wrong place, somewhere I shouldn't have been, doing something I shouldn't have done, all of it illegal. The authorities will never believe the truth. If I come forward now, I'm looking at a life behind bars based on a misunderstanding, just so I can feel a clear conscience, just so I can ... what, exactly? What would be accomplished? What would they do to me?"

"You're the lawyer. How do you think it would go?" Julio asked.

"They'll charge me with murder right from the start, for sure, at least second-degree. Plus, Cervera was a well-connected man. The maximum sentence is life in prison. The Jamaicans aren't big on plea bargaining. Best case, I receive an offer and plead guilty to manslaughter and get a reduced sentence of at least four years. Worst case, they don't want to deal with it and find some reason to send me back to Cuba. That's as good as a death sentence."

Julio felt sick at the thought. None of these options were good. He took a deep breath and thought about it.

"Listen, Marco. This is what you need to know, but it doesn't fix your immediate predicament. There's no contest over the gravity of our sin one way or another. By God's standard of righteousness, we all come up short. For the redeemed, our sins — past, present, and future — are all covered by the blood of Christ Jesus. We will stand before God, robed in the righteousness of the perfect Lamb."

"God has forgiven me, this I know — there is no sin in my life not covered at the cross of Christ Jesus. So then, why does this devastation follow me?" Marco begged for answers. "I have been so foolish. I just want this feeling of being stained and broken, this guilt, to leave me — this torture ..."

He kept replaying the events of that night in his mind, thinking about what different choices he could have made. Withholding the truth from Jhas wasn't malicious dishonesty, but his negligence in omitting these significant facts had serious consequences.

"Sin brings suffering. There are still temporal consequences for sin in this world. Two thieves were on either side of our Lord when He was crucified," Julio reminded his brother. "One was repentant, but his confession did not deliver his flesh. He endured the punishment but did so with the promise that Christ Jesus would remember him, and that day, he went to be with the King in Paradise."

"It's not fair to Jhas. She didn't sign up for this," Marco argued.

"But she did," Julio replied instantly. "When she vowed before God and witnesses at your wedding, 'Til death do us part — I do,' she signed up for it — and so did you.

"It may not be fair — I'll grant you that much. But it's one of those things in life that many couples do not anticipate before marriage. What if an accident left her paralyzed, and she required your care for her every need, every hour of every day, for the rest of your life? You didn't know that was going to happen, and you may not feel that's fair, but you did sign up for it."

Marco drew in a sharp breath, close to tears.

"Another way of looking at this is, does she have a right to know? She does, and so do the authorities."

Julio elaborated on this assertion. "I once had a patient with a chronic, debilitating disease that she had found out about before she married. She didn't tell her husband-to-be for fear he wouldn't want her. Her condition progressed, and the truth eventually came out."

"That's horrible," Marco admitted, temporarily jolted out of his own tragic situation.

"Did he have a right to know? Of course, he did. She had deceived him about her physical well-being, which had huge implications in their lives. The question then arose for the husband as to how he would deal with her sin? Would he also forgive her for a legitimate sin that caused him great suffering? Or would he compound her sin with unforgiveness, bitterness, or perhaps retribution? — all for which he would give an account before God."

Marco understood Julio's point in the anecdote but still felt the dread of shame he would endure when the truth was exposed. Jhas would lose faith in him, and rightly so. His honesty would always be in question. He loved Jhas, and he loved her family. They would lose all respect for him. He was sure to be a pariah after disappointing them this way. It left him questioning his worth as a husband and a father.

Marco explained sorrowfully, "It was an accident years ago. I'm not the same man — well, I am, but I'm not. I didn't intend to deceive Jhas by keeping this from her. I just wanted a fresh start."

"I'm sure you didn't intend it that way, but that's what happened. God knew this would transpire, and yet He allowed it to be so. From our vantage point, we don't know why, but He does. And He is trustworthy," Julio reminded him.

Julio felt for his brother — he was aching inside himself. He tried to explain, "My relationship with God will always include aspects I experience on a private, individual, and inward level. It exists between God and me, hidden from the view and knowledge of others. Additionally, there will always be a component of our walk with God that includes other people. It hurts others when we sin."

"Like my son — oh, Nemesio!" Marco cried now, a bitter tear rolling down his stubbled cheek. "The boy is only three years old. What will he think of his father? It's not fair to him."

A haunting memory flashed into Marco's mind of the man he had prosecuted long ago in Cuba for possessing a Bible. He remembered the faces of his wife and children when the man was sentenced — how he had been personally responsible for destroying that family. Marco knew he may not have deliberately committed the crime in question, but he had committed other acts that caused others to suffer unfairly.

"You're right, brother. It's not fair to him," Julio agreed. "When King David committed adultery with Bathsheba and arranged the murder of her husband, his sin affected the lives of people around him. He had to deal with it.

"We know God can bring judgment down on our heads at any time in this world — and David knew his sin deserved judgment. In Psalm fifty-one, we see clearly that he identified sin for what it is — evil. Seeing the gravity of his sin, his only option was an appeal to mercy and grace. He didn't blame God or anyone else. His guilt was personal, and he accepted full responsibility. He didn't tell himself that he was basically a good person who made a mistake. He understood his inherent depravity as intrinsic to his character. This is a true confession."

"I know ... I know," Marco said, sobbing quietly.

Julio continued, "David recognized God's desire for holiness in our innermost being — in our hidden parts. He looks at the heart — it must be true, free from deception or hiding. We don't cover up anything. Ultimately, He knows all. We know what He has said is true, which is why we're compelled to repent. God is not interested in some superficial cleaning. Rather, He desires to purify us on the inside.

"David knew God was willing — He is by nature a forgiving God. David wanted to serve God and please Him. After all, the Bible says he was a man after God's own heart. Convicted of his sin, he was broken and repentant. David wanted restoration, and he recognized God's power to do that."

"This is where I question, is my faith real?" Marco went on, "Am I willing to bear the consequences because that's what God requires? Because if it's not real, I'd be a fool to breathe a word about what happened."

"Marco, it is God who explains your repentance," Julio assured him. "You're on a new path, walking in the light. It's impossible to be saved without first being convinced of your own sinfulness. And we can take comfort in knowing that God chastises His own children for our good. He doesn't bother with the devil's children, leaving them to their own destruction. Their stubbornness and unrepentant hearts are storing up wrath for a day when it is all revealed at the righteous judgment of God."

"Could I just be one of those? Maybe it is my destiny?" Marco asked, questioning his own salvation.

"No, brother. All believers go through struggles, and you are now. I would be more concerned if you weren't torn and troubled about this.

"It's a reasonable assumption that the apostle Paul struggled with reminders of the terrible things he had done before his conversion. Yet, he was the one who wrote to the church in Rome, 'there is now no condemnation for those who are in Christ Jesus.' Perhaps recollection of those awful sins was something God the Holy Spirit applied to work in Paul's heart for the rest of his life, ensuring he would never underestimate the magnitude of his deliverance."

"Yes, but how bad was he really? I didn't realize ... but there's blood on my hands," Marco choked out. "He was Paul, an apostle in the Bible. I'm just Marco."

"Marco, Paul needed forgiveness for serious offenses against both God and man. That forgiveness wasn't withheld from him. Only a few verses later in the same chapter of that letter, Paul made it clear that he considered himself to be a child of God and a fellow heir with Christ Jesus. The 'chief of sinners' was crucified with Christ Jesus, and Paul was a new creature in Him. 'All of the old things have passed away.' The Bible assures us of this.

"A short while later, in the third chapter of Paul's letter to fellow believers at Philippi, he told them that he 'pressed on toward the prize of the upward call of God in Christ Jesus.' He said he did so 'forgetting what lies behind and reaching forward to what lies ahead.'"

"That's just it, brother," Marco said, his voice broken. "What does lie ahead? I'm so confused. I don't know ..."

"God can use our past sufferings to remind us of our dependence on Him, and He can use those past sins to humble us. But you must believe God's Word. He has given us the promise of the Lamb of God who takes away the sins of the world — He bore your sins at the crucifixion. You can have confidence that you have been completely forgiven, brother. What lies ahead for you, and me, and every genuine believer is Christ Jesus, Himself.

"Remember this, our Lord is compassionate and merciful in ways that never diminish His righteousness. He is concerned about our plight — He knows that you're in trouble, and He cares. You're meant to walk with Him right here, right now, in this world. This is all crazy talk to natural men — to unbelievers in the world. But we have a Good Shepherd to whom we run when others would be afraid.

"Is there any safer place than the knowledge that our Lord deals generously with us? He loves His children, and He'll never abandon you, Marco. Amid life's storms, we rest in the knowledge of God's love and sovereign authority."

Julio paused as though he might say something else, but decided this was a good place to leave the conversation.

"Marco, you know I'll be praying with you about this. My heart is grieved."

"Yes, I know. You just keep reminding me — our Lord will lead me in His righteous ways. I need to do what's right ..."

"Yes, you do. I know that you can — and you will," Julio said.

"I will trust Him and follow. I have a little time to think about how that happens."

"Do that — and pray about it. I can't give you all the answers, but God can."

"Right now, we need to get Vladi's son back to him," Marco said.

"Hey, Marco — I love you."

Those words caught Marco off guard, but he didn't hesitate before speaking them back and meaning each one.

"I love you too, Julio."

PART IV

CARIBBEAN LIONS

40

CORNERED

Marco was once again on his routine morning walk to get the newspaper. He stopped at the fruit vendor's cart, extended a friendly "Good morning," and bought his usual two bananas before continuing on his way.

He was preoccupied with peeling his breakfast when a homeless man aggressively approached him, shuffling like some kind of frenetic zombie. Marco had seen mentally unstable behavior among the indigents before and wasn't alarmed. Instead, his first thought was to offer the man his spare banana to placate him.

"Hey, man — how about some breakfast?" Marco held the fruit out toward him. He was stunned when the stranger suddenly produced a gun and pointed it at him.

Marco dropped the outstretched banana and raised his hands to show he was not returning the aggression. "Hey, I don't want any trouble. I just thought you might want some help," he said, slowly backing away.

"Marco Rivera, you're under arrest." In one smooth motion, the man grabbed Marco's arm and whirled him around, attempting to handcuff him. The restraint failed to engage, but the stranger had a hold on Marco.

"What are you doi—? Get away from me!" Confused, Marco struggled as he tried to make sense of what was happening. *Why is a homeless man trying to arrest me?*

"Shut up!" the vagrant shouted.

Marco was deeply confused. The guy was strong and didn't sound like the typical homeless man. Twisting himself around, he got a better look at the stranger who had accosted him. His eyes just about bugged out of his head when he realized this certainly wasn't a vagrant — it was none other than Detective Inspector Cato. His heart thumped hard. *OH, NO!*

"You have the right to make a phone call upon arrival in custody to a person of your choosing," Cato informed him, as per the law. "We will now enter my police vehicle and drive directly to legal custodial confinement in a locked facility, where you will be held pending official charges."

"Custod—?"

"It means jail, Rivera," Cato snapped. "You're the lawyer, supposedly — you should know that."

A homeless man, a real one, with whom Marco had kindly shared his bananas on many mornings in the past, was looking on from a distance.

"Help! Help!" Desperate shouts came from a half-block north. "Help!"

Cato hesitated. He was torn between following through on the arrest and contending with what could be another crime in progress. He gave a low growl and commanded Marco, "Don't move! You move an inch and I'll nail you twice as hard." Cato then turned, scarcely noticing that his handcuffs fell to the ground, and sprinted toward the pleas for help.

That was one ridiculous command he surely couldn't have expected Marco to obey. *Yea, right, I'm outta here!* Marco spun around and made a break for it, reflexively running from the scene. He fled in the opposite direction — south — then zigzagged west — as fast as his short legs could take him.

When Cato reached the man calling for help, he was still holding his gun. The homeless man immediately raised his hands, one still grasping a running water hose, drenching Cato's front.

"What? What's the problem?" Cato demanded, panting.

The man focused his eyes on the gun, which Cato had inadvertently pointed in his direction. "I, uhm, uhm ..." he stammered.

Cato stared at him intently, trying to catch his breath while waiting for the man to get an answer out. The man was afraid to talk.

"What is it?" Cato growled impatiently.

"I, uh ... I couldn't turn the hose ... I ... I ... I couldn't get the water spigot to turn. I was hoping someone could help me, suh."

Cato slumped, but only for a brief second. What an idiot. He had no more time to waste.

Snapping his attention back to the ongoing arrest, he whipped his head around and looked over his shoulder toward where Marco was supposed to be. There was no sign of the suspect besides a half-eaten banana on the ground.

Infernal scoundrel! Cato took off running south. His eyes scanned the shadows for any sign of his quarry. In motion, the man was a fearsome sight. His face was etched with the determination of one who would not be denied. His long legs ate up city blocks rapidly, stride by stride. Every pounding footstep echoed his unyielding resolve not to let Marco slip away yet again.

Cato caught a glimpse of Marco fleeing into the Tivoli Gardens garrison and pursued him with even greater vigor.

You're on my turf now, Rivera. These were Cato's old stomping grounds.

Marco ran through the open courtyard of a dilapidated, mint-colored apartment building pockmarked with bullet holes. The rusted jungle gym was a blur as he panted past.

Emerging out onto the street again, Marco's legs burned as they pumped down the asphalt. A mangy stray mutt, seeing him run, gave chase, as any dog would do. He growled and nipped viciously at Marco's heels. On the third try, his teeth caught the hem of Marco's pants and tore them, causing Marco to stumble several steps and lose speed.

Arrrgghhh! "Go away! Away! Away!" Marco shouted. Several people looked out of nearby apartment windows as they heard his panicked yells. *Just what I need now, to be chased by that mad dog, Cato — and this crazy dog, too.*

Not sure he could outrun either for long, Marco knew he had to change course. A tall, white cinderblock wall surrounded another apartment building, the design of which included decorative gaps in the blocks. He ran and jumped, immediately finding a foothold and hopping over, hoping he could easily disappear from the sight of both of his pursuers.

The dog gave up, but Cato would not. What was more, he was quick, and he saw Marco maneuver over the wall. *He's going to trap himself,* Cato noted with satisfaction, as his mouth turned to a sneering grin. Maniacally focused on catching Marco, he scaled the cinderblock wall in a different spot at a corner where he could get an easy foothold. His error was in doing so without checking to see what was on the other side.

When he landed, Cato found himself in the middle of a group of lounging ruffians, peeved at the intrusion of a stranger in the hood. Several were sprawled on a half-disemboweled blue sofa, smoking ganja, while another was swigging from a bottle of rum and listening to crude Jamaican dancehall music on an old portable boombox. Cato might as well have jumped into a hornet nest — it would have been friendlier. Five miscreants from the Shower Posse surrounded him.

"Hey!" shouted one particularly indignant young man, "Ya almos' jump on mi head! Yu have a death wish?" Instinctively, Cato drew his service pistol in one fluid motion, a Colt 1911. At the same moment, the barrel of a

Desert Eagle 44 Magnum was pointed back at him, trained directly at his forehead. The man drinking rum had also been playing around with his weapon at the same time, and he was known in the garrison for being a very quick draw. The others stood around casually fingering weapons of various types.

The gang had Cato backed into the corner of the wall as "rum boy" kept the Eagle trained on him. They outnumbered him and felt no fear that Cato might pull the trigger. In fact, they were enjoying this surprise encounter. Another young man with short dreadlocks and a red bandana flipped open his switchblade with one easy flick of the wrist and waved it menacingly, indicating for Cato to drop his weapon and step back.

"I'll be takin' that." The red bandana hoodlum reached down and snatched up Cato's service arm, pointing it back at him while grinning in victory.

The rum-drinking fellow let out a long hoot as "red bandana" delivered the line, followed by the fellow gang members hollering as if they'd scored in a sports match.

Marco had already reached the opposite corner of the building when he heard the commotion. Skidding around the corner, he stopped and ducked behind the building wall to catch his breath. He cautiously peered around to see if Cato was close. It didn't take long for him to make out that the detective was in deep trouble.

Marco's first instinct was to keep running. *How the tables have turned. He's hung up, and this is my chance to get away. He's a police officer, and he has a weapon. He can handle himself,* Marco rationalized. *Maybe God is just giving me a way out? ...*

But another quick look told him that Cato would not be fine. The man was surrounded by five armed men, and his defenseless hands were raised. *Maybe he can talk his way out,* Marco told himself. But deep down, he knew the detective wasn't about to have a friendly chat and get out.

*Ughhh! I can't just leave him. Those guys are like hyenas — he's as good as dead, es*pecially *if they discover he's a cop. Abandoning him would be turning your back on a murder about to happen.* Without further deliberation, Marco made his move.

In a performance worthy of Hollywood, Marco strode back down the alley between the cinderblock wall and the building. He approached Cato confidently and began acting like they were both being pursued by the police.

"You fool! I told you to put that piece away — keep it out of sight!" He got up in Cato's face. Cato's expression was a mix of surprise and bewilderment. He stared at Marco, speechless. Barely moving his lips, Marco indicated for him to just go along with it.

Turning to the young men, Marco asked them coyly, "Seen any squaddie around here?" For added effect, he got up on his tiptoes, pretending as if he were trying to see over the wall. He dropped back down and postured, "Thanks to this joker, every 'red stripe' in West Kingston is hot on our tails, looking for that sidearm he jacked from 'em."

At the mention of the police in possible pursuit, the five scanned their surroundings and hurriedly dispersed into the shadows without another word. Marco watched for a moment while they all disappeared.

Satisfied that the crisis was over, Marco turned and walked away alone, leaving Cato to contemplate what had just happened.

41
UNFINISHED FORGIVING

Marco met the men at the airport on Monday afternoon. He was already emotionally spent from his talk with Julio and the harrowing encounter with Cato. He knew this meeting would bring its own challenges and tried to prepare himself.

Marco was leaning against the outside of his car when Vladi and the others walked out of the Kingston airport. Seeing each other face-to-face again was awkward for both Vladi and Marco. The last time they had laid eyes on each other was at a tribunal in Havana when Marco handed Vladi a death sentence.

Vladi paused when he saw Marco, his dark brown eyes passing over his former nemesis. The men stared at each other in silence, so many thoughts running through both minds. Vladi had wanted to move on from what transpired in the past with Marco. While on the plane, he had prayed and repeatedly rehearsed this meeting in his mind. He needed to see Marco as the man he was in this present moment. But that was easier said from a seat at thirty-thousand feet than face-to-face with reality.

There was such a complex storm of unresolved emotions involved — anger, grief, horror, confusion — forgiveness was always swallowed up before it could ever take hold.

When he thought about it, Vladi wasn't sure he was being oversensitive. After all, he had endured Marco's abuse and suffered much at his hands. That mistreatment had left an indelible mark on him. Why should he let this guy back into his life? Then again, it was Marco who had arranged for Vladi to return to his family. This complicated Vladi's thoughts even further. Marco wasn't his enemy, at least not anymore. This left a burning question — *What am I to think of this man?*

The moment he had laid eyes on Marco, he had an involuntary visceral reaction. It was like a trigger had been pulled, and every emotion and memory he had tried to suppress for years shot through him with a force he had not expected. *I knew this would be difficult, but I did not understand how gut-punched I would feel.*

It was obvious that Marco was uncomfortable as well — his face was drawn, and his once-full cheeks seemed gaunt and hollow. He opened the car door and motioned for them to get in. The men momentarily looked each other in the eye as they shook hands. Vladi politely thanked him as he got in. Thankfully Jorge had the grace to get in the front passenger seat and made small talk with Marco along the way. Vladi felt grateful relief as he gazed out the window in silence.

Vladi occasionally glanced at Marco from the back seat. Could he trust this man who had once betrayed him so deeply? Even now, he couldn't shake the feeling of suspicion that clung to him like a second skin. They sped west along the A4 and Marcus Garvey Drive across Kingston, then toward the causeway to Portmore. Marco seemed focused on the task at hand, and Vladi pretended to catch some shut-eye.

Marco drove them directly to Frank Díaz's compound in Hellshire Hills. Vladi didn't realize his mouth was agape as he pulled up. Díaz's place made Vladi's home look like a shack in the orchards. The men got out of the car in the circular driveway, and Díaz was there to greet them, standing next to a large palm tree and a fountain with a brilliant turquoise dolphin spouting water. Vladi shook hands with Díaz and thanked him for his help.

"Save the thanks until you hear the rest of the plan," Díaz told him in a somewhat ominous tone.

"I want to know something first," Vladi insisted. "How is it that you can get through to someone in this organization? You cannot just look up the cartel's phone number in the Yellow Pages."

Díaz gave the deadpan reply, "I could tell you, but then I'd have to kill you." When Vladi's eyes widened slightly, Díaz gave him a quick wink.

"Seriously, it is important for me to know what you are doing," Vladi insisted.

"Look, we've circumvented your man, Pablo Noriega, by going over his head. I went directly to his boss, Osiel Cárdenas."

"How in the world did you gain access to Cárdenas?" Marco asked, astounded.

"Wait, who is Cárdenas?" Vladi asked.

"Gulf Cartel kingpin," Marco quickly answered, filling in the details for Vladi. They turned their attention back to Díaz, eager for him to continue.

"The word is that the one thing this cartel boss is most passionate about is quarter horses," Díaz explained. "I have a contact who is a racehorse trainer in central Texas. This guy is good, perhaps the best in the world. He has a lead on a prize mare out of an all-time winning racing quarter horse. Everyone wants this blood. She's foaled twice and consistently throws winners."

"What do horses have to do with anything?" Vladi was dubious — his skepticism was reasonable under the circumstances.

"Simple. In exchange for the lead on the horse, I got a phone call — direct," Díaz stated with a gleam of pride, "... with Cárdenas."

Marco was impressed. Cárdenas's obsession with racehorses had made controversial news in years past when a well-known trainer in Texas got himself embroiled in questionable dealings with him.

"Cárdenas has given me his word that they will make the deal, even though it's now slightly different than you initially proposed, Marco. He wants the horse more than he wants your son or the money," Díaz reassured Vladi. "Pablo Noriega takes his orders from Cárdenas, so I am confident this will go down as planned. Noriega will do what he's told — he won't cross Cárdenas. It's that simple."

The other men exchanged satisfied glances. It was apparent that they all recognized the brilliance of Díaz's approach. Vladi was feeling more confident in him now. Indeed, this mysterious attorney embodied his reputation as "The Boss" in every respect.

In his behind-the-scenes negotiations, Díaz had brokered a deal in which the cartel kidnappers would deliver Aleksey in exchange for the lesser amount of ransom money. When they pushed back, he offered to sweeten the deal with a load of the Rastas' sinsemilla Lamb's Bread. The farmers were growing ganja in abundance, so it was dirt cheap for them to produce in Jamaica, but the cartels didn't have access to the same high-grade product in Mexico. The cartel would move it north, across the border, and this would fetch a big markup stateside. It was practically free money, Díaz emphasized. The cartels liked money, and this got their ear.

Plus, the farmers would cut them a deal on the goods. Besides a little cash, they were taking delivery on forty Colt 1911 45s and Desert Eagle 44 Magnum handguns. The cartel had acquired the pieces in Texas and Arizona — all stolen or procured through black market dealers in the Rio Grande Valley. The cartel smugglers were to put the guns on the boat heading to Jamaica. The Rastas could then trade these in the garrisons along the wharves at Kingston for profits much greater than "juggling" ganja.

The cartel guys and the Rastas both got a win, and Vladi would get his son back alive. At least, that was the plan.

When Díaz finished talking, Erik and Vladi looked at each other. There was no doubt they felt the same reservations. Without a word, each could read the concern on the other's face. No one had said anything up to this point, but the contraband deal that Díaz had arranged crossed moral boundaries that made the men uncomfortable. For one thing, a lot of other people would doubtless be caught up in the fallout when that contraband hit the streets. It was Jorge who voiced what Vladi and his brother were thinking.

"I don't ... this is different from what I was expecting," Jorge tried to be tactful. "It goes without saying, we are dealing with evildoers who have no conscience or morals of their own, yet it appears we're also turning to measures that are ... not quite right."

Díaz was listening but with an incredulous look.

"Not 'right'? My man, we are bargaining with the worst people on the planet," Díaz reminded him. "If you hope to save this kid's life, you're going to have to be prepared to get your hands dirty."

"I mean ... It is one thing to give money to these swine to get Aleksey back — but trading drugs and weapons? Those days are behind me," Jorge said. "It is like making a deal that trades one evil for another. No disrespect, Señor Díaz. I ... I refuse to bring myself to that level."

Díaz waved it off easily. He was as unoffended as one could be. He saw the deal through a pragmatic lens, not a moral one. However, he did acknowledge their moral anxiety and responded to Jorge's concerns thoughtfully, while remaining firm in his own convictions.

"Listen, I understand what you are saying. This is not the kind of life you live — I get that. But here's the thing — in all my years, I've learned a hard and inescapable truth. If you want to get to bad guys like this, you must do business with unsavory people."

"Business, sure," Jorge said, "but this crosses the line. We're trading arms and drugs."

"There are no white knights in the cartel world — only scum and other lowlifes who help run their operations," Díaz insisted emphatically. "If you want to penetrate these organizations, you have no choice but to use these resources. My grandfather back in Cuba used to say, 'If you want to take down a pig, you can't be afraid of the mud.' There is no other way."

Vladi and Marco looked at Jorge, impressed by his moral passion but hesitant to commit to the same idealism.

"Have we considered all the other possibilities, maybe another option for the guns?" Vladi asked. "We are supposed to be the good guys, so I can see what Jorge is saying here ..."

Díaz raised his eyebrows and shook his head.

"Being a decent person neither brings justice nor does it get your boy back alive. You're contending with people who recognize no moral absolutes. These are hardened marauders who spend all day every day thinking about how to plunder and lay waste to everything in their path. If you happen to be in the way, they'll kill you in the most savage way without blinking an eye.

"Dark forces must be confronted with equal ferocity. These are villains, and you better be ready to be skull-splitting bad guy stompers yourselves. Otherwise, they will mess you up and take you down hard, because that's what they do. If you hope to come back alive and bring this young man home, you need to recognize how severe you'll need to be."

Vladi stood with his arms crossed and exhaled a deep breath through his nostrils. He and Marco knew this to be true — both had dealt with their fair share of bad guys. Even if they didn't like it, the men understood Díaz was right. Now wasn't the time to second-guess the plan or try to dissect it piece by piece.

"You're fighting evil now — they've chosen their path, and bad choices have consequences, which they will soon find out," Díaz continued.

"All those guns on the streets of Kingston, though — I can't stop thinking of it," Jorge said. "... the people they'll harm ... the crimes they'll be used for."

"If it helps you feel better, let me give you the big picture. The guns will never hit the streets," Díaz assured him. "We're taking forty handguns away from the most dangerous criminals on the planet. My own security team will make a deal with the Rastas later for the 1911s and Desert Eagles.

"As for the ganja, it was a bargaining chip to get them on our turf. We have a surprise for them that will ensure their drugs never leave the island, let alone find their way onto the street."

"A surprise?" Jorge asked.

"Indeed, the ganja's not going anywhere either. Remember, our primary objective is to extract Aleksey without casualties on our side. When we're done, the bad guys will lose their hostage, money, firearms, the boat, and the ganja — and they may not even get away with their lives. Is everyone on board with that?"

Everyone nodded except Marco, but no one else noticed his reluctance.

"All right, *señor*, what is the plan?" Intently focused, Vladi was eager to be done with the moral quandary and hear what Díaz had cooked up.

Díaz laid out the operation in detail, assigning to each man his role. The rendezvous point with the cartel was on the docks at Oracabessa, where they loaded bananas. It would take place in the wee hours at 03:00 on Tuesday morning.

"Perhaps the biggest wild card is that we don't know how many cartel operatives will be on the boat. Given the size of the vessel, we should assume at least five but not over seven. There's no way to know for sure," Díaz told the others. "There is one thing you can be sure about — every one of them will be armed to the teeth with automatic weapons — and they know how to use them.

"They will only expect Vladi to bring cash and whoever comes in the delivery truck for loading. The Rastas won't know what's going down, but they're used to making deliveries to shady characters at night. They won't suspect anything out of the ordinary.

"Marco and Erik will ride with the Rastas, who will help load the boat," Díaz explained. "Erik should remain concealed, maybe under the tarp behind the bales of weed or somewhere near the vehicle."

Erik couldn't swim, so they had already discussed that it was best to keep him on land.

"Vladi and Jorge will already be there. Jorge is to make himself appear as a dock worker patrolling for routine security purposes, otherwise minding his own business."

Díaz took the money that Vladi brought and divided out four thousand U.S. dollars for the Rastas. After all, they expected to be paid upfront. He bound the other thousand together with counterfeit currency and put it into a small knapsack with a special surprise for the pirates — the bottom of the case was lined with a plastic explosive set on a timer.

"Best case for these pirates is that they'll have to swim back to Mexico. Worst case, well ... the sharks occasionally need to be fed around here. The rumor is that they enjoy Mexican food," Díaz said with a wink.

"Wait," Vladi belatedly realized what Díaz was saying. "You are going to blow up my boat?"

"No, you are going to blow up your boat," Díaz told him. "You know they aren't giving it back to you, no matter what happens. If things were to go according to their plan, they would be leaving with it."

Vladi sighed.

"Write it off as a casualty of the operation. Better the boat than your son, right — or any of these brave men?" Díaz reasoned.

Vladi nodded, but he wasn't happy. Díaz was spot-on — although Vladi hoped for a more ideal outcome, he knew on some level that the *Skipper Dan* was a loss.

Vladi replied, "I concur. As long as Aleksey comes home safe — I do not care what else happens. That is enough."

Díaz gave them confidence that the details were being handled. He also proved to be hospitable, providing a place for the men to rest and eat at the compound.

"Everyone, try to get some sleep early this evening," he advised. "I'll have someone come for you at midnight. Meanwhile, if you need anything, let me know. You have a big night ahead."

"I can't."

Everyone was leaving, but at the sound of these words, they turned around.

"Who said that?" asked Díaz.

It was Marco.

"I'm not going — I'm not doing that." Marco's words stumbled out of his mouth awkwardly.

"Marco, this was your plan," Díaz pointed out.

"Look, guys, I want to help Vladi, but this is as far as I go." The men gave him piercing stares that felt like daggers in his heart.

"I understand the desperation you're feeling, Vladi." He paused. Inside, Marco was torn. Deep down, he felt indebted to Vladi. He turned to speak directly to Vladi in a low voice. "I regret how I treated you. As much as anything in the world, I hope for your forgiveness." Nothing he wanted to say sounded right at the moment. Marco felt like he was running out of words.

But even more than that, he had a wife and his own son at home. Today was Nemesio's third birthday, and Jhas had family coming down from Trinity for a celebration tonight. His son wasn't going to have a birthday party without his daddy there. It wasn't just about the birthday party, though — it was about the danger. Other people depended on him now, and he had new responsibilities to consider.

"I'm sorry, I can't," Marco reluctantly declined again. "I know I said I would do this ... and I truly want to be there for you now. But this is where I need to get off. I will help in whatever other ways I can."

The men shook their heads in disappointment and began to walk away.

Marco pulled Vladi aside to speak with him away from the others. He looked Vladi in the eyes. "Vladi, I'm sorry. I'm sorry this has happened to you. And this doesn't feel like an ideal time to have this conversation. I know your mind is in many different places right now. But this has been hanging over my head for years, and I'm not sure when I may have another chance to talk with you."

"What are you saying?" Vladi's eyes bored into his soul.

"I just want you to know that I am sorry for all the pain and injustice I caused you before. Now, I'm even more sorry that I will not accompany you."

"You do what you have to," Vladi told him with feigned indifference. "I care about one thing only — that I return home with my son."

Marco nodded. "I hope you will somehow find it in your heart to forgive me."

Vladi was at a loss for words. In his present frame of mind, he was not emotionally ready to have the discussion of forgiveness with Marco. He didn't say anything for a moment, his eyes fixed on Marco as his mind searched for a response. Marco didn't give him the chance.

He looked down and patted Vladi's shoulder before turning to leave for his son's birthday party. Unable to process his thoughts, Vladi stared dumbfounded as Marco walked away. He'd reached no conclusions of his own. *I have too much to think about right now to deal with him.*

42

TORMENTED BY MERCY

Despite Marco's surprising intervention to save him in the alley in Tivoli Gardens, Cato doggedly persisted, eventually trailing him to the airport.

Wonder who he's waiting for? Cato pondered suspiciously. At first, he thought Marco might be trying to make a run for it — fleeing the country. But his assumptions proved wrong. Marco was casually leaning against his blue Mitsubishi Lancer, waiting for someone at the Arrivals terminal. Cato watched from several cars back as three men exited the building and approached Marco.

There was something odd and uncomfortable in the demeanor of the tall, older man as he approached. *Perhaps he's nervous,* Cato thought as he jotted notes in the small notepad that he always kept with him.

As all three men got into Marco's vehicle, Cato wondered if they had any connection to the "boatload" of illegal cannabis that he'd overheard Marco brokering with the Rastafarians.

These guys don't look like dealers. He conjectured that maybe they were involved in some part of the financial or business end of this drug operation.

Cato had developed a Captain Ahab-like obsession with this elusive suspect, one he wouldn't let go of. He needed to know why this was happening and put a stop to whatever crime was underway.

Cato moved through the world with the calculated precision of an automaton, his thoughts and actions guided by the unshakable principles of the law. Though he possessed a conscience and the ability to think, his actions seemed almost mechanical, as if driven by an unseen force. He'd always acted with confidence and decisiveness, never doubting himself once a decision had been made.

That's why his mind was continually and irresistibly drawn to that fateful encounter with Marco in Tivoli Gardens. Marco had saved him from the clutches of a ruthless gang and challenged everything he had ever believed in. Yet he had simply walked away, making no demands or threats, extracting no promises ... nothing. It made no sense.

Why did he do that? Cato was perplexed and obsessed with the question. *He could have fled. Anyone else, criminal or not, would have saved himself and left me there to die. Why?*

As an officer, Cato had experienced his fair share of criminals making futile attempts to bargain with him. But Marco's actions, in the course of saving his life, had thrown him for a loop. Marco was the lawbreaker, the bad guy. Yet he had risked his life to save his persecutor from almost certain death. Cato's mind kept circling the contradiction — a criminal saving a policeman. *Why? In what universe?*

Marco had voluntarily shown him mercy and compassion, qualities that were at odds with the murderer he thought he understood. Even more baffling, Marco had shown these qualities in direct contradiction to his own self-interest and self-preservation. It vexed Cato's rational mind.

Marco's actions revealed to him that perhaps his strict devotion to the law was imperfect, that there were times when even a criminal may do what is right, or a law-abider may have to break the law to do the morally right thing. Cato was mystified at this sudden epiphany — *Could it be that Rivera is simultaneously a criminal and a good person? Perhaps. But this man is an alleged murderer!* Cato had only ever seen the world in black and white — he had no mental categories for someone like Marco.

Not since arresting his brother had Cato found himself in a situation like this — one that called his beliefs into question. Even so, this was far different, and it threatened to turn his worldview on its head.

It was frightening to him in some aspects. The static nature of law and order meant there was one right way, and one didn't have to think past the rules. They were either followed or they weren't — there were no messy, philosophical notions of morality to consider.

But now that was up in the air.

Cato was torn between his desire to let Marco go free and dishonoring his profession. After all, to what extent did owing this man his life change Cato's duty to imprison him for murder?

The deeper he delved into this incongruity, the more it suggested the existence of a superior moral system that transcended the law. His encounter with Marco forced him to confront the limitations of his understanding and question the foundations of his beliefs. Cato was left with a feeling of uncertainty but also with a newfound desire to seek out the truth ... someday.

For now, Cato remained a man of singular vision. His cold temperament hadn't thawed even a single degree. Even though mercy had spared his life, for Cato, there was no place for such compassion when one was upholding the law. He still viewed it as a weakness and approached his duties with unfeeling punctiliousness. Mercy would have to wait — bad things were taking place. He continued in his determination to be a force of order in a world of chaos.

Cato tried to quiet his thoughts as he sat near the airport, assessing the situation until the men clambered into Marco's Lancer and left. The inspector gunned the engine to follow, trailing at a discreet distance.

"Get a grip on yourself, old man," he muttered to himself, shaking his head as if clearing out his muddled mind. He was the law, and the law was him, and nothing else mattered but the upholding of that sacred trust. The "moral" dimension to all this could come later — now was the time for justice.

I vowed to protect and to serve, and I will do that until the day I die.

Cato tailed Marco westbound across Kingston for more than half an hour. He was suddenly snapped out of his introspection when he saw Marco's car pull into Frank Díaz's compound in Hellshire.

Frank Díaz! Cato punched his dash. *I should have known he was part of the whole suspicious picture. I'm doing the right thing by not giving this renegade the benefit of the doubt,* Cato reassured himself. *This is leading to all the worst people ...*

To avoid being seen by Díaz's security team guarding the Hellshire compound, Cato drove to a spot away from the entrance where he had a comfortable view. He retrieved his binoculars from behind the seat and focused on the end of the long driveway on the hilltop. As he observed, someone he thought could be Díaz came to meet Marco and the men he brought from the airport. Cato's mind swam.

So, is that "The Boss," the legendary merchant of contraband, himself?

As Cato speculated on what they could be talking about, he still couldn't stop wondering about Marco Rivera. Why in the world would this man, who had no doubt committed murder and was acquainted with ganja farmers and lowlifes like Frank Díaz, have helped him escape the clutches of those thugs back in Tivoli Gardens?

On the one hand, he felt compelled to arrest Marco, a probable criminal by the law's standards. On the other hand, he struggled to come to terms with the reality that the man who had saved his life should also be behind bars. Cato couldn't bring himself to turn in a man who had essentially risked his own neck to preserve his.

Yet there Marco was, with his DNA at the murder scene ...

And now, here Marco was with Díaz, a man who thought he was above the law, who represented the exact arrogance and lawlessness that Cato so despised.

In Cato's eyes, Díaz represented an element that lived outside the law, a force that threatened to undermine the very foundations of society. Although little or no crime had been committed that Cato was aware of, there were plenty of anecdotal stories that circulated within Jamaica's law enforcement community — smuggling Cuban refugees, maintaining cartel alliances, and maybe even bootlegging Cuban cigars. As far as Cato was concerned, it mattered less what exactly Díaz had done or not done — it was the underground, the black market, the way he did it.

Who was to really know how much of it was true and how much of it was the stuff of unsubstantiated legend? Cato had never personally met the man or even seen him before today, yet he tended to believe the stories were rooted in truth. Anyone who lived and worked that deep in the shadows was probably into dubious activities.

The only thing Cato felt certain about was that Díaz's world represented a lack of control, which Cato perceived as a threat to the very principle that guided his life — the rule of law.

43

THE AWAKENING

Aleksey awoke again on the deck of the *Skipper Dan* moments after the sun had peeked over the eastern horizon. In the initial moments of consciousness, he was happy and content. This was the way it should be. A slight tang of saltwater spray on his skin, a breeze passing by. His mind recognized he was on his boat, and his ears picked up the ever-familiar rumble of the *Skipper Dan's* twin diesel engines as it cut through the sea with the salty, cool morning air washing over his face.

I wonder if Papa is awake yet. He has probably already caught several —. Reality slammed into Aleksey so hard that it jarred his mind. "Ughh!"

Between the evaporation of those pleasant thoughts and the thorough exhaustion of never really knowing what was happening, a stinging mist formed beneath Aleksey's half-closed eyes. He shook it off and forced them open to meet the jagged reality of the new day.

No time to be emotional — you are a Gavrilov man.

Aleksey's whole body ached from sleeping on the hard deck — alongside the wooden coffin, no less. With a soft grunt, he struggled to sit up. He was momentarily dizzy as the blood drained from his head to the rest of his body. From an upright position, he had a better vantage point from which to observe what was happening on the boat and in his surroundings.

Once Aleksey's headrush subsided, he could see the horizon line. A deep red color began to seep into the sky, silhouetting the wispy fishbone clouds that stretched parallel to the horizon.

The old maritime adage popped into Aleksey's mind — *Red sky in morning, sailors take warning. Hmmm, I wouldn't mind some rain after days in the blistering sun.*

Aleksey's kidnappers had throttled back some, but they were still heading in the same direction.

Are they taking me back to Florida? he wondered.

A short while later, one man came back for him again, and they repeated the same sequence as the night before — a trip to the head, then more water and, *surprise*, cold cabrito. The cartel member in his ever-present Bull's jersey tossed him the food as if doing him a favor and gave a thumb's up before guffawing with his buddies.

If they let me move around, I could at least show them how to warm up breakfast.

Aleksey stared at the coffin on the deck while he ate. *What are they doing?* he wondered over and over. *What is the deal with that thing? I thought it was an intimidation tactic at first, or worse. But neither seems to be the case. I'm dying to know what's in there ... no, poor choice of words.*

More hours went by — the sun reached its apex. Aleksey's head was getting hotter as it soaked in the sun's rays, sending sweat pouring down his neck.

If they would slow down, I could enlighten them about fishing. There must be some good 'finnys' out here. That's what he'd heard Vladi call them. Perhaps it was an odd thing to be thinking about now — maybe his brain was getting baked. Not only the heat, but the beatings, the psychological tactics — it had all begun to take a toll on Aleksey's mind. He was genuinely exhausted through and through, to the extent that even death seemed kind of abstract and irrelevant at this point. He was almost too tired to feel fear anymore — almost.

"*Permiso*," he caught the attention of one of the men, "I need to move into the shade. I am going to be sick from the heat."

It was the truth and something he should have asked about sooner. But Aleksey hated to have to ask them for anything, since it put him in the weakened position of wanting something from them. He had concerns that they might react to any request he made with mean spite, adding to his misery for their own amusement. However, at this point, it was worth the risk.

The man didn't say anything but untied him and nudged Aleksey with his foot, allowing him to scoot over into the shady area as requested. Aleksey's hands remained bound behind his back, but he was no longer tied off and bound to the boat.

Thank God for small miracles. The thought formed in Aleksey's head as an exclamation. He didn't literally wish to "thank God," but the words rumbled around now in his mind. *God ... whoever or whatever God is ... or is not.* He recalled the conversation with his father about the difference between prayer and wishes. Wasn't it just the same? He still didn't know.

From where they had moved Aleksey into the shade, he could see his pocket watch out of the corner of his eye. Instantly, his heart warmed — a comforting reminder of his father's love. He marveled at the fact that it was still in the place he had pushed it with his foot when he and his father had first been surprised by these men days earlier. He tried not to make it obvious that he noticed it, lest one of the men follow his gaze and grab it for themselves.

Keeping an eye on the smugglers, he made his move when he was sure they weren't watching. Discreetly, he adjusted his position until he was seated on the deck within reach of the watch. With his hands still bound, Aleksey awkwardly grasped the watch with a couple of fingers and slipped it into the back pocket of his trousers.

Dusk was closing in and the sky began to darken. Again, Aleksey's mind drifted to a canyon, where he heard the shots cracking from all directions. Snippets of Russian and far-off Pashto melded into a sick medley of manic poetry. He snapped back out of his daze.

Present reality was scarcely better. Here he still was, on the deck of this boat, tied up as though he were livestock. If there had ever been a time to try out praying for real, this was it.

Aleksey observed the sky for a while, watching for shooting stars. He thought again about the conversation he had with his father the last night they were together about whether prayers were just wishes.

I had silently mocked Papa in my heart when he said that sometimes God answers prayers, not by altering our circumstances but by transforming us amid the situations that God arranges. Could it be true? Did God let this happen to me?

Aleksey had heard Tetya pray. He had heard his parents pray. But he always dismissed it as religious ritualism — empty words. Now he was reconsidering his assumptions. He thought he would pray, and perhaps he could know whether God might hear him.

Aleksey began quietly mouthing the words that came to him.

"My Heavenly Father ... Our God ... just, well ... God ... If You are up there, I need Your help. I have not asked You for anything before, and that is my fault. I hope You know who I am and can hear me. Being God, You know my life is in danger and, well, I do not know about my father. I hope that he is okay.

"I know he is doing whatever he can to help me. Okay, but I am scared now. I fear for my life ending at the hands of these vicious men. I think my future is lost, whatever You have made me for, God ..."

Aleksey paused to take a breath, his mouth dry and his eyes moist with unexpected emotion.

"You owe me nothing. And I have nothing to offer to You. God, I am pleading with You to save my life. But whether or not You save my life, do save my soul. Amen."

Night had now fully fallen, onyx and chilling, and Aleksey was relieved by the cooler air. It helped revive his senses, so he had better mental clarity. He again looked to the stars to gain their bearings. *We are much too far south to be heading toward Florida.* His mind was straining to figure out what they were doing. He listened carefully to the conversations between the men, hoping to catch a clue about their destination and plans.

I should have practiced my Spanish with Antonio more when I had the chance, Aleksey thought regretfully. Their Spanish was so rapid, making it difficult for Aleksey to understand clearly. He could only catch a phrase here and there, but not enough to piece together anything meaningful. However, in the process, he did pick up something that he found interesting. He heard one man address Cucuy as "Pablo."

So, the big guy has a name. It was the first time he'd heard anyone say it during his captivity, and somehow it made him seem just a little more human. The name "Cucuy" was already imprinted on Aleksey's mind, though. Thinking of this man as Pablo might never stick now, as if it really mattered.

High clouds began rolling in, blocking off the glimmer of his guiding nightlights. *I guess the red morning sky was right after all.* With nothing much left to observe in the night, Aleksey dozed off to sleep. He was awakened when the incessant droning of the engines went silent.

I hope these fools have not run out of fuel or broken my boat, was his first thought. *But then they would have to radio for help.* MAYDAY *is good!* He was optimistic. Then he thought about it more — *Help could not arrive to find a person tied up and a coffin on the deck. That means they would have to get rid of me first. That is not good.*

As the craft bobbed in the wake, he caught a glimpse over the bow. *Lights!* They shined in the distant darkness all along their port side.

Land! But where? If I can work my hands out of these bindings, maybe I can swim for it. I do not care where we are as long as it is away from these thugs.

For the first time since his abduction, Aleksey felt a surge of energy. *Did God hear my prayer? Is this an answer already? Papa did say that sometimes God does not answer prayers in the way we expect.*

Aleksey could see that the smugglers were becoming more active. They were getting close to something, but what?

One smuggler approached Aleksey and looked him over, ensuring he was securely bound, hand and foot. He gagged Aleksey again. This left Aleksey with an ominous sense that something was up ... and that something would be bad for him. Then, without warning, the black hood was pulled over Aleksey's head. Complete darkness once again.

44

A PERFECT HUSBAND

Marco and Jhas hosted all her family that came down from Trinity for Nemesio's birthday party. Jhas had made a cute submarine-shaped cake for the occasion. "Happy Birthday Nemo" was written in colorful turquoise and orange script on the icing.

"His name is Nemesio," Marco protested.

"There wasn't enough room to write 'Nemesio.' He'd need a bigger submarine," Jhas joked.

Marco didn't find humor in her remark. Although he was present at the party, his mind was elsewhere. All evening, Marco had been troubled about what to do about the *Daily Gleaner* newspaper story and his conversation with Julio. Added to that, he kept thinking about Vladi and the other men.

You are exactly where you should be — with your wife and son and the rest of the family, he reminded himself. But it wasn't enough. The thought that he needed to be with Vladi and his men persisted. Marco prayed for them but was still consumed with guilt and worry — about everything.

Every time Marco looked at Nemesio, he thought about Vladi and his son. Every time he looked at Jhas, he thought about the implications of a confession about Michael Cervera. The prospect of confession felt like a ton of bricks oppressing his whole being.

"Are you okay, love?" Jhas asked. "You aren't your usual self. I hope you're not coming down with something."

Marco insensitively brushed her hand from his forehead and dismissed her thoughtful concern, perhaps with more brusqueness than he intended. "I'm fine. Just distracted."

Marco was being a poor host, and he knew it. Jhas had a wonderful family — joyful people. Meeting them, it was easy to see how she was the way she was. Her mother, Jaynee, was a fine Christian lady. She was all smiles and doted on Marco, the man who loved her daughter so dearly.

"I hope all my nieces find a husband as perfect as you, Marco," his mother-in-law fawned. She was so impressed with him and thrilled to see her daughter in a happy, secure marriage. As Jaynee turned to other family members, she held his arm and remarked, "This right here is a real man — how a husband ought to be."

Marco was pained. *If she only knew. I'm such a fraud — always have been. Hiding my sins behind this mask of a great husband and father. It makes me sick to hear her talk about me this way. She doesn't know.*

"I wish my dear Herschel was here to meet you. He would love you as much as we do," Jaynee continued to gush.

Marco had always wished he could have known Jhas's father. A former Vietnam POW and sheriff until he died of cancer, the stories of Herschel "Bear" Campbell seemed legendary. He overcame great obstacles and was truly a courageous man. Bear had been a real man, a hero, and Marco was nothing in comparison to him.

Marco thought about his own situation, lamenting that Mr. Campbell's daughter deserved better than the husband she had now.

If she only knew ...

Marco's smile was thin as he gently unhooked his mother-in-law's hand from his arm. He kissed it and excused himself, saying he needed to check on something in the house.

Walking across the yard, he was stopped by Jhas's uncles. They were true gentlemen themselves and kept company with other men they believed were of the same character. One patted him on the back while the other extended a firm handshake.

"Heyyy, this guy here! A class act if I do say so myself." The men chuckled. "Sit down," they invited warmly, beckoning to Marco. "Tell us how your trade initiative has been going. How are the wheels of bureaucracy turning for you?"

Marco politely demurred, still insisting that he needed to take care of something in the house. He excused himself, hoping that wouldn't be met with protest from the congenial men. He didn't feel up to chatting and engaging in small talk, even for a few minutes.

He went into the house to take a breath and collect his thoughts. Instead of finding himself alone when he closed the door, Jhas's brother Hudson was sitting at Marco's work desk. He was so absorbed in his task that he hadn't noticed Marco's entrance.

"What are you doing?" Marco asked. Hud, as they called him, peeked out from behind Marco's computer monitor. Realizing his question sounded sharp, Marco softened his tone.

"Come, you should be outside enjoying yourself with the family, buddy. Nemesio already doesn't get to spend nearly enough time with his uncle."

"He's a cute kid, for sure, but I ..."

"You're good for him, Hud — he can learn a thing or two from you."

"It's just that Jhas said you were having problems with the computer, so I told her I'd fix it while I'm here."

Hud was an exceptionally smart young man. He had been tinkering with computer programs before anyone knew they needed a computer. Then again, Hud hardly needed one because he could figure numbers in his head faster than anyone else. Mostly self-taught, he was the family's go-to tech wiz.

Any other time, this would have been an opportunity to look over Hud's shoulder and maybe learn something novel, but Marco simply nodded and walked away. He wasn't inclined to engage in conversation or interact with anyone. Hud was charming and brilliant, but talking over the specifics of his computer issues right now was the last thing on Marco's mind. He decided that if he couldn't get a moment to himself, he'd sit and just watch his son for a while. Nemesio was a never-ending source of delight for him.

By eight o'clock, Nemesio was getting tired, even though it was his own birthday party. Jhas changed him into some cute new pajamas with a submarine print. Everyone ooh-ed and ah-ed and squealed with delight as the toddler gave them all kisses on his way to bed. Marco took him from Jhas's arms, wanting to hold on to him for as long as possible.

He took Nemesio to his twin bed and tucked him under a thin blanket. Marco sat on the edge of his bed, looking at his son more closely than usual, soaking in the moment. His son's cute button nose was just begging to be kissed, and Marco felt his throat constrict with emotion.

"Daddy, whatcha doin'?" Nemesio asked, his little senses picking up that something was unusual about his father tonight.

"Nothing, little man. I just love you." He leaned over and kissed Nemesio's forehead before closing the door behind him. He paused just outside the door. He could hear Nemo softly singing a silly little ditty.

Daddy's big belly, round and strong,

Makes me laugh and dance along.

He hugs me tight so I can see,

How much love he has for me.

Daddy's big belly, soft and round,

A cozy place to lay me down.

I wanna snuggle close and see,

How near to Daddy I can be,

Daddy's big belly is full of love,

Makes me grateful for this gift from above.

I love my Daddy, from head to toe,

And his big ol' belly makes me love him so!

He heard Nemesio squeal with delight and burst into laughter. It was something Jhas would sing with him from time to time to keep his attention. Sometimes they changed the words or added another line, but it always ended the same — with them collapsing into giggles. Marco smiled. These days, his belly could stand to shed a few pounds, it was true.

Jaynee helped Jhas clean up, and everyone else went home within an hour. Later that night, Marco and Jhas lay in bed. She was exhausted from an evening of entertaining guests. Marco, however, was in a cold sweat beside her. He lay with his eyes open, staring at the ceiling.

Finally, he pushed the words out as if shoveling hard cement. "Jhas, there's something I need to talk with you about."

Half-asleep, she mustered a bleary reply. "You don't say. Now you want to talk? You sat there like a bump on a log and hardly said a word to my family all night."

"I'm sorry," he apologized flatly.

"If I'd known the name on a birthday cake would be such a big deal to you, I would have just left it off!"

"It wasn't a big deal. I'm sorry I gave you that impression." His apology was more sincere this time.

"Honey, I know you've been stressed. It happens. Please don't worry about it. I forgive you. Now, can we just get some sleep?" she pleaded. "We have a three-year-old who will be up bright and early in the morning, ready or not."

"Sure. I'll leave you be. I'm having a hard time sleeping," he told her as he sat up and swung his legs over the edge of the bed. "I need to go out for a while. I love you." He leaned over and kissed her cheek.

"I love you too," she replied groggily.

Marco got dressed, then kissed her again as she rested peacefully on her pillow. He softly walked out of the room and closed the door without a sound.

He went to his desk and pulled a locked box out of the bottom drawer. Even though he knew Hud would never look through his stuff, and even if he did, he would never be able to open the box, Marco had felt highly uneasy with his brother-in-law so close to it.

Marco unlocked it himself now and pulled out its sole content. He held the loaded Glock 26 subcompact 9mm handgun, feeling its dense weight in his palm. Earlier, when he was leaving the compound, Díaz had pulled him aside and given him the piece.

"Insurance. In case you change your mind," Díaz told him as he handed the weapon to Marco. Marco didn't want to take it at first, but Díaz wasn't the type of fellow to argue with.

"Just in case," Díaz insisted as he pushed the weapon into Marco's hand.

Just in case. Just in case. Those words played over and over in Marco's mind. Had Díaz expected Marco to change his mind? Could he read the conflict that Marco was contending with?

Marco checked to ensure the safety was on before tucking the weapon into his waistband. He looked in on Nemesio one more time to ensure he was still covered up. Then he walked out the door.

45

RELENTLESS PURSUIT

Dressed in black, Cato drove through the night alone with his thoughts. He was careful to keep enough distance from the vehicle he was tailing to avoid calling attention to his pursuit. He was bent on interdicting a drug deal that he was convinced was about to go down. Why else would Marco Rivera drive north to the coast in the middle of the night?

Why have I been so emotional about this crook? He's obviously contributing to the flood of dangerous and illegal activities on this island. Surely, I'm not getting that soft, Cato worried. He steadied his breathing and blinked his eyes tightly and rapidly as if resetting his vision.

Inept constables may have allowed this murderous, drug trafficking, phony lawyer to slip past the law all these years, but he'll face justice once and for all. And when I get him in the interrogation room, it will all spill out, including the details of his underground activities with Frank Díaz.

Cato gritted his teeth and gripped the steering wheel as if he were on edge with suspense. Despite his resolve, the encounter with Marco in Tivoli Gardens kept replaying in his mind.

Just because he did one good thing, he isn't absolved of his crimes, especially murder, Cato reasoned. *He probably did it hoping that it would save his own rotten skin, knowing that the law would catch up to him sooner or later.*

Cato had given this matter a lot of thought, but still, he defaulted to his usual black-and-white thinking. If someone "bad" did something "good," there must be a selfish motive. There always was. There was no other way he could reconcile two vastly different behaviors in one person.

So why did this endless loop in his mind never find a resolution? The incident persistently troubled his conscience. He had no patience for moral dilemmas or complexities — there were no "complexities." For Cato, there was no middle ground. That left no room for leniency or understanding.

In the normal course of his daily life, Cato was a man of few distractions. He rarely indulged in anything unrelated to his job. His focus on his duties left little time for reading or listening to anything irrelevant to his work. Yet, tonight, he turned on the radio.

He randomly twirled the dial until he came across the only strong signal he could pick up as he drove through the mountain foothills. The clear voice of a preacher came through the speakers. Cato might have simply turned it off, except the first few words caught his attention. There was that word again — "mercy":

"But God, being rich in mercy because of His great love with which He loved us," the preacher said. "Ephesians chapter two verse four — 'But God,' the most hopeful two words in all the Bible. 'But God ...'

"God has mercy on whomever He chooses," the voice continued. "The apostle Paul, a righteous man by the standards of this world, learned this on the road to Damascus. Mercy — you can't earn it, you can't buy it, and you don't deserve it.

"Sovereign mercy is not owed to men. We don't deserve God's mercy — we can't demand it. If so, then it's no longer mercy. Some people think that everyone has a right to receive God's mercy. That viewpoint is deeply ingrained in fallen humanity. This is why the gospel is offensive to people. People get mercy when they don't deserve it. If they did deserve it, then it would no longer be mercy."

Cato strained his ears. This was making more sense than it should.

Of course, Cato knew that some people got into this religious stuff, but it had never come through to him in such a lucid, plain way, speaking straight to his heart and pertaining directly to his current situation. He turned the volume up slightly to catch what this preacher was saying more clearly.

"Mercy is in the nail-scarred hands of the God-man in glory. It cannot be obtained in any other way," the preacher continued. "At the crucifixion, God the Father turned His back on His innocent Son, letting the only sinless man in history bear the full punishment for someone else's sin ... my sin ... before being resurrected to life. The sun refused to shine on that scene, while the earth trembled. You ignore that fact at your own eternal peril. We are all condemned without divine mercy, which no man has ever received apart from the crucified and resurrected Son of God — the living Lord.

"There is no such thing as salvation by demand, nor by chance — only by God's grace and sovereign will. A sinner's only hope is to submit to God's verdict on him, lay himself on the mercy of the court, and plead with an empty hand. God alone receives the glory for having mercy on the worst of sinners. That scares some people to death, I'll tell you. But that, dear listener, gives me hope."

The words penetrated Cato's heart. He contemplated what he heard, how it shed light on this ordeal he'd been struggling over. Religion still struck him as fanciful, but something in what the preacher was saying had penetrated Cato's defensiveness. He desired to know more, but for now, he was a man with a job to do — simple as that.

Cato turned off the radio as Marco's car pulled off onto the James Bond Beach Service Road near Oracabessa. He couldn't see where Marco had parked, so he simply continued a little further, finding an inconspicuous place to park along Wharf Road, a fair distance beyond the piers. Cato put the car in park, turned off the lights, climbed out, and locked the doors. From there, he crept back on foot to the area where he'd seen Marco pull off the road, being careful to remain in the shadows.

46

RENDEZVOUS POINT

As midnight approached, Díaz reviewed the plan with the men one last time. The tension was palpable. Vladi had more than his share of combat experience, but Erik and Jorge had never faced anything like this. Not knowing what to anticipate, they were apprehensive.

You have wrestled four-hundred-pound tusked boars—you can take a two-hundred-pound man, Erik reassured himself. *But then, I only had to tackle one boar at a time, and they never shot at me.*

"*Khorosho!*" Erik clapped his hands together. "Let us get our boy back," he said as Díaz concluded. Erik hadn't come all this way for nothing. If he was afraid, it came across with a mix of molten adrenaline. He wanted this done and done.

Jorge gave Erik a sidelong examination, sizing him up. *He doesn't seem to be nervous at all. I hope his skill is equal to his confidence.*

Jorge knew and trusted Vladi, but he had just met Erik a few days prior.

Vladi always spoke so highly of his brother, and Jorge hoped that it was all true and more. If they came under fire, they needed to know they could depend on each other. *We're all placing our lives in each other's hands.*

Díaz's driver held open the rear door of his black 1997 Rolls-Royce Phantom. As the men climbed into the car, they felt less like commandos and more like dignitaries, at least for the moment. They had never seen such a luxurious automobile, especially not in Russia or Cuba.

"This feels like we are riding around in a living room in someone's house!" Erik remarked with his usual humor.

Díaz rode along with the team as an observer, although he had no intentions of getting his hands dirty. Still, he thought it would be helpful if he were available for any last-minute coordination.

Díaz's driver chauffeured while Jorge prayed with the men along the way, asking for safety and favor in their mission. Erik was dropped off at Tom's River to meet the Rastas, and then the driver took Vladi and Jorge to the produce docks at Oracabessa.

The roadside fruit stand at Tom's River, designated as their meeting place, was pitch black at that hour of the night. Erik didn't have to wait there for long. Delroy and Ras Iyah appeared right on time. With them, in the back of the little truck, were seven pressed bales of their best produce — 280 pounds of premium Jamaican "Lamb's Bread" ganja, wrapped in cellophane and then encased in canvas and bound with sturdy twine.

Erik climbed into the tiny truck cab and squeezed between Delroy and Ras Iyah, congenially placing a hand on each man's shoulder. "How are you men doing tonight? Ready to make some money?" Erik asked them lightheartedly.

The Rastas laughed. "Yea, mon. Ya know we do like dat." Delroy turned to Ras Iyah, "I like dis guy already. He seem like di type we can get down wit."

Turning back to Erik, they asked him, "Ya like di herb, mon? We got di best — we can get into some a dis good stuff togedda after di deal go down."

Erik looked back and forth between the men. "Sorry, my English is not so good," he confessed.

The Rasta's strong *patois* had Erik struggling to figure out what they were saying. His grasp of English was fair, but whatever they were saying was downright confusing.

Still, he understood the words "good stuff," and surmised that what they were offering must be something "good" ... like pork roast. *We should be finished in time for breakfast*, he imagined. A hearty meal sounded great to him, and an invitation like that was something he would definitely accept.

"Yes, good stuff. I like the 'good stuff,'" he affirmed.

The Rastas burst into laughter. "Yeaaaa, boy, dat's wha' we talkin' about. We all gonna have di good stuff real soon, bruh!"

Since they were already friends who shared what they had, Erik decided to show what he brought with him — his own something "good," he thought.

"I have — 'good stuff' — here," he told them proudly as he unsheathed his boar knife and held it out in front of the men. The blade glinted in the moonlight streaming into the cab of their little truck.

The Rastas gasped in stereo, "Yow, mon, whatchu doin' wit dat ting?"

Erik chuckled at the reaction. "It is my boar hunting knife, and we are going to meet Mexican cartel pigs. You know ... swine." Erik snorted, making grunting noises like a hog. "It is ... protection."

"Dat's a sword yu have dere, masqueradin' as a knife! Jus' don't bring any swine near to we, mon. Rasta don't deal wit' swine. An' don't be wavin' dat ting around here. Ya might accidentally cut off mi gorgeous locks!" Delroy half-joked as he touched his hair.

"Dat frizzy nest could use a trim," Ras Iyah teased. "Here, gimme dat ting, I'll do it fer ya." He playfully went to take the knife from Erik. Delroy leaned into his window, trying to get as far away as possible.

"Get outta here wit' dat. Di ladies love dees locks." Delroy waved him away. Ras Iyah laughed and took his hand off the knife. He started the truck and put it in gear, driving away while continuing to needle his friend.

"I ain't seen no ladies lovin' yer locks. In fact, I ain't seen no ladies round ya at all!"

Slightly offended, Delroy returned barb for barb, "Well, I ain't seen you killin' di ladies in decades either, breddah. Come to tink of it, I don't tink ya ever had one!"

"Get outta here, mon! I had plenty. Da fines—"

"Oh?" Delroy affected an expression of mock surprise.

"Get real, mon. What about Sharisha? And Latoria? Remember dat catch? Mi know yu was jealous ..."

"Ahhck!" Delroy waved him off. "Dey was just looking fer yu money!"

"What money? Mon, you don't know di first ting bout dem honeys."

"What money, dat's right!" Delroy laughed, stifling a deep cough. "I always knew you wuz a poor one under dat fake 'wash-over' jewelry mon!"

Erik had little idea what they were arguing about, but the tone of their conversation had him laughing as they bantered back and forth. At least it was going to be an entertaining ride, and it was a welcome distraction from the tension he'd been feeling before now. He was thoroughly enjoying this kind of lighthearted, laughter-filled atmosphere with the Rastas.

Meanwhile, Vladi anxiously paced the docks at Oracabessa, checking his watch every few minutes. *Where are they?* The question pounded itself into his head again. *Where are they? They should be here already. This is not the time to be late! This place is so remote and quiet at this time of night. Still, I do not hear any boat engines, even in the distance.*

Three AM came and went with no sign of the cartel. *Were we played for fools?* The knot of anxiety in Vladi's gut continued to claw at him. *We should never have trusted that lying cartel trash! They could have just killed Aleksey and taken the boat. Lowlife animals.* His imagination went into overdrive and began spiraling through all sorts of scenarios, none of which ended happily.

Vladi walked up the hill to where Díaz was parked. "The Boss" was calmly sitting in his black Rolls Royce Phantom, wreathed in shadows, beneath the awning of a nearby warehouse. *How can he be so relaxed?* Vladi thought with annoyance as he saw Díaz slightly reclined in his seat.

"Díaz!" he whispered loudly, rapping on the window. Díaz took his time rolling it down. "Are these guys really going to show up or not?"

"They said they would be coming," Díaz replied all too casually for Vladi's liking. "Just wait."

"Well, it is far past the designated time." Vladi's sense of military punctuality was violated. But more than that, he worried about what they would do if no one came. "Do we have a contingency plan if they do not show?" he asked anxiously.

Díaz was unruffled. "These types of guys don't care about what your watch says. They work on their own timetable. They come when they come — if they feel like coming. All we can do is stick to our plan and hope they want to collect their prize."

"I do not like this," Vladi protested. "This is not how this deal is supposed to go."

"Just try to be patient. We will worry about what to do if and when it comes to that."

Vladi reluctantly returned to his restless watch at the edge of the dock. The sound of the wind whistling through the palms and the endless crashing of waves on the shore did nothing to calm his frayed nerves. Every slight rustle in the night or faraway sound of a bird cawing got his attention as he strained to hear even the slightest hint of a boat engine.

At 4:10 AM, he finally heard the familiar purr of the *Skipper Dan*, its twin diesel engines idling, just moments before it chugged into sight and docked at the far, dark end of the pier.

47

CHECK!

Vladi hurried out to meet the boat as it entered the harbor at Oracabessa. As far as the cartel guys could see, he was alone on the pier. They had no idea that a very stealthy Jorge was watching out of sight from a nearby boat docked about midway along the pier. This had been well planned, and Vladi was grateful to have a second set of eyes so close to the situation and someone as keen as the boxer ready to spring into action if necessary.

As he got closer, Vladi did a quick sweep of the boat with his eyes, trying to assess the situation before he got there. As far as he could tell, at least four armed men were on board. His eyes scanned beyond the thugs, searching for the person he was really hoping to find — but he didn't see Aleksey. His heart rate quickened even more.

Did they come without Aleksey? Those worthless rats! Do they dare double-cross us? Vladi's thoughts jumped straight to the worst-case scenarios he'd been rehearsing in his mind while pacing the dock — his face was flush with anger as he approached the craft.

In fact, Aleksey was tied and positioned against the gunnel again, where he couldn't be seen from the pier. With the hood over his head, he only knew that the boat had stopped and that there was activity among the men. He had no idea where they were or who else was there, apart from feeling and hearing the boat docking.

As Vladi approached the craft, one smuggler called out, "*Alto!*"

Vladi's feet squeaked to a halt.

"Don't come any closer until we tell you!" Vladi remained rooted to the ground.

"Pablo Noriega!" Vladi's voice thundered over the lapping water. He did not want to trifle with minions.

"*Sí, señor*," his greeting was reciprocated, calling out of the darkness. "Ready to pay, Ruso?"

"Where is my son?" Vladi demanded.

"We will get to you!" Pablo bellowed back in his deep, gruff voice. "You have something for me?"

"Yes, all your money — right here." Vladi held up the knapsack with the cash so the kidnappers could clearly see it.

"Set it on the dock alongside the boat," Pablo directed Vladi. "Slowly!"

"What about your cargo?" Vladi asked.

"Leave it and go. We'll come for that when we're ready."

"Okay, but make it quick!" Vladi demanded.

Aleksey sat up straighter when he heard the exchange. *Papa? That must be him!* Hearing his father's voice, Aleksey was infused with hope. If anyone could get him out of this, it was Vladislav Gavrilov. Now, maybe this ordeal would come to an end.

Aleksey felt the boat rock as two of the smugglers jumped off.

Vladi strained to see their faces in the dark. He recognized a couple of them as the guys who had raided the *Skipper Dan* back in the Bay of Campeche, which now felt like a lifetime ago. Without realizing it, he clenched his fist at his side. His instinct was to fight, but he knew he had to hold that in check.

Vermin! Vladi deemed them, though he discreetly kept the thought to himself.

One man opened the knapsack and thumbed through the cash. He didn't bother to count — it looked like what they expected, and time was of the essence. "It's all here!" he declared, calling back toward the boat. He tossed it onto the *Skipper Dan's* deck. Vladi's heart skipped a beat — the explosive-laden knapsack landed with a dull thud.

Nothing happened, but the clock was now ticking on that explosive charge. *If Aleksey is somewhere on the boat, his time is running out, too.* Vladi now felt the urgency of the situation even more keenly than before.

Two armed cartel operatives ran up the pier to the waiting truck, one of them the thug who always wore his ratty Bulls jersey. They were happily waved down by the Rastas. "Over here, mon! We got what yu lookin' fa."

The cartel operatives ordered the Rastas to transfer the load from the truck. Vladi "supervised" the transfer while Erik hid in the blackness behind the thick cluster of low-growing fan palms and hanging vines near the parked truck. Armed and alert, he would be ready to back Vladi if things went sideways.

While the cartel smugglers were busy with everything else going on, Jorge slipped into the water and quietly swam to the back of the *Skipper Dan*, now bobbing dockside. He wasn't ready to board, but he held onto the ladder, half of his head sticking above the surface from his nose up.

The smugglers escorted the Rastas, one in front, the other behind. They deposited one bale on the deck of the *Skipper Dan* and were going back for another when the armed smugglers motioned aggressively with their weapons, stopping them. Vladi's heart jumped again.

What is wrong now? Did they see Jorge or Erik? Is there something wrong with the bales?

"You two." The Rastas turned their attention to the man who spoke to them. "Each of you grab a corner of that coffin!" Delroy and Ras Iyah looked at each other, then warily at the men, who repeated the instruction. They cautiously walked over to the boat. It wasn't like they had any real choice.

Together, the four men — two Rastas and two smugglers — hauled the coffin onto the dock and back to the truck where Vladi was waiting. He could see the men carrying something large and heavy. *What is this now?* He was confounded.

When Vladi saw the coffin, his heart sank into the pit of his stomach, and rage forced it back into his throat. Tears threatened to well up in his angry eyes. The men walked over and set the coffin down at his feet. Then one smuggler nodded to the other to unlatch it. Anxiety and frothing anger vibrated through Vladi's whole body. Delroy and Ras Iyah closed their eyes, preparing for the worst.

Vladi let out a small, strangled sound as the lid opened. He thought his legs might buckle. It was certainly not what he had expected. *Did they do this to taunt me? Why a coffin? Those despicable vermin!*

Handguns — forty, if the men had been true to the agreement — lay packed into the coffin. Vladi reached in and picked out one to inspect. He picked up another and passed it over to Delroy and Ras Iyah for them to evaluate. They expressed their approval, and Vladi gave the smugglers the nod that this was good — they could go ahead and latch it back closed.

Back on the boat, Pablo pulled the hood off Aleksey's head.

"It looks like we are going to make a deal after all," Pablo told him. "Fortunately for you, this was not a wasted trip."

Aleksey didn't know what he meant, but the first thing he noticed was that the coffin was gone. He wasn't sure what to think about that. He thought he heard the men dragging it around a few minutes earlier, but he couldn't tell what they were doing. *Hopefully, they are not still planning to use it..*

Things were going well up to this point. Everyone was not quite as guarded as they had been initially. But they still didn't have Aleksey and weren't certain where he was.

When the second bale of ganja was pulled off the back of the little truck, a small commotion occurred in the bushes. The smugglers dropped the bale and immediately drew their guns, pointing toward the rustling vegetation.

While Erik had been carefully watching the scene on the dock, he had not noticed a wharf rat sniffing around his pant leg. He felt the tickle and brushed it off, remaining crouched and never taking his eyes from what was going on between the truck and the dock.

The rodent scurried up Erik's pants leg at his calf. It got stuck at Erik's bent knee and bit him. Erik cursed under his breath and slapped at the rat through his pants leg, but the agitated rodent bit him harder. It happened so fast — Erik stood more upright and tried to shake it loose.

He almost had the rat out when *thwack!* Something fell from the tree above and gave him a glancing blow off his brow before landing on the front of his shirt. Erik gasped without thinking. Looking down, he saw the biggest cockroach he had never known existed.

Startled, he tried to swat it off his shirt just as the rodent gave him a parting bite on the ankle. Losing his balance, Erik tumbled through the palms and vines. The smugglers instinctively swung their weapons toward Erik, ready to fire.

Adrenaline caused Vladi to witness the situation in a sort of slow-motion. With no further time to think, his military training and defensive instincts kicked in to save his brother.

In a flash, Vladi reached around with a knife and slit the closest smuggler's throat, blood bubbling out in dark crimson. The other smuggler swung his weapon toward Vladi, who then had a split second to make a decision. Before he had the chance, a decision was made for him.

A dark figure emerged from behind the truck, and all heads turned his way. He had the Glock that Díaz had offered him as "insurance" drawn on the smuggler, holding it steady.

"Marco?" Vladi shouted in surprise. He was the last person Vladi expected to see.

Marco didn't want to pull the trigger, hoping not to compound his troubles by killing anyone — intentionally this time. He, too, hesitated for a fraction of a second.

Unlike Marco, Cato showed no hesitation when it came time to act. He had watched it all go down from the shadows in the vegetation behind Marco and Erik. Now, he was making his move.

Fluidly, he drew his weapon on one of Cucuy's thugs and fired three rounds from his concealed position in the darkness. Muzzle flashes accompanied the deafening report of the weapon, one of the rounds having found its mark. Instantly, a hole opened through the smuggler's abdomen — blood and tissue flew as the bullet tore through him. The smuggler dropped to the ground, a bloom of dark red soaking his shirt from the wound in his torso.

Not knowing whether Cato was a friend or foe, Vladi moved quickly to disarm him. An epic struggle ensued, a battle of titans, as the veteran Soviet special forces officer took on the hardened police investigator, who had the relative advantage of youth. In the midst of the scuffle, Vladi didn't see that the wounded smuggler, coursed with adrenaline, had shakily risen back to his feet and pointed his weapon toward the men. Erik, however, did see it.

Regaining his footing, Erik leaped onto the gunman, knife at the ready. With the maneuver he had used many times while hunting wild, tusked boars in Russia, he embedded the knife into the heart of the man who threatened his brother. He twisted the blade, a boar hunting technique to ensure maximal damage. The cartel thug gulped his last and slumped to the ground.

Moments later, Vladi had disarmed Cato and thrown his service weapon into the vegetation. Whether he was there for good or bad, whoever this man was, it was going to take him a while to find his gun in the darkness. Vladi had no time to ask questions. The sound of the *Skipper Dan's* engines roaring to life became an immediate problem that commanded his attention.

48

CHECKMATE

Pablo and the other remaining smuggler had started the boat after hearing the commotion onshore. It was apparent that things were deteriorating rapidly — gunshots alerted them to flee, and they were preparing to do just that.

The *Skipper Dan's* engines were deafening as they lit up beside Jorge's ear, where he remained hovering at the waterline. Still hanging onto the ladder, he now had to make a move one way or another — either to board or swim away. Not one to give up on his mission, Jorge threw himself onto the deck of the *Skipper Dan* and commando-crawled his way into the shadows. He made his way to Aleksey, who wriggled back into a corner to get away.

Only Aleksey saw him, but he was gagged and had his hands and feet tied. Jorge could tell by Aleksey's wide eyes that he was startled and confused. He didn't know who Jorge was, but Jorge put his finger to his lips, signaling for Aleksey to remain quiet.

Back on the pier, the battle continued. Vladi was hard as oak and fearless in a firefight. Years of military training came back to him in an instant, and his measured approach to mortal danger was textbook soldiering. He grabbed the AK-47 that lay beside the fallen smuggler and ran down the pier as fast as he could toward the boat.

There was no thought to how many weapons could be pointing at him from the vessel — all that mattered was that his son was presumably on that boat. With the timer set on the explosives, he couldn't let the boat leave with Aleksey onboard.

Vladi could see muzzle flashes as one pirate shot toward him from the vessel. He responded instinctively, squeezing the trigger as rapidly as possible in the direction of the hostile fire.

As the pirate emptied his magazine, spent shell casings flew out of his receiver and onto the deck beside Aleksey — *tink, tink, tink*. Fortunately for Vladi, the gunman couldn't see well enough in the dark to strike a target. The shooter was also preoccupied with trying to untie the boat without exposing himself on the dock.

Dripping wet, his dark clothing plastered to his body, Jorge slowly and silently stood up from his commando crawl, emerging like a swamp monster behind the unsuspecting gunman.

Before the smuggler could raise his weapon, Jorge landed a brutal blow with his fist, striking the side of the gunman's head. The thug collapsed instantly, laid out cold on the deck.

That left only the big man, Pablo, desperate to get out of the harbor. He didn't wait to untie the boat. Instead, Pablo slammed the throttle forward until the ropes began to snap, and the dock cleats broke loose. Several boards buckled in protest and gave way a few seconds later. Within seconds, the *Skipper Dan* was pulling away from the Oracabessa docks at full throttle.

Jorge grabbed his knife and quickly cut through the bindings around Aleksey's legs. As Jorge stood up, the boat lurched forward, knocking him off balance. He landed on his side and skidded across the deck.

Aleksey scrambled to his feet. The boat was moving now, and he wasn't sure what to do.

I cannot swim with my hands tied together — I will drown for sure. Can I maybe take out Cucuy and get control of the boat? ...

Before Aleksey could decide, he saw Jorge push himself up from the deck, regain his footing in the accelerating boat, and come rushing toward him. The speed with which he moved told Aleksey what was about to happen. Eyes wide, Aleksey shook his head adamantly, his scream of protest muffled by the gag still in his mouth.

"My hands are tied!" Aleksey tried to shout. But all that came out were muffled grunting shouts, "Mmmmaahh haddd ideeedd!"

Jorge barreled into Aleksey palms-out, and just like that, with a mighty shove, he sent Aleskey tumbling over the edge of the boat.

Aleksey felt a sting as his body slapped into the water from the speeding boat. Disoriented, he twisted and struggled for several panicked seconds, instinctively kicking his feet toward the surface.

Jorge jumped into the water right after pushing Aleksey overboard, but the speed the boat was traveling had put some distance between them. He quickly resurfaced and searched the inky water for any sign of Aleksey. The dark sky offered no contrast against the black water, making it difficult to discern his location. Then, a flash of orange light.

The sound of a deafening explosion raced across the water. A wave of superheated air rushed over the docks as the sky and the water lit up. Steam hissed up from the surface as the *Skipper Dan* was completely engulfed in flames.

Concussive waves rocked Jorge, and the intense heat reached his face a split second later. Fiery debris began to rain down around him. He dove below the surface to avoid being struck, and in the process, he swam toward where he assumed Aleksey had hit the water.

When Jorge came back up, the burning boat created enough torchlight for him to distinguish bubbles coming to the surface. Diving down again below the bubbles, Jorge strained to see through the water. Though there was a faint light from the burning surface, it was nearly impossible to see where Aleksey had gone.

Another burst of bubbles tickled Jorge's arms from directly below him. It was only then that he could discern that Aleksey was just beneath him. He swam down further, blindly reaching around until his hands hit a struggling Aleksey. Jorge's powerful arms latched onto Aleksey with a viselike grip and pulled him toward the surface.

Back above water, Aleksey struggled to get enough air into his lungs. Jorge ripped the drenched gag from his mouth, and Aleksey gasped. He wheezed, attempting to suck in as much oxygen as possible while coughing out the seawater that had filled him. Jorge held him afloat and gave him a moment to collect his breath. But a moment was all he got.

A flaming piece of debris floated toward a streak of oily fuel that sat atop the water, igniting the flammable pool. A band of fire now lapped between the men and solid ground. Jorge pulled Aleksey back under the surface without warning and dragged him through the water underneath the twisting line of flames. Caught off guard, Aleksey instinctively thrashed in the water, but he remained secure in Jorge's strong grasp. By the time they resurfaced on the other side, Aleksey no longer struggled. In fact, he wasn't moving at all.

Back on the pier, Vladi had also felt the heat of the explosion as it rushed over him and sucked the breath out of his body. He shielded his eyes and face with his arms, turning away from its intensity. He looked up to see his beloved boat engulfed in an inferno, but he hardly gave the boat a second thought out of concern for his son.

Aleksey was on the boat, wasn't he? ... and Jorge. Where is Jorge? Not knowing what had become of either of them, Vladi frantically scanned the water's surface for any sign of the men.

There! Was that a person's head bobbing in the water? Vladi's shoulders slumped as he realized it was only floating debris. Pieces of the boat, many of them on fire, littered the surface. Although the explosion's aftermath provided some light, it was difficult to distinguish what he was seeing. Streams of fire snaked around the water's surface.

Vladi begged God, "Please, he has to have made it off. He has to be alive. We did not come for him to die — and by my own hand."

Vladi sank to his knees. With every moment that passed, despair set in. *I planted the bomb that killed my own son!* he screamed inside. "Ahhhhhh!" an audible wail escaped from his throat. "No! No!" Grief tightened around his heart — oppressive and leaden.

Figuratively, this would be the kill shot — the lone bullet that could bring Vladi to the ground. If Aleksey were gone ...

What will I tell Irina? She will never forgive me. I have failed her again. My poor judgment has killed our son. I will never forgive myself! I can never face her. I might as well just throw myself into this water and never come back up ...

A splashing sound caught his attention. Vladi put his hands on the edge of the deck and strained his neck forward. Silhouetted against the fire in the distance, a black figure moved through the water. It looked like he was dragging a body behind him, pulling it along the surface of the water.

"Jorge?" Vladi whispered. Unable to wait to find out, Vladi dove in and swam to meet the shadows in the water. He saw the fire's reflection in the wet face of his son as he was dragged by Jorge. There was no movement and no answer as Vladi repeatedly called his name.

Moments later, the three reached the pier. Vladi clambered out, then helped Jorge get Aleksey out of the water, haul him onto the pier, and lay him on his side. Right away, Aleksey sputtered and gagged as he coughed up salty water. Vladi almost collapsed with relief to hear signs of life. He knelt next to him and put a hand on his face.

"Aleksey? Can you hear me?" Vladi was desperate to hear his voice. He held his son by the shoulders, panting. Aleksey couldn't get any words out but nodded yes.

Aleksey coughed and gasped again. "Papa ... you are here," he eked out weakly.

Still shaking from the ordeal, Vladi put a trembling hand on his son's shoulder. He grappled at his boar knife and cut Aleksey's hands loose from his rope bindings.

Aleksey made a wobbly attempt to push himself up, but his arms gave out immediately.

"Hey, hey, give yourself a minute," Vladi told him.

Vladi then turned to Jorge, "I can never thank you enough. I—" His voice caught. "I did not know if either of you made it."

Exhausted, Jorge nodded in acknowledgment. Then he, too, flopped onto the pier on his back.

Vladi raised his hands to the sky, turned his tearful eyes toward Heaven, and gave thanks to the Lord.

After several more minutes of recovery, Aleksey and Jorge were able to sit upright. Vladi hugged his son close — long and firm — something only moments before he wasn't sure he would ever be able to do again. Almost lulled into a comfortable state, he suddenly remembered his old adversary — a man who had put his life on the line for all of them.

"Marco!" Vladi suddenly shouted as he gently pushed himself away from Aleksey. This crisis was over, but he remembered the scene back at the truck. Jorge looked up in surprise. "Marco?"

Vladi scrambled to his feet and ran back to where he had last seen Marco. In fact, it wasn't only Marco who needed to be found. There were many questions waiting to be answered for him back around the truck.

Where is Erik? Who was the other gunman? Where did he come from?

49

STANDOFF

Cato and Erik locked eyes, each man convinced the other was a dangerous threat. They were both wrong. Neither knew the full story. Cato believed that Erik was part of a failed drug deal, while Erik thought Cato was a backup for the cartel smugglers. Only Marco knew the truth.

The lifeless bodies of two cartel smugglers lying between them were a grim reminder of the violence that had erupted only moments before and only fueled their mistaken beliefs. Vladi had taken the Kalashnikov AK-47 rifle that belonged to one of the slain smugglers before he took off running down the pier. That left the other dead man's rifle on the ground beside his body.

Volatile, dangerous, unpredictable — the men listened to the sounds of deep breaths and their own pounding hearts as each weighed his options and and sized up their opponent. They were both ready to fight — it was only a matter of who would make the first move.

Erik maintained a firm overhand grip on his boar knife. Cato had already seen that he knew how to use it — he wasn't willing to take on Erik hand-to-hand.

Cato kept his eye on the knife, assessing whether he could get to the dead man's weapons faster than the agitated Russian.

"Stay. Right. There," Cato intoned. "And put your hands right where I can see them in the air. Slowly."

Erik just glared at Cato. Although he didn't comprehend much English, he could surmise the meaning of Cato's commands. He wasn't willing to comply, regardless. This stranger had just appeared unexpectedly at a supposedly secret rendezvous. Erik wasn't about to start taking orders from him.

Erik looked down briefly, apparently having the same thoughts as Cato. Cato's gaze followed Erik's back to the AK-47 lying an equal distance between them, begging to be claimed. The detective could see that Erik wasn't going down without a fight.

At that moment, the prize of the rifle represented the balance of power between them. Whoever had the rifle had the power, simple as that.

In a blur of motion, Erik and Cato simultaneously lunged for the weapon. With lightning speed, Erik's hand closed around the stock first, pointing it directly at Cato with his finger hovering over the trigger.

Marco perceived the standoff happening before his eyes — it was as though the world around them seemed to slow down. Marco knew he had to act. As the only one who knew the identity and intentions of both men, Marco wasn't about to let them kill each other. It was a delicate situation that needed to be defused quickly and completely.

Marco stepped between the two men, putting himself in the line of fire. At this point, he needed to protect Cato and believed it would be easier to reason with Erik. Cato — not so much — he was more unpredictable.

"Put it down, Erik," Marco said slowly and gently, using hand gestures to indicate what he wanted him to do. He knew that Erik's grasp of English was limited, but he hoped that by motioning and speaking in a calm tone, Erik would get the idea.

Erik wouldn't be persuaded, his finger tightening around the trigger. It was like a switch had flipped into kill mode, and Marco didn't know how to switch it back. Fueled by adrenaline, Erik was too wound up to listen. He was beyond reasoning, and his grip on the rifle was unwavering. His eyes were wild and ferocious. He panted and squinted at Cato like he'd cornered a dangerous beast.

Marco continued to face Erik, pleading with him again to lower his weapon, trying desperately to explain that Cato wasn't a threat to him or the mission.

"Erik, listen to me. He doesn't want to hurt you. He just wants me," Marco told him. Again, Marco tried using hand gestures to communicate his point.

Marco's words fell on deaf ears. Erik stood his ground. His posture revealed the Russian's volatile agitation, heightened by a language barrier that left him feeling like one of his senses had been taken away. Erik was taking all his cues from his environment. Beyond voice tone and facial expressions, he was operating on pure instinct.

Just then, Cato took a step forward, combative as ever in his demeanor — ready to make a move and take on anyone who stood in his way. Marco knew that if Cato attempted to wrest the gun from Erik, it would end with one or both of them dead.

Marco was left with no other choice. In a bold, desperate decision to prevent more bloodshed, Marco turned to face Cato and held up his hands in a gesture of surrender.

"Take me. I'm all yours, Cato. Arrest me. That's what you want. Just let these guys go."

Marco had already concluded that running was futile — he was as good as caught anyway. Delaying the inevitable wouldn't benefit anyone. He at least hoped that if he could show Erik that Cato was just there to arrest him, it would convince Erik to stand down, seeing that the danger had passed.

"I don't think so, Rivera. Your buddy has a weapon — he's just itching to use it. Tell him to put it down." Cato retorted. He wasn't about to turn his back on a crazed individual with a weapon trained on him.

"He doesn't want to hurt you. He doesn't know enough English to understand what you're doing. You've got him convinced you're a threat to us. When he sees you're just here to arrest me and nothing more, I think he'll stand down," Marco explained.

"You think?" Cato scoffed. That wasn't reassuring enough to the cynical lawman.

"Yes, he will," Marco promised blindly. He didn't really know what Erik would do. He might shoot Cato to free Marco, but it was the best plan Marco could come up with under pressure. So, he committed to that approach — all in.

Hidden in the bushes as the intense standoff played out, the Rastas watched the scene unfold in stunned disbelief. Back when the shooting began, they had taken cover in the bushes where Erik had been hiding. Still concealed, they looked on in horror, whisper-arguing nervously about what was happening.

"He's takin' down Cheeko, mon," Delroy whispered, awe in his voice.

Ras Iyah was stunned. "What? No way! Who gonna make da next movie fa him?" he asked, his voice filled with concern.

Delroy jokingly suggested, "Hey, maybe you could be his stand-in, like a stunt double."

Ras Iyah was having none of that. He lightly punched Delroy's arm, solemnly scolding, "Das not funny, mon. Dis ain't a movie — dis is real life. Cheeko life!"

As the two men continued to banter, Cato relented and tossed his cuffs to Marco.

"Put them on," he commanded.

Marco obeyed, sliding them on and ratcheting them closed. Erik's breath began to calm, and he lowered the barrel of the AK-47.

Nonetheless, Erik was confused by this turn of events. It appeared that imminent danger had passed. Yet, what was happening to Marco? Now Erik began to wonder if he needed to rescue Marco from this belligerent stranger. Marco, for his part, looked resigned to his fate. But why? Was he in trouble because of their mission? Was Marco taking the fall for the whole affair? So many questions, none of which could be answered at the moment.

Erik took a step toward Marco and reached out his hand, unsure of what to do. Marco put his cuffed hands up in a gesture meant to reassure Erik.

"It's okay, it's okay, Erik." Erik put his hand down — he could at least understand these words.

"Stay here. Wait for Vladi. Help him get home safe with his son." Cato then gripped Marco's arm to lead him away while Erik watched, helpless to comprehend and therefore intervene for Marco.

Erik hadn't understood everything that had happened, but he did realize that Marco's quick thinking and self-sacrifice saved the men from doing further harm to one another. Deep down, Cato knew it too.

50

AFTERSHOCK

A shard of sunlight peeked over the horizon, casting a golden hue over the pier. Vladi had returned just in time to see Marco handcuffed, about to be led away by the stranger who had appeared out of nowhere. He didn't know what this man wanted with Marco, but he intended to find out.

"Marco?"

Erik turned around at the sound of Vladi's voice. By the look on Erik's face, Vladi could tell that his brother didn't have any answers either. As he drew closer, the situation became even less clear.

Initially, Vladi thought that the tall man attired in black was one of Díaz's security team. Marco didn't struggle but hung his head as if he knew the game was over for him — as if he had given up. But given up on what? What was this about? Vladi was thoroughly confused.

A rustling in the bushes caught Vladi and Erik's attention. Everyone was already on edge. They were relieved to see it was just Delroy and Ras Iyah emerging from the nearby vegetation. With the commotion having died down, they peeked out to check if the coast was clear. Seeing Vladi return, they felt it was safe enough now to come out of hiding.

"What in di world? Mon, you guys almos' got wi killed!" Delroy was indignant and shaken.

"I didn't sign up for dis, mon. All di shootin' and explodin' and carryin' on! Dis ain't wort no amount o' money!" Ras Iyah was equally indignant.

"Mon, errybody be havin' guns up in heah!" Delroy pointed this out with a salty attitude.

"Except us!" Ras Iyah chimed in. They both nodded solemnly in agreement.

Yet for all their indignation, their curiosity over the situation with Marco got the better of them. Delroy and Ras Iyah moved closer to where Marco stood. "Marco Rivera, you are under arrest," was all they heard. And that was all they needed to hear.

At the first sign that law enforcement was present, they were already scrambling. "Wi ain't no parta dis," Delroy asserted, holding his hands up as he and Ras Iyah backed away several steps. Spontaneously, the Rastas turned on their heels and bumbled past each other in their haste to flee. Delroy's feet lost purchase on the shell surface, causing him to slip through several steps before he regained balance. His companion wasn't waiting to see if he got himself together. Ras Iyah was already in the driver's seat starting the engine when Delroy dove into their little truck and slammed the rusted door.

Their spinning tires kicked up dust clouds as they peeled out, heading into the hills toward home. Cato might just deal with them later, but for the moment, he wasn't concerned — he had his man.

Vladi, on the other hand, had stopped short when he heard Cato's words. Erik, just behind him, stopped as well. The men watched the arrest, dumbfounded. Vladi strode right up to Marco.

"Marco? What is this? Who is this?" Then, turning to Cato, Vladi questioned him directly. "Who are you to be taking him? He did not shoot anyone!" The intensity in Vladi's dark eyes matched the iciness of Cato's frigid stare.

"I'm Detective Inspector Cato, JCF Kingston. You need to step back," Cato spat out brusquely.

"Marco?" Vladi turned back with a softer, pleading voice. The very same questions Erik had been unable to verbalize now raced through Vladi's mind.

Marco looked up at Vladi with sorrow in his eyes.

"Your son." Marco struggled to say anything. "He's all right?"

"He will be fine," Vladi assured him. "Everyone is fine. We did not even know you were here." Marco's appearance had diverted a disaster, and they all knew it.

"Very well," Marco answered. "Vladi." Marco's eyes were glassy. "I have one thing to ask from you, although I don't deserve it."

"Wait — explain to me why you are here now. And why is this ...?" Vladi looked toward Cato.

"Detective Inspector," Cato injected.

"Okay, whatever," Vladi shot back with disdain. "Why does this 'Detective Inspector' have you handcuffed?"

Marco shook his head. "The past has returned to torment me. Unfortunate matters have begun to surface, for which I'm responsible."

Even more bewildered, Vladi's eyes widened. Marco's short answer was far from adequate.

"It's too much, Vladi. That's all I can explain in this moment. But I need something from you ... *comrade*" — the word came with an affectionate tone. "One thing, although I understand it may be something you aren't willing to give to me."

"What is that, Marco?" Vladi prompted with a tone of uncertainty, caught between emotion and confusion. Marco had just saved their lives. What could he possibly want from him right now?

"Forgive me," Marco asked in a weak voice.

Vladi was nodding his head before the words were out. Somewhere deep inside, he'd known that this was coming and mentally prepared himself. Yet, the moment still brought with it heavy emotion. Vladi swallowed hard, and his eyes began to water.

Even until now, Vladi hadn't known how he would respond. His stubborn flesh wanted to hold on to the bitterness, rationalizing that what Marco had done was unforgivable. Vladi also knew how the Lord had forgiven him. This reality was also once unimaginable. Here was a man who needed forgiveness the way a dying man in the desert needed water.

"I do," Vladi replied, trying hard to keep his voice steady. "I will."

"Say it — I want to hear you say it," Marco urged softly. "Please."

Vladi cleared his throat. Saying the words was not as hard as he had thought it would be. In all sincerity, he verbalized what this desperate man had needed to hear for many years.

"I forgive you, Marco. It is true — you have my forgiveness." Vladi added, "It is over."

Marco gave a feeble nod of his head as Cato jerked on his cuffs. The emotions inside Vladi began to break at the sight.

Speaking in Russian, Erik asked Vladi to tell him what was happening. Vladi didn't have all the answers his brother was looking for, but he assured him that he would explain more later.

Satisfied for the moment, Erik crouched next to the lifeless smugglers, blood-soaked earth beneath them. In a gesture he knew was almost certainly futile, he checked them for pulses.

Dripping wet, Jorge and Aleksey made their way up the pier.

"Dyadya!" Aleksey's eyes were wide with surprise. "How did you get here?"

Erik jumped up and grabbed Aleksey in the greatest bear hug he could muster. The sopping wet Aleksey now soaked his clothes as well, but Erik hardly gave it a thought.

"I would not leave you if I had to go to the end of the earth to find you, my boy," Erik assured his nephew as he put an affectionate hand on his head. Erik then turned and thanked Jorge for a job well done, and the men exchanged pats on the back. The moment was emotional but also matter-of-fact. The job was done. Lives were saved.

A well-dressed Caucasian gentleman with a graying beard walked up on the men, seemingly out of nowhere, confidently giving orders with a Cockney accent.

"Freeze! Let's see some hands. Get 'em up!" he ordered.

Everyone was quick to comply, except for Cato, who took his time as he studied the interloper.

"Inspector Richard Mason, NCA." He flashed identification, although it was too fast for any of the startled men to examine it in any detail.

"NCA?" Aleksey questioned, looking over at Vladi. No one had a clue what was going on, least of all Aleksey. Mason might as well have said he was from another planet for all the sense it made to them.

"National Crime Agency," Cato spoke up, the only one who recognized the acronym. "... New Scotland Yard."

The Glock that Mason was holding was all the identification he needed to present to establish that he was in charge of this affair. And he had the weapon trained on Cato, the only wildcard present.

"Who are you?" Mason asked.

"Detective Inspector Winston Cato, JCF Kingston," Cato said with a twist of sourness in his voice. He was used to being known. He reached for his identification.

"Whoa! Nice ... and ... easy," Mason cautioned as he peered around behind Cato.

"Kingston, eh? What's your business this far north, Cujo?" Mason pressed.

"It's Cato ... Detective Inspector Winston Cato."

"Roger that." Mason continued to toy with the stiff cop, maintaining his composure.

"I —" Cato started to explain. Mason cut him off.

"I'll have you know ... Mr. Cato ... we've been watching this ring for a long time. Now ... you ... have single-handedly blown our whole operation," he chastised with masterful condescension while simultaneously looking over at the *Skipper Dan* burning in the water.

"We've seized this crate of weapons," Mason said, flicking his wrist in the direction of the guns, "but this case could have — should have — yielded more answers than I expect it will now." Mason pursed his lips in mock dissatisfaction.

Cato raised his eyebrows slightly.

"Had we been able to apprehend one or more of these cartel operatives, we could have extracted insights to aid in neutralizing their operation, at least as they extend to Jamaica's shores." He paused, glancing toward the smuggler Cato had shot. "I see you have ensured that will not be possible."

Cato was not impressed, nor was he swayed by the man's words.

"Mason, I'm taking this man into custody," Cato stated with unwavering defiance. "An array of criminal charges will be brought against the 'suspect,' up to and including murder."

"By all means ... go ahead. I'll call in support from Ocho Rios and file our report."

"You do that," Cato told him dryly.

"Right. We'll have someone reach out to your office before the end of the day."

"You'll get your report. Be sure of that," Cato quipped.

"Very well. I'll expect that within forty-eight hours." Mason turned stern. "Let's hope there is a very good explanation for why you have your nose stuck in our operation," he added.

With that, Cato turned Marco toward where he'd parked the car and escorted him away without any further discussion as everyone else helplessly looked on.

"The watch!" Aleksey suddenly exclaimed, looking in the direction of what remained of the smoldering wreckage on the sea.

From the way he said it, Vladi assumed it had been lost on the boat. Every head turned toward the *Skipper Dan* in the distance, burning to the waterline.

Instead, Aleksey reached into his trousers and pulled out the old pocket watch. He examined it to see what he already knew. Water had penetrated the timepiece — it had stopped. He showed the watch to Vladi.

"Papa, I am sorry. It was ruined in the water." Aleksey felt guilty, despite his efforts to save the heirloom.

Vladi hugged his son tightly, laughing.

"It is not the first time that watch has been in the water, son." He gave Aleksey an affectionate rub on his head. "I know what to do."

51

THE BOSS AND THE LAWMAN

A breeze blowing in from the sea whipped around as he led Marco to his parked car. The morning air was cool and crisp. It was the perfect backdrop for Cato's moment of glory — much like his ego, full of bluster and bravado. Cato's chest swelled with pride to be walking away with Marco in custody, further bolstering his confidence in his dominance over society's foes. The law wins, and the criminal loses. Again.

Except for the sound of waves gently lapping against the shore, the area was secluded and quiet, with only a few parked cars and boats in sight. To avoid detection, Cato had parked quite a distance from the docks along Wharf Road on the outskirts of town, where he couldn't easily be seen. It would be a fairly long trek back toward Oracabessa town to reach his car with his prisoner, Marco, in tow.

Cato had the sensation of being watched. He quickly spun his head around to look over his shoulder but saw nothing except an empty road. He chalked it up to the stress of the previous few hours. Shrugging it off, he continued onward.

As they walked, Cato maintained a tight grip on Marco's arm, a physical reminder that he was in control. He relished the power he held over this criminal fugitive who had eluded justice for a decade. Lost in his own glory, Cato felt untouchable, bearing the sense of invincibility that came with a big catch like this. Nothing could stop him now.

Or so he thought.

Looks like we have a situation on our hands. Díaz ruminated. The cigar clenched between his teeth was nearly chewed to a stub as he studied the affair. Unbeknownst to Cato, Díaz had been watching the entire scene unfold from a distance. His keen eyes missed nothing. His mind batted around a multitude of possibilities. Although he had an uncanny ability to read people and situations, for the moment, Díaz lacked the crucial bits of information to make a meaningful assessment. He could only assume that Marco had been singled out and arrested in connection with this operation. That wasn't good, to say the least.

Díaz stepped out of the Rolls to get some fresh air and maybe a fresh perspective. He began pacing quietly, his clean linen suit soundless and crisp. His pacing turned into walking, half-consciously making his way in the direction the lawman was moving with Marco. Díaz's mind was busy moving around the people and events like pieces on a chessboard, calculating every move, anticipating every possibility.

The lawman's unexpected interference had caught Díaz flat-footed, and that was unacceptable. Díaz had no idea who the man was, nor had he anticipated the unpredictable meddling in their carefully laid plan. This twist counted as a failure in his book, and Díaz didn't do failure.

Marco's potential transfer to Kingston in handcuffs was a new problem with potentially far-reaching consequences. Díaz needed to get Marco loose from the clutches of this troublesome lawman. If Marco cratered under interrogation, it could spell disaster for all of them.

But Díaz wasn't one who gave up easily, nor was he ever fully without resources. As he figured it, the greatest resource on earth was resourcefulness, and he had plenty of that. He was a man who invariably turned the tide of battle in his favor, no matter how dire the situation appeared. He unfailingly had another trick up his sleeve, an ace in the hole. He was nothing if not adaptable, always ready to adjust his strategy on the fly.

Subconsciously, Díaz tapped the face of his watch as he quickened his steps, still pondering. Indeed, time was an unyielding and problematic factor in all of this.

In any other situation, he might lie low and wait until the perfect opportunity presented itself, but there was no time for that. Yet an immediate attempt to rescue Marco was also a risky move that could put them in jeopardy. The stakes were too high for errors or poor decisions. This needed to be done right ... and fast.

At once, his feet abruptly stopped on the seashell-strewn roadway, and Díaz deftly spun out of sight with the smooth precision of a tango dancer. He'd sighted his target. From behind the cover of the corrugated tin bus shelter and some foliage, Díaz could see the lawman closing the back door of his car and getting into the driver's seat. Marco's head and shoulders were vaguely apparent in the back seat. Díaz made a mental note of the make and model of the vehicle — *black Toyota Corolla — as unflashy and practical as they come.*

Sizing up the lawman like a prizefighter assessing his opponent, Díaz watched him drive off with Marco.

"You've got guts, lawman," Díaz muttered to himself with disdain. He was simultaneously impressed and displeased by the man who had so brazenly intervened. This maverick cop was indeed gutsy — he had to give him that — but Díaz didn't like surprises.

Guts alone won't get you far in this game, Díaz opined. *More like reckless arrogance.* He'd seen such "Lone Ranger" types before, loose cannons in the name of justice. Men who thought they had it all under control but were, in reality, wildly out of bounds. *He'll be a victim of his own hubris, just like the others.*

Contemplating his options, Díaz walked back toward his car and then stared out into the sea for a moment, scanning the horizon as the rising sun cast a crimson glow over the scene. He needed a plan, and he needed it now.

With the fierce elegance of a panther, Díaz was on the move. He slid into the driver's seat and turned the ignition on his sleek black sedan — the Rolls' V8 engine purred like a caged animal eager to be unleashed. That made two of them.

Díaz cruised toward the end of the pier where Mason stood with the other men, waiting for orders.

All eyes were on "The Boss" as he emerged from the driver's seat — his calm yet commanding presence was impossible to ignore. He was in his element. "The Boss" wasted no time. He was back in charge of the situation like a seasoned general directing his troops in battle.

"Quick!" he directed Mason, signaling for him to get in the car as he climbed out. Díaz twisted his pinky ring and sauntered around the car as if it really were just a day at the beach. Mason held open the back door for Díaz, and it was clear that he was leaving the others behind.

Vladi furrowed his brow in concern. "Wait. You are leaving? But how do we get back?"

Díaz was a man of few words and had no time for trivial details. He produced a crisp hundred-dollar bill with the flick of a wrist. "You'll get a ride back with this," he said, pressing the fresh Benjamin into Vladi's hand, "... and don't forget the guns!"

"But what about the coffin?" Vladi persisted.

Díaz didn't hesitate. "Russians put the first man in space. Did he get back?"

Vladi nodded, puzzled by Díaz's insinuation.

"See what I mean. You guys are smart." Díaz arched an eyebrow to punctuate his thought. "You'll figure it out," he told Vladi, waving his cigar casually as if the matter were settled.

Mason nodded curtly, silently affirming that "The Boss" had made a convincing point.

"We need to intercept this 'Dick Tracy wannabe' before he gets to Kingston with Marco," Díaz told Mason, slapping the hood of his Rolls Phantom like it was a disobedient donkey.

Mason was always ready for whatever "The Boss" had in mind next. He'd seen Díaz move mountains before and had no doubt he could do it again. Mason knew that when his boss got this intense, something was about to go down.

"Let's move," Díaz instructed through his cigar-clenched teeth, his voice ringing with authority. Mason hit the accelerator. Díaz was ready to play this game of cat and mouse, and the lawman was about to find out who the real cat was.

"Stop!" Díaz suddenly called out, causing Mason to slam on the brakes, sliding to a stop.

"There — that's Marco's car." Díaz reached forward, pointing to the dark blue Mitsubishi Lancer parked at the turnoff to the James Bond Beach Service Road.

"Change of plan," he told Mason, who didn't even know the original plan. Díaz's charisma was usually enough for people to readily follow him, so he rarely spelled out his thinking.

"Whatcha got in mind, Boss?" Mason waited for further instructions.

"What a stroke of luck! You head down to Kingston. I'll take Marco's car. We have a chance to cut them off — we can intercept them before they arrive."

Mason nodded in agreement but then cocked his head to the side, prompting for clarification about exactly what Díaz had in mind.

"How so, Boss?"

"He'll take the A3 to Kingston. We need to catch up before he reaches City Centre Police Station. The best place to position yourself is Old Stony Hill. Get your map from the glove box." Mason opened the map, and Díaz pointed out the Old Stony Hill cutoff.

"You'll park there. Watch for Wyatt Earp in his uninspiring black Toyota Corolla — just look for the most boring and practical car on the road at this hour of the morning ... it's probably him.

"Once you see him, don't let him out of your sight and wait for further instructions."

"Will do, Boss," Mason responded.

"Call me on the Nokia immediately," Díaz said, already climbing out of the car. "I'll give you further instructions. Just don't let him out of sight."

"Got it, Boss!"

Mason's knowledge of the plan was limited to what Díaz had just told him, but he was perfectly confident that his boss had the situation under control. A strategist of the highest order, Díaz was always one step ahead. His confidence was infectious, and his men trusted him implicitly.

Mason waited as Díaz opened the trunk. Grabbing a slim-jim from the back, he gave a thumbs up to Mason and sauntered over to Marco's car.

Díaz easily unlocked the driver's side door of Marco's blue Lancer and got in. His head disappeared from view under the steering wheel, his fingers dancing over the wires beneath the dashboard. With a few deft flicks, he sparked the right connection, and the engine revved to life.

Watching from the driver-side window of the black Rolls, Mason could see Díaz give a sly smile.

"You're about to meet your match, lawman," Díaz said to himself with a half grin.

Díaz cruised the Lancer aside his own luxurious black sedan and rolled down the passenger side window for some final words to Mason. "I've got some calls to make and things to do. I have to make this airtight. We can't afford any more trouble," Díaz said.

"Get moving, and don't let him catch you trailing him. You never know if 'Sherlock Holmes' here is trigger-happy. Call me the second you see him."

Mason nodded in the affirmative and hit the gas in the Rolls Phantom. The chase was on, and Díaz was determined to come out on top. Cato had no idea they were coming for him.

52

UNDER ARREST

Cato put Marco in the back of his car and turned back toward Kingston, his grip on the steering wheel resolute and his countenance expressionless.

"You saved my life back there," Marco admitted. "Thank you."

"Makes us even," was Cato's concise reply. He thought for a moment, then continued, "Then again, getting between me and 'Crazy Ivan' back there ... I think you've still got one up on me."

It was uncomfortable talking to the cold figure of Cato while staring at the back of his head. Marco made efforts to meet the man's eyes in the rearview mirror. Cato, however, maintained focus on the winding mountain road ahead. Marco still tried to converse with him. There was a lot on his mind.

"Back there, that wasn't what it looked like," Marco started out.

"Oh? I very much doubt that." Cato was as cynical as they came.

"Neither was Michael Cervera." Marco diverted his eyes from the mirror as he said the name. This time, Cato did glance up into the rearview, his stony glare reflecting back at Marco.

"I've heard every excuse in the book. Everyone is always 'innocent' of the crimes they commit. So don't bother," Cato intoned coldly. "The prisons are full of convicted criminals who maintain their innocence. Save your breath. I don't need to hear another criminal try to justify what he did. I'll not feel one ounce of sympathy for you."

Marco took a deep breath. He needed a different approach. "It was a rescue mission," he stated, hoping to catch Cato's attention. It sort of worked.

"What? Are you trying to tell me you were trying to save Cervera and just happened to murder him instead? You are more absurd than I thought."

"I'm not talking about Michael Cervera. I guess that's part of the story, going back, but just not this part. I'm talking about what you think was a drug deal back at the docks."

"What do you mean?" Cato demanded.

"It was a front to rescue a friend's kidnapped son from the Gulf Cartel. None of the authorities in the US or Mexico could help — so my friend, the tall Russian, was left to his own resources. I owe him ... I owe him more than my life, so I came to the docks in case they needed me."

"His son was kidnapped, you say?" Cato asked.

"Yes. He's been held hostage in Mexico for weeks — the cartel made absurd ransom demands for his return. We all feared for his life. This deal was a ruse arranged to persuade the cartel ... and explode the boat ..."

Cato narrowed his eyes. He knew of similar scenarios where law enforcement used contraband to set up a sting operation. He wasn't sure what to believe, yet this wasn't the usual justification. Marco was spinning a yarn more intricate than what he was accustomed to hearing. He couldn't help his amusement at what a creative liar Marco was if he was making it up.

"I care less about what happened at the dock. They can sort it out," he told Marco. "You're in trouble for that, but that isn't why I came after you. You're here for Cervera."

"Yeah, about that ..."

"Listen, the law allows you to get an attorney and mount your defense. You don't have to say a word. But we have a long drive, so if you want to talk ... go right ahead. Eventually, it'll all come out in court anyway," Cato said. "I want to know about Cervera and what you had to do with it. You said it's a part of the story — so, what's the connection?"

If what Marco was saying was true, Cato could see that he was missing vital pieces of this story. With confidence bordering on recklessness, he'd been quick to condemn — at least to assume he knew the context. He glanced back in the mirror. Cato had left the conversation open for Marco to continue, and he would listen more attentively now.

If anything, the suspect may just hang himself. Let him talk.

Marco was encouraged by the implication that Cato wanted him to continue with the story instead of just shutting him down. But if the man wanted the truth, he was going to get it all, starting with when he and Julio first left Cuba.

"I have a lot to tell you — if you will indulge me, it will all begin to make more sense."

"I'm listening," Cato said, his voice gravelly. "But keep in mind, I deal in facts. So if you're going to give me a sob story, just save it."

"Fair enough. What I have to say will probably answer many of the questions you have. In the end, all the pieces are going to connect." Marco offered, hoping Cato would be patient enough to hear him through. Cato gave a brief nod, and Marco took it as his cue to start.

"Before my brother and I were smuggled out of Cuba as refugees, I was one of the top prosecutors in Havana ... perhaps all of Cuba," Marco began. Immediately, Cato connected why Marco had said he was an attorney.

"A Cuban lawyer, not Jamaican — right?"

Marco went on to tell Cato how, in his former life, he effectively carried out his assigned responsibilities for Castro's government. He had been proud of his misused talent, which had fueled his zeal. In the course of time, he had done much irrevocable harm.

Ah, this is already interesting, Cato thought shrewdly. He remained silent as he let Marco talk.

"I destroyed many lives, and I was proud of it," Marco told him flatly as he continued his empty stare out of the window. His mind was deep in his memories, and that was all he saw.

He continued, telling Cato why and how they had left Cuba, about Vladi and their life in Florida, and how he eventually fled, landing in Jamaica with nothing.

"Why would you leave the States ... and return to Cuba?" Cato demanded.

"It was pride, really. Nothing but stubborn, stupid pride. And it caused me to leave my own brother, the one I persuaded to come with me to the States. He always showed love to me and others, despite my own selfish character. I just left him wondering whether I was dead or alive for so many years." Marco sighed at the foolishness of his former self.

He briefly told Cato about being robbed by the driver and his accomplices, being stranded on the jungle road, and how he ended up meeting the Rastafarian men.

"They really are a couple of okay guys. Funny even. They saved me without knowing it."

Cato made a *harrumph* sound deep in his throat but continued listening.

"And today they helped save this kidnapping victim too." They hadn't known the role of their participation, but Marco gave credit where it was due.

"But this is all to say that it was what first brought me to the travel agency and Michael Cervera's office. It was nothing personal — I was only there looking for what I needed — supplies to forge the documents that would get me back to Cuba and help me slip back into my old life as if I had never left. I was hoping I could get everything I needed without being seen."

Marco then described in detail the night he broke into the travel agency for documents to return home to Cuba, how he was cornered in Michael's office, and how a struggle in the dark resulted in the tragic accident.

"I never intended to hurt him, let alone for him to die," Marco recounted, his voice thick with sorrow. "I panicked, and he fell ... And as you know, I was able to flee before his driver could get a good look at me in the dark."

"So, you got back to Havana?" Cato asked.

"Yes, I made it back to Cuba and returned to my former life — no one ever knew. Then one day, the Cuban coast guard picked up someone I had been longing to exact my revenge upon ... the Russian man whose son we rescued, Vladi. 'What good fortune,' I thought." Marco's face flushed with shame at having felt the way he did. It was so ... dark-hearted and malicious.

"What was your problem with the Russian?" Cato asked.

"Pride, again, it was my pride. Vladi had a successful life in America, and I envied him. I also felt he was exploiting my brother and me, using our status as illegal immigrants to chain us to his citrus business and pay us less than fairly. In retrospect, I can see that, while he is imperfect, Vladi was never the ogre I made him out to be."

"I see," Cato said, his voice slightly softening.

"But during that time, when Vladi fell into my hands in Cuba, something brought me to a crossroads. For the first time, I saw clearly who I was ... what I was ..."

Marco then told of how the Lord had changed him. He wasn't doing this to persuade the officer toward lenience. Instead, he shared this testimony for the benefit of the man driving the car — a fellow human — a soul who needed to hear, to know, what the Lord had done.

Marco was compelled to speak of the glory of the One to whom he now belonged. This gave Marco peace about the ordeal for the first time, because he knew that even if he were convicted, he would be God's man in prison.

Marco went on to tell how his transformation had saved Vladi's life too.

"I owe him many lifetimes over for the harm I did to him, for the persecution I visited upon him. And that is what landed me on the pier tonight. Truth be told, I worried about losing my own family by doing this, but in the end, my heart was pulled to help him save his son's life. Even though that ended up with me here, in this car, I have peace knowing that I did the right thing and his son, an innocent man, is alive."

Marco continued talking, going into detail about the efforts to save Aleksey, the pain the Gavrilov family had endured, and the circle of friends and fellow Christians, including Jorge, who had prayed and had a part in the rescue.

Cato didn't utter a single word, not even a sound, during the remainder of the story — he just listened in stony silence. Marco was perplexed by the lack of any acknowledgment of his words.

Is he even listening? I think if someone told me a story like this, I would have at least something to say about it.

Marco had been so preoccupied with recounting everything that he had paid no attention to where they were going. Cato stopped the car. Marco snapped out of his thoughts, startled to realize they were ... in front of his home. Cato got out and opened Marco's door.

Why did he bring me here? Marco stared up into the detective's implacable face, wholly unsure of Cato's intent. *Is this some kind of trap?* Marco wondered nervously. He didn't make a move out of concern that the officer would say he was trying to escape. Cato ordered him out of the car, and Marco slowly complied.

"I don't understand. Why are we here?" he asked. Cato didn't answer. Instead, he turned Marco around and unlocked his handcuffs. Marco was petrified.

Cato's lack of communication only intensified that feeling. Marco had no way of knowing what this dispassionate detective could be thinking.

Cato looked him in the eye and finally spoke, "You are free to go. I believe you." Marco blinked and stared back at Cato. Was he hearing this right?

It must be some sort of trick. Is he really letting me go, just like that?

"One question." Cato paused. "The NCA guy posing as Scotland Yard ... Frank Díaz?"

For a half-second, Marco considered whether there was any harm in divulging the man's identity. Amused after he thought about it, Marco replied, "No."

Cato cocked his head, perplexed. After his entire confession, was Marco Rivera going to lie to him now?

"Almost ..." Marco filled in the blank for him. "Frank's driver."

"Okay." Cato pursed his lips and shook his head. "Just confirming the ruse."

"What about Michael Cervera?" Marco asked.

"The case will never see the light of day," Cato assured him.

Without another word, he turned, got back into the car, and drove away.

53

FOREVER A PARDON

J has watched the whole scene from the window of their home. Anxiety had been eating her up inside ever since Marco had left, and her heart raced when she saw the black Toyota Corolla pull up in front of the house.

Where did Marco go last night? She tried to calm herself. *Don't assume the worst.* Her anxiety turned more into confusion when she saw Marco get out of the car.

Oh dear, Marco is handcuffed!

She recognized Detective Inspector Cato as she watched him uncuff her husband's wrists. As soon as he drove away, the front door flew open, and she ran out to Marco.

"Marco, what's going on? Is everything okay?"

Marco held up a hand to ask for a minute — feeling overwhelmed.

"Why did he drive you home? Where is our car? What have you done?" Her mind was racing, and the words couldn't come out fast enough.

"Let's go in the house and put on some coffee," Marco told her in a calm voice as he lightly gripped her arms in a bid to soothe her. "There's a lot I need to tell you."

Marco went into their home and showered while Jhas made the coffee. He had time to reflect on what he would say to Jhas and how he would say it. To avoid it now would be to regress back into his old self — somewhere he didn't want to go.

Still, he lamented the thought that divulging the truth would likely cost him his family. He sighed and dried himself off. He lifted his head and took a long look at himself in the mirror before sighing once more.

Better to just get on with it. She is already frantic. Unfortunately, what I must tell her is probably far worse than she could ever guess.

He felt pity for Jhas because, in revealing the truth, her life would also be irrevocably changed through no fault of her own.

She doesn't deserve this. And I never deserved her.

"Marco, there's someone here," Jhas called up through the door, shaking Marco from his thoughts. "And, why is somebody else driving our car?"

Marco threw on his clothes and stepped out onto the door stoop. His car was in the driveway, but how did it get there from Oracabessa? The car door opened, and Frank Díaz stepped out onto the Riveras' lawn.

"It's okay, honey. I'll explain everything. Wait for me inside, please. I'll be right there."

Jhas had an unconvinced look but retreated into the kitchen.

"I have the keys. How did you start the car?" Marco called over to him.

Díaz rolled his eyes as though Marco should know better. "It's not the first time I've hotwired a car, *amigo*."

As soon as he finished the words, a black Rolls-Royce Phantom pulled up in front of the house. With a small nod of his head, Díaz got into the back of the car and rode off. Hands on hips, Marco stared at the vehicle as it drove away.

That is one interesting character.

Marco went back inside and sat at the kitchen table, where Jhas had two cups of fresh coffee waiting. From across the table, he took her hands in his. "My love, what happened today is actually just the culmination of a very long story — one I am ashamed to say I have not been honest with you about from the beginning."

Jhas took a sharp breath as if to say something, but Marco stopped her. "I know you have and will have a thousand questions. Please let me speak — for once, all of them will be answered."

Jhas nodded her silent assent. Then, for the second time that morning, Marco recounted everything that had happened from the very beginning. He was deeply sorrowful that he had not been forthcoming before now, and tears welled up in his eyes several times as he confessed the full truth.

Just having to see the shock and sadness he was inflicting on Jhas was almost more than he could bear.

"I understand if you can't forgive me for not telling you. I can also understand that you'll see me differently now. I wasn't the person you thought I was when we married."

Jhas had listened attentively, though so much of it was hard to hear. She had a hard time believing some parts of the story could be true. The questions that kept queuing up in her mind were ... *Why? ... And also, why would he lie about that?*

Her emotions moved across a whole spectrum — from anger, to uncertainty, to sorrow, to empathy, to compassion, to tears for reasons she couldn't tell. Marco confessed every detail until he was sure every question was answered for Jhas. He would prefer that she didn't have to ask anything.

They could hear Nemesio beginning to stir in the other room. But before the conversation concluded, Jhas took his hand and looked deeply into Marco's eyes. She took a long breath.

"I need a little time to process all this. It is ... a lot to take in," Jhas finally spoke. Marco shook his head sadly but didn't look up to meet her eyes.

Here it is, Marco dreaded what was coming.

Jhas took in and let out another deep breath. "Honestly, this is ... I don't know ... shocking, to say the very least. Never in my life could I have expected anything like ... this. So much is swirling around my mind now. And I'd be lying if I said there isn't anger mixed in there."

"I know." Marco's whisper was almost inaudible. Jhas had never seen him looking so dejected. Her heart broke for him.

"I can leave if you want ... for a few days," Marco offered, trying to head off the worst. "I probably wouldn't want to look at me after hearing this either."

"Look at me," Jhas said firmly but kindly. It felt so heavy, but Marco picked up his head, just meeting her eyes. "Marco, this must have been an oppressive burden on you. I appreciate that you've told me everything and did not try to continue to hide it. It tells me a lot about who you are now. I just ... I wish you would have told me all this long ago — but then again, our marriage has needed time to season. Maybe I would not have taken it the same before now."

Marco's face showed surprise at her words, but he remained silent.

"You are my husband — you are Nemo's father — and you are a child of the living God. We've lived together for enough years that I know the man you are."

Marco blinked back the tears forming in the corners of his eyes.

"So, you ... you're saying ... ?"

"Marco. I'm saying that I'll need some time. But I can forgive you — and I will forgive you."

"I can't change the past, and I can't change the fact that I haven't told you so much all these years. But you can rest certain it won't be an issue moving forward. I don't deserve your forgiveness or understanding. I do want to be here — with you at my side."

"Of course," said Jhas. "We made a covenant before God — 'til death. What kind of person would I be if I would easily forsake that? Truth is, I'm committed to you, Marco — to the 'you' of now — to the 'you' that you have been throughout our marriage. And the past will never change that.

"You're a new creation in Christ Jesus — not the old one improved. I will never doubt that for a moment. I have more confidence in you now than ever."

As Marco listened to what Jhas was saying, he hung his head and cried without shame. This was salve for his heart. This was his home, his love, his life — and the mercy of God, who had heard every breath of his desperate prayers. The struggle ended with his confession, and the burden of guilt was lifted completely.

"Our Redeemer has granted to us everything pertaining to life and godliness," Jhas continued. "And if you ever have doubts about us — you and me — just know I can trust you because I trust Him.

"God has forgiven you — and I can too," she reassured him. "I love you, Marco."

Therefore if anyone is in Christ, he is a new creation;
the old things passed away; behold, new things have come.

God's Holy Word — 2 Corinthians 5:17

EPILOGUE

Vladi, Erik, Jorge, and Aleksey found themselves in a predicament. How were they going to get a coffin containing a cache of contraband firearms back to Díaz's compound in Hellshire Hills? Who in their right mind would give them a ride?

"Well, we are not going to find a ride standing around here," the ever-pragmatic Vladi said, resuming charge. "We will pack this into town with us." Without other options, the men concurred.

The men picked up the heavy coffin and started the hike toward Oracabessa town, looking like a group of pallbearers who had skipped their morning coffee. With biceps like boulders, the brawny Jorge hoisted the foot of the coffin with one arm while Vladi and Erik grunted and struggled to keep it steady at the front. Aleksey, too frail to bear a load, led the way.

It was impossible for them to go unnoticed carrying the coffin. They trudged along with haggard, dust-streaked, sweat-stained faces set in solemn determination, looking like a sad, small funeral procession of ragtag mourners.

Aleksey flailed his arms like a windmill, trying to flag down a ride. It only added to the spectacle. He looked more like he was doing the YMCA dance at a funeral.

Drivers misinterpreted his gestures as some odd mourning ritual. Passersby slowed in their tracks, their eyes transfixed on the strange group carrying the coffin. Mistaking them for a real funeral procession, drivers tapped the horn lightly and waved with condolences. The sympathetic gestures made the men feel even more exposed. The only reason people weren't asking them questions and interrupting the proceeding was out of respect.

The weary men stumbled along DaCosta Drive into the heart of Oracabessa. The weight of the coffin felt heavier with each step away from the docks. Heaving with exhaustion, their faces contorted and red from exertion, the men sat on the coffin to rest and catch their breath.

Jorge, the only one with experience in the matter, shared his knowledge in the Cuban art of *botello* — catching rides from strangers.

"Guys, just hold out your thumb like this," Jorge said, thrusting his thumb up in the air. And so, they did — just four guys sitting on a coffin in the center of town with their thumbs up. They could have passed as a band posing for an album cover.

The men drew stares from curious onlookers, including one tourist who took photos thinking it was some quirky local custom for paying tribute to the deceased. Although the friendly locals were intrigued by the curiosity before them, nobody dared stop to give a ride to an odd group of fellows resting on a coffin. It became clear that their method wasn't working.

Aleksey was the first to catch on to the problem and state the obvious. "Guys," he said, "I think the coffin is scaring off drivers."

"So what do we do then? We can't just leave it on the street," Jorge countered.

Aleksey checked their surroundings for a moment. "There. We can stash it behind that closed fruit stand. At least it won't be in plain sight."

The other men shrugged. With their brains running on no sleep and their stomachs devoid of food, that suggestion was as good as any.

The locals watched with amusement as the men moved the coffin and emerged from behind the fruit stand. They stood lined up on the side of the road, each leaning to the right with his thumb held high. Several passersby chuckled, while others were simply bewildered at the cartoonish sight.

Before long, a car pulled over to where they stood. The men examined their thumbs and turned to each other with incredulous looks. The squeaky driver's side door opened, and a tall, lanky man in his mid-twenties popped out. With a wild shock of dreadlocks, a green tank top, and faded jeans that hung precariously low, he looked like he'd just come from a Bob Marley concert.

Friendly, he greeted them in a thick *patois* accent laced with Rastafarian slang, making it especially difficult for the Russians to decipher.

"Hey, mon! You boys needin' a ride?" he called out, offering his services as a driver.

The driver's small, shrewd eyes flicked over the foreigners. Sizing them up to be tourists, he grinned, smelling easy marks.

Jorge was quick to speak up. He was best able to understand the Jamaican's patois-laced English and knew the negotiation game better than anyone. "Fifty bucks U.S. to Hellshire Hills," he offered confidently.

The driver shook his head like they were asking him to drive to the moon. "Nah, mon, dat's too far. And dere's four of you, so dat's two hundred. Minimum."

Jamaican men — they are all laid-back, no? ... Apparently not all of them, reflected an annoyed Vladi.

Jorge wasn't fazed. "How about sixty? Fifteen each."

The driver countered with a hundred, twenty-five each.

Jorge met him in the middle at eighty, twenty bucks each.

"Deal," the driver conceded, reasoning that he was either going to get eighty or nothing today from these odd tourists.

Then came the tricky part. Once the driver was locked in, Jorge dropped the bomb about their cargo. "We have some, uh, luggage, we need to bring with us."

"Dat's fine. Yu can just chuck it in di trunk."

"Ummm, yeah. We'll do what we can," Jorge told him. "Just wait one moment while we grab everything."

The guys went behind the fruit stand to retrieve the coffin.

The driver took one look, and his eyes nearly bugged out of his head.

"Oh no. No, no, no. No way, mon. I ain' puttn' no coffin in dis car. Are yu high?" The driver held up his hands and backed away. "Don' wan' no duppy spirit, and ain' seekin' no trouble wit di law."

"Of course, we don't want to put it in the car with you," Jorge reassured him. "What do you think? Maybe we can secure it to the roof."

The superstitious driver remained unyielding. "I not drivin' no coffin 'round! Dat's jus bad luck, mon. Di last ting I wan' is a duppy slappin' mi in mi face in mi sleep."

Erik, clever as ever, played on the driver's sympathies. He launched into melodramatic sobbing, mumbling something about *Tetya*. Aleksey immediately caught on to his uncle's performance.

"Oh, poor dear Aunt Gunny," Aleksey wailed, playing along.

Jorge looked at Vladi for cues. "He says it is his aunt," Vladi dutifully translated, "and the driver is heartless."

Aleksey and Vladi played their roles perfectly, adding their own embellishments to the tale.

Jorge explained further to the driver, "Ah. He says it's his Aunt Gunny. They came to Jamaica on holiday. Being Russian, she tragically succumbed after unknowingly eating some deadly ackee fruit."

The driver practically jumped backward.

"Unripe ackee? Jah save us ... yu never touch dat stuff, less yu know wat yu doin', mon. Evrybaddy know dat!"

The Russians lowered their heads as if ashamed, and Jorge continued.

"They spent all their money on doctors and a coffin. Now, they have to get Aunt Gunny back to Russia."

"Gunny? I dunno, dat don't sound much like no Russian name."

"Oh, it's a nickname. Her real name was Olga," Jorge explained. It was just the first name for a Russian woman that popped into his head. Vladi and Erik simultaneously furrowed their brows, giving Jorge a stern side-glance.

The driver nodded.

"Oooolgahh ... yeah ... Dat sound more like a Russian name."

The driver gave Jorge a skeptical look. It was then that he noticed Aleksey's bruised and battered face. "Well, what happen to dat guy? Some fight broke out at di wake?"

"Oh, uh, well. Um, he was the one who climbed the ackee tree to grab the fruit. He fell out of the tree, that's why he looks like that. But despite the fall, he managed to save the ackee. It was their aunt's greatest wish to try everything about Jamaica. And even as he lay on the ground, hurting, he proudly held it out to her like this," Jorge gestured dramatically. "Of course, he had no idea it was poisonous. He's just been torn to pieces over it." Both men looked back over at Aleksey who, on cue, put his head in his hands and broke into fake but convincing sobs.

"I dunno, mon ... Yu guys jus have di bad luck all over yu," the driver stated nervously.

"Well, we did . . . until you came along. Our luck has turned around, thanks to you! We needed a ride, and you appeared. That is the best of luck!" Jorge smiled hopefully at the driver.

"Fine, but she have to pay too," the driver relented with a sigh, nodding toward the coffin. "Anudda twenty fo' aunty." Bingo — exactly one hundred.

Now that they had a driver, they had to figure out how to transport the coffin atop the compact car. The driver didn't have anything strong enough to tie it down.

"She's just going to have to go in the trunk," Jorge told the chagrined driver. Leaving him no time to object, Jorge directed the guys to bring the coffin around to the back of the car.

With much shoving and maneuvering, they managed to cram Aunt Gunny's coffin into the trunk of the car. It was impossible for it to fit all the way in, so one end of the coffin jutted out from the trunk.

"But, yu just gonna leave 'er hangin' out like dat, mon?" the driver asked quizzically. "Dat' jus' disrespectful if yu ask me."

"She'll be fine, it's just her feet hanging out," Erik quipped. "She was always hard as steel."

"And feisty too," Aleksey added. "She could be a real pistol."

Vladi translated the one-liners exchanged between Erik and Aleksey as everyone tried to keep their composure.

The driver pulled out a thin, frayed rope he kept to tie down passengers' luggage, mainly so he could make off with their belongings in addition to their fare. In this case, he used it to lash the coffin to the bumper and hold the trunk lid down.

The guys piled into the car, a vehicle in dubious mechanical condition at best. Vladi slid into the front passenger seat while Erik, Jorge, and Aleksey jammed themselves into the rear seat. Big Jorge was sandwiched in the middle. The shock absorbers on the compact car were already shot. With all the added weight, the suspension completely bottomed out and the rear of the car sagged just above the ground.

Still concerned about how secure the coffin was back in the trunk, Vladi remarked, "As long as Aunt Gunny does not fall out of the trunk, we will be fine."

The driver smiled. "Don' worry, mon. She safe an' soun' back dere." But the way he said it didn't give anyone confidence.

They gave the driver the whole hundred-dollar bill upfront since nobody had change, which was perfect for him.

The driver turned up the reggae music on the radio, and the car suddenly lurched forward, sending the passengers bouncing in their seats as they sped off into the Jamaican countryside. The driver grinned at them through the rearview mirror, his eyes glinting with mischief.

The thing was a deathtrap with a busted suspension and a clattering engine that sounded like it was coughing up its last breaths. Careening around sharp corners and barreling down steep hills at breakneck speed, they were in for a wild ride. But at least they had "Aunt Gunny," and they were on their way.

Outside of town, the twisted roads were pocked with potholes, large and small. The driver's absurdly reckless driving had them all hanging on for dear life. They gripped onto anything they could — door handles, the seats, each other. With every dip and rut, the rear bumper dragged across the ground.

As they careened around a hairpin turn, the car hit a hole big enough to swallow an elephant. A collective grunt sounded out as everyone's heads hit the ceiling, and the trunk lid flew up.

"Hey, take it easy — we don't want to lose Aunt Gunny!" Jorge shouted. Vladi ordered the driver to stop. The last thing they needed was for the coffin to fall out, spilling the cache of contraband handguns onto the road.

The driver slammed on the brakes, and they skidded to a stop merely inches from a steep cliff. The coffin teetered dangerously on the edge of the trunk. Vladi leaped out of the passenger door to secure the trunk lid back down on the coffin.

As they hurtled toward their destination, Erik found himself seated right over the rusted-out spots in the floorboard. He could smell the heat from the engine exhaust melting the soles of his shoes. But that did nothing to dampen his humor. Erik spent the ride trying to keep their spirits up with jokes and one-liners. Now, he peered down through the holes where he could see the rush of the road beneath them and chuckled, "Hey look, we are getting a ground-level tour of Jamaica!"

Without warning, the driver stopped short, and Erik's bent-over head bashed the back of the seat. "Hey!" Holding his neck, he shot up to see that they were on a remote stretch of road.

Immediately sensing something was wrong, Vladi turned to the driver and asked with curiosity, "Is there a problem with the car? Did we run out of gas?"

The driver didn't answer, his eyes fixed on the rearview mirror. He was expressionless, and looked almost bored — like he was waiting on something.

Two burly men with machetes emerged from opposite sides of the road. One wore tattered trousers and a black tank top, stretched taut over biceps the size of coconuts. The other man had a gleaming bald head and wore a gray shirt with frayed cut-off sleeves. He sported reflective sunglasses that appeared to take up half his face, and a snarl that could curdle milk.

The men moved with an eerie grace. Their glinting blades flashed in the hot Jamaican sun. With unexpected speed, the two ruffians yanked open one of the rear car doors. The bandits felt confident as they grabbed a shocked Aleksey, dragging him out by his shirt like helpless prey. He spilled out of the car onto the ground, his shirt sleeve still clutched in their grip.

Oh no — you do not! You get your hands off my son! Vladi's protective instincts took over immediately, and his combat training flowed like second nature. He lunged from the vehicle and stood face-to-face with the assailants, ready to protect Aleksey at any cost. He wasn't going to lose his son now — not after all this.

Erik followed suit. With an angry growl, he leaped out of the car to take on the bandits. He, too, was not to be underestimated.

In swift unison, the brothers unsheathed their boar knives, already stained with the blood of the cartel smugglers. The bandits hesitated for a moment — Erik and Vladi made it obvious that they weren't playing games. But the bandits didn't back down. The men circled each other like pumas preparing to pounce.

Jorge then emerged from the back of the car, his teeth bared with ferocity. His fiery gaze locked onto one of the thugs, his silent challenge clear: "Come at me if you dare."

The bandits now realized that these weren't a bunch of weak, stupid tourists who would cower and give up whatever they had. The blood-stained boar knives they wielded were no mere props. The would-be robbers' initial bravado crumbled in the face of their unyielding opponents and, slowly, they backed away. They turned on their heels and sprang for the little car, hoping to make a getaway. But their escape plan hit a snag — Aunt Gunny's coffin was still tied to the trunk.

As soon as the car started to move, Erik and Jorge were on it. They threw themselves onto the coffin. Their weight caused the bumper of the little car to drag along the ground, momentarily slowing its acceleration. The coffin slid out of the trunk onto the ground, still tethered by the rope.

Erik and Jorge clung on to the coffin, being dragged behind the car like a sled. They jostled and bounced along the rough terrain, the pebbly road tearing through their jeans and slicing their skin into shallow ribbons of red. Erik struggled to hold on with just one hand as he gripped his knife with the other. Finally, with one swift stroke against the rope, he freed the coffin, and the bandits sped off into the distance.

Now the men were stranded yet again, lost beneath the scorching Jamaican sun with neither money nor transportation. They picked up the heavy coffin and started walking, but with every step, they were swallowed further into the mountain jungle.

"I do not think we are going the right way," Erik observed.

They looked around, trying to get their bearings. They knew they needed to end up at the coast, but the road undulated up and down and around curves. Finally, Vladi shrugged. "We have no idea which way to go, but anywhere is better than staying here." Everyone agreed.

As they walked along the mountain road, the sounds of nature rang clear and vibrant. The chattering of small mammals scurrying about and the distant calls of birds surrounded them.

It was far from a comfortable situation but, instead of worrying, Vladi had a sense of peace about him now. He contemplated the ordeal. He could see how, despite his own weak faith, everything that happened had only reinforced his confidence in the sovereign hand of God.

Vladi's life had been filled with suffering, but he could have never foreseen what lay ahead — and, he wouldn't trade his life now for any other. It was a path that had led him to his family and, much more importantly, to the Lord. He would exchange neither his best days nor his worst days for fellowship with God and eternity future in His accepting presence.

Vladi observed vultures swooping down on carrion. It reminded him of the ones he'd seen on his first night in Florida, when he came ashore after surviving the plane crash. He had walked on that dark, lonely road, not yet realizing all the ways that tragedy was to change the whole trajectory of his life. No, this was not the time to lose hope.

The hours stretched on as they trekked deeper into the thick jungle, their throats parched and their stomachs growling. Aunt Gunny was getting heavier by the minute. The sun sank lower, ducking behind the forest canopy and casting long shadows across the road.

Then, out of nowhere, the sound of reggae music pierced the air, blaring a high-pitched throb from tinny speakers. The crunching of rock and dirt told the men that a vehicle was approaching. They turned to look.

A compact truck rounded the bend and kicked up a cloud of dust as it braked to a hard stop. Delroy and Ras Iyah spotted them, their faces wreathed with broad grins.

"Yoooo, it's you guys!" Delroy called out the window.

"What are the chances?" Jorge muttered in astonishment. "God is good."

"What yu doin' all di way out here? It's almos' dark. Yu lookin' to get yuselves eaten up by di jungle?" Ras Iyah asked.

"It's a long story," Vladi told them.

"Mus be, at dat!" Delroy agreed.

"We will tell you all about it," Vladi promised. "How about giving us a ride back to Hellshire Hills?"

"Yea, mon. Hop in di back and wi get you outta here," Delroy said with a toothy grin and a wink.

Together, they loaded Aunt Gunny into the bed of the compact truck. The four men sat atop the coffin, including Aleksey, who felt like he'd ridden this coffin halfway around the world. Their bodies racked with exhaustion, they jostled along in the back of the truck on the bumpy ride toward Díaz's compound.

"At least we are not walking anymore," Erik noted as he caught himself to keep from sliding off.

They rode down out of the mountains mostly in silence, each man lost in his own thoughts. Vladi reflected on the twists and turns that had led them to this point. It was a reminder that life is unpredictable, and that one never knows what is waiting around the next bend. His heart swelled with gratitude for the precious moments of life that they had been given.

One thing was for certain, the harrowing trial they'd endured had brought Vladi and Aleksey even closer together. After the long decades apart, all the life they'd missed together, their bond had been forged and tested — proven stronger than either had known. Aleksey knew he could count on his father no matter what. And Vladi had found that his Father also would be with him amid any ordeal.

The setting Jamaican sun cast a fiery glow on the horizon, igniting the sky in shades of orange and pink. Vladi could hardly wait to get to a phone to call home. He longed to hear Irina's voice, to let her know their family was safe.

"Mama will be overjoyed to hear your voice," he told Aleksey.

"It is quite a story. She will never believe what happened," Aleksey replied.

"But she will sleep well tonight. As will we all," Vladi added. His voice was filled with the certainty of a man who had once again stared death in the face and come out on the other side.

Aleksey sat looking up at the sky. He had no doubts anymore.

"Papa." Aleksey looked over at his father with eyes full of wonder. "God … our God … hears our prayers. I know that now."

Vladi pulled his son close, embracing him with a love that transcended words. This moment — etched into their souls forever.

AUTHOR'S NOTE

RECONCILIATION is a central theme in God's Word, where He tells us about reconciling sinful man to Himself. From the moment of the Fall, the default setting of the universe has been movement away from God's order and toward chaos and destruction. A right reading of God's Word reveals His will for us is to be reconciled to Him and with one another. What does that look like?

Literature today, with the exception of the Bible, seems to give not enough treatment to such a vital aspect of the human experience. We have libraries full of tales with man's concepts of love, death, good versus evil, power and corruption, survival, courage and heroism, prejudice, and war. But what about forgiveness? We almost have to go back to Victorian literature, to the era of Charles Dickens and Victor Hugo, to find thought-provoking stories of redemption and forgiveness, something so essential to our existence.

Forgiveness, in the true biblical sense, is hardly a household word in our day - and that's not good for us. More than anything in this world, we need to receive God's mercy, His pardon — and the real forgiveness that comes with that.

From there, God's children are required to forgive others — continually. That may be the hardest command to impose on the vestiges of sin in our flesh. It does leave us with the understanding that God's forgiveness was no small thing — but we rationalize that He is God — and we are not. We would almost rather walk over hot coals than fully forgive someone who hurt us. It's nearly as difficult to accept forgiveness when we're hounded by guilt and the consequences of sin.

THE RANSOM offers some helpful takeaways. For one, let's consider Marco's problem — plagued with the aftermath of sin for which he was already grace-forgiven.

Our Creator is both all-wise and all-powerful, and He has decreed that sin has repercussions. We harm ourselves by revolting against any aspect of God's rule over life. Our offenses cause difficulties, some of which we experience even after we have received a divine pardon. Despite being forgiven and reconciled with God, we may still have to deal with temporal and literal consequences of what we've already done. For example:

- mental and physical damage from abusing alcohol or other drugs
- unplanned pregnancy as a result of fornication
- a broken home after marital infidelity
- juvenile delinquency arising out of failure to discipline children
- deception, cheating, stealing
- sins of the tongue ... sinful thoughts spoken aloud have a vicious proclivity to haunt us.

If that were not enough, our sins cause the innocent to suffer physically, emotionally, financially, and in a myriad of other ways. It's painful for all involved.

I'm adding an encouraging note here that God can redeem those circumstances for our good and His glory — we've all seen Him work that way. But, for us to bear those consequences without complaining about how God governs the universe requires an act of faith. If we have such faith in God, we'll proclaim His justice and mercy even as we endure the earthly repercussions of our sins. We'll use the example of those consequences to warn others not to follow in our footsteps.

King David affirmed that all of God's judgments are just and true even as he was experiencing the consequences of his transgressions. He also voiced his trust in God's kindness and grace. As the Psalmist wrote:

Be gracious to me, O God, according to Your lovingkindness;
According to the abundance of Your compassion blot out my transgressions.

Wash me thoroughly from my iniquity
And cleanse me from my sin.

For I know my transgressions,
And my sin is ever before me.

Against You, You only, I have sinned
And done what is evil in Your sight,
So that You are justified when You speak
And pure when You judge.

God's Holy Word — Psalm 51:1-4

Marco, particularly, struggled with his own sense of freedom from guilt. A quote attributed to Ed Welch speaks crisply and truly to this — "God forgives completely because He is the forgiver, not because you are forgivable."

In the story, Vladi gave us an example of an earthly father's devotion to his son. He demonstrated the lengths to which even a sinful man will go to rescue and redeem the son of his flesh. In reality, the severity of our sin necessitates a much higher ransom. The penalty for sin is so great that we can never hope to satisfy that debt ourselves. There is, thankfully, a way through this seeming impossibility.

"In Him [that is, Christ Jesus] we have redemption through His blood, the forgiveness of our transgressions, according to the riches of His grace." — Ephesians 1:7

Think of redemption as the payment of ransom. God's just ransom demand for our eternal salvation was satisfied in Christ Jesus, who gave His life in the place of those who belong to Him. In other words, "God paid God" — He paid this ransom to Himself on our behalf.

Our sin violates God's perfect justice — thus, He has every right to require a penalty that satisfies His holy righteousness. The price was Christ Jesus' death, which was the ransom that bought His people out of the bondage of sin's enslavement and damnation.

Because Christ Jesus died for the sins of all who will trust Him, we have the freedom to obey our Creator. A genuine believer will endeavor to do so now, repenting of sin and praying for God the Holy Spirit to fill us to live for His glory forever.

When Christ Jesus was crucified, He shouted from the cross, "It is finished!" — and that is to say, "Paid in full."

Christ Jesus is King — and He will be for all eternity.

THE RANSOM was paid, and the work of redemption is done!

— Rodney Powell

www.ingramcontent.com/pod-product-compliance
Lightning Source LLC
Chambersburg PA
CBHW030419310726
48979CB00009B/1528/J

* 9 7 9 8 9 8 7 6 2 3 3 4 3 *